HOW IT HAD TO BE

THIS ONE IS FOR ME

HOW IT HAD TO BE

A NOVEL

MARISSA VANSKIKE

Incoming Text Message from Mark Palmer (11:37pm):

Megs... my Megs. I need you to know I've always loved you. I'm sorry I haven't been there for you. But I promise if you search your heart, I'll never be too far away again. You just have to know where to look. My time is up. But there's still time left for you. Megs, this isn't goodbye, it's see you later. I'll see you again one day, in Heaven.

CHAPTER 1

SUNDAY, AUGUST 30TH

Megan Palmer leans against the counter across from her coffee maker, her favorite white speckled stoneware mug with a red clay bottom clutched between her palms. Her first cup of birthday coffee is nearly ready. She's twenty-seven years old today.

She should be sleeping in, but she always wakes early on her birthday to have a few moments to herself before the onslaught of well-wishes. Any minute, the phone calls and text messages will start to pour in, but they can wait. Her day can't start without this first cup. She listens to the steady drip of the coffee as it runs into the pot and the hiss of the steam releasing from the vent. The warm, nutty, slightly caramel scent of the elixir fills her tiny kitchenette.

Megan frowns when she hears her phone vibrating from her bedroom. It hammers away, unrelenting, on the weathered white oak nightstand around the corner.

She taps her foot rapidly, unable to decide if she should abandon her coffee to see who is calling. *Am I crazy? I can't do that.* Her day never starts before coffee.

The phone continues to rumble louder, demanding her attention. She cranes her neck around the corner toward the bedroom, knowing that even if she could see the phone, the screen would still be laying facedown, the way she leaves it, so she's not distracted by lights and notifications while she sleeps.

Call ended.

She turns her attention back to the pot brewing in front of her. Her phone rings again. She drums her fingernails on the empty mug.

Call ended.

She plays this game twice more before finally pulling the coffee pot out before it's full to fill her mug, supremely irritated that whoever it is refuses to leave a voicemail like a normal human. Her first sip of coffee is rushed and nearly ruined.

She pads down the tiny hallway, ready to give the poor caller a very groggy piece of her mind. It's 7:30 in the morning, on a Sunday, no less. No one should be awake at this hour, let alone waking others with their very irritating phone calls. Even if it is to wish them a happy birthday. The display shows a number Megan thinks she may recognize, but the thought leaves as quickly as it came, since the number isn't saved in her contacts.

"Hello?" she croaks. Her throat is dry and feels like sand, but her water glass is empty. She left her coffee on the counter so she swallows a few times, hoping it will soften her rasp.

It's her stepmom, Annie. Megan deleted her number from her phone a long time ago, around the same time she severed ties with her father. Annie had always been nice enough to her, but it had been too complicated for Megan to keep Annie while she let go of her dad. After that fateful fight with Mark, Megan needed a clean break.

She is about to ask what Annie wants before reminding herself that it's her birthday. Once a year, Megan ignores the familiar phone number, along with every other number not saved in her contacts, and waits for the inevitable voicemail message that follows. Annie always wishes Megan a happy birthday while her dad always forgets, or more likely, just doesn't care.

"Megan. I have some terrible news." Annie's voice is thick and broken, sounding a bit as if she has a lump in her throat.

"Ok... what's going on? What happened?" Megan's heart is suddenly racing. Annie nearly never calls her and never with bad news. Megan's heart hammers against her ribs. She clears the remaining sleep from her eyes with the backs of her first two fingers, and lowers herself onto her bed.

"Your dad passed away last night." Annie pushes the words out slowly, with an odd rhythm. Megan notices the beats come out steadily. Their delivery feels practiced. Perhaps Annie is trying not to fall apart. For Annie's benefit or her own, Megan isn't sure. Annie offers no further explanation, allowing space for Megan to process what she has just heard.

Megan could have answered any number of ways after cutting herself out of her dad's life for the past seven years. She thinks about how "passed away" feels most appropriately used to describe the elderly who fall asleep and never wake up. Or for the family being told their terminally ill loved one has lost their battle. Megan's dad was neither elderly nor ill. Megan honestly does not know what Annie means when she says her dad "passed away last night".

"Wait, what are you talking about? How?" Megan closes her eyes, breathing on purpose, in case her body forgets in the wake of this shock. Megan pinches the bridge of her nose and shuts her eyes.

"He killed himself. The police found him last night and just contacted me. Megan, I'm so sorry." Annie's breathing has leveled out, and she sounds strangely neutral, devoid of any strong feeling one way or another. As if she's instantly been put back together. For the way she sounds to Megan, Annie could be talking about a complete stranger.

"Where——" Megan is suddenly desperate for more details, but her voice catches. She's always lived better with more information rather than less and prefers a carefully choreographed response over a knee-jerk reaction. Once she has all the puzzle pieces put together, she'll figure out how to feel about the picture they create.

Megan pushes down the feelings expanding in her chest and forces herself to focus on facts, using practicality as a shield. Becoming overly emotional right now won't help her understand what happened to her dad, so she asks questions instead.

"Where did they find him? How did they know who he was? What time did they find him? Why did they just now call you?"

Her questions come out rapid fire, far more like an interrogation than curiosity.

"They found him in the parking garage of the Viva Las Vegas Wedding Chapel," Annie answers the first question and ignores the rest, which irks Megan to no end. Megan shoves her annoyance aside because the information Annie just gave her feels far too heavy to carry alone. *He killed himself where they were married? How is Annie able to hold on to that by herself?*

Megan's unflagging need to understand doesn't subside. The choice to search for answers in a situation offering no promise of any seems to be made without her consent, or even her knowledge. She needs logic to propel her far away from the hole left by the absence of her father, now gone too soon at forty-nine years old. To face this truth alone, right now, is too much.

Megan leans forward, resting her elbows on her knees, which she's drawn up to her chest. "He drove for ten hours, all the way out to Las Vegas to kill himself where you guys got married? He wouldn't. Why would he do something like that? And where are you right now?" Megan feels as though she's grilling her stepmother, freshly widowed, in a case only Megan is beginning to suspect needs solving. She should probably feel guilty, but this was her father, and Megan deserves answers she's convinced she isn't getting.

It feels like Annie is leaving out important pieces to the story and Megan is growing increasingly agitated. Annie was the closest person to him in the end and must have some idea of what might have led her dad to this. It is crazy to Megan that she should even have to ask these questions. Surely, her stepmom must know how strange this all sounds.

"Well, honestly, we had an argument two nights ago. He'd been drinking, and he wasn't making much sense. He stormed out and didn't come home the next day. I noticed his gun was missing. So I called the police. I told them where he was going so they could find him before he hurt himself."

Megan can tell Annie's words are careful, still possessing a rehearsed quality even though Annie has no way of knowing what questions Megan will have, if any. She speaks in a deliberate procession of relaxed notes, arranged in the same short sentences a mother might drum up when her kindergartner suddenly asks where babies come from. Megan notices Annie offers no extra information beyond the answer to the question posed.

"What made you think to look for his gun? And why didn't you call the police sooner? You said he didn't come home the next day and *then* you called." Megan had forgotten until this moment her father owned a firearm. It was rarely mentioned or talked about growing up in their house. Though it wasn't unusual. Many Army veterans keep guns in their homes.

"Well, he went to the bedroom and he stayed in there for a little while before he left. I'm not sure what he was doing while he was in there. But, he had a small bag of his stuff with him when he walked out. This wasn't the first time he'd left the house with his gun."

"Oh," is all Megan offers.

This is news to Megan. Then again, Megan has been avoiding her father for nearly seven years now.

Growing up, her relationship with her dad was complicated. She loved him, while he seemed only occasionally interested in her. On the best days, she could convince herself that he loved her. She held onto those days so tightly, knowing how Mark's moods flickered on and off and soon enough, she'd be left to navigate them by herself. It always felt as though a stranger had taken control of her dad, and she was never sure how to bring him back to her.

She dragged the weight of this burden around until the pain finally became unbearable. By the time Megan could admit she was broken, the only solution she saw was to put space between them. She realized that while she wasn't allowed to choose the father she was born to, she could choose to walk away from him.

And Megan did.

She told herself she had to let go of the father she dreamed of him becoming; to walk away from the father he was. She told herself she was punishing him for what he had done to her, and for the horrible things he said to her the last time she saw him. But was it really a punishment if the consequences didn't bother him?

Megan tried to convince herself that she was better off. And somehow, the pain of that felt worse because in spite of everything, she still loved him. She only wished he'd loved her in return.

But this? The announcement of his suicide reverberates through her body like a shock wave. It's as if someone has used a defibrillator to resuscitate her past, drawing history up to the surface. Memories flood Megan's mind, clearing the path for her to see the one unimagined consequence of her decision to walk away: ambivalence in her father's death. The truth is, she grieved the loss of him years ago.

Megan blinks away the thought, clinging to the facts. "What else was in the bag? Did the police tell you? Did you notice anything else missing from your bedroom?" Megan can't stop thinking they are missing the bigger picture here. Her father was many things, but suicidal wasn't one of them. Could he really have changed so drastically while her back was turned? She can't focus on anything else except *why*. Perhaps her brain is protecting her from this devastating news thrust upon her, unwanted and unmanageable, before she has even had her first cup of coffee.

Her father is dead now. By his own hand. *Does it matter at all what was in his bag when he left? He ran away to kill himself. What matters is why. Why? And he took a bag? Had he been planning this with a bag packed for the moment he decided it was time? Were the items in the bag meaningful to him, or meant to be significant to those he left behind, so he took them where he knew they'd be found?* Her mind races with an endless string of questions.

"I don't know, Megan. I didn't ask what was in the bag." Annie lets out a sigh, sounding almost relieved, Megan thinks. Or irritated? She decides she must be misplacing the emotion. Maybe Annie is just exhausted. She has every reason to be.

Megan knows she will not get any more answers out of her stepmom right now.

"Ok. Well, look, I need to get going." Megan doesn't bother making an excuse. "Talk to you later?" Megan's voice surprises her. It sounds calm. It should sound wrecked, or at the very least, sad.

Truthfully, she's ashamed of the indifference she feels. She tucks those feelings into her back pocket, so no one discovers the calluses she's grown.

Part of the problem had been how similar Megan and her father were. When the push and pull of their relationship finally collided, they'd each been too stubborn to admit fault. There were no apologies, no attempts at reconciliation. She hadn't even talked to him in years. They say everybody processes grief and trauma differently. She wonders how many people are like her, broken and numbing themselves to it from the start, so when the day inevitably comes, there is no pain to feel.

"Ok, sure. Megan, are you alright?" Annie seems as confused by Megan's reaction as Megan is.

"Yeah, I'm fine. Call you later, ok?"

"Ok, any time you want. I'll be here." Megan instantly remembers how good Annie has always been to her. Though Megan also recalls that Annie has a darker side, she's never found herself on the receiving end of it.

"I know. Thanks." Megan goes to hang up the phone, shaking off a foreboding feeling whispering to her something is wrong, when a thought strikes. "Annie, wait!" Megan yells into the phone, hoping Annie will hear even if her phone is no longer pressed to her ear.

"Yes?"

"How did you know where Dad was going?" The question has been poking the back of Megan's mind. She'd nearly forgotten to ask.

"What?"

"You said you told the police where he was going so they could check on him. How did you know where he was going?"

"Did I say that?"

"Yes, you did. Just a moment ago." *What the hell?*

"Oh, I guess it was just a hunch. Maybe he mentioned it on his way out." Megan hears a small huff on the other side of the phone.

Megan decides to deal with that later. She has too much to think about right now as it is. But now she is certain Annie is not telling her everything. "Ok, I was just curious. I'm going to go now."

"Ok, I'm sorry Megan."

"Thanks. Bye, Annie." Megan hangs up the phone and tosses it to the side. Somewhere in the distance, she hears the crunch of her down comforter crinkling as her cell phone lands on it. She glances over at the screen lit up. A notification previously hidden by the phone call is now visible. A text message from an unknown number is waiting for her response.

Weird. Must have come in while I was asleep.

Megan leans forward to see who the message is from. Probably some drunk person who texted someone they met at a bar. It wouldn't be the first, or even second, time someone named Jessie used Megan's number instead of their own.

Megan pauses and scowls at her phone when she reads the first line. *Megs… my Megs.*

It's not a drunk dial. The familiar nickname is used only by her close friends. And her family.

Her pulse throbs inside her ears and tears fill behind her eyes when she realizes she knows this number. Every year, she hopes to see it on her birthday. But not like this.

It's true. He killed himself. If only Megan had seen this text come in last night. She could have saved him. She knows she could have. Megan is sick as the guilt of this missed opportunity overwhelms her and her chest begins to tighten.

She can't breathe.

She drops the phone and buries her face in her hands. She focuses on pulling oxygen into her lungs, and releasing it again so slowly it takes all her effort.

She isn't sure how long she takes to come back to the room. Picking up the phone once more, she stares at the message, waiting for something to happen. She prays for those three little dots at the bottom to appear, showing he's sending another message. Perhaps to tell her he'd reconsidered. To tell her it was a fleeting moment of temporary insanity and what he'd really wanted to say was he regrets not fighting for her after she left.

Megan shakes the fantasy out of her head, feeling childish. She reads the message once more before deciding she needs to get up and do something, anything. But as she stands, something else strikes her.

Something is wrong. Her dad's text message makes sense on the surface. It's his final goodbye. But something doesn't feel quite right. The words themselves give Megan pause.

He mentions "Heaven," but Mark wasn't a religious man by any means. What's more is a familiar sense lingering, making Megan feel like she's read these exact words before.

Megan chalks it up to an odd sort of written déjà vu, but she can't shake the feeling that there is something else here. Her dad's text message might be more than a simple goodbye.

Megan marches to the kitchen to grab her coffee and takes a deep drink. She pulls out her hair-tie and shakes what's left of her messy bun loose. Chest-length strands of thick, ash blonde hair fall forward, framing her face with an air of privacy. Her head aches in random places where her hair has been pulled too tightly for too long, telling her she's overdue for a shampoo. Megan glances down as she rubs her scalp and notices her toenail polish has chipped away a great deal, and it feels absurdly important it gets fixed immediately. Ever the meticulous organizer, she begins a mental checklist of tasks for the day.

Call Smalls and Mom to tell them about Dad.
Check on Grandma Barb.
Call boss and tell her what happened but that I'll still be in on Monday.
Call Katie and Josh.
Get a pedicure.
Oh, and since it's been a week, wash hair.

Megan walks to the bathroom to take a shower and turns the hot water on full blast. As she waits for it to warm up, she can hear her mother in her ear complaining about how much water she's wasting. As she lifts her eyes, her reflection stops her in her tracks. Her deep brown eyes are a stark reminder of the way her mother has always told her, "you look so much like your father. It's the eyes, mostly". It is never a compliment. Her mother's voice drips with disappointment on every occasion, as if it physically pains her to see Mark when she looks at her daughter.

Megan realizes she's been standing there for a while when the mirror fogs over. She runs her hand over the glass, creating a single palm-sized streak across the otherwise uniform surface. And she relishes the imperfection.

She sits there for a minute, maybe longer, her mind swirling. She can feel an idea taking root in her head and growing stronger.

There's still time left for you.

CHAPTER 2

Half an hour passes by in the blink of an eye and painfully slowly all at once before Megan draws up the courage to call her brother, Jonathan, to tell him what happened.

Megan's parents divorced when Megan was just seven years old. Her brother was five when their dad left them, and he hasn't been in contact with their father in as many years. At twenty-five years old now, he's grown up, and he did it with no help from their dad.

She isn't sure what she expects him to say.

Megan dials his number, feeling nervous. Not knowing what to expect from him leaves her feeling woefully unprepared for the conversation they're about to have. She hates being unprepared. Her coffee has grown cold sitting on the table in front of her. She's left it untouched after discovering the rich body of her favorite morning blend is oddly devoid of any flavor this morning.

"Hey, sis. You know you're not supposed to call people so they can wish you a happy birthday. It takes the fun out of it." Jonathan teases.

"Awe, Smalls, I wish that was why I was calling. I have something kind of crazy to tell you and I'm not sure how I'm supposed to do this, so I'm just going to say it." Megan sighs and closes her eyes.

"Well, now you're just making me worry. Everything ok?"

"Dad died, Smalls. I just got the call this morning. He killed himself last night." Megan waits for his reaction and tries to remove any expectation from it. She isn't sure whether he'll be sad, or angry, or nothing at all.

"Wow. Ok, shit. Are you alright? That must have sucked to hear today, though I'll admit, it tracks, I guess." Jonathan's voice is seething.

"What do you mean?" The two little vertical lines pinch together between Megan's brows.

"Mark has always been a selfish asshole. It's just not shocking to me that if he was going to off himself, he'd do it the night before your birthday. The ultimate dick move." It isn't lost on Megan how Jonathan continues to call their dad by his first name. She ought to be used to it by now, but it somehow surprises her every time.

"I actually hadn't thought about it." And she hadn't. It never occurred to Megan that her father might have chosen this day on purpose. "I just assumed maybe he didn't think about what day it was at all. It just kind of happened."

"That's a different problem. But same result, right? Basic narcissism." Jonathan snorts. "Megs, he forgot your birthday again, and it never occurred to him he's leaving you with this reminder every year on a day you should be celebrating? Seriously messed up."

"I guess so." Megan knows her brother means well. He is on her side here. But the sting of this new bite catches her off guard. She needs to suck the poison out and close the wound. "I don't want to think about it right now."

"Shit, sorry, sis. I didn't mean to make you feel bad or anything. I just…"

"It's fine, really." Megan cuts him off. "I just don't want to dwell on that right now. I appreciate you having my back, though. Anyway, I just thought you should know, and I felt like it should come from me so…" Megan wraps up the conversation, ready to move down the list of calls she needs to make.

"Right. Of course. Thanks for telling me. If you need anything, want to talk or something, you can call. I promise I'll just listen next time."

"I'll keep that in mind, Smalls. I need to call mom now."

"Alright. And sis, happy birthday."

Megan says goodbye and hangs up the phone with a sad smile. She and Jonathan hadn't been close growing up. Megan was busy working hard to earn her father's affection. Meanwhile, her mom overcompensated for his absence and focused the overwhelming majority of her parenting on Jonathan, leaving just scraps of her motherliness for Megan. As a result, Megan and Jonathan lived very different childhoods, despite the fact they are siblings.

But they love each other. And as they grew to understand their parents as people rather than their parents, they reconnected and found some common ground. Their bond is fragile, but they are working on it.

CHAPTER 3

The weather is all wrong today. The sun shines without creating too much heat. Megan can hear the birds chirping happily, despite the turmoil rolling inside her stomach. The perfect Sacramento breeze coasts alongside Megan as she shuffles along the few blocks to meet Katie at Bean, her favorite coffee shop. All she can think about is how the weather gods missed the memo.

Megan's mind grabs wildly at the thoughts sparking inside of her head, but it fails to hold on to any single one long enough to ignite a flame. Her life flashes before her eyes, but through a filter, removing anything her dad was absent from. She catches glimpses of what their relationship could have been today, and fantasizes about what her future might have looked like if her father had been a better man.

His message is nagging at her. Taunting her, daring her to understand. Those who knew Mark, for any significant amount of time, also knew he'd been fighting his own demons his whole life. It's fair to say this news probably shouldn't have felt so jarring.

By most standards, he wasn't a great dad. By some standards, he would be considered a really poor one. At his best, he was mostly absent. But he wasn't suicidal. Megan swims through her past looking for the signs, but everything looks blurry.

Bean is busy this morning. Megan inhales the scent of espresso laced with too many colognes and perfumes, overlaid with new asphalt from the recently repaved parking spaces.

A crowd of people huddle outside the door, waiting for the line to move enough that they can step inside. Megan's entire body wilts, as if it weren't enough she should lose her dad today, but that she should also have to wait thirty minutes for coffee.

Standing near this many people is making her anxious. She is surrounded by crowds that have no idea what happened to her, and even if they did, it would mean nothing to them. Her father has been plucked from this world, and the world didn't even bat an eyelash. It flows just the way it always has. It's oddly comforting given Megan's preference to ignore complicated feelings. At the same time, Megan has never felt this lonely.

"Megs!"

Megan moves toward the back of the crowd where she finds Katie seated at their favorite outdoor patio table, her arm outstretched, waving high in the air. The table is tucked away, surrounded by privacy screen trellises full of ivy and flowers except on the one side, which is open and provides optimal people watching. Their spot is always in high demand, but the early bird catches the best seating. Two twin lattes sit side by side on the tabletop, paired with two blueberry muffins. Megan could have cried right there. Crowds be damned.

Katie stands, wrapping Megan in one of her very best hugs, letting Megan pull away first before they sit down. "Hey there, birthday girl," Katie offers sadly. "Megs, I am so sorry. How are you doing? Really." Katie asks while her voice fills to the brim with her natural warmth, which is arguably more comforting than the coffee now in Megan's hands.

Katie has been Megan's best friend since the fifth grade when, before a math test, Megan nervously batted all five of the sharpened pencils off her desktop, sending them flying in all directions. The teacher shot Megan a scowl of annoyance at the disruption. Instead of crawling around under her classmates' desks, Megan froze. Just when she thought she might melt into a puddle, causing an even bigger scene, a hand shot out from the side and Megan looked over to find Katie holding her own pencil out for Megan to take. When Megan whispered to ask what she would use, Katie smirked and said, "I've got something in my backpack". Katie reached down and pulled out a thick red marker. "This will work," she said with a smirk. Megan put a hand over her mouth to keep from giggling. Katie had to retake the test using the correct medium, but she never complained about it to Megan.

"I'm fine, you know, given the circumstances. Except, everyone keeps apologizing. Like it fixes things."

"Remember who you're talking to right now. You know that *I'm fine* thing doesn't work on me." Katie brushes her hair back behind her shoulder.

Megan has always marveled at Katie's casual beauty. It takes no effort at all because Katie was born beautiful. Her mahogany-colored hair has rich copper streaks woven in and cascades past her shoulders. Despite its thickness, it curls with an ease Megan can never achieve with her own hair. Katie's eyes are brown, but not like Megan's. Katie's are a deep brown you sink down into, intensifying the longer you look at them. Her olive skin always looks as though she's been laying in the sun for the perfect amount of time, and the couple handfuls of freckles she has are perfectly scattered across the bridge of her nose. Her only imperfection is a single mole, roughly the size of a pencil eraser, just underneath the far corner of her right eye. Katie has always been self-conscious of it but refuses to have it removed because of its proximity to her eye, fearing permanent damage to her vision. Megan thinks Katie's affinity for watching shows about botched surgeries has a lot to do with her fear, far more so than the statistical likelihood that her eye may be damaged in the routine removal of a beauty mark.

For one fleeting moment, Megan nearly forgets Katie always knows when Megan is retreating into herself and is happy to call her out for it, knowing Megan will only get worse until she blows up.

Megan takes a long drink of her coffee. It's the same brew she always orders, but like her home brew, it doesn't taste as good as it normally does. Like some vital ingredient is missing. She pauses, trying to put her thoughts in some semblance of order.

"God, I honestly don't know. I have so many things running through my mind, and it feels like they're all going at Mach speed." Megan looks at the muffin in front of her, mentally estimating how many calories it's worth. *At least 350, possibly more.* She picks absentmindedly at it without taking a bite.

"I can only imagine. It's been so long since you've talked to him and now this." Katie's arm stretches across the table as if reaching for Megan. She lays her palm down on the table, pulling Megan's focus away from her food. Megan notices her nails are freshly done; the long blush-colored acrylics shine in front of Megan as she looks down at her own bare nails cut short because long nails get in her way. "I know you think you're good at compartmentalizing and brushing things off to the side, but this just sucks. It really sucks, Megs." Katie's head shakes gently, looking defeated.

"I keep thinking when I was little, I thought I was so lucky. I had this dad who felt way more like a friend than he probably should have. He was never annoyed when I talked his ear off or climbed up onto his lap without asking. He always gave his full attention when I asked for it. Well, when his head was clear, I guess." It feels only fair to include the disclaimer since he wasn't always sober. "My point is, when I was little, it was easy to overlook his shortcomings. When I got older, I started seeing both sides more clearly. But it was too late. I was so attached to him. Every time he bailed on me, or yelled, it hurt ten times worse because I just wanted him to love me like I loved him. The last time I saw him, I was so angry." Megan looks down at the table. "I said the worst thing I could have possibly said to him. I can't stop thinking about it, Katie."

"Hey, your dad said some pretty hurtful things to you, too. Don't forget that. But you are allowed to hold both good and bad memories at once. People change all the time. He made a lot of bad choices. And he shared a lot of his good days." Katie adds, acknowledging the truth of her friend's layered memories. Katie leans back in her chair. "I'll never forget the day I came over after school and he had a set of plastic dishes with my name on them just like you and Smalls had." Katie looks down at her lap, embarrassed, like she just realized what she'd said. She and Megan both knew Smalls' set of personalized dishes never ended up being used. Megan can't recall when she noticed they weren't in the cabinets alongside hers anymore.

Katie shakes her head and quickly continues, pretending like nothing had happened. "He told me I was welcome anytime. He included me. Always bringing home a souvenir when he went on work trips, just like he did for you." Katie stops there to take a bite of her muffin and waits, which feels to Megan like Katie's way of gently nudging Megan to take over.

Megan isn't sure what to say and she ends up blurting out the thought sitting closest to her lips. "It's been years since he had called me on my birthday. I knew better than to hope for anything different." Megan shifts in her seat and puts her sunglasses on, relishing the feeling of anonymity, giving her the courage to be even more vulnerable. "This is so stupid. But even after everything, year after year, I would watch the text messages and the calls coming in, from random Facebook friends, and my closest friends and family, like you." Megan pauses, smiling at the recollection, alleviating some of the heaviness in her confession. "And every year, I'd wait, wondering if this would be the year he cared enough to wish his only daughter a 'happy birthday'. Or hell, if this was the year he'd even remember me. The first couple of years, I even stayed awake until midnight. It's not over until the bell rings, right?" Megan chuffs, trying and failing to keep things light, but her chin betrays her, quivering just enough to reveal the pain that had lain dormant for so long.

"It's not stupid, Megs. He was your dad. Remembering a child's birthday is one of the most fundamental dad jobs every kid should be able to count on." Katie looks at Megan directly in the eyes, after gently tugging Megan's sunglasses from her face, as if the message would penetrate more deeply.

"You know, the weirdest thing happened on the way over here, too. The old Van Morrison song, *Brown-Eyed Girl*, came on the radio. I can't tell you the last time I heard it. Probably back when my dad used to sing it to me. He always said it reminded him of me. How crazy is it that I heard it today, of all days?" As she grew older, Megan avoided the song every time she heard one of its familiar riffs. Its sentiment had been ruined when her father began to fail her more often than he cared for her. Hearing it was painful.

A coffee shop employee passes by their table, cheerfully asking how they are doing and if they needed anything else. Megan shakes her head as Katie tells the worker they are doing fine and thanks her before the girl moves on to the next table.

Megan spent most of her life being hurt repeatedly by people she should have been able to count on. There were the girls growing up who were friends with her at school but excluded her from every sleepover and get together outside the school walls. There were the boyfriends who would imply she was stupid because, unlike them, she went to a junior college before transferring to a four-year school. Megan was smart enough to understand when they were belittling her. There was the guy who told her she had an amazing body, but she would be perfect if she lost just five pounds. At 105 pounds soaking wet, Megan didn't have the weight to spare, though she tried her hardest.

She reinforced the walls that guarded her heart, putting a little more distance between herself and her most frequent offenders. Mostly men, but a lot of women, too. She learned early on humans have a finite amount of strength. If they aren't careful, cracks in the wall will give way, leaving them more vulnerable than ever. That protection means the difference between the resilient and the broken. She would not be broken again.

Megan ran with the wrong crowds as a teen, experimented with alcohol at too young an age, and she made damn sure, by any means necessary, that her scale never tipped higher than 110 pounds. At five feet four inches tall, moving any higher in the normal BMI range meant relinquishing too much control. Megan couldn't afford to do that. She knows now that a few extra pounds won't hurt her. In fact, they might suit her slender frame, but years old habits are hard to break and she determined long ago that no food was worth tipping the scale.

Megan shoves a tiny piece of her muffin in her mouth, just so Katie won't ask questions about whether she's eating.

A few minutes pass before Megan speaks again. She and Katie sip their coffees in silence. The pair know each other well enough to understand when talking was less important than listening. Waiting. Mulling. Giving space.

"I guess we can't be too surprised, right?" Megan jumps right in. "There were the DUI's, the stints in county jail, the endless court hearings where he had to be ordered by a judge to show up as a father financially, if in no other way. Those are cries for help, aren't they? Shit, maybe I should have known." Megan rubs her eyes with the pads of her thumb and pointer finger, distracting herself from the unexpected wave of responsibility that just crashed down on her.

"I don't know, Megs. He was troubled, yes. But none of those things scream *suicide risk* to me. You can't blame yourself or anyone else. You can't predict when someone is going to take their own life. And even if you think you can, you still end up reading about parents doing everything they could to protect their suicidal kids from making an irreversible mistake, and they still couldn't prevent it." Katie shifts in her seat, sitting up a little straighter. "When someone is determined, they find a way. I think it's part of the tragedy. In hindsight, the signs seem painfully clear. But people hardly ever see it coming in real time. Even if you can, it's just not enough."

Megan appreciates the effort, though they both realize it won't assuage Megan's guilt. Guilt doesn't make sense at all. Its existence depends on nothing in particular, but it's there, weighing you down, squeezing you like a fist.

Megan runs her finger along the rim of her coffee cup, not looking up when she asks, "Do you think it's hereditary? That being suicidal can be passed down?"

An alarmed expression veils Katie's face. "What do you mean?"

Megan realizes instantly how the question must sound and scrambles to put Katie at ease. "Not me, Katie. I swear. Relax." Once Katie looks less tense, Megan continues. "There is something I never told you, but when my dad was sixteen, my grandpa killed himself. I hadn't given it much thought before, but now, I wonder. I don't know, Katie. I never imagined he would follow in his father's footsteps. He knew the unique trauma of surviving your parent's suicide. He was still a kid when he became the man of the house. But I'd think he would have known better than to put his own family through the same thing." Megan isn't sure if he knew better or not. She has so many things she needs to know, and the one person who can answer her questions is gone.

Katie nods in total support, allowing Megan complete freedom to hash out each individual feeling.

"Does Josh know?" Katie asks, breaking her commitment to the dedicated silence as Megan returns her cup to the table.

"Yeah, I called him right after I called Smalls. He told me he's here for whatever I need, any time, day or night." Megan feels Katie's eyes burning on her face. Or maybe it's Megan's face flushing, knowing what Katie is going to say next.

"Of course he did. That's very Josh…" Katie lets the thought dangle in the air, unfinished.

"Come on, Katie. Don't start. Josh is just being a good friend. The best kind of friend really, since he and my dad didn't even really like each other in the end, though I never knew why." Megan takes a sip of her coffee, remembering the last time Josh came to her dad's front door. Josh left before Megan got the chance to see him that day, but she still remembers hearing his voice outside of her bedroom window as he and Mark took turns shouting at each other.

Katie sets her cup down a little harder than intended and the thump of the cup connecting with the table jolts Megan back to present. "Sure, they butted heads a lot," Katie is saying, "but Mark was like a father to Josh." Katie stops abruptly, as if she made a mistake, but Megan knows that it's true. Mark was more of a father to Josh than he was to his own biological son.

Katie continues, sounding much more thoughtful. "What I'm saying is Josh needed someone to be tough on him with the direction he was headed. But seriously, when are you going to admit to yourself that Josh has been in love with you since we were all kids—"

Megan cuts her off there. "Josh loves me. He's not *in love* with me. I love him too, as a friend. And I love you, even when you're super annoying." Megan tosses a piece of muffin at Katie to end the discussion.

"Ok," Katie changes the topic. "How did your brother take the news? And your mom?"

"My mom just wanted to know if I was ok. It doesn't surprise me she seemed unperturbed by it. She's known him since they were teenagers, you know? She was there when his dad died." A thought surprises Megan, having never occurred to her before. "She probably knows his pain better than any of us now that I think about it."

"And my brother sounded shocked. But in the way you'd be shocked to hear someone super famous died. Smalls knows who this man is, but he never really knew him."

"Yeah, I get that. He was a little boy when your dad bailed on him. Of course, it feels more like hearing about a stranger than his own dad."

Megan nods and they sit there in silence, taking a moment to let the heaviness subside before continuing. She listens to the chatter of the people around them. She inhales the scent of the flowers in the trellises next to her.

Megan leans forward, resting her elbows on the table. "Can you believe my boss told me not to come into work on Monday? She told me to take a minimum of two weeks bereavement leave and strongly recommended I take longer. 'As long as you need' is what she said." Megan rolls her eyes and lets out an indignant huff.

Katie nods. "Not only do I believe it, but I wholeheartedly agree with her. You work way too much, especially for a dental office manager. You do tasks way above, and below, your pay grade, you never take time off, and this is a major trauma you're dealing with now. You need a break and a huge raise while we're talking about it. I'm already worried about you." Katie wears her concern openly on her face. The sincerity of her words is palpable.

"What do you mean? I'm fine. And I could use the distraction, to be honest."

"Megs, you work yourself to the bone, and you lock all your feelings away until they explode. And you haven't taken even a single bite of your muffin." Katie holds up her hand while shaking her head, to stop Megan before Megan can start arguing about it. "Yes, I noticed. And you're paper thin already. You need to take care of yourself. Do it for the people who love you if you can't do it for yourself."

"Ok, Katie. Don't get worked up. I'll take care of myself. Promise." Megan concedes, looking Katie in the eye while forcing down a bite of muffin, *30 calories*, so Katie will relax. "I can't believe you have to work today. It's Sunday."

Katie is head of the billing department for a popular pediatrics group downtown. "I know, I'm sorry. Weekend work isn't typical, but we're horribly behind on client billing since Dr. Hodges put the wrong codes on a bunch of patient care summaries. If I don't go today, we'll never get caught up. I'm tired of dealing with angry moms calling about the error on their statement. It should only take a few hours, though. Do you want to come with? You can hang out and read in the lobby and then we can go grab lunch? I hate the thought of leaving you alone today."

"No, it's alright. I appreciate it though. I'm good. Just text me when you're done."

Megan knows Katie needs to go to work, but the heaviest thought Megan is carrying around comes tumbling out of her mouth before Megan can form a conscious thought about it. As if the thought itself needs to be heard, regardless of Megan's opinion on the matter.

"There's one more thing I haven't told you yet." Megan swallows the last of her latte. "My dad sent me a text message last night." She pulls out her phone, flipping the screen around to allow Katie to read the message verbatim.

Katie's eyes go wide. "You got a suicide note from him? That's what this is, right? After all this time?"

"That isn't even the weird part. I feel like I've read it before. The words sound so familiar, but I can't figure out why. I finally chalked it up to some strange déjà vu. But also the apology. He *apologizes*."

Megan waits for some acknowledgment that Katie understands. However tiny, only two words, after all, she can't recall a single occasion her dad has ever apologized to her for anything.

Katie reaches for an explanation and Megan gets the feeling Katie is trying to follow Megan's thoughts. "Is a deathbed apology odd? Maybe this was his last plea for forgiveness, for years of mistakes and pain, and he didn't know how else to apologize. I mean, it's not uncommon for that to be in a letter left behind, right?"

"Alright, Katie. I'm going to tell you something now. And it's the craziest idea, but I just can't let go of it. Not since Annie called me. I've been thinking about it all morning." Megan stops to take a breath to steady herself. "I don't think my dad killed himself. And I don't know why, yet, but I think this text was his way of telling me."

Katie says nothing for a minute. Megan suspects she is ranking her on a scale of one to insane. Megan watches Katie finish her coffee, screaming inside for Katie to say something. Anything will do at this point.

Katie's mouth finally opens and Megan scoots forward to the edge of her chair. "Megs, I love you. But are you hearing yourself right now? Are you sure this isn't your way of avoiding the massive amount of baggage that just got dropped in your lap?"

Megan shakes her head. "I know how this must sound, but I am telling you, Katie. Annie's hiding something. And this text is weird, right? You can't deny that. It's beyond a standard suicide note. He talks about seeing me again, in Heaven." Megan's arms gesture wildly. "He wasn't religious. At all. And there's still time left for me? What the hell does that mean? Is there a clock somewhere ticking down the minutes until something bad happens to me?" Megan pleads. "Something isn't right."

"A lot of people find religion when they're about to die."

Megan wonders if Katie might be right. "Look, I don't even know why I care. I shouldn't care. But I'm in this. My dad is making sure of it. He wouldn't have killed himself. He wasn't perfect, but he wasn't suicidal either." Megan slumps against the seat back. "If I don't find out what happened, everyone is just going to remember him as the guy who abandoned his kids and killed himself the night before his daughter's birthday. And maybe that's the truth, but I have to know." She pinches pieces of her muffin, squishing them flat between her fingers and avoiding Katie's gaze.

Katie stares at Megan and Megan feels like she can see Katie considering what to do. Then Katie does exactly what Megan expects, because Katie is selfless to a fault. "Ok, Megs. How do we figure out what happened? Maybe we should call Josh again. Use his police connections?"

Megan nods, giving Katie a smile which she hopes conveys her gratitude as she picks up her phone and dials Josh's number.

CHAPTER 4

SATURDAY, SEPTEMBER 5TH

There isn't a traditional viewing of the body. The mortician noted in his report he'd been unable to reconstruct Mark's face, given the extent of the damage from the gunshot wound. When the need to discuss how to proceed came up, he was kind. Making it seem as if having a closed casket was more of a gentle suggestion rather than absolute necessity.

Megan understands that, her brain ever eager to rationalize and remain practical. But the fact that there isn't a viewing makes her restless. The viewing is the first piece of the process providing closure.

Without it, and knowing it sounds at least a little crazy, it's difficult for Megan to accept her dad is truly gone. Over the course of the week, she swears she would catch glimpses of him. She would see him in her peripheral vision at a stoplight, seated on the driver's side of the car next to hers. Waiting in line at the grocery store, she'd see the back of a man wearing similar clothes to those in her memories of him, a healthy mixture of salt and pepper hair peeking out from underneath his Oakland A's ball cap. She can't count the number of double-takes she's made, or how many times she'd quickened her pace to a near run to catch up to a man walking away from her who was possibly her father but, of course, always a stranger.

Before Megan had a chance to view her dad's body, and against the mortician's suggestion, Annie had Mark's body cremated in lieu of a closed casket ceremony. Annie claimed she viewed the body once the body removal technician transported it to the morgue and verified Mark's identity. Furious seems too light a word for how Megan feels. She couldn't hit the button to end the call fast enough when Annie had told Megan she could not view Mark's body for herself.

Now, Megan is expected to move through the acceptance stage of grief, while she remains unconvinced Annie has told her the truth about the events leading up to her father's death. Annie avoided Megan's calls throughout the week, despite her declaration of availability to Megan. The one time she answered, Annie got frustrated when Megan asked again how Annie knew her dad would go to the wedding chapel in Las Vegas. Before ending the call, Megan tried to offer her help with the funeral arrangements, but Annie cut her off, telling Megan she and Dan had everything under control.

Today, family and friends gather for the celebration of Mark's life Annie threw together. Megan cannot wrap her mind around how Annie accomplished this in a week. Annie is supposed to be grieving, not planning a party with her friends.

Who am I to judge? I'm not mourning properly, either. Megan scolds herself for criticizing the way a person navigates something they never imagined they'd need to navigate.

Megan parks by the activity center of the mobile home park where Annie's mother, Mary, lives. She sits in her car, just for a moment, before plucking up the courage to walk inside.

The room is a decent size. Megan counts ten round tables. A game area off to the side houses both a ping-pong table and a pool table where few people are already playing pool. A short table sits along a side wall displaying various photos of Mark. One from his time in the Army, another of him in an eighties Gold's Gym muscle tank top straddling his Ninja motorcycle, and Megan's favorite photo of him. He was in his late thirties, and he was leaning up against a tree. The picture was taken in the early fall. He was wearing a plaid cutoff shirt, the top two buttons opened since he'd been working out regularly, with his favorite pair of Levi's. His hair is nearly all black with just the faintest hint of grey streaking the front and his smile is genuine, not the kind produced on demand. His cheeks are full and when Megan leans closer, she can see the way his eyes crinkle in the outer corners. He's handsome. He looks happy. A guest book sits next to the photos so guests can leave their mark. Proof they were good enough to come.

Megan notices a small kitchen at the front of the room. It sits behind a half wall with a chef's window. A couple of folding tables sit underneath the window with cold sandwiches, buckets filled with ice and beverages, a few fruit trays, and cupcakes on top. As if this were an actual celebration. Megan feels her face heating, her eyes narrowing with a sudden urge to overturn the cupcakes and smash them on the floor. She shoves the feeling down and looks at the people gathered around the room. Some are in seats, eating the food provided. Others huddle together in groups, talking amongst themselves.

Megan asked Katie to come with her, knowing her best friend wouldn't say *no*. Megan had always envied Katie's effortless ability to let other people in. Katie doesn't have an issue telling people how she feels or empathizing with others. She never worries someone on the receiving end of an emotional outburst will find her silly or irrational, or worse, write her off all together.

Megan's phone dings and she pulls it out to find a text message from Katie apologizing for being late. She had to stop and put gas in her car and now she is sitting in traffic because of some accident up ahead. Megan tells her not to worry and slides her phone back into her back pocket. Megan already decided to hide herself behind Katie today, once Katie arrives. Perhaps then no one will notice how very much Megan doesn't want to be here.

There are more people in attendance than Megan expected. Most of whom Megan doesn't recognize.

She scans the room quickly and locates her grandmother, Barbara, with her short, stark white crop of hair. She is the person Megan most wants to be with today. Megan's Grandma Barb lost her husband to a self-inflicted gunshot wound before Megan was born, and now she's lost her son the same way. Megan can't help but reflect on how unbearable her pain must be today. It's a wonder Grandma Barb can stand here today, accepting offerings of condolences, each surely a sharp reminder of not just her most recent loss, but of her first loss, too.

Grandma Barb is a force of nature. A powerhouse born in the deep Arkansas backwoods. She is a strong but gentle matriarch who sits at the head of her family, quietly overseeing the goings on. Both tough as nails, and kind as could be. She makes the best twelve-hour salad at holidays and always has a pitcher of sweet tea in the Frigidaire. Whenever Megan was at her grandma's house growing up, she'd ask for a bologna and cheese sandwich for lunch. Grandma Barb made them with Miracle Whip. According to her, mayonnaise has a great many uses, but not a single one is on a sandwich.

It doesn't escape Megan's notice that Grandma Barb stands on the side of the room opposite Annie. Megan assumes this is intentional since Grandma Barb has never been a fan of Annie's. She always said a woman should trust her intuition. It's rarely wrong, and she didn't trust Annie because Annie never showed much interest in Mark's family. What kind of woman tells a man she loves him and then isolates him from his family, forcing him to choose between them? Grandma Barb will do anything to protect her family. She's proven that more than once.

Family legend has it on good authority that once, when Grandma Barb learned Mrs. Maverly, Mark's eighth grade teacher, was plotting to have Mark expelled for frequently disrupting class, Grandma Barb marched into a meeting with Mrs. Maverly and the principal and screamed at the poor woman. Mrs. Maverly quit on the spot. On her way out the door, one parent swears they heard Grandma Barb sweetly suggest to the principal that the next teacher has a pair of balls and is a little more interesting. Maybe then Mark wouldn't feel the need to entertain the class. Another time, when Megan was just a kid, she heard a rumor that her Grandma Barb caught her grandpa fooling around with the woman next door. When he told Grandma Barb he was leaving, Grandma Barb cut off his *thing*, and that's why her husband ended up killing himself. Because he couldn't possibly live without it. Whatever would he whip out in the next dick measuring contest? Megan sometimes wonders what it would be like to get on Grandma Barb's bad side, but she never dwelled there for long because it always sent a shiver down her spine. Megan adores her.

When Megan called her grandma a couple of days prior to see how she was holding up, she learned her grandmother was the one who had been called out to Las Vegas to identify and claim the body. Annie hadn't been involved in the process until after he was transported back to Sacramento for the autopsy. According to Grandma Barb, Mark was cremated before Annie showed up. "Some mix up with the paperwork," Barb said, waving the explanation away as if it were no matter.

Megan weighs whether Annie lied to her about identifying his remains and having him cremated, or if she just didn't tell Megan the entire truth. It says something to Megan that her stepmother is not the person who the police contacted first. As his wife, Annie should have been the one to receive the call. Maybe she didn't answer her phone and they moved to the next closest relative. Was she glossed over by accident? It seems unlikely the police would have forgotten to call her. She claimed to have been the one who called the police to do a welfare check on Mark. Is there some reason she would have been skipped intentionally?

Megan is about to ask her grandma if she knows why she was called instead of Annie when her grandma asks, "Did Johnny come with you?" Barb's voice is laced with grace, knowing the answer but seemingly unable to let go of the sliver of hope that Jonathan would be here today. She and Megan both know it makes no sense for him to come. He hasn't had a relationship with his dad since he was a little boy. Jonathan is grown now, an adult by law.

"No, Grandma. He didn't. He doesn't know dad." Smalls probably can't imagine anything worse than standing here pretending to understand the grief shared by the strangers in this room. Megan doesn't blame him. Not even a little. She can't find a single reason to expect Smalls to show up now for a man who made it a point not to show up for Smalls.

Grandma Barb nods and pulls Megan into her arms. "I'm so sorry, baby."

Barb knows what kind of father Mark was to Megan and her brother, Jonathan. However, she never pushed her granddaughter to see Mark or to make amends after their fight. She never forced them together. Grandma Barb let her son lie in the bed he made, and Megan loves her dearly for it. In her own quiet way, Grandma Barb was the first person in Megan's life who placed the blame where it belonged, on the adult. When Megan needed space, she always gave it to her, all the while making sure she stayed closely connected to both Megan's life and to Jonathan's.

She clings to her grandma for a minute, or an hour, she can't be sure. They collect themselves before turning to face the room together. Megan scrambles to choose a few questions about some guests she knows Grandma Barb can answer, hopefully before she is pulled away to tend to other well-wishers.

Many family members whom Megan hasn't seen since she was a little girl have traveled a long way on short notice to pay their respects. Her heart warms at the sight of those she remembers most fondly. She plucks a few of her favorites and asks her grandma to give her an update on their lives.

Megan's uncle Nick, who isn't really her uncle, but Mark's cousin-in-law, is here, but there is one thing remarkably different about him. He is sitting in a wheelchair. Grandma Barb explains he was in a construction accident, leaving him bitter and a paraplegic. Nick was a good family man. Megan can't remember her uncle without his distinctive smile filled with pearly white teeth. His smile alone had a way of making Megan feel as if she were cuddled up on the couch under her favorite blanket, watching a movie on a rainy day. That something could steal his smile away was a heavy reminder. Tragedy doesn't discern between those who are more or less deserving of its destruction.

Heather is here. Heather married Mark's cousin, Paul. Megan always wondered how that happened. Paul had a horrible temper, and Heather was always too good for him. Too beautiful for him and he knew it. So, he controlled her, demanding she look unattractive so no one would be stupid enough to pay her a compliment. Not that the offending party would ever pay the price for their kindness. It was always Heather who paid. A vivid memory flashes in Megan's head, of looking at Heather's face curiously when she arrived at a family gathering with subtle yellows and purples around her eyes. The skin around her eyes was painted thick with makeup, as if she was trying to hide a dark part of her, both physically and emotionally. Heather would say she was tired or clumsy. As an adult, Megan understands what the truth of those occasions must have been. Today, Heather looks stunning while her ex-husband looks pathetic and ill. Megan tracks his pitiful eye line as he follows Heather around the room, while Grandma Barb recounts how Heather finally called the police on Paul. While he sat in a jail cell that night, Heather packed a bag, took their two children, and left him. Heather never looked back. Paul was so depressed he paid for weight loss surgery. It worked well enough until he got an infection, which left him weak and sickly looking. Heather floats around the room, offering help and comfort. Megan loves this version of her.

When Grandma Barb finally gets pulled away, Megan walks over to the refreshments to grab a bottle of water. She scans the room and takes a sip of the ice-cold drink, savoring the chill as it cools the heat from the anxiety of being in this room.

The conversations around her become white noise. She notices Annie and Mary sitting in a corner, along with several other faces she hasn't seen before. Megan's eyes eventually land on Dan.

Dan Walker dated Annie long before Mark had ever come into the picture. But Dan and Annie remained close friends and, over time, Dan became the closest friend Megan knew her dad to have as well.

Megan has always felt like Dan has a charming quality. It's the kind that's hard to put her finger on, but she can remember watching people light up when they talk to him. His hair is still sandy brown, though it's lighter now. Yet, he somehow looks the same. Dan's face is round, soft and kind. His blue eyes sparkle when he listens to you, as if the words you speak breathe life into him. Dan seems to draw out emotion from every person he encounters, making them comfortable enough to accidentally overshare their thoughts, good or bad. People always seem to leave a little warmer than when they arrived at his side. Megan watches him now, taking in every word from the woman he's chatting with, as if it's the most important things he's ever heard. The woman smiles at him, too much.

Megan wades through the guests, pulled by some invisible force, seemingly against her will. She isn't sure what she wants from him, and she doesn't acknowledge anyone else on her way over. Before she has even fully realized where she is going, Meg is standing just a few feet away from Dan, staring at his profile.

He turns and looks right into her eyes, as if he's been expecting her. His face softens and his eyebrows pinch in the middle, as if he's looking right through her. "Hey kiddo, how are you doing?"

Megan is reminded of the tale of the Little Dutch Boy who put his finger into a pebble-size hole in a dike to stop the angry sea from breaking through and flooding the town. The boy waited there for so long his finger went numb, and his arm began to tingle. But he held steady until help arrived, refusing to let the water crash down and destroy the only place he'd ever called "home".

Megan can't say exactly what she's angry about. The way her father wasn't really a father at all or the way he bowed out of her life forever. The way Annie threw a party today or the way she's alone in her thoughts about what happened. Perhaps it's because a part of her cares so damn much about any of this. She isn't sure. But she knows her heart is a sea of rage threatening to destroy anyone who comes too close, with only a finger keeping it from storming down on everyone around her. Dan never even hesitates, unafraid of what it may unleash. With that simple question, Dan removes the finger stopping the flood.

For the first time since her birthday, Megan breaks.

Before she cries, he closes the gap between them, wrapping her in a hug. Everything else disappears for a few kind minutes. He holds her close whispering, "it's ok, Megs. It's ok."

As she stands there, it doesn't feel like someone is holding her. It's more like Dan created a tangible space where Megan feels like she can be vulnerable—a literal safe space for her emotions. For a moment, it is like Megan has been hypnotized, the world around her falling away in bits and pieces, like a broken windowpane dropping shards of glass, one sliver at a time, while a quiet voice gives her permission to let go. That's the magical quality Megan has a hard time describing when she thinks about Dan Walker.

When Megan finally steps back, no words come out, and she sits there silently, while Dan tells her she can call him anytime or come out on his boat with his family and Annie. "Your dad is gone, kiddo. And I am so sorry. But it doesn't mean we're gone too." *Another apology.*

"Thanks, Dan." Megan manages the smallest smile for him, knowing she'll never take him up on his offer. She hadn't been able to bring herself to be in the same space as her dad when he was alive. It was too hard. To be in a space devoid of him when it shouldn't be feels unbearable. Megan raises her chin slowly, wiping her eyes. "Dan, did you get a message from my dad?"

Dan's eyebrows pinch together. "What kind of message, kiddo?" When Megan doesn't respond right away, he shifts his stance and stands up a little straighter. "Megan, did you get a message?"

Megan's spine tingles. "No, no. Forget it. I was just hoping someone could tell me what happened." Megan looks around the room, wondering how many of these people had known something was wrong with her dad. Did anyone else get a text message from him? Her dad's message said he ran out of time. Would anyone have been able to save him? To buy him a little more time? What would he have done with it? Would he ever have tried to fix what was broken between them? Would it have made a difference if he had tried?

Megan likes to think if her dad had tried hard enough, she could have forgiven him, and they would have been good. Or at the very least, they could have been ok. They'd never have been as close as Megan expected a father and daughter should be. Her dad wasn't cut from the same cloth as most others. But they could have tried.

CHAPTER 5

Megan is drained and ready to call it a day. Katie still hasn't arrived, but Megan doesn't want to stay just so Katie can make an appearance. Megan taps out a quick apology text message letting Katie know she can't be here anymore. She asks if Katie can meet her for a late lunch instead.

Megan is saying her goodbyes when Josh walks through the front doors in his full police uniform. Megan hadn't been expecting him to be here today since he was on duty. To say he draws a few eyes wherever he goes would be an understatement. He is a good-looking guy in his own right, but the police uniform makes him truly stand out in a crowd. His soft brown hair is brushed neatly to one side, but with no hair product as far as Megan can tell, so it looks like he didn't try at all. It's hard to ignore the way his eyes change from blue to green depending on his mood or the color of his shirt. Today his uniform draws out the blue. He takes care to stay physically fit and the muscles in his arms peek out from the bottom of his sleeves. His cheekbones and chin are chiseled with definition and women tell him frequently he reminds them of that one guy from that one show.

Katie constantly wonders out loud why Josh and Megan aren't a couple, but the truth is, Megan has never seen him romantically. She grew up with Josh, alongside Katie. His family lived a few duplexes down from Annie's. There weren't many kids Megan's age, and none she saw with any kind of consistency. When Megan started staying with her dad regularly, Josh was the first close friend she made and truthfully, a big part of why Megan continued to visit, even when her dad had other things going on. Josh went to the same schools as Megan and Katie, but he was in the grade above them, so their paths didn't cross often. Eventually, Josh became Megan and Katie's third musketeer. It's hard for Megan to see him as anything other than a slightly older brother.

Josh waves as he walks over to where Megan is saying goodbye to her grandma.

"Hey, Megs. Mrs. B," He nods courteously to Megan before pulling Grandma Barb into a big hug. "I'm sorry for your loss. I can't imagine how hard this must be for you."

"Thank you, sweetheart. It's so good of you to come by, Officer Pierce. Or should I say 'Detective Pierce'?" Barb's eyes twinkle with pride. She's known Josh since he was a young boy. She'd give him and Katie rides home from school when she picked up Megan and Jonathan, insisting Megan invite her friends to family dinners and special occasions. He's every bit one of her own grandkids.

"Ah, cut it out, Mrs. B. You don't need to do that." Josh's cheeks turn scarlet. "Besides, I'm not a detective yet. I still have a lot to learn." Though she's rooted him firmly in the friend zone, Megan can understand why women find him so charming. "Megs, are you leaving?"

"I was just about to."

"Can I walk you out? There's something I want to talk to you about." His voice sounds forcibly light, like he's not wanting to draw any attention to their conversation. "Dinner this week, Mrs. B.?"

"Anytime, dear. Just give me a day's notice so I can have your favorite lasagna ready."

Josh gives her a wink and turns to walk slowly away, out of earshot of any eavesdroppers.

Megan follows, just a half step behind him. "I didn't know you'd be by."

"I was passing by on my route so I wanted to see if I could catch you and say hi to Mrs. B." Josh answers easily without turning to look at Megan.

Josh lowers his voice and tilts his head casually in Megan's direction. "You know how you asked me to look into the night your dad was found and who got the call to claim him?" Josh reaches behind Megan and rests a hand lightly on her lower back, guiding her further away from the guests. "I pulled the police reports from the night he died, and everything looked normal—"

"Really?" Megan bursts out, cutting him off. "Nothing unusual? Nothing about why my grandma got called instead of Annie? Shouldn't Annie have been notified first?" Megan peppers him with rapid-fire questions, forgetting she needs to look normal in the process. She is failing miserably.

"I was just getting there. Stay cool, Megs." Josh crouches down so he can speak more quietly. "I can get into a lot of trouble if anyone finds out I'm digging into a closed case for you. My personal connection to the case alone is enough to put me in hot water with Chief." Josh and Megan both know he is taking a calculated risk to his career, but then, he's never been able to refuse Megan. He had said as much on the phone when Megan called him. Megan makes sure she never really needs him, so when she called, pleading with him to help her find out what happened to her dad, she knew he wouldn't turn her away.

"I know, I know. Sorry. Keep going."

"Well, I was looking through the report and stuck to the back of one page was a yellow post-it note that said 'call mom' and it had your Grandma Barb's number on it. I'm not sure who wrote it because it isn't mentioned in the report, but someone gave the order to call Grandma

Barb instead of Annie." Josh watches Megan, as if he's waiting for the information to sink in.

"Is it unusual someone would give that order in a case like this?" Megan asks.

"No, not necessarily. The unusual part is that the order is laying there on a sticky note and not mentioned in the police report at all. As far as the official report is concerned, the note doesn't exist. I called the officer who signed the report to ask about it, but he didn't know what I was talking about. Though, he didn't seem concerned. He said he took the required statements, so he signed the report, but he didn't put together the completed file. His guess is someone added it after the fact. I'll keep digging."

Not being in law enforcement herself, or having dealt with anything like this before, Megan isn't sure what to make of it yet. But she files away the explanation in the back of her mind to sort out later.

"Thanks, Josh. I really appreciate this. I know this isn't easy for you, considering the falling out you had."

Josh grew up in a broken home—in every sense of the word. His father was a drug addict and his mother turned a blind eye to that and the physical abuse that came along with it. When they were just kids, Josh latched onto Megan, Mark and Annie and they were all happy to have him. Things didn't start getting rocky between them until Josh and Megan were teenagers. Josh and Mark butted heads regularly over little things like whether Josh completed his homework, and then over bigger things like why Josh was knocking on their door at midnight, drunk when he was fourteen. They left Megan out of it, often taming their tempers when she entered a room, so she never quite understood what the problem was.

Until one day, when Josh was about seventeen years old, Megan heard Josh and her dad arguing out in the driveway. She ran to her room and opened the window to hear better. She caught the end of the exchange.

"Nothing I do is going to be enough for you, is it?" Josh yelled.

"Go home, Josh. And stay away from her." Mark's voice was like steel.

Megan couldn't hear Josh's response. His voice sounded far away. But she heard her father once last time. "I mean it, Josh!"

Neither Josh nor her dad ever explained to her what the fight was about, but Josh stopped coming over. He went straight into the Sacramento Police Academy after high school the following year, wanting to put people like his dad away where they couldn't hurt anyone. Now, he's gunning to become one of the youngest detectives on the force. Josh's heart is golden. He's nothing like his father, which is a miracle considering Josh's upbringing.

Megan wasn't willing to let Josh go so easily. After high school, she stayed in Sacramento and went to college locally with Katie. The three of them remained as close as ever.

Megan picks at a fingernail on one hand, trying to smooth the rough edge with her opposite thumb nail. "You know, you've never told me what happened between you guys. Why you stopped coming over." Megan looks up at his face, searching for the story.

"It doesn't matter, Megs. It's ancient history."

"I know it sounds crazy to think maybe he didn't kill himself. All signs point to it…"

Josh puts an arm around her shoulders. "Megs, crazier things have happened in this world. You have a right to know what happened to your dad. If I can help you, you know I'm going to. I made you a copy of the papers in his file. They're out in my car. Can I walk you out?"

"Of course. That'd be great." Megan turns and gives the mourners one last look before following Josh out the door. Her whole body freezes when she sees Annie. Annie isn't looking at her, she's engrossed in a conversation with Heather. But standing next to her, Dan is staring directly at Megan.

As if snapping back to reality, Dan shakes his head and returns to focus on Heather. Megan spins on her heels and hightails it out the door.

Had he been watching us the whole time?

CHAPTER 6

TUESDAY, SEPTEMBER 8TH

A couple of days later, Megan is preparing to walk into her first appointment with a therapist. The appointment was Katie's suggestion, recommending that Megan talk to an objective professional, and stop pretending none of this was bothering her. Megan felt she owed it to her friend to try.

Megan had no idea where to find a good therapist, or what makes a therapist any good. But she found out Annie had already started attending a support group last week for Widows Initiated From Execrable Suicide (WIFES). Megan made it a point of silently judging these women because *what kind of people sit around figuring out a way to give their grief group an incorrectly spelled acronym so suicide support feels cute and cozy?* Regardless, against every one of her natural instincts, she called Annie the day after her dad's memorial service and asked if one of Annie's group members could refer her to a decent therapist.

Annie practically squealed into the phone at the opportunity to help, which sent a pang of guilt reverberating through Megan. But she shook off the feeling, reminding herself Annie still owes her answers.

Later that same day, Annie texted Megan the name and number of Dr. Hannah Glover. "A friend of mine said she's fantastic and kind. Try her out. I hope this helps."

It feels as though for the last ten days, Megan has done little more than search through her mental catalogue of media, experiences, and conversations that might be the source of the familiar words in her dad's text message. Focusing on something else may be good for her.

But when Megan sits down in the waiting room, she immediately regrets her decision to listen to Katie. There is no way she can do this. If she can't even explain to her best friend all the delicate and complicated intricacies of her thoughts and feelings about her dad, how can she possibly open up to a stranger? And anyway, how will talking about it be of any help? *This is a colossal waste of time.* She should be home trying to figure out the next move in her own private investigation of her father's suicide.

His *alleged* suicide.

"Megan Palmer?" A woman appears in the doorway, ready to see her now. Megan stands and follows the woman through the door.

Hannah's office looks nothing like Megan imagined. It has all the trimmings of a warm, welcoming living room. The room is on the fourth floor and filled with natural light pouring in from the floor to ceiling windows. There is some artwork, but it's minimal. A different photo of the beach in the soft light of sunrise hangs on each wall save for the one by the entrance, which displays framed copies of Hannah's diplomas and therapy license.

Hannah extends an arm towards the center of the room, seeming to point at everything and nothing all at once. "Please, take a seat. Make yourself comfortable."

Megan immediately wonders if this is her first test. If Hannah is evaluating which seat Megan chooses and what her choice must suggest about her mental state. Megan makes a snap decision in case her inability to decide suggests she is unstable or possibly insane.

Megan walks over to the side of the room with a single ultra-plush grey couch. A large cable knit cream colored pillow and a medium plain coral pillow are propped up at either end. She takes a seat at the far side of the couch, nearest the windows, and next to a small wooden side table with a box of tissues on top. Megan regrets her choice as soon as she sees the box, but she can't change seats now. How would *that* look? Hannah might assume Megan anticipates becoming overly emotional. But Megan won't need any tissues today because she is not an emotional breakdown sort of girl. She will make sure of it.

Megan watches as Hannah strolls to the opposite side of the room and sits in one of two cobalt blue swiveling armchairs before setting her notebook down on the small accent table between the chairs. Megan wonders whether Hannah would have chosen the other blue chair or the grey sofa had Megan chosen a blue chair instead.

Her new therapist insists Megan call her Hannah, not Dr. Glover, and Megan assumes it is some kind of mind trick designed to elicit a false sense of familiarity.

"What brings you here today?" Hannah asks, pushing her perfectly coiffed silver wedge haircut away from her face. Her voice is gentle, offering neither expectation nor suggestion.

Unsure of where to begin, Megan blurts out her first thought before she can consider it. "I'm not sure. Actually, I don't want to be here. My best friend told me I should come."

Hannah seems unfazed by Megan's response. "Why did she suggest you come to therapy today?"

"My dad just died." Megan keeps her answers as short as possible, not nearly ready to trust Hannah with her thoughts. Not nearly ready to trust herself not to fall apart and unload the full weight of her emotions onto a stranger.

"I'm sorry to hear that. How long ago?"

"Ten days ago."

"How are you feeling?"

Megan looks out the windows, shifting in her seat while contemplating Hannah's question. How does she explain she feels twenty different things all at once? How deeply ashamed she feels that it was no longer enough for him to forget her birthday all together. But he'd rather die before her next one than try to have any kind of relationship with her. Or how pissed she is that she'll never get to tell him how she feels about the dad he turned out to be. Is she most bothered because it had all been pointless, her trying to be perfect every single day so he might love her? Forget about love. Megan would have settled for half-interested in her. How could Hannah possibly understand that despite everything he put Megan through, she loved him throughout it all?

Instead, she replies, "He killed himself. I was told about it on the morning of my birthday," as if that explained everything in one short, neatly packaged answer.

There. Megan decides it was blunt enough for Hannah to think it's the reason Megan seems suddenly inattentive, and not because she is dissecting her dad's text message in her mind and having trouble focusing on much else.

"How do you feel about that?"

Really? Megan assumed the whole *how does it make you feel* thing from the movies was just an exaggerated impression of a therapist done for comedic effect. Then again, she's also heard all good comedy stems from a little truth. That's what makes it funny.

But this? Megan isn't sure she can handle it if this is what their sessions are going to look like going forward.

"It doesn't matter. I've never been big on celebrating my birthday, anyway. And neither was he so…" Megan trails off from her half-truth and lets the thought hang there, incomplete. In order to avoid making eye contact, Megan shifts her eyes to the nearest object. A short, square crystal vase with a peach and pastel yellow floral arrangement sits artfully next to the teardrop-shaped sea glass lamp on top of the tiny table next to Hannah. *That'll do.*

When Hannah doesn't attempt to get Megan's attention back, Megan gives up and turns her focus to Hannah, feeling like she'd lost a game perhaps only she had been playing. Hannah's face is stoic, revealing nothing. Megan figures it's her job. She is supposed to sit there, without judgment, and without projecting her own feelings into Megan's story. This must be what makes her such a good therapist, Megan decides. Megan wouldn't be able to hear other people's troubles without trying to take them on herself.

Hannah waits, as if she intuitively knows there is more bubbling up in Megan's throat.

Megan releases a long, cleansing breath to clear the tightness that had been building in her chest. Inhaling again, she smells the strong floral stench of lavender. Megan sees the lavender candle sitting on top of Hannah's desk, its scent filling the room and assaulting Megan's nostrils, making her feel like Hannah must be a good twenty years older than she looks. *Only old people love the scent of lavender. An ocean scented candle would have suited the room better.*

"Look, he hasn't contacted me in longer than I can remember. I don't know when the last time he said happy birthday to me was." Except she does, and it was when she turned fifteen. Megan is on the verge of either crying or screaming and she isn't sure which. She stuffs both urges back down and wonders if Hannah would show any kind of response to a twenty-seven-year-old screaming at her about something she had nothing to do with. Hannah would indeed be phenomenal at her job if she could maintain her composure.

"Your answers feel measured and incomplete. This suggests to me you're unsettled when it comes to these issues," Hannah observes, pushing her round glasses frames up the bridge of her nose.

It's not a question. It's a statement. A very generic statement. *What does that even mean? Unsettled. That could describe any set of emotions beyond the realm of happy.*

"Yeah, well, he wasn't exactly a great guy." Megan huffs, sounding childish.

"You're judging. Does your judgment of your dad make you feel better?"

It takes all the self-control Megan can muster not to roll her eyes at Hannah, which would not only be unhelpful to this session, but downright rude when she knows Hannah is trying to help her.

"No, it doesn't make me feel better. But it *is* how I feel. Isn't that what you keep asking me to talk about? How I feel?" Megan's shoulders sag a little and she leans further back into the couch, like a small child who has just been reprimanded and made to apologize. And in her head, she does roll her eyes while she responds, hoping Hannah can feel it. *That* would make her feel a little better, she suspects.

"It's not uncommon for women with profiles similar to your own to have underlying issues with their father figure," Hannah prompts.

It's insulting to have someone box her into such a neat little category. She is a human being. How dare these shrinks just organize people in her Rolodex like a color-coded sticky note.

And so what if Hannah's right?

"What is the first memory you have involving your father?" Hannah asks.

Megan stares blankly ahead at the photo of the ocean hanging on the wall opposite her. She wonders if Hannah chose photos of the ocean at sunrise on purpose, rather than sunset. Megan prefers the sunrise with its fresh sparkle of a new beginning.

Megan realizes her mind has wandered when she hears Hannah continue pressing. "Is it a happy one? Or is it a painful memory?" She gestures to the pillow next to Megan, offering to have Megan recline on the couch and close her eyes. *Another cliché.*

"Almost all my memories of my dad are difficult. How is it helpful to bring them up?" Megan doesn't want to go back to those places, preferring to leave them where they belong. In the past.

"It's important you're able to understand your anger and assign it to the person with whom it belongs. You are not responsible for your father's actions or behavior."

Megan is stalling because the task at hand requires no thought. She knows her first memory well. The memory is embedded in her, marrow deep. It is the same memory that appears in her dreams. Her mind wanders back to it regularly, without Megan's permission. Each time, Megan tries to recall anything before it. Something good. Something normal. And each time, she comes up empty-handed. "There's better material to study in more recent years. Do we really need to go back that far?"

"Is there a more suitable place to begin than at the beginning?" Hannah retorts.

Megan's pragmatism knows Hannah is probably right. But getting her heart to follow suit is a fresh challenge. Her heart is not so easily swayed.

The entire room is soft and inviting, intending to coax the patient into relaxing. So much so they'll forget they've come here to put their inner workings on display and share the sordid details of their life with a total stranger. Hannah's diplomas and desk disrupt the soothing atmosphere. They are clinical. The desk is simple, with a white desktop and four legs made of natural wood jutting out from the bottom at forty-five-degree angles to provide stability. Megan looks at the desk and diplomas frequently, actively focusing on the only items in the room that remind her she is not home. She is in therapy.

Megan recalls her vow to give therapy a fair shot, if not for herself, then for Katie.

Fine, Megan submits. "My first memory…"

I was about 7 years old. I know that, not because I remember I was 7, but because I know what year my parents separated.

It was the middle of the night. I don't know how long I had been asleep for. I woke up because someone was yelling.

It took me a second, a minute, maybe, to remember where I was. I looked around and saw the familiar surroundings of my bedroom. The pink metal canopy bed had no canopy on it but framed my white bedsheets with pictures of The Little Mermaid all over them. Everything was The Little Mermaid for me. Maybe because the water has always calmed me. Everything seems so much more peaceful in the water. It's as if the water knows you came seeking comfort, letting you float there, small and weightless in its vastness. The water is dependable. Its waves don't know how to stop coming back to the shore after receding out into the deep. The water doesn't know how to disappoint you. As a child, I'd pretend to be a mermaid, even refusing to speak to my mother until she called me Ariel, instead of my given name.

The screaming frightened me. I wasn't sure at first if I was dreaming or if the sound was real. Was it coming from the TV?

No, it was much closer.

If things like this had happened before this night, my parents must have been good at hiding it from me and my brother. Or perhaps this is the one I remember because I became directly involved in it.

The shouting came into focus, the words became sharp. My bedroom was directly across the hallway from theirs. I doubt anyone outside knew what went on inside. Maybe not even my grandparents on my mom's side who lived just down the street.

"Mark, please!" my mother begged.

I tried so hard not to cry. To make myself small, praying not to be noticed. I didn't want to cause any more trouble for my mom than it sounded like she was already in.

When the first sob escaped my lips, it felt like my body had betrayed me. I had so little control over what was happening across the hallway, and even less control over how I responded to it.

After the first cry, the dam had shattered, and I sobbed uncontrollably and pulled my blanket up close to my face to hide the sound. I was so little. I tried to stay as quiet as I could, I did. But he heard me.

"Your daughter needs you!" he roared. I had never heard him so angry. His voice was wild.

"Your daughter", he had said. Not "our daughter". Not even "Megan". He claimed no ownership of anything or anyone he didn't want to deal with. Not then, not ever.

That's when I heard the crying. My cheeks were wet, but this new sound was not my own. This sound belonged to my mother. She was still pleading with my father to calm down and stop yelling. Even as she was being dragged across the floor, like a rag doll, by one arm into my room while he continued to scream.

I didn't recognize this person. He was a madman, unhinged. I still don't remember the extent of the damage my mother sustained that night. I never asked.

"I SAID YOUR DAUGHTER NEEDS YOU!"

She climbed up into my bed and held my tiny body. We cried together, waiting for whatever came next, our shaking bodies pressed closer and our tears mixed so we couldn't tell which were mine and which were hers. It didn't matter anyway.

She tried her best to soothe me. To explain what was happening in words a seven-year-old could understand. "He's tired. We had a disagreement. It's ok. He'll calm down. Shhh."

There was banging. Maybe dresser drawers being slammed shut. I can't be certain. He stormed past my bedroom door in a rage, banging the walls with his suitcase. He didn't say a word.

The front door slammed shut, and he was gone. How my brother slept through it, I am not sure. Maybe he didn't. Every time we changed homes, my brother and I always hoped for the bedroom closest to our parents'. It made for quick access should a nightmare sneak into our dreams, or a monster decide to come into the house. I never considered how it would feel if the monster lived across the hall. Perhaps my brother was lucky he lived at the end of the hallway.

I'm not sure what the fight was about that night. But I know it was the last one they had together in that house.

"Can you remember something good before that incident?" Hannah inquires.

"No. At least not anything specific. I grew up a daddy's girl, or so I've always been told. But I can't think of a better memory before the night he left. Maybe there weren't many of those".

Megan's mind is stuck back in the memory she just relived. Her seven-year-old self is awake and staring at the floor, afraid to look up. Her bedroom was separated from her parents' by just three feet of old, brown carpet that was always clean but stiff and sturdy, as if it needed to support not just the family living between its walls, but the weight of their secrets too.

Megan realizes Hannah is talking to her. "It's often the distressing experiences that stay with us more readily. Good memories are often lost in the wake of them because, by comparison, they seem mundane." Hannah explains.

People are supposed to be grateful for the experiences, good or bad, that shape them into the better people they become in the end. Megan wishes her life had been a little more mundane.

CHAPTER 7

WEDNESDAY, SEPTEMBER 9TH

A nnie called me yesterday after I got out of therapy, asking if I could come over. She was going through my dad's things and found some stuff I may want," Megan explains to Katie on the other end of the phone as she sits in the driver's seat of her car, willing the car to magically start on its own. If it did, the decision to go back to her father's house after all these years would be made for her. She'd be following the universe's orders rather than returning, of her own volition, to the house that broke her.

"How was your first therapy session, by the way?" Megan purposefully hadn't called Katie after her session. Not because she didn't want to share with Katie. She knows Katie always has her best interest at heart. But Megan didn't know how to feel about any of it.

On one hand, she feels like they accomplished little during their first session. She isn't sure what she had expected, but the feeling she didn't achieve what she set out to never sits well with Megan. On the other hand, being made to search for the place where her childhood memories begin and discover how the scars on her heart were formed was more traumatic than she'd thought it would be, considering how skilled she'd become at burying her feelings so deeply they were often forgotten with time.

"I meant to call, but it was just a lot." Megan answers truthfully, chewing on a fingernail that's grown too long. She stopped biting her nails when she was a teenager with the aid of the acetone flavor of nail polish. But she's so nervous she didn't even notice when her hand flew up to her mouth. "Can we grab coffee later and catch up?"

"Of course we can! I'm free all day tomorrow. Usual spot in the morning?"

"Sounds good. I'll be there at 9." Megan pauses, not quite ready to hang up the phone. "I don't want to go over there, Katie. But a couple of things popped up in my head and I can't decide if I want them. I should grab them just in case, right? People always regret it later, not saving things. Don't they?" Megan isn't sure if she is convincing herself to go, or if she is giving herself permission to want something of her dad's. In either case, she suddenly needs affirmation that going over to Annie's house is the right decision.

"Go, Megan. I know you were on the outs with your dad for a long time. But it's ok if you still want to keep a piece of him. To remember the wonderful moments. If you get there and you want nothing, that's ok too. But you owe it to yourself to see. Maybe say goodbye. To that place. To those memories."

Damn it if Katie isn't always right.

Megan pulls up to Annie's duplex an hour later and parks at the end of the carport. She cuts the ignition and waits. Hannah told her to take three deep breaths when she's feeling anxious but, everyone says that.

Sometimes Megan can't believe how many therapists get paid to spout off common knowledge. What Megan does find helpful is her new grounding strategy. While breathing, she is supposed to identify something she can see, something she can touch, something she can hear, taste, and smell. After that, she is free to continue her day. She closes her eyes and feels the steady rhythm of her heart pumping inside her chest. She hears the hum of the cars flying by on the main road on the opposite side of the concrete retaining wall to her right. She smells the slightly smoky smell of a barbecue drifting through the vents. She tastes remnants of the coffee she gulped down just before she arrived. Megan slowly flutters her eyelids open to take in her surroundings, noticing the tiny trees that line the front yards.

She gets out and trudges up to the door. Megan takes her house key in her hand and lifts it to the lock above the handle. She'd wanted to return it to her dad. A final dagger after their fight. But she couldn't, so it sat on her keyring for seven years, unused. Annie wouldn't mind if she let herself in, but after all this time, she feels like an intruder. She shakes her head, sliding the key back in her pocket and knocks on the door.

A few moments and a second knock pass but, Annie still doesn't come. Megan presses her ear to the door and listens. She can hear the TV, or more likely, music, playing in the house. Annie was always listening to music. She had hundreds of CDs, all arranged in alphabetical order. She would deep clean the house every few weeks. It would take her all weekend between cleaning and caring for the small jungle she kept in the house, and she would play her CDs one by one, in alphabetical order. It feels oddly important now, to complete the memory, but Megan can't remember how long it took her to listen to them all.

Megan knocks a little louder and when the door opens, Annie pulls her inside the doorway and into a deep hug.

Annie's eyes look red rimmed and tired, as if she's been crying all morning. "Do you still have your house key? Why didn't you just let yourself in?" She seems to have forgotten Megan hasn't visited in seven years, save for the occasional trip between classes to grab some food. The junior college Megan attended was right down the road and even though their relationship was already becoming strained, driving here saved her a lot of time and money on food. She knew when her dad and Annie would be at work. If Megan saw either of their cars parked in front of the house, she'd turn around to drive to the McDonald's near campus.

Megan follows Annie down the narrow hallway, towards the living room, intentionally avoiding looking into the master bedroom lying directly across the hallway from the front door. To peer inside feels wrong, like crossing the line somehow.

Uncomplimentary scents accost Megan, each vying for real estate in her memory. She recognizes the clean, citrus scents of lemon Pine-sol and orange Pledge. Two of Annie's cleaning staples. As Megan floats closer to the kitchen area, she picks up the warm, sweet smell of Annie's pineapple upside-down cake and then the peanut butter and butterscotch cornflake balls, one of Megan's favorite treats around the holidays. As she peeks around the corner and into the kitchen, she sees both desserts resting atop the counter. It occurs to Megan Annie must be in a deep state of distress as she remembers both cleaning and cooking were forms of stress relief for Annie.

In the living room, the TV is on. Annie's watching a home movie that features Mark, and Megan's legs stop working when she sees the face she remembers so vividly staring back at her.

"I'm just going through some videos. You wouldn't have seen these." Annie's eyes narrow ever so slightly. "Sit down."

Megan realizes, when Annie tells her this, Annie is very much aware of how long it's been since Megan was a regular guest in her house. It's always been Annie's house, and Megan has always been just a visitor.

Annie nudges a box of tissues closer to Megan on the coffee table as Megan obediently sits on the plush brown couch. The gesture strikes Megan as odd. As if Annie is predicting it will wreck Megan the way it has Annie.

It's strange to see Annie in this state. The woman Megan knew growing up was tough as nails.

Annie grew up poor in a small country town. She has grit from learning early on how to get ahead in a ruthless world and how to keep others from underestimating you. From the stories Megan heard, Annie did this mostly with her fists growing up. She was scrappy, and she didn't take shit from anyone. Not as a child, and certainly not as an adult. She had mellowed a lot with age, probably from all the weed she smoked, but some of the hardness was part of her now.

Annie had her own set of morals. Her humanity seemed to sputter along a spectrum of goodness. Like she hand-selected which pieces of being a quality human she most liked, and which she discarded as unnecessary.

She never spanked or smacked a child, but she also disciplined her dogs with an old piece of cable cord folded in half. Megan recalls at some point, the simple act of Annie standing with the cable in her hand was enough to redirect the dog's behavior. Megan supposes that was Annie's goal all along.

Annie was an assistant at a medical practice where she took great pride in helping their impoverished clientele and then billing their services to those who could afford to pay the bills they received from their insurance companies without verifying the bills were correct. Megan overheard Annie explaining her new work initiative to Mark one evening when they were smoking out on the back porch. Annie also had an entire hall closet filled with what she said were unwanted medical supplies and expired medications an average person cannot get without a prescription.

A breach of ethics, such as this, was handy when Megan had a cold as a kid, but there were so many pills Megan couldn't pronounce and was told *never* to touch. As a child, Megan never understood the implications of a closet like that, but as an adult, in hindsight, she could venture more than one guess as to its purpose.

If Megan had stuck around longer, she may have tried to Google the names to learn what each pill and liquid was meant to aid and what a person might act like if they were abusing them. It may have explained some things. Or it may not have.

Megan sits there entranced by the movie Annie has on. The scene playing when Megan arrived is just finishing, and when the next clip begins, Megan's jaw falls open.

Her father is swimming in a pool with two small children, perhaps around six and three years old. Only seven years have passed since she last saw Mark, but he looks much older in this video. He is tossing them high into the air and then catching them, slowing them down as they hit the waterline until they squeal with delight, yelling "Again! Again!".

Megan feels as though she is watching a group of strangers in the video, even though she knows who many of the people are. Nikki giggles as she sits on the edge of the pool, her toes tracing the surface of the water. Nikki is Annie's daughter. Megan never saw much of her growing up since Nikki was quite a bit older than Megan. Annie explains that the video was recorded earlier in the year at a barbecue Nikki hosted and that these were Mark's grandkids. They're adorable. Megan nods just enough to acknowledge she's heard Annie, but she also stops listening to her after that. She can't pull her eyes away from the screen.

A rush of confusing emotions flood Megan, filling her to the brim and threatening to spill over. She'd always been curious, if she were being entirely honest, about what her dad's life was like after she removed herself from the picture. But upon seeing it, she is seething. Megan's separation was meant to be a punishment. How dare he just move on without his own children, his flesh and blood, and become content in a life devoid of Megan and Smalls. Perhaps the worst thing of all, is how happy he looks. *Why couldn't he be happy with me?*

A grinding noise rings out in Megan's head. Too loud. It takes her a minute to realize she's gnashing her teeth together.

Megan sees Dan in the background. He's standing in a cluster of people Megan doesn't recognize. Dan appeared to be nursing a beer and cheering on her dad. He is laughing, his eyes crinkle in the corners, twinkling, but his eyes are fixated on something just beyond Mark. Megan can't determine what. Dan sits in a chair, leaning forward, his elbows resting casually on his knees, his middle finger wrapped around the long neck of the beer bottle. He seems carefree, and yet, the intensity of his focus leaves Megan a little unnerved. Perhaps he's just staring off into space.

And then, of course, there is Mark. Unmistakably the same person Megan grew up with, though his hair is far whiter with a smattering of dark grey than the pepper with a healthy dash of salt she remembers. He'd began greying prematurely. More than once when she was young, Megan would find him at the bathroom sink, a box of black hair dye in his hand, trying to decide whether to cover up the light strands or embrace them.

Mark's smile radiates a warmth for these two grandkids who don't belong to him. In their time apart, Megan's dad had chosen a new family. And why wouldn't he? When given the chance, it's far easier to choose a family who wanted him, one who had not been with him long enough to know how undependable and destructive he could be, rather than stick with the family he would have to work far too hard to fix.

Indignation at this injustice smothers the other feelings swimming around in Megan's mind, choking her until she can't breathe. Rather than watch his own daughter grow up, walk her down the aisle, or play with his real grandkids in a pool, he picked another family. The simple choice, as always. He never did the harder, more meaningful things.

We all have choices. He made his.

Fine, Megan decides to herself. If he didn't want her, she can't change that now. And if Annie is expecting Megan to ask for a tissue because she misses him terribly, then Annie is sorely mistaken. Suddenly, Megan's rage is winning out, pushing viciously against the dam. Tears hot with anger are flooding in behind her eyes as Megan tries desperately to hold them back. Annie will not have the satisfaction of witnessing her grief. It always sneaks up on Megan now and she hates how unstable she feels.

Megan regains control, pointing her outrage at Annie. Annie should have been encouraging him to make amends with Megan. She could have told him to try harder. Reminded him Megan was his only daughter and of how much Megan loved him and needed him as a kid. Reminded him it was never too late to try.

Instead, it seems like Annie decided this way was better for her, too. She could focus on the family that belonged to her rather than repair a blended, but very broken, family. Annie capitalized on the separation between Megan and her father. As Megan sits here, being made to watch this picture-perfect home movie, she doubts very much whether Annie feels even marginally bad about it. As always, Annie gets what she wants, no matter the fallout.

Megan stands up abruptly. "I'm done watching this. Can we go look through his stuff now? I thought of a couple of things I'd like to have". Megan can't rip her eyes away from this video, as much as she wants to, so she removes herself to wait near the hallway and her eyes are forced to follow. She had wanted to remain composed, but Annie made her watch this movie. Megan's words are caustic, though she can't bring herself to feel sorry for it.

Annie says nothing. Megan can feel Annie's gaze, heavy and intense in her peripheral. But when Megan turns to look at her, a wide grin is painted across Annie's face. When Megan blinks, it's gone. Annie sits there looking hurt.

"Sure, it's in the spare bedroom".

Annie means Megan's old room. Megan trails after Annie, leaving plenty of space between them.

CHAPTER 8

Megan doesn't believe in ghosts, but when she steps inside the room, her father's presence settles over her like a thick fog. She rationalizes it only feels like his spirit remains here because it's obvious this is where he'd been staying. Her mind involuntarily begins devising some theories explaining why he may have moved into this room, but she has no actual knowledge to confirm any of them.

There are pieces of him everywhere and Megan finds it hard to believe Annie moved all his belonging in here so quickly.

"Did my dad move into this bedroom at some point? Why is all of his stuff in here?" Megan asks without turning around to look at Annie.

Annie doesn't miss a beat, as if she expected this question. "He slept in here sometimes. You remember how he snored? He never wanted to keep me awake."

Megan's brows knit together. She'd never known her dad to snore, but she decides not to push it right now since clearly Annie just lied. It's been too long since Megan has been in touch with Annie, and Megan has no idea how far Annie will go for her story.

Megan scans the room slowly and then turns to face the open closet. His clothes hang inside, frozen in time, awaiting his return. She runs her fingers over the tops of the garments, taking in the familiar textures and colors. His favorite blue and grey plaid vest hangs in the front, the one with the grey cutoff sleeves he wore in the picture of him Megan loves. Next to it hangs his vintage Harley Davidson leather jacket. He owned a motorcycle for many years, but it wasn't a Harley. He had always wanted one, but he could never afford it. His army green garrison cap sits on the shelf above the hangers, in front of his framed military headshot. He was so young. So alive.

When Megan finally spins back around, she clocks his *Star Trek* memorabilia. Things he paid ridiculous amounts of money for. A replica of Worf's Starfleet badge. The Klingons were his favorite *Star Trek* characters, Worf, in particular. There is a replica of Lieutenant Commander Geordi La Forge's visor, and of course, there is his multi-board *Star Trek* themed chess set. He had promised for years to teach Megan how to play. That day never came. The chess board sat unused, serving as a bookend for his collection of *Star Trek* books, all tattered, worn-out copies from the second-hand stores he and Megan would frequent growing up. Some of Megan's fondest memories were of going to thrift stores and shopping for books with her dad. They would come home with armfuls and have reading days where they'd lie around on the couch together with a book in one hand, the other hand reaching into the shared snack bowl between them.

The bed has a large box style headboard, open on one side where the mattress slides in. Sitting on the top of the headboard are a few framed pictures. One of Mark as a young boy from his years in the Army. One of Mark, Megan and Jonathan, on an Easter Sunday standing in front of his old 1992 sky-blue Ford Mustang white top convertible. They'd taken the photo outside Annie's duplex, but Megan and Jonathan were still very young, around six and four years old, respectively. *We all looked so happy*. And one photo was of him with Annie at a holiday party. That picture has been around longer than Megan can remember.

Looking at the photos he kept displayed leaves a hollow feeling in Megan's chest. It's like he didn't have any recent memories he loved enough to keep. Could he have been depressed, and no one had noticed? Maybe he just loved these moments that much. Maybe he loved his kids once.

Megan buries the idea, feeling childish, and decides he just couldn't be bothered to swap the photos. Megan has no way of knowing now, and she felt the sharp bite of sadness once more.

Megan continues to look around, taking in every piece of him left behind before she decides what to look through. None of these things feel like something she should be allowed to take with her. She has no attachment to his stuff, and it is painful seeing the only things he held onto were from so long ago. As if nothing beyond these frozen moments was special enough to keep.

Then Megan spies some photo albums on the lowest floating shelf attached to the wall. She walks over and sits cross-legged on the floor in front of the albums. Annie sorts through the clothing behind her.

Megan pulls out the last album on the shelf, assuming it contains the most recent photos. It'd been painful watching the videos, but she seeks the albums all the same. As angry as she is, a part of her wonders if she deserves to be punished after the things she'd said to him.

When she peels back the thick maroon cover to skim through the pages, the photos inside make her stop abruptly. The pictures in this album are from Megan's childhood. They end rather suddenly around the time she stopped visiting regularly. The last set of photos marks an occasion they'd all gone out to the ranch where Annie boarded her horse, Justice. Megan was around fourteen then. She's always wondered what happened to him.

The albums must be in the wrong order. She selects another and opens to the first page. It is even older. She shrugs and looks through it anyway. Something feels off as she skims through the pages. She isn't sure what it is, though.

"Are these all the photo albums you guys have?" Megan asks, hopeful that Annie has some stashed away somewhere else.

"We have a few more, but…" Annie cuts herself off, as if she hadn't meant to divulge that information. She coughs to clear her throat. "They're in the outside storage closet. Your dad wasn't a big part of those albums." It doesn't escape Megan's notice how carefully Annie is speaking, as if each word means something important Megan isn't privy to.

"What do you mean? Like he's not in the pictures?" Megan tries to pull more information out of her without pushing too hard in case Annie clams up the way she did when she called Megan just days ago.

"Your dad and I went through a rough patch. He came and went for a while. The albums in the outside closet don't have many photos of him." Annie's voice sounds casual. Too casual. Annie still isn't telling her everything, but the things left unsaid ring so loudly in Megan's head she isn't sure how Annie can't hear them.

"He came and went for a while? Went where? Can I see the pictures he's in?" Megan pushes back. Fatigue is setting in from Annie's dishonesty and that alone upsets Megan more than whatever Annie is hiding possibly could. When Annie doesn't respond right away, Megan tries a different tactic. Taking a deep breath, she turns to look Annie in the eye and, with all the doggedness she can muster, says, "Look, I'm an adult, Annie. I'm not the fragile, sweet little child you knew. Can you please not treat me like one? Not about this."

Annie sighs and lets her head tilt to the side ever so slightly. "Honestly, it's mostly just pictures I took on walks with Kona, or when I'd visit Justice at the stables. Some pictures of the grandkids. Things like that. Mark wasn't one for having his photo taken anymore." Annie adds the last part tentatively, Megan notices. Annie looks unsure of how she will react to the information. The realization surprises Megan because Annie has never tiptoed around other people's feelings.

"Why do you keep them in the outside closet? Why not just keep them with all the others?" Megan cocks her head, her brow furrowing, creating lines of genuine curiosity across her face. She doesn't understand why recent albums are being stored outside while such old photos live here in his bedroom and, frankly, it sounds bizarre.

The smallest twitch in Annie's jaw fires off as she sets her mouth into a firm line. If Megan didn't know better, it seems like Annie is getting nervous. At the very least, annoyed by Megan's questions. But Annie, Megan recalls, is not an anxious person.

"We were running out of space in here, so I moved a few things to the outside storage area. I didn't give it much thought." Annie shrugs off the answer and waves a hand in the air as if dismissing the discussion.

Megan lets it go, unsure of how to pry deeper without upsetting Annie. Besides, she has more things to look through. But she can't shake the feeling that whatever Annie has in the closet, Annie wants it to remain hidden. Something Megan has no business knowing about since she's the one who pushed them away.

Megan turns her attention back to the shelves in front of her, pulling one final photo album to look through. She turns a few pages when it finally strikes her, the odd thing about these albums. She can't believe she didn't notice right away. Now painfully obvious is the fact that Smalls is missing from every page. Like he never existed.

Megan returns the album to its space and moves up to the next shelf displaying Mark's favorite books. Beside his collection of thin, old *Star Trek* stories, is his set of *Mania* novels. The books are the huge, heavy hardback editions Megan remembers him reading when she was younger. The jackets are tattered and ripped just enough that it seems intentional, producing an excellent condition, vintage appearance.

When Megan closes her eyes, she sees him again. He's wearing a Chicago Bears t-shirt and a pair of what he called his "rich man sweatpants", which were really just sweatpants with pockets. He's laying sideways on the couch with his legs stretched out, reclined on the arm, always with two pillows under his back. She watches as his eyes track the words from top to bottom, and his mouth moves just a little, as if it's dying to read the beautiful words aloud so anyone nearby can enjoy them, each sentence carefully selected by the author to paint a world you can lose yourself in.

Megan grazes her fingers down the spines, one by one. Memories flood her brain as if the books themselves hold them inside and spark them back to life, one at a time and then all at once.

She sees herself and her dad sitting together on the couch in the living room, her dad slowly becoming more and more reclined until he finally dozes off, his book laying open and face down, pages flush against his chest.

Her mind jumps, forward or backward, she can't be sure, to a picture of them holding hands while she skips along next to him, partly to keep up with his long strides, partly because she was so excited to be searching at their favorite second-hand store for any R. L. Stine books that hadn't yet found their way into her collection.

In a flash, she is back in her room, huddled under her comforter with a flashlight and her dad's copy of *Children of Mania*. Somewhere far away, she hears her dad's voice and Annie's. They're fighting again and Megan sinks deeper into the story she holds in her hands. She never understood the entire story on her own, but her dad would describe the books to her. She would scan through the pages looking at the infrequent black and white illustrations, making up her own version of the story by interpreting the pictures in a way that provided warmth. The children always found their way home to the waiting arms of parents overwhelmed with joy at the sight of the children they believed to be lost.

Megan snaps back to present when a question sneaks into her mind. It whispers to her, reminding her the next book in the *Mania* series is slated to release later this year. Now she wonders how many books in her dad's favorite science fiction series would he never get to read. The question is insignificant enough that Megan feels silly for wondering, but it is important enough to remind her that the world doesn't wait for you to catch up.

Megan picks up *Children of Mania* carefully. The book is heavy with significance and fragile in her hands. She opens the cover where she sees he has written his name at the top of the inside cover with a date. Megan forgot that she'd watched him pen this information inside his books, the way a person would sign the card inside of a library book so the librarian would have a record of those who borrowed that story. Megan never asked about it and it occurs to her now it was a very childish thing to do.

As if this grown man was afraid to lose his favorite book.

But perhaps it was his small way of leaving a physical mark on the world, offering proof he once existed, afraid the world would forget him one day.

After sliding *Children of Mania* back into its spot, Megan picks up his first *Star Trek* book to see when he finished the first of the series. How long had he been doing this? She opens the cover, but the inside is empty. She randomly plucks two more volumes and checks them for his signature.

Nothing.

She pulls a few miscellaneous science fiction books from his shelf, but they're all empty, too. Her memory must be wrong.

Could it be this was a marking reserved only for the *Mania* series, which she knows meant something to him? She picks up the book furthest to the left on the shelf and gently pulls back the cover.

Mark Calum Palmer 02-03-94.

There are sixteen *Mania* books on the shelf. Megan chooses a few more at random and, one by one, cautiously opens to the first page, half expecting one book to betray her with a blank cover. It's peculiar that he felt compelled to note the date he read these books specifically, but more than that, something about the books themselves niggles at the back of her mind. She can't quite tell what it is, but a nagging itch to figure it out grows stronger each time she opens another book.

Maybe it's nothing. Megan's mind merely trying to focus its energy on something tangible to calm to the sea of confusion swirling inside her. Trying to make sense of things she isn't sure need making sense of. The truth could be that these signatures had no deeper meaning than he wanted to remember something special to him. Megan knows she won't be able to shake the feeling until she checks them all to see if she can sharpen the blurry idea formulating in the corner of her mind.

"Hey, Annie? Do you know why did my dad only dated his *Mania* books when he was done reading them? It doesn't look like he did this with any of his other books here." Megan relaxes her voice to mask the unease tightening in her throat.

"I'm not sure what you mean." Annie reaches out her hand for the book Megan was holding. Her brow pinch together, further stressing the two vertical lines that live between them. Megan passes the book to Annie, reluctant to let it go, but she wants the answer. "I'm not sure. I don't remember him reading this book around the time it's dated. But I could be wrong." Annie hesitates before passing the book back to Megan. Her eyes are wide as she shifts from side to side, glancing around the room. She looks scared. But Annie has never been afraid of anything, least of all Mark.

"Is there is anything of Mark's you'd like before I sort through everything?" Annie gestures to the boxes labeled "donate", "keep", and "trash".

Megan came to this house wanting his hardcover collection of *Mania* books. It's the one connection she has to him she can hold in her hands and look back on with fondness. Seeing this unique tag inside the covers makes Megan want them even more. She must tread lightly, though. She doesn't know what it means, if anything, and she still hasn't made sense of Annie's reaction to this discovery. Megan can't alert Annie to her suspicion that the dates are important.

"Honestly, the only thing I wanted when I came here was his *Mania* collection. The best memories I have with him are the times we spent together reading, and I'd like to read the stories he loved the most. It would mean a lot to me. I don't need anything else." Megan waits anxiously, hoping since she didn't ask for much, Annie will grant her one request.

Annie seems to consider it for a moment. "I can give those to you, but I want to read them first." Annie looks down on the floor and sniffles. "I want to feel what he felt when he read them so I can be close to him one more time."

"Wow…" Megan mutters under her breath. And since Megan knows she doesn't stand a chance at winning an argument over it, she bites her tongue, a little too hard, the metallic tang of blood forming on the tip.

"What was that?"

"Oh, I didn't say anything. Just me know when I can come pick them up?" Annie gives a curt nod.

Still sitting cross-legged on the floor, Megan puts the book gently back on the shelf. She looks over the volumes again, noticing a tiny sliver of paper peeking out ever so slightly from the top of one book, and pulls that volume gently into her lap.

There are two kinds of people in the world: those who use a proper bookmark, and monsters. Megan had always been a fan of real bookmarks, all the better if she could find a bookmark related to the book she was reading. Her dad, however, used whatever random receipt, coupon, or sticky note he could find to mark his place. Occasionally, and she shudders at the memory, he would dog-ear the page to hold his place.

Megan peels back the cover and snaps a mental picture of the date written inside, 03-02-00, before fanning the sheets of paper between the covers. She revels in the scent of the old pages, inhaling as it wafts up into her nose. It's been said that scent is one of the strongest memory triggers. Megan believes it.

She pulls the paper out to see what he used this time. A receipt from their favorite place to get burgers, Lou's Drive-In, with something written on the backside. Her breath catches as she reads her dad's familiar scrawl.

There's not much time left. Come find me.

Megan wonders who this message was meant for. Though her insides are screaming, *"It's for you"*. Megan starts to ask Annie if she knows what this paper means, but something stops her. Instead, she quickly glances over her shoulder and finds Annie has her back to Megan as she goes through Mark's clothes in the closet, folding articles neatly and packing them into the "donate" box.

Annie reacted strangely when Megan showed her the dates inside of the book covers. Maybe Annie doesn't know about this either, and Megan wants a chance to figure out what it is. Annie's cell phone is ringing in another room, so she steps out to take the call. Megan uses the opportunity to slip the paper into her back pocket, wondering all the while if any other books have secrets tucked away inside them. She doesn't have time to find out today.

She can hear Annie, catching clips and pieces of what sounds like a frantic conversation before Annie's voice drops into a hushed tone. Annie returns just a moment later and explains that she must go. She's forgotten she needed to pick up some dry cleaning.

Urgent dry cleaning emergency? Come on, Annie, you're not even trying.

Megan purses her lips and stands up to leave, reminding Annie to text her when she can come back to get the books she wants. Annie nods and asks if she wants to take any of the photo albums from when she was a kid.

Megan considers the option but immediately rejects it. Her mind drifts again to the photo albums locked away in the front closet, thinking she would rather see those. "No, that's alright." Megan makes her way to the front door, apparently not fast enough because Annie is urging her out the door with a hand on her back as she talks.

"Are you sure? I can make copies."

"Don't worry about it. I just want the books."

Annie steps around Megan to open the front door. "Don't be a stranger, ok? Just because he's gone... I'm here for you." Annie sounds deeply sad. Megan wonders if Annie regrets not having tried to mediate any kind of reconciliation between the two of them. But then, it's too late now. Megan isn't interested anymore. As far as Megan is concerned, the connection between her and Annie died with Mark. They can go their separate ways. Just as soon as Megan gets the answers to the questions burrowing deeper into her brain.

Megan backs out of the carport and coasts down the street. She rolls to a stop at the end of the road and pulls the paper out of her pocket, turning it over in her hand.

This note. Her dad's text message. The dates.

Megan's mind swirls with questions but she's jolted from her thoughts when a horn honks from a car that's pulled up behind her. She waves a quick apology before putting her car back in gear and driving off.

CHAPTER 9

THURSDAY, SEPTEMBER 10TH

I can't believe she wouldn't give you the freaking books! It's not right! It's not like you asked for everything. You asked for one thing. What the hell?" Katie takes an indignant sip of her coffee, a hot chestnut praline latte. The first of the season. It's both Megan and Katie's favorite drink. They wait every year for the sacred flavor to return and rarely deviate from it while it's in season. The nutty warmth provides a thick, tasty comfort.

Megan adores Katie's more than appropriate level of righteous outrage as Megan recounts the details of how her visit with Annie went, leaving out the discovery of the dates inside the book covers.

"I'm not surprised. She's always been that way. She has the final say and anyone who feels differently can take a walk." Megan shrugs and tries to wash down her frustration with a deep gulp.

"But you're his daughter! Surely you have some rights when your dad dies." Logically, that should be true. But the law doesn't always follow logic.

"Not when he didn't have a will in place. Apparently, everything gets passed to the surviving spouse before the children. She can legally hold his stuff hostage if she wants. She was probably trying to hook me into coming over just so she could show me what I missed out on all those years. Annie had those movies on and, I swear, it was like she was rubbing my face in it." Megan knows Katie won't appreciate the casual tone in her voice, but none of this came as a shock to Megan.

"She was tough, sure. But she never struck me as being malicious. And especially not to you."

"No, you're right. But you should've seen the look on her face. She was generally decent to me, but she did small things here and there just to keep you in check. There were also some bigger things I still wish I'd never seen." Megan shakes off the thought.

"Like what?" Katie's eyes grow wide.

From any normal person, Megan would interpret Katie's response as fishing for a juicy piece of gossip that could become the hot anecdote at the next social gathering. But from Katie, Megan knows she is genuinely interested in her life and the history that shaped her best friend. Plus, Katie is probably shocked there are secrets Megan still hasn't told her.

"Well, for example, she used to keep this piece of old black cable cord folded up in half on a shelf in her entertainment center." Megan gives Katie the abbreviated version of how the cord was regularly used to educate Annie's dogs. "I mean, her dog spilled some dirt from one of Annie's giant potted plants. It would have been an easy fix with a vacuum, but she acted like her dog was mauling a baby."

Katie sits there, looking stunned. "I don't even know what to say... What kind of psychopath beats an animal like that? I'm having a hard time reconciling the Annie I knew with this version".

Megan nods her understanding at Katie's distress.

"I know, but that's my point. It sounds crazy that she won't give me some books, but she also has some ugly parts to her most people don't know about." Megan won't expand any more today.

Megan's phone vibrates on the table. She flips it over to check the caller ID.

"Speak of the devil." She shows Katie the screen.

"What do you think she wants? You just saw her yesterday."

"I honestly don't know. She said she didn't want to be strangers anymore. I don't want to talk to her right now. Or ever." Megan flips the phone back over, waiting for the call to roll to voicemail, when Katie intercepts her thoughts.

"Just answer it, see what she wants. I'm right here with you." Megan waits, her finger hovering over the answer button. "Hurry! Before the call ends!"

Megan hits the button to accept the call. "Hello? Yeah, I'm fine. How are you?" Megan notices Katie watching intently, as if she focuses hard enough, she'll hear the other half of the dialogue. "Really? Why the sudden change of heart?" Katie looks to be getting impatient listening to a one-sided conversation. If Megan wasn't so confused by what Annie was telling her, Megan might have chuckled at Katie's growing anxiousness, unable to wait the extra sixty seconds for Megan to hang up and explain. "Ok, if you're sure, yeah. Great, thanks. I'll be by later today. Bye."

"Well?"

"She said I could have the books." Megan shrugs as she sets her phone back down on the table.

"Just like that?" Katie snaps her fingers. "She just changed her mind?"

Megan shrugs. "I guess so. She said she thought about it, and it felt like the right thing to do. Besides, it would take her forever to read all of them herself. I can come by later today to pick them up. Who knows, maybe my grandma got under her skin. I know my grandma has been pressuring her to give back his pictures and medals from the army, along with some other things. She can be a tough woman to deal with," Megan hypothesizes.

"True." Katie concedes. "Your grandma is Southern Strong through and through. She probably 'ran her through the warsh and hung her out to dry'." Katie's accent couldn't have been worse, but she nails the extra letter Arkansans add for no good reason. Megan tries to keep it together, but Katie's earnestness breaks her facade. They both double over while their eyes fill up with tears. Megan hasn't laughed like this in weeks. It feels good.

Megan polishes off the last of her latte. "Ok then, I guess I'll go pick up my inheritance after therapy today. Annie said she'd be gone most of the afternoon so I could come by anytime and let myself in."

"You're back at therapy already? You haven't even told me how your first session went!" Katie exclaims.

"I know, sorry. Yesterday was just so overwhelming and the first session the other day just brought up a lot of shit…" Megan's thought trails off, unfinished, and dissipates into the air.

"I understand if you don't want to talk about it even more than you already have." Katie offers, letting Megan off the hook.

"It's not that. I just… I haven't made sense of it yet." Megan tells Katie how it felt for her to sit in a room with a stranger who expected her to unearth secrets Megan didn't even realize she was keeping. And about the memory that surfaced when Megan opened the door to her past. "It's like I worked so hard to remember only the good bits, as fractured as they were, I forgot a darkness always lived inside him at least a little. Maybe he wasn't really the person I remember at all." Megan's sentences come out in stops and starts, like she can't decide what order to put them in, or if she wants to say them at all.

"Megs. I can't believe you've been carrying this with you your whole life. I'm so sorry."

Megan shakes her head, brushing off the sympathy. "It was a long time ago. But it freaked me out, knowing the viciousness he was capable of." Megan sits reflecting for a moment. "Anyhow, afterwards, Hannah suggested I come twice a week, at least for now, and I thought maybe it wasn't a bad idea. She had a cancellation for today, so I took it."

"I think that's smart. It seems like there's a lot for you to unpack and I'm so happy you're going to keep going. I'm proud of you, Megs." Katie smiles, but Megan notices it doesn't quite reach all the way to her eyes. It looks sad and Megan wonders if it's pity she's reading on Katie's face. Megan can't stand the thought of Katie feeling sorry for her and scrambles to turn the conversation around before she leaves.

"On another note, I read through the police report Josh gave me. Josh said he hadn't noticed anything off. He is supposed to be talking to some officers on the scene to see if anyone can tell him about the random *call mom* sticky note in the file. I should check in with him." The new information does exactly what Megan was hoping it would. Katie appears to be coming back to her, a little less sorrowful and the tiniest bit hopeful.

"Oh my god, yes, you need to text him! Someone must know something, right? Someone handled the note and put it in the file."

"Exactly! We just need to figure out who. The officer whose name was on the report told Josh he didn't know. So, fingers crossed for a lead there. That could be huge." Megan's eyes catch hold of Katie's, silently stealing some of Katie's optimism for herself.

Megan glances at the time on her phone, realizing she's stayed ten minutes longer than she should have. She huffs, "I'm late. I don't want to go yet, but I need to get moving if I want to make my appointment. Call you after?" Megan scoots her chair away from the table and stands up. Katie follows her lead.

"Definitely. Go do some good work in there," Katie throws out casually with a pump of her arm, as if Megan was off to high school soccer practice. Katie adds a little wink.

Megan slides her phone into her purse where her hand grazes the note from her dad. She feels a jolt of recognition blindsiding her like a bolt of lightning. She rights herself and grabs Katie's arm to stop her from leaving. "Oh my god, Katie. I think I know where I've seen my dad's text message before." She can't be certain yet, but at least she might know where to start looking.

"Where?" The excitement and hope in Katie's voice is undeniable.

"I'm not positive yet, but I need to get to Annie's ASAP. I've got to run to meet Hannah, but I'll call you on the way to Annie's house!" Megan is already turning to jog to her car, waving her arm in the air hoping it would pass as both a goodbye and an apology.

"You better!" Megan hears Katie yell after her.

CHAPTER 10

Sinking back into the couch in Hannah's office, Megan feels the anxiety bubble up in her throat again. It's aggressive today. Having been here before, the expectation of what they might find today is both comforting and frightening. Megan can only hope that following the dark path laying in front of her will lead her to the truth, whatever it is.

"And what about your brother? What was his relationship with your father like?" Hannah asks.

"Why does that matter? Aren't we here to analyze *my* relationship?" Megan agreed to come more frequently since it's an opportunity to explore her memories and maybe put a few of the broken pieces back together. But she is still skeptical about this entire ordeal.

"Sibling dynamics with the same parental figure can be a valuable tool in understanding your own experience. Your brother's relationship to your parents plays a role in your own, whether or not you see it." Hannah's explanations always feel unnecessarily complicated, but Megan appreciates an answer to her questions, rather than some vague shrinky nonsense.

"Well, that may be true, but Smalls and our dad don't have a relationship. Or they didn't," Megan adds the correction as an afterthought.

Jonathan and Mark hadn't spent any significant amount of time together since her brother was a young child. As she grew older, Megan understood it had emotionally stunted her dad when his own father committed suicide. Frozen in time at just sixteen years old, Mark had no idea how to be a proper father or how to handle complex emotions intensifying within himself, let alone within his two children.

"Why do you think that is?" The classic Hannah follow-up question has been served, awaiting Megan's volley back.

I remember the night that split my dad and my brother into a man and child. No longer a father and son. The chasm had opened too wide to be repaired.

My dad and Annie had run off to get married. The decision was made without our knowledge, let alone our stamp of approval. This woman our dad had been having an affair with would officially become part of the family.

Smalls and I were told the joyful news when my father sat us down one evening and showed us a picture taken at the Viva Las Vegas Wedding Chapel.

Even as a little girl, I remember thinking how silly it looked. To be dressed, head to toe, in an Egyptian prince and Arabian princess costume with someone they called "King Tut" standing between them. They called it a wedding photo, but I saw grown-ups ready to trick-or-treat on Halloween.

The four of us sat down at the dinner table as a new family that night. My brother was a very picky eater as a child and our new step-mommy had no tolerance for it. He was to eat his food, or he could sit at the table all night. It felt cruel.

I remember feeling heartbroken as I watched him sit there crying the stubborn tears of a five-year-old, giving his best effort to win this battle.

Later that evening, I was getting ready for bed. Our bed then was a futon mattress laid out on the living room floor, while my brother was still at the table, exhausted and nodding off from his effort. He was called back to our father's room to talk. I remember feeling stiff, my body tingling with anxious energy. I wasn't sure if he was going to endure a lecture or face an additional consequence for not having eaten his food. And I didn't know how long I was going to have to sit in the living room alone. I didn't want to be alone there.

When my brother came out just a few minutes later, he had an odd look on his face, or rather, he had no look on his face at all.

I asked him what happened, but before he could tell me, I heard our dad crying.

I walked down the hallway, so slowly, each tiny step trying to decide if I should go back into the bedroom or not. Unsure and a little afraid of what I would find.

I peeked in and saw my dad sitting on the floor. He propped his back up against the old brown wooden dresser, his knees pulled up to his chest and his face buried in them. He wrapped his arms around his legs as if he couldn't hug them tight enough.

I must have made a noise because his head snapped up the instant I was in the room. He looked up, and I saw his face, puffy and splotched with red. Two distinct streams of water ran down either cheek, flowing completely uninhibited and without end.

He told me to come sit with him, so I did. He let go of his knees and stretched his legs out in front of him.

"Daddy, why are you crying?" I asked.

I realize now, as I'm telling you this, he didn't give me much of the story at all, only the part that hurt him the most. "Do you know what your brother just told me?"

"No."

"He told me he hates me, and he hates it here and he never wants to come back here ever again." His words came out broken up in the way that only sobbing can cause.

"Daddy, Smalls didn't mean it. He was just mad." My brother was only five years old, after all. How was it possible I knew this at only eight-years-old, but the venom of a little boy left our father tattered and broken?

My dad was destroyed. Utterly defeated.

That was the last night my brother spent at our dad's house. A five-year-old dictated what their relationship would be like, and our father never questioned it. He never fought for my brother. I wonder if Annie influenced him, or if he was simply too broken to know how.

Before we went back to our mom the next day, our dad gave us each a little token. It was a poker chip engraved with our initials.

I don't think my dad ever knew Smalls took his everywhere. It lived in his pocket for longer than I can remember. He would fiddle with it constantly. We were just kids, though. Kids lose things. I don't remember when I stopped seeing it.

They still saw each other occasionally, often when my dad would come pick me up or my mom would drop me off for the weekend. Sometimes Dad would randomly take me and Smalls out for ice cream, but he'd take us back to our mom when we were finished. Never to Annie's. Those special trips stopped shortly after my brother could verbalize he didn't want to go any places with our dad. I never faulted Jonathan for any of it. Whatever the reason, our new stepmom didn't seem to like him much. But his own father never tried to fix what was broken between them. And that was Dad's job, not Smalls'. Smalls was just a kid.

From then on, I fought for as long as I could to make sure my father knew I still loved him. At least he would have one of us. I assumed it would be important to him. I'd never leave him or disappoint him, even though he let me down more times than I could count.

No one told me it wasn't my responsibility. No one told me even the best child can't fix a broken parent. Why did no one tell me?

"Children always have different parents. Even within the same family." Hannah observes without expanding. "And how did your brother react when he learned about your father's death?"

"It didn't seem to have any impact on him. Why should it? He hadn't spoken to or heard from our dad since he was a small boy. The man could have been a stranger on the street for all he knew," Megan answers flatly. She hadn't expected it to be so draining to dive into the past and she's exhausted now as their hour mark closes in. What's more, Megan is angry.

She is angry with her father, but she isn't sure which father deserved her current fury the most. The father she had nearly twenty years ago who was a child himself? The father she had a few weeks ago, who'd left a bigger mess in the aftermath of his death than she could have ever imagined? Or the father she's learning about now as she looks backwards in time. The one, it turns out, she might never have known at all.

CHAPTER 11

Megan calls Katie, but she doesn't answer. Megan sends out a quick text message telling Katie she is on her way to pick up the books from Annie and will ring her again afterwards.

Megan has a heavy feeling in the pit of her stomach. The same gnawing in your gut alerting you something bad is going to happen. She chalks it up to anxiety about her investigation, which feels like it's at a standstill.

Megan hopes Annie isn't home. She arrived later than she expected, but Annie said she'd be gone most of the afternoon. Relief washes over Megan when she pulls up to the duplex and sees Annie's car is gone. She relaxes a bit, but her insides remain tangled with nerves, feeling as if she is breaking and entering somehow.

Megan knows why she feels like a burglar. She isn't planning on only grabbing the books. There is one other thing she's come for.

Megan parks at the end of the driveway, nearest to the street, and when she gets out of her car, she takes a panoramic look around. Out of the corner of her eye, a movement catches her attention. A shared wall facing the street attaches the two master bedrooms of the duplex. The blinds in the next-door neighbor's bedroom are swaying back and forth. Megan doesn't see any cars in the carport next door. She never saw a face, but her spine started tingling. Awareness of her surroundings is on high alert now.

Megan walks up to the front door and lets herself in.

In the middle of her dad's bedroom, on the floor, is a box labeled "Mark's Books". The room has been mostly cleared out and what's left stands neat and orderly, save for this one box. It's as if it didn't want to be missed. The box looks out of place and lonely. Megan shoots her eyes down to the floor just to avoid the way the box seems to reflect how her dad must have felt in his last moments; surrounded by life, but utterly alone.

Megan gathers herself and steps over to the box. She pops the top off to see if any books are missing. Everything looks to be in order, so she pulls one book out to see if it also contains a date inside the cover.

It does.

She slips the book back into its space and scoops up the box. As she shuffles to her car, she thinks about how she's carrying with her the only piece of her dad she'll ever have again.

Once the books are safely in her trunk, she takes a deep breath, looks around, and steels herself for her next task.

She walks to the side gate, the entryway to the backyard and, surprisingly, it's unlocked. She passes through and stalks to the storage closet. With each step, she grows more tense thinking about the photo albums hidden inside. The ones supposedly containing pictures of nature and things from Annie's walks with her dog. The knot in her stomach tightens a little more with every inch closer, unsure of what she'll find, but certain it isn't Annie's amateur submission to *National Geographic Magazine*.

The lock on the outside closet had been the same as the front door when Megan was growing up. She hopes, by some miracle, they haven't been changed as she raises her key to unlock the door and rummage through its secrets.

The lock clicks opens and she sighs, relieved, as she steps inside to assess the labels on the storage bins, looking for the one she wants. She scans the shelves for the hidden photo albums but finds nothing obvious at first glance.

Unsure of how much time she has before Annie comes home, Megan starts again more carefully. By her estimation, even if Annie were to pull up right now, she'd hear the car and have at least a minute before Annie makes it to the closet to see what Megan was doing. Megan doesn't have a good excuse for being in the closet. She can feign ignorance, saying she was trying to find the box of *Mania* books, but as soon as they go into the house, Annie will know she was lying.

Megan shakes off the thought. *Focus.* She's wasting precious time. Megan moves stacks around, careful to replace anything she touches exactly as she found it.

She is just about to throw in the towel when she sees it. A box tucked away on a middle shelf with "FALL" written on it in thick black sharpie. It catches her eye because growing up, Annie always decorated the house according to holiday, not to an entire season. Megan glances around to validate her memory and notices, sure enough, other boxes in the closet are labeled things like "Halloween", "Thanksgiving", and "Christmas".

She pulls the box down and peaks over her shoulder. She feels like a child snooping for Christmas presents in her parent's closet.

When she lifts the lid, she spies them. The box is filled with photo albums that hadn't been in her father's room yesterday, all neatly organized in a row with the spines facing up. Three slim photo albums are missing labels, while the rest have a neatly written tags protected by a thin plastic slip. Megan slides one out to open it. Her hand shakes. She stops unexpectedly, afraid of what might lurk inside. She is confident it isn't pictures of the great outdoors. But the consequence of what it may hide inside feels grave.

She takes a breath to ease the tension in her chest and peels back the cover.

What she finds knocks that breath, and each subsequent breath, right out of her. Page after page, stealing a little more oxygen from her lungs. She isn't sure what she expected, but it wasn't this.

This can't be real. It doesn't make sense.

She pulls the other two albums out and quickly flips through their contents.

Those eyes. What could have done this?

Megan's head is swimming, or perhaps more accurately, drowning, trying to come up to the surface for air. The face laid out on the pages before her is nearly unrecognizable.

The deep rumbling of a car snaps her back to reality, and she scrambles to put the albums back quickly, carefully, and close the box. She slips the box back into its place, closes the closet, and walks out of the yard, acting as relaxed as she can. She can't unsee the photos, and now she can't remember what normal is.

The engine she'd heard turns out to be a neighbor pulling out of their driveway and heading down the street. As grateful as she is it hadn't been Annie returning, she is perhaps even more thankful for the warning it provided telling her time was up. About thirty seconds later, Annie's car is headed straight towards her.

Annie parks her car and gets out. She must have seen something odd in Megan's face because when she gets closer, her head tilts to the side and she frowns a bit as she talks.

"Hi Megan! Oh good, are you here for the books? I…" Annie trails off. "Are you ok? You look pale."

"Oh yeah, I'm fine. Maybe a touch of the flu or something coming on. I was just making sure I locked up behind me."

"Come back inside. I'll fix you some soup and you can rest on the couch until you feel well enough to drive," Annie offers.

It's a kind gesture, but Megan doesn't trust its sincerity.

Megan steals a glance back at the closet involuntarily and scolds herself for the slip up when she notices Annie clocked it. "That's a nice offer, but I just want to go home and lay down. Thanks again for the books. I appreciate it." Megan steps backwards slowly towards her car so Annie can reply if she wants, and Megan isn't acting like a suspicious jerk storming off.

Annie watches her, never breaking eye contact. "Of course, no problem. Maybe we can have lunch sometime."

"Yeah sure, maybe sometime. Later." Megan quickens her pace and climbs into her car as quickly as possible, fumbling to get her keys in the engine. She can't hold on to one thought long enough to process it before she is bombarded by another.

As she drives down the street, she steals a glace in the rearview mirror. Annie hasn't left her spot on the sidewalk.

She tucks her theories away and determines she will come back for the albums later. Right now, she needs to figure out what is happening with the dates written in these books.

Something about them feels like a key that will unlock the door to understanding what happened to her dad.

Speaking of locks, did I remember to lock the storage closet?... Shit. I can't go back and check now...

Megan dials Katie again. *Please pick up.*

CHAPTER 12

Katie doesn't answer. Megan tries again, but no luck. The phone rings, over and over until on the fourth attempt, Katie finally picks up and Megan feels relief wash over her.

"Hey, Megs! How did everything go?" Katie's voice is bright and chipper, much to Megan's annoyance.

"Katie, where the hell have you been?" Megan screams.

"Calm down. I'm at work, Megan. Is everything ok?"

Guilt washes over Megan for forgetting not everyone is on bereavement leave. "Sorry. I forgot... Can you come over tonight? I need to talk to someone, and you're the only one I trust." Megan's voice gives away how unsteady she feels, but she knows Katie won't begrudge her anxiousness.

"Of course! I'm off work at 5:00pm. I can come over then. Did you get the books?"

"I got the books, but there was something I didn't tell you before. About my first visit. Look, I don't want to talk about it over the phone." Megan is trembling and trying to keep her focus on the road. She's almost at her apartment. She swallows down the lump filling her throat, but it grows back larger each time. "But you'll come?" Megan asks again, overlooking that Katie had already answered the question. Megan's voice is dry and cracking as she pulls into her parking space. She closes her eyes and lays her head on top of her hands on the steering wheel.

Katie repeats her previous answer, though now she sounds far more concerned. "Megan, you're freaking me out. What's going on? Are you alright?"

Megan gathers herself and walks into her apartment with her phone pressed to her ear, paranoia creeping inside her. Someone may overhear. What anyone around here could possibly know about, let alone do with the information, she knows is nothing. But the feeling remains.

She kicks her shoes off and sinks into her couch, letting out a sigh. "I'll be fine. And I'll explain everything when you get here. I promise." Megan closes her eyes, trying to unsee but remembering in vivid detail, page after page, photos, each crashing down on her like waves when you've stepped out into the ocean too far and it takes hold of you.

Have I been wrong about Annie?

"Ok, Megs. I'll be there as soon as I can."

Megan walks over to her sliding back door to close the blinds before making her way back to her master bathroom. She flicks the hot water on and grabs her phone once more to call Josh to ask if he will come over too. On second thought, she fires off a quick text, unable to talk anymore about it until she's calmed down. Megan tosses her cell phone down on her nightstand and steps into her shower. She turns her back to the stream and sits down on the floor of the tub, bracing her hands against the wall and the edge of the bathtub. Megan's never been claustrophobic before, but she's suddenly feeling like the walls are closing in around her.

A few hours later, Katie is sitting with Megan on her small, blue tufted couch when Josh knocks on the door. Megan's apartment is modest, minimalistic in both layout and décor. Megan could never decide how she wanted to decorate when she got her own place, so she ended up not doing much at all. She has a couple of large fake plants in two corners just to give some life to the place without having to commit to keeping them alive. Then Katie brought some color to the room with a housewarming gift of two bright yellow throw pillows for the couch and a cream-colored Sherpa blanket to drape over the back. Megan's TV sits on a small, rectangular entertainment center with a drawer for movies and a couple of shelves she keeps a few books on.

Megan lets Josh in. Bless him, he brought food. And drinks. "I got your favorite! Hawaiian style, with black olives and pepperoni." His full open mouth smile shows off a top row of beautifully straight teeth except for one fang, which tilts just enough to disrupt the perfection. Megan adores that tooth. He thrusts the box forward for Megan to take. Megan smiles, aware of how good it feels not to fake it.

She takes the pizza from his hands and makes a show of taking in how good it smells, savory with a layer of sweetness from the pineapples, as she turns to put the box on the coffee table in front of the couch. Josh follows her inside and greets Katie.

"Beer?" Katie raises an eyebrow and nods her head toward the six-pack in his hand. "Did you bring anything for us?" She makes a mock gagging noise at the idea of drinking beer.

"Come on, Katie." Josh sets the six-pack down on the tiny bar top in the kitchen area and pulls two cans out of their slots, holding them up so Megan and Katie can both see. They are hard seltzers, mango flavor.

Megan and Katie's favorites. A smug grin spreads across his face. "You know I'd never forget my girls."

Megan brings over paper plates and napkins and plops down on the couch. Josh takes a seat on the floor opposite the girls.

Josh breaks the palpable tension in the room first. "How are you doing, Megs? You didn't give me much in your message."

Megan considers for a moment but can't quite verbalize what she's feeling. She buys herself some time when she declares, "Pizza first." She gives a firm nod, and it's decided. As they eat, the silence looms thick, but the three of them have known each other long enough that none of them feels a need to fill it.

The three of them finish eating. Megan knows she can't put off the discussion any longer. "Ok, there's something I haven't told either of you yet from when I went to Annie's yesterday." Megan shifts, sitting up a little straighter. "When I was going through my dad's photo albums, I asked Annie if there were any more recent pictures I could look at to see what my dad was like these last few years." Megan pauses to take a sip of her drink so her throat won't dry out. "When I asked, Annie got all dodgy like she was hiding something and she told me she had some recent albums out in the outside closet, but they didn't have my dad in them."

Megan relays Annie's story about the photos taken on her walks with her dog. "Well, I got a terrible feeling about it. It just didn't make sense, and she sounded almost nervous… and so I got into the closet today when I went back and found the albums and oh my god…" Megan's breath catches before she can continue. Katie and Josh are focused intently on her, but they don't interrupt. "There were photos. So many photos of Annie. It looked like a catalogue of injuries. One black eye, then a second. A split and swollen lip. Bruises on her forearms were the rough size and shape of a man's fingers. Ribbons of bruised skin wrapping around her ribs. Huge cuts with staples holding them together hidden in hair." Megan's fingers graze the different parts of her body as she recounts the images, as if she can feel the pain herself as she describes the wounds.

"Who could have done that to her?" Megan looks to Josh just as a dark look flashes across his face.

He presses his lips into a sad, thin line. "It's common for victims of domestic abuse to keep a record of their injuries. Unfortunately, the legal system doesn't always do its job protecting those who need it most. Having photographic evidence can help them get the courts on their side."

"But my dad never abused her." Megan stops abruptly. She only just realized it's possible she could be wrong. "I guess, not that I knew of. But if that's true, why would Annie keep a sick diary like this? Why didn't she ever report him?"

Katie answers, her voice soft. "I don't know. It's so hard to say, Megs, or even guess, when you haven't been around them much since you were sixteen. If this is even true, of course."

Megan nods her acceptance of the fact. "You're right. I thought maybe they were really old photos, like before my dad got together with her, but the second album I pulled out looked darn near new and had date stamped pictures. They were all from a period when she was married to my father." Megan continues, laboring through the details aloud.

Katie jumps in. "Maybe it's something else. Maybe she was in a car accident and was taking photos for a lawsuit."

Something sparks inside Megan. She will not admit it, given the circumstances, but she's excited. Excited at the idea of this truth coming out after it had been locked away. Perhaps she was on the right path to the answers she needs, no matter how ugly. Bouncing ideas around with Katie and Josh feels natural. It's something they've always done. Megan realizes how much she'd needed to feel that. She'd felt stalled before. This spark will keep her going.

"Could be," Megan replies. "But three separate accidents?" Megan thinks for a moment, sorting through other explanations for the next most likely scenario. "Maybe she was dealing with violent patients at her office. Her clinic wasn't in a safe area of town." Megan turns to Josh. "You've been quiet this entire time. What do you think?"

Josh looks at Megan. His face looks pained. "I think it's one possibility. But it's unlikely. Again, three separate patients? Or the same patient three times? Maybe." Josh pauses, glancing at the floor for just a moment before adding, "But Megs, I think it's irresponsible to throw out the idea…"

Megan cuts in, though she's reluctant to admit to it, "I know, I know. We can't ignore that *maybe*, Annie was documenting a string of instances where my dad lost his temper with her in case she decided to report it. I'd seen him unhinged before." The memory of her mom being dragged into her bedroom creeps into her mind. "It's not an entirely unreasonable thought to entertain. He just never seemed violent. But I guess abusers often don't…" Megan looks back at Josh, who is quiet again.

Megan wonders if they believe her dad was not only capable, but guilty of domestic violence and neither wants to say it out loud.

Josh is nodding his head slowly, his face veiled in sadness. "Shit, Megs. This is heavy. Do you really think your dad might have done it?" he asks.

"I really don't know anymore. It feels like I might finally be onto something, but I think my wheels are spinning in the wrong direction. My dad and I had our issues, but it's hard to believe this is who he turned into when I wasn't looking."

"I get it," Josh offers with a nod. "I remember what it felt like when I saw who my dad really was. For what it's worth, Megs, I wouldn't have thought your dad was capable of this, either. I mean," Josh's eye flick down to the floor before he continues. "He helped me so much. When I asked about joining my dad's drug business, your dad paid me to do odd jobs around the house instead. When I was getting into fights at school, Mark reigned me in. To this day, I don't know why he did it, honestly. He was there for me when my own dad wasn't."

Josh's reminder hits Megan's heart like a knife.

When Mark and Megan moved in with Annie, Josh spent a lot of time at their house. Megan thought he was just excited there was finally a kid his own age on the street to play with.

Josh never asked Megan to come to his house to play. Once when Megan asked, he nearly jumped out of skin before screaming, "no!" As Megan grew older, she started noticing the kinds of people who flitted in and out of Josh's house. They were loud, spewing angry, colorful words Megan had never heard before. They partied late into the night, and it wasn't unusual to find empty liquor bottles littering their lawn.

Over time, Megan noticed how much Josh hated to go home. He'd ask, beg really, to stay the night and he could just sleep on the couch. Some days his lip would be cut, or his eyebrow swollen and purple. He always had an explanation. But when he turned up one afternoon with fresh burn marks on his skin, dime sized and cherry red, Mark disappeared to Josh's house for a while, claiming he wanted to borrow some milk from Josh's mom. He returned home without milk, but with a fresh set of angry crimson knuckles. He filled up a plastic bag with ice cubes and plunged his fist into the bag. When Megan asked him what happened, he chuckled and told her he had been silly and closed the door on his hand by accident.

Megan breaks the tension, overwhelmed with a need to lighten the mood. "There's one other thing I found in the closet, and I might have swiped it…" Megan looks back and forth at her friends mischievously.

Katie looks at Josh, silently asking him if he knows anything about this. When he shrugs, she turns to Megan. "Well… what is it?" Kate sucks in a breath of excited air and sits up a little straighter. The mood shifts exactly as Megan had hoped it would.

Megan pulls a photo out of her back pocket and presses it to her chest, hiding the image. "It was sitting in a pocket inside the front cover and I panicked when I hear a car coming and shoved it in my back pocket."

She turns it slowly, teasing Josh and Katie. When it's almost facing them, she flips it around quickly with a dramatic unveiling. "Ta-da!"

"No way!" Josh says. His eyes light up.

"I can't believe it!" Katie covers her mouth with one hand, stifling a giggle that slipped out.

"Do you guys remember this picture?" Megan tries to forget, for just a moment, about the frightening photos, and focus on the playful one in her hands. It half works.

It's a copy of Mark and Annie's wedding photo. The trio drinks it in.

Annie and Mark pose in the center of the photo, Annie on the left and Mark on the right, dressed head to toe in Egyptian garbs. Mark looks like he may have been auditioning to play Aladdin at Disneyland, while Annie is a casual Cleopatra.

Standing between, but slightly behind them, is a large man dressed like a Pharaoh, holding an old, tattered book laying open in his palms. Megan remembers wondering as a girl if a priest was allowed to dress up in silly costumes when they married a couple. It wasn't until she was much older, she learned anyone could be ordained on the internet for a nominal fee.

Three women stand to the left of Annie, and three men to the right side of Mark. They all recognize Dan. He was around often when they were growing up and he knew them well, too. As well as you can know three kids who don't belong to you.

"I can't believe you found this!" Katie exclaims.

It surprises Megan how contented she feels in this moment, reminiscing about sillier things, and happier memories with two of the people she loves most in the world. "Do you guys remember they brought back those poker chips for us?" Megan leaves out the part where she remembered this detail while reflecting on her dad's relationship with Smalls in therapy just hours ago.

"Oh! They had our initials, right? And I think their wedding date is on the other side?" Katie recalls.

Josh chimes in, "Yeah! That's right. I probably still have mine in a box somewhere. I don't remember for sure." He trails off in thought.

Katie is smiling, her sweetest closed-mouth smile. "I always thought it was so nice of your dad, bringing one back for me and Josh, too. You know, since we weren't his kids."

"Yeah, but he always thought of you guys as family. Annie too." Megan remembers this with fondness. It feels only fair she includes Annie, since it's the truth. At least, she thinks so.

Megan continues, slowly inching her way back to the mystery she has to solve. "Do either of you have any memory of who the other people in the picture are? We know Dan, but for the life of me, I can't remember the others." Megan points to the man standing just to the right of Dan. "This guy looks vaguely familiar, but I can't say why." The man's dark, slightly wavy hair has been slicked back neatly. He stands taller than the rest, with impeccable posture. His arms stick out from under his Egyptian vest and are chiseled in a way that makes Megan assume the rest of his broad body is equally defined. His hands appear to be clasped behind his back and he has a wide, tight-lipped smile stretching across his face.

Josh and Katie both take their time studying each of the faces, but they didn't recognize the others. They shake their heads simultaneously, looking at each other, each hopeful the other has something to offer Megan.

"Sorry, Megs. I don't remember them at all. Maybe they weren't very close," Katie suggests.

Megan considers this for a moment. "It's possible, I suppose. But they were in their wedding, for god's sake. You don't just ask random people to stand next to you while you get married. Right?" Megan looks at Katie and Josh for affirmation.

Josh nods his head. "Yeah. You probably wouldn't normally. It's just surprising we don't recognize anyone aside from Dan."

Megan looks at Josh, pleading with her eyes. She doesn't want to ask because she knows how much he's already risking to help her. His career is on the line when he's worked so hard, against the odds, to get where he is today. But she doesn't know where to turn next, and she has to know the truth. All she can hope is that she isn't asking too much. "Josh, do you think maybe you can look into these other people? They can't be strangers. And maybe one of them is still around and can tell me about my dad in those later years, or about his relationship with Annie and what they were like together."

Considering if it is worth exploring, she adds, "Maybe look at Annie and Dan too? Please. Given Annie's secret albums." *And how Dan was staring at me at the wake.* "I'm just not sure what to believe. I've known them for most of my life, but maybe I really don't know them as well as I'd thought."

"Of course I will, Megs. Don't worry." Josh's face is soft, his eyes telling Megan she can count on him.

"Thanks, Josh. I know you're not authorized to use your resources for personal matters."

"I mean, guys do it all the time, right?" Josh shrugs as though it's common knowledge many officers abuse their privilege when it suits them. He doesn't look away from her, holding her gaze while guilt coils around Megan's neck, knowing he's slowly becoming one of those officers and it's because she's asking him to.

"Anyway, I'm glad you called tonight, Megs, because I wanted to talk to you about the police report." Josh changes the topic, brushing aside the charge Megan feels buzzing in the air around them. Seems she's the only one who noticed.

"Oh yeah? Did you find anything new?"

Josh shifts his weight on the floor, aiming his body more directly at Megan. "I was looking through the report again and I noticed a couple of things that don't sit right with me. Can you grab your copy?"

Megan walks over to the dinette area and grabs the manilla file folder from behind the box of books. She tosses it lightly onto the coffee table in front of Josh and he opens it up to the second page. "First, look here," he says, pointing to a spot about halfway down the page, "there's a sentence that been crossed out. At first glance, you might just think the officer taking down the report wrote the wrong thing and was correcting the statement. But he used liquid paper to ensure it was entirely covered instead of just striking through with his pen. See how some letters peak out from the top? That was weird to me so, I checked it out. Turns out, the original sentence was scribbled with a pen pretty hard and it left an impression."

Josh flips the page over to demonstrate, running his finger across the backside, even though Megan's page was a photocopy. "I took it and put a piece of transfer paper behind it and took a pencil etching. When I flipped it around, it looked like the report previously mentioned there was gunpowder residue in two different places near your dad's body, but only one bullet casing found. That casing came from the gun found at the scene." Josh pauses and looks at Megan, studying her reaction.

"It's ok, Josh. Keep going." Megan swallows.

"Right. I went to the reporting officer and asked why he scratched it from the record. He said his superior told him the suicide rate in Las Vegas is exceptionally high. It's more likely the extra residue was from some other incident and it wasn't relevant to Mark's case."

Megan nods her understanding. "And what do you think?" She wants Josh's opinion, knowing how seriously he takes his job and how meticulous he is. More than that, she knows he will be honest with her.

"I think it sounds fishy. It's not protocol to scratch information from the record. Even if it may be irrelevant. It's better to have too much information than not enough. You can toss out the parts that don't matter later."

"Makes sense," Katie agrees, as if to show she is following along with them. Katie had been so quiet, and Megan had been so attentive to Josh, she nearly forgot Katie was sitting next to her.

"The other thing I noticed was on this page, here," Josh flips to the photocopy of the coroner's report and points to the bottom corner. "See how a few letters stick out? Like someone has folded over the corner and there is a page behind this one. Maybe the pages got stuck together during copying. Who knows? But the point is, the page behind it isn't included in the report at all. I couldn't find any other pages with the same lettering shown in the corner of this copy."

"What do you think it means?" Megan is trying to follow Josh's train of thought but hasn't arrived at a conclusion yet.

"I can't be sure just yet, but I got a friend to pull the original file for me again. I thought maybe I missed it when I made copies for you. But the original file has photocopies of the coroner's report as well. That's highly unusual. We typically hold the original documents so they can't be tampered with during an investigation. The coroner said he submitted the original report and corroborated everything on the page we're looking at when I called him, but I haven't found out where the original exam report is or why we have a copy on file instead."

Katie leans forward, interrupting before they continue. "So, if I'm understanding, you think there is a page of the coroner's report that was deliberately left out when he photocopied it? And maybe someone in the department is aiding in covering up that same information?"

Josh nods. "Maybe. I don't have nearly enough detail to form a solid theory yet, but it's definitely bringing up questions I think are worth answering."

"Ok, this is good. Right? We have some leads." Unease pools in Megan's stomach. Though she feels like they are getting somewhere, she's starting to second guess if it's a place she wants to go. "I'm going to dig into my dad's books and see if I can make any sense of the dates in them tomorrow. If there's any sense to be made of them anyhow. And then I have a family dinner with my mom and brother tomorrow night." Megan forces a fake smile to pair with the falsified excitement in her voice. "Wish me luck?"

Josh and Katie help Megan clean up and begin making their way to the door.

"Thank you both for coming. It really means a lot to me. I hope you know that." Megan blinks back the tears filling behind her eyes.

"Of course, Megs. We're always here for you." Katie squeezes her tight and then steps back to hold her by the shoulders, letting the truth of it sink in.

"We'll figure this out, Megs." Josh is hugging her, and she's momentarily taken aback by how big he truly is, and how comfortable it feels to be in his arms. It's like she's noticing it for the first time.

"I'll call you tomorrow." Megan locks the door behind them and turns around, taking in the emptiness of the spaces where they sat. She can't bear to sit there alone with this new information right now, so she grabs the box of books off the living room floor and heads back to her bedroom to get started.

CHAPTER 13

Megan sits on her bed and slides the first book from the *Mania* series out of the box. It feels far heavier than it should, the gravity of its secrets pulling it down. The moment she pulled the book from the shelf in her dad's bedroom, her mind wandered back to where her dad sat with his feet thrown casually onto the coffee table. *Mania* is in his hands. She can see him reading the story, glancing up at her every so often, smiling. She can't understand the words he's speaking. They sound far away and garbled like he's underwater.

But when Megan sat with Katie at Bean yesterday, she heard the words, crisp and clear, as if her dad were standing just next to her. She isn't sure why, but Megan suspects this is exactly where her dad was trying to lead her in his last message. Validating her memory feels like a daunting, if not impossible, task, but she has to start somewhere.

She lays the book on her lap and closes her eyes, letting her mind drift back once more to when she was a little girl, and she'd noticed her father reading *Mania* for the first time. His eyes glide smoothly over the pages. He stops and looks up at Megan, his smile stretching all the way up to his eyes.

She sees herself ask him what he is reading. He pats the couch cushion next to him and beckons her, "come sit. I'll tell you." Megan plops herself down on the couch and he tells her about the fantastical science fiction world made up of things only the most vivid imaginations could create.

The *Mania* novels tell the story of a group of angels, led by the archangel Mania, tasked with coming down to earth to sort the righteous humans from the evil. When the world tipped too far in either direction, this sect of angels plucked out the humans doing too much good, or too much wrong, and disposed of them to restore balance. Mania became enamored with one human in particular and decided not to return to Heaven when their job was complete. Mania's loyal army remained with them, becoming increasingly interested in the human species. The angels began to reproduce with the humans creating a new species, the likes of which, God could never have imagined. The balance of angels living in heaven and the angels living on earth became so skewed that earth became Heaven and Mania became God. As a result of Mania's betrayal, God waged war on earth and all its creatures, human and celestial alike, hunting down Mania, in order to take back Heaven for itself.

"But some of it isn't so fantastical. I just read about a father who had a daughter he loved very much. But he had to leave her, even though he didn't want to…" Megan sees his mouth moving, reciting the words she remembers, but there's no sound. Her mind's eye drinks in his image. She's staring at him, watching the corners of his eyes crinkle as he smiles, feeling the way her heart swells at his words. This is the version of him she wishes had stayed. When the sound flicks back on, she hears his voice. "That makes me smile because it's how I feel about you. My sweet girl."

This isn't goodbye, it's see you later.

She inhales the memory, savoring the sweetness of their special goodbye, echoed in his text message to her, then she tucks it away where she can see it again if she wishes. Her dad loved her. He'd told her as much. But which was more truthful? His words or his actions?

Megan's memories of her father over the years are inconsistent, at odds with each other, and Megan still isn't sure which version of Mark was real, and which lived only in her head.

She pushes the thought away and scans the black and white text, praying she finds what she hopes is hidden in this story somewhere. Answers.

She skims the pages, seeing the words, but reading none of them until she finally changes tasks. Maybe she's wrong, searching for things that aren't here. Or maybe they are here, but she's looking in the wrong place.

No.

I'll see you again one day, in Heaven.

This is it. Mania's battle for the Heavens. It must be here.

You just have to know where to look.

Megan is confident she's hovering in the right place. She just doesn't know what she's looking for yet. Megan decides instead to sift through the dates in the covers of the books, rather than its text. The dates may not be what she thinks, or they may be exactly what she thinks, which isn't very helpful. Upon looking at three of the dates, she notices they don't make sense chronologically. If they were the dates on which he finished the book, then he'd have read these epic novels very much out of order. When she can't think of any good reason for him to do so, her mind flits to the possibility that these are not dates at all. An idea whispers to her. *Perhaps they are some kind of code.* But for what? She hasn't the faintest idea. Nor has she any idea how to decrypt them.

She gets up and walks out to her kitchen to get a notepad and a pen. Megan recalls Josh once telling her how his job was not to find evidence to fit his theory, but to find a theory that fit the evidence. She dutifully ignores any theories she's posited at this point before opening the books, one at a time, and jotting down all the dates from the covers.

01-01-93

01-05-04

03-02-00

02-09-92

01-08-03

02-03-94

05-04-76

05-10-05

03-07-01

04-06-87

She already knows the dates aren't in chronological order, but now, after collecting them all, she also notes only the first ten volumes have dates while sixteen volumes sit in the box. Had he stopped reading them at some point but continued collecting the books, hoping to catch up one day?

Megan is starting to think maybe they are indeed some sort of code, dressed up to look like calendar dates at a quick glance. No one would suspect otherwise, especially if they didn't know the order in which they should read the books. She puts the books back in the box. It's getting late and her brain isn't operating at full capacity anymore. She knows sleep will help a great deal and since she has nothing on her agenda for tomorrow until family dinner in the evening, she decides to start again in the morning.

CHAPTER 14

FRIDAY, SEPTEMBER 11TH

When Megan wakes up the next day, she gets to work immediately. Well, almost immediately anyway. Coffee always comes first.

She brings the books out to the living room while the coffee brews, reveling in the way the warm scent fills her small apartment. She always prepares a full pot of coffee because she can never get by with a single cup and it's far too costly and time-consuming to use the single serve pods everyone seems to covet.

Once she's had her extra-large cup of coffee, she gets to work.

She considers what other combinations of numbers might be laid out in date format. *Combination locks?* She can't fathom any reason a single human would need ten separate combination locks. They may still be dates, but unrelated to dates on which he completed the books. He was a former military man. They could have something to do with military time. Or coordinates, intentionally separated to appear as though they are dates. Megan scribbles a note to google some numbers as coordinates to see if it sheds any light one way or another.

Another possibility that occurred to her, which is taking a stronger hold as she eliminates other hypotheses, is they're a kind of code her father created, for what she isn't sure. Mark had been a computer programmer. A damn good one, too. Megan remembers seeing enormous stacks of programming books on his desk at home. The books may as well have been written in Greek for all she could glean from them, even as she got older. But her dad was creative. If this was a system he created for himself, Megan is sure she stands no chance of understanding it. Her heart sinks.

After a few hours and several pencil eraser drum sessions, Megan concludes exactly zero progress has been made. She gets up, pacing the room in a last-ditch effort to get her thoughts flowing, but again, comes up empty-handed. Or more accurately, empty-headed.

She stretches and refills her coffee mug before deciding to relax and start reading the first book. Inspiration often strikes when you least expect it, she reasons. Maybe if she can get her brain to stop thinking about it, some idea will make an appearance and she can follow up on it.

Megan reads for most of the afternoon with nothing new to report. She checks the time and sees she should have started getting ready for dinner with her mom and Smalls at least thirty minutes ago. As if reading her mind, her phone lights up. Her mom's picture appears on the screen.

"Hey mom, I was just about to leave."

"You haven't even left yet? Megan, honestly, you're going to be late now." Kathy scolds.

Megan turns on the speakerphone so she can set her phone down and change her clothes while her mom is talking, deciding mentally to skip the shower and just splash some cool water on her face to save time.

"I won't be late. I just need to grab my keys. What's the big deal?" Megan throws on a minimal amount of makeup. Just enough to look fresh. She runs an eyebrow pencil through her brows and swipes a quick layer of mascara over her pitifully short eyelashes as she hears her mom sigh loudly on the other end of the phone. "Nothing, it's fine, really. Your brother is just getting fidgety. I'm sure he's just hungry."

"Ok, well, tell him to get a snack. I'm on my way." Megan hops a few times to pull her jeans on and flops backwards onto her bed to button them, cursing herself for eating so much pizza last night and making a mental note to be mindful of what she eats tonight.

"Alright. See you soon. Hurry, please, but drive safely." Kathy hangs up before Megan can reply.

"Here we go again," Megan whispers to herself.

CHAPTER 15

Friday night family dinner was born of a shared love of *The Gilmore Girls* between Megan and her mom. Though she isn't nearly as ritualistic or strict about their dinner dates, Kathy tries to gather her two children together on a semi-regular basis to catch up on their lives and check in with them.

It isn't that Megan doesn't enjoy dinner with her mom and brother. It's that she and her brother have very different relationships with their mom, and Megan always feels like an outsider when the three of them get together. At these get togethers, Megan often learns about important or exciting things in her mother's life that Smalls had been privy to all along. Once, Megan showed up for dinner to discover her mom had recently adopted a new cat. Rather than Kathy bombarding Megan with photos or even sending a quick text to announce the recent addition, it was Smalls who explained how their mom had adopted Reginald two weeks earlier and gave Megan a complete rundown of what the cat was like. Since their dad died, Megan feels even further removed from them.

Megan arrives at her mom's house and sees Smalls' car parked outside. He's often there hours beforehand, dutifully keeping their mother company.

Megan gets out and walks up to the door. She lets herself in and sees her brother first, in the plain black zip up hoodie he seems to live in as of late from what Megan gathers from recent family dinners and their occasional FaceTime calls, and his favorite pair of jeans which somehow make him appear even taller, as if that were possible. He's hovering near the entryway like he's been waiting for her. When he sees her, he turns and takes just a couple of long strides to reach her.

"Hey, sis." He envelops her and holds onto her for just a beat longer than he normally would. It feels like he's telling her he means it. He's good that way.

"Hey, Smalls." It always amazed her how they could possibly have come from the same parents. While she is slender and on the short side, Jonathan stands nearly six feet, three inches tall. He is solid. His size may feel imposing to a stranger, but he is soft as a teddy bear. He is reserved, but never rude.

When they were little, they watched *The Sandlot* together for the first time and Megan began calling her baby brother Smalls, since he was half her size at the time. The nickname stuck around his whole life and became even more endearing when he surpassed her in height with no sign of stopping. He towers over her now, but he is still Smalls.

"How are you holding up?" His soft brown eyes glisten. Megan knows her brother's nonchalance at the news of their dad doesn't mean he doesn't care. Maybe he never cared much for Mark, but he cares about Megan.

"I'm doing alright." Megan bats him lightly on the shoulder. "You need a haircut." Megan says, playfully changing the subject and staring pointedly at his chocolate brown hair, which spirals and bounces along softly when it grows longer than a couple of inches.

Jonathan runs his fingers through his curls, as if such a mild brushing could ever tame them. He chuckles. "Yeah, yeah. I know. Mom already got onto me about it."

"Where is she? In the kitchen?"

He nods. "Just finishing up a few things."

Megan heads down the short entryway to the kitchen and dining area. Kathy is behind the counter dumping a cutting board full of chopped veggies into a large salad bowl.

"Hey, Mom!" Megan moves closer and throws her arm around her shoulder, pulling her into an affectionate side hug.

Kathy leans over and kisses her cheek, then makes a production of her arrival time. "Oh, Megan. How kind of you to finally grace us with your presence," Kathy says dramatically. Megan is never sure if her mom's jabs are playful or pointed.

Jonathan appears, putting his elbows on the counter. "Mom, can we help you with anything?"

"Oh no. No, I've got it all covered. You go sit down in the living room and relax. I'll call you when we're ready to set the table."

Jonathan turns to go, as instructed. Megan spins to follow him when Kathy stops her. "Oh Megan, could you just stay and stir the meat sauce for me? And then take some plates and silverware to the table."

"Of course." Megan turns her back to her mom and rolls her eyes. It's typical Kathy to dismiss Jonathan, but put Megan to work. Jonathan is still Kathy's baby. Their whole lives, where Megan was more independent, Jonathan was doted on.

Megan usually chalks up the discrepancy in how Kathy treats her children to the estrangement between Jonathan and their father. Kathy overcompensated for his missing relationship, and doing everything on Jonathan's behalf became second nature at some point. Jonathan is twenty-five now and had moved out three years prior, just after his twenty-second birthday. Megan thought it was going to do their mom in. Kathy would keep Jonathan under her roof forever if given the choice, while Megan only occasionally chats with her on the phone. The scarcity of their conversations seems even more glaring since her dad's death.

When dinner is ready, Kathy calls Jonathan to the table while she and Megan bring the food over.

Jonathan sits and Kathy reaches in front of him, picking up his plate to dish food onto it for him. It's a comical sight since Kathy is even more petite than Megan, and Jonathan is nearly as tall as their mom when he's seated.

Kathy floats around the table, her short platinum blonde hair standing tall on the top, curled under on the bottom, unmoving because she's doused it in Aquanet. She moves from dish to dish, putting each item on his plate, not bothering to ask whether he wants it.

"Go ahead and just help yourself, Megan." Kathy instructs, as she sets Jonathan's plate down in front of him.

Kathy has never been one for cooking complicated meals. But her few go to dishes always feel like home to Megan. The warm, earthy scent of cooked tomatoes paired with the pungent aroma of garlic and onion mixed into the meat sauce tonight transports Megan to much larger family gatherings when she was a little girl. The spaghetti recipe her mom uses was passed down by Megan's great grandmother. When her great grandma passed away when Megan was eight, Megan began requesting spaghetti once a week because the taste reminded her of the afternoons spent with her great grandma after school.

Once everyone has their food, Megan weighs how to start the conversation she really wants to have. She has questions about her dad, but she needs to tread lightly since Kathy isn't privy to Megan digging around in Mark's life, let alone his death. Megan had told Jonathan briefly during a FaceTime call earlier that week, wondering if he'd be interested at all in knowing what happened. He wasn't. He couldn't understand why Megan didn't believe the police report. Their dad's suicide wasn't surprising to him and there is no reason to suspect otherwise, in his opinion.

"So mom, how's work?" Megan tosses out, casually. Kathy works as a veterinary technician. She's always had a soft spot for animals but got a late start in her career after raising two kids, nearly entirely by herself. Megan was proud of her for pursuing her dream later in life.

"Oh, just wonderful. Mrs. Stable brought in yet another cat she saved from the streets. I keep telling her she can't save them all, but bless her heart, she keeps trying. The woman is breaking about nine city ordinances with the number of animals she keeps on her property. But it's none of my business, mind you."

Megan and Jonathan exchange a knowing smirk, each fully aware that their mom not only feels like it is, in fact, her business, but that she also adores Mrs. Stable for her efforts.

Jonathan winks at Megan before looking down at his plate as he asks, "And how many animals have you maxed out at, mom?" It's a running joke that their mom couldn't even keep track of the number of animals in the house at any given time.

Kathy doesn't even bat an eyelash at the question as she points her fork in Jonathan's direction. "Now that's a different situation and you know it. I take in animals temporarily to find them new homes. Mrs. Stable has no intention of re-homing."

Silence settles over the dinner table and when no one says a word for what feels like an eternity, Megan speaks tentatively.

"Mom, can I ask you some questions about dad?" Megan tests the waters to see if the topic is open for discussion as she pushes the food around on her plate. Her mother's voice sings out in Megan's head, *a moment on the lips, a lifetime on the hips.*

"Sure sweetie. You can ask me anything. Though I'm not sure how much help I can be. You know we haven't communicated since you kids were teenagers."

Jonathan shifts in his chair at the change in topic but he keeps his head down, focusing intently on the plate of food in front of him.

"What was he like when you first got together?"

"Oh goodness. Well, he was charming. We worked at a local pizza place together, and he'd just come home from the army. He looked quite dashing with his cropped haircut and his muscular arms. I was a little wary when he started flirting with me. Your grandma always cautioned me to be careful around overly charming men. But I never noticed him flirting with the other girls." Kathy sets her fork down and takes a sip from her water glass before continuing. "Anyhow, I was smitten and one thing led to another and before I knew it, we were walking down the aisle. Soon after, you popped into my belly and the rest is history." Kathy smiles at the memory. "There isn't much to tell. It all happened very fast. We were young, but we were in love…" Kathy stares off somewhere else, seeming to drift away to another place. Or perhaps another time.

Megan takes a bite of her salad—*fifteen calories*—and looks at Jonathan to see if this was something he knew before she did. When he looks up at Megan, he shrugs and shakes his head. Megan is about to ask another question when her mom speaks up again.

"But I'll tell you kids a secret." Kathy says coyly when Megan looks at her, unable to hide her intrigue. "You're old enough to hear this now. When your dad asked me to marry him, I was already engaged to someone else. I had to break things off with him first. Your grandmother was none too pleased, let me tell you."

Megan gasps. "Mom! Scandalous. Are you serious?"

"Oh yes. Don't look so surprised. I was quite the dish in my day." Kathy sips her water innocently before returning to her food. Jonathan looks just as shocked.

"So then, what happened? You guys were married for… nearly eight years, right? What caused the divorce?"

Kathy's expression betrays nothing. "That's a story for another day. Sometimes things just aren't what they seem. People change." Kathy takes a bite of spaghetti as if closing the discussion. Megan lets it go but tries again, still invested in gathering the information she needs, not caring much about the rest.

"What was he like after the divorce? I don't remember too much from those first few years."

Kathy seems to consider the question for a moment before deciding whether she'd answer. "Well, I won't pretend it was amiable. It wasn't easy. Seemed like everything was a battle. We were in and out of court for years. Custody was a battle, but ultimately, kids need to be with their mother. The visitation schedule was a battle. Child support was a battle. Lord, child support was a battle. He didn't pay a dime for years, despite the judge telling him to, repeatedly. He claimed he was having trouble finding steady work, but I knew he was working under the table so he wouldn't have his wages garnished."

Kathy shakes her head disapprovingly. She seems to realize she'd drifted off, and snaps back, her face relaxed as if she's telling any old story. "Then one day, out of the blue, he just started paying again. Maybe a year after he got together with Annie. He paid in full and even some extra as a show of good faith. We never had an issue with it again, which goes to show you I was right all along. He was just choosing not to pay what he owed." Kathy moves a piece of lettuce onto her fork before looking up. Megan notices she and Smalls share the same tiny snarl in their upper lip when irritated.

Kathy scrambles to add, "Course, none of the ugly pieces had anything to do with you kids. The ugly parts were between me and him. Amongst it all, he loved you both. I know it may not have felt like it sometimes, but he did. Children always suffer in divorce…" she seems to say to no one in particular.

Megan lets the story marinate for a moment while Kathy turns back to her meal. It occurs to her that her mother hid everything rather well when Megan was growing up. She can't recall a time where her mother spoke ill of her father in front of her and she can't remember a single fight between them after her dad left.

Feeling an overwhelming urge to brighten the atmosphere, Megan turns to Jonathan, smiling. "Want to guess what I found when I went to look at his stuff?" Jonathan likely has zero interest in knowing, but Megan knows he will humor her, anyway.

"Um…. I have no idea. Sex handcuffs?" Jonathan jokes.

Kathy's fork clangs loudly on her plate. "Jonathan! I never…" she exclaims, not bothering to hide her shock.

Megan nearly chokes on her food. "Oh, my god! No! Smalls, that's disgusting! What is the matter with you?" Jonathan doubles over in laughter, beyond pleased with himself. "Anyway…" Megan continues, "No, I found dad and Annie's wedding photo. Do you remember it? The Egyptian themed one?"

"No, can't say I do. But it sounds hysterical." Jonathan offers without looking up from his plate.

"It is. You must have been too young. I was in a hurry the other day, but I swiped it. I'll show you next time I see you."

"Sounds great, sis."

Megan can read people fairly well and Jonathan makes no effort to hide the fact he can't possibly care any less about seeing the photo. It shouldn't surprise Megan, but she's disappointed, hoping she'd be able to connect with Jonathan a bit this way. She checks on their mom, who appears unbothered by the conversation, and tries again.

"Do you remember the poker chips with our initials on them they brought back from Vegas? Josh, Katie and I were talking about them yesterday and how silly they were, but also a little thoughtful."

"Nope, doesn't ring a bell. Sounds super cheesy, though." Jonathan mutters, his mouth full of food.

"Really? You don't remember those? Gosh, you carried yours around with you for forever. I wasn't sure you'd ever leave it behind."

Kathy looks up. "That's true, honey. You took it everywhere with you. I'm surprised you don't remember. You were quite a bit older when I stopped noticing it." Kathy offers a tiny contribution to a discussion she otherwise wouldn't have a reason to be included in.

Megan turns to face her mom. "When did you stop noticing it, mom? Do you remember? Did he lose it?" Megan takes a deep gulp from her water glass. "Josh was saying he thought he might still have his in a box somewhere."

"Oh goodness, I'm not sure. I just know he used to play with it a lot, pulling it out of his pocket, examining it, toying with it absentmindedly before putting it back. It was quite adorable." Kathy turns to Jonathan. "Like your own little piece of treasure." She looks back at Megan. "At some point, I just stopped seeing it."

"Jesus, who cares? It's just a stupid poker chip. Kids lose stuff all the time." Jonathan interjects.

Megan holds her hands up in mock surrender. "Sorry, Smalls. I was just making conversation. It's not a big deal." She looks at her mom for help, and Kathy hurries to change the topic.

The three of them carry on, back and forth, in polite conversation, catching each other up on their respective jobs, aspirations, and extracurriculars. Jonathan shares that he's taken up boxing at a local gym. "It's great exercise. Plus, it helps me blow off steam."

Megan furrows her brow as she finishes up the bite of salad in her mouth. "What exactly has you so steamed these days?" It's news that her brother is wound up about anything. As far as she can tell, he's fairly unflappable.

"Just work. My boss has been riding me, telling me I'm not getting repairs done fast enough. I think she's still got a stick up her ass about the time off I took a couple of weeks ago. She said she didn't approve it, but I told her Brad gave me the green light." Jonathan grumbles, his mouth full of food. "It's not my fault her second in command is a complete idiot and didn't run it by her first."

Jonathan is an apprentice at an auto mechanic shop in downtown Sacramento. He seems to be a natural, which makes sense to Megan. Jonathan was always fiddling with things growing up. Taking things apart and putting them back together. Studying how they worked. Building complicated Lego structures well beyond his age bracket.

"You took some time off a couple of weeks ago?" Megan perks up at the timing of his trip.

"Yeah, it was just a few days. A couple of buddies wanted to drive up to Comanche Hills to go hunting."

"Hunting? But you hate guns. Since when do you hunt?" Megan is floored by the admission, knowing that for his whole life, Jonathan has stayed far away from guns, alcohol, and drugs.

Kathy seems just as surprised and equally disappointed. "Jonathan, I can't believe this. You know what I do for a living. To think you're out there just killing wild animals for fun."

Jonathan lowers his eyes, glaring at Megan. "I don't hate guns themselves. And I *do* think it's stupid to hunt animals unless you need to. Like in a survival situation. What kind of sport is it to shoot an unarmed animal with a rifle? Takes a real tough guy." Sarcasm drips thickly off his words. "But Chad and Tommy are into it, so I thought I'd tag along and just shoot at some targets. Can't hurt to learn basic gun safety."

Jonathan closes the discussion. He seems more than irritated Megan has called him out in front of their mom. Returning fire, he sits up straight and with an artificial politeness, asks, "So, Megs, how's the investigation going?" successfully diverting attention away from himself.

Megan's jaw hits the floor and her nostrils flare. She shoots Jonathan a look, needing no explanation. "Thanks a lot!" Megan throws a piece of bread at her brother. Jonathan shrugs in faux apology.

Megan tries not to, but her face tilts just enough to catch her mom staring at her anxiously.

"Investigation? What investigation? Megan, you didn't tell me about any kind of investigation. Are you in some kind of trouble?"

Megan can't believe her brother went there. "No, mom. It's nothing like that." Megan shakes her head, exasperated. "I promise," she adds quickly after seeing her mother isn't buying it.

"Then what is it like, Megan? What does Jonathan mean by *your investigation?*"

Megan sighs. "Nothing, mom, it's just… god this is going to sound so stupid." Megan makes a split-second decision to blurt it out and be done with it. It was foolish of her to think they could get through one family dinner without Kathy and Smalls reminding her that the three of them together do not create a triangle. Instead, her mom and brother are wheels on a bicycle, each needing the other to move forward. Megan is a spare tire, kept in storage until they need her to set the table or deflect an uncomfortable conversation. "I have this hunch maybe Dad didn't kill himself. That maybe something awful happened, and I've been asking around a little just to see what I can find. That's all." Megan waves her hand, minimizing the idea.

Kathy and Jonathan are silent. If Jonathan had meant to push Megan away, he's succeeding. "It's crazy, I know," Megan says as she shoots her chair back abruptly to get up and refill her water.

She walks over to the refrigerator and puts her glass under the water dispenser. She breathes deeply, mesmerized, as she watches the water stream slowly and steadily reach the top. Steeling herself, she turns to rejoin the table. She's halted in her tracks just as quickly, having caught the tail end of her mom and brother righting themselves as though they were huddled together, talking in secret, and pulled themselves apart at the last second so Megan wouldn't overhear.

Megan deflates as she returns to the table.

Kathy looks at her with affection in her eyes. "Megan, we don't think you're crazy. I know it must be hard to accept what happened. Especially when you hadn't been in touch for so long. But this is not your fault, and it's not something for you to fix."

I didn't say you thought I was crazy.

Megan feels her face growing hot. Her mother thinks she's delusional and she just can't handle the fact that her father committed suicide. She has half a mind to unload everything she's found out so far. To scream at her mom. *Josh and Katie believe me!* She looks down, collecting herself, being mindful of how she'll respond. The last thing she needs right now is to isolate herself from her mom and brother. They mean well. She knows they love her, even if they love each other more.

As hard as she tries, she hears her voice rising in volume and her tone darkening. "It's not like that, mom. I'm not chasing some situation I imagined! I know neither of you cares that he's dead, but I'd appreciate if you didn't treat me like I'm stupid for wanting to know the truth. If the truth is he killed himself, then so be it. But I don't think it is, and you don't get to sit there and judge me right now." Megan's outburst is layered with years' worth of buried feelings of being an unimportant part of their world. She's barely a part of it at all. But on the surface, she knows her words will be interpreted one way only and taken at face value.

Megan feels lighter after having unloaded her unfiltered opinion for once. Though, she also wants to shove the words back down as soon as they leave her mouth so as not to give her mother and Smalls any reason to push her further outside of their tiny bubble.

"Megs." Jonathan's voice is gentle as he reaches across the table to squeeze her hand. He is treading carefully, and Megan hates it even more than if he'd started arguing with her. She can win an argument, even if she is inherently wrong because Smalls will stop fighting before she does. But this. That he feels sorry for her, she can't stomach his pity.

He drops her hand and slowly drags his back across the table as he locks eyes with Kathy in a moment of agreement. Megan knows instantly she hadn't imagined the exchange she caught earlier.

Kathy nods, apparently giving Jonathan an encouraging push because he looks back at Megan. His brow lowers as he tilts his head. "We don't think you're crazy. We're worried about you. This just seems like a fruitless endeavor ultimately holding you back from moving on. He's gone, Megs. And we're sorry you're hurting." He looks back at their mom and Megan watches as Kathy gives him a sad smile, as if he'd delivered his lines flawlessly.

Megan assumes her mother's concern is genuine, having not been privy to what Megan is up to before tonight's fiasco. But Smalls knew. That he would go along with this charade and gaslight Megan now, Megan wonders if he realizes how cruel he's being.

Megan has had enough. What little composure she has left is gone. "A fruitless endeavor? That's ultimately holding me back from moving on. Are you my shrink now? You're twenty-five years old, Jonathan." Megan watches as he winces under her use of his given name. "You know nothing. You had your whole life to get used to the idea of not having a dad. This is new for some of us."

Megan is hitting way below the belt now. She knows. But he started this when he violated her trust by telling their mom what she has been up to and then tried to make her feel crazy for it.

She stands up, moving away from the table. "As usual, this has been lovely. Thanks for dinner, mom. I'll call you later."

Megan shoots one final dagger from her eyes in Jonathan's direction. He'd been trying to turn their mother's focus away from himself. He couldn't possibly have predicted how badly Megan would take it. But right now, she doesn't care if she is supposed to be his protective big sister or that she'd never let anyone treat Smalls this way. She'll call him tomorrow. She is in no condition to talk to either of them until she sleeps off the emotional hangover of this evening.

CHAPTER 16

SATURDAY, SEPTEMBER 12TH

By the following morning, Megan has felt the grime of last night's family dinner dissipate with a hot bath and a full night's sleep. She leaves the comfort of her bed only long enough to fill a mug with coffee and walk back to her room. Megan opts to stay in bed a while longer today, with no obligations on her agenda. She looks over the list of dates collected from her dad's books once more, hoping for a flicker of understanding that hasn't yet surfaced, before pushing the list off to the side of her nightstand.

She picks up the first volume and begins reading from where she left off yesterday, remembering with each page the sound of her father's deep, soothing voice reciting the story to her when she asked. Him reading to her was her favorite pastime as a kid. He'd create a fresh voice for each character, rattling off each line as if the words did not belong to the entire world. As if the story was written especially for her.

She could hear when he was smiling by the way it changed the shape of his words. A tear rolls silently down her cheek. She hadn't realized she was crying until she saw the wet splotch on the page laying open in her lap.

Her hand lifts to her face, and she smooths away the streak left by the grief that always seems to surface while she is alone. It seems to know when her mind has nowhere to run.

She searches the pages, not quite taking in the full story. She is hunting for the words echoed in her father's text message—*this isn't goodbye, it's see you later*—to confirm her memory of them, knowing it will be proof enough that she is looking in the right place. Proof her hunt is not some inane distraction from processing the pain that remains in the hole her father's death left behind.

Her mind is a jumble of thoughts, distracting her from her pursuit. Smalls pops into her mind among the mess.

Damn it. I need to call my brother to apologize.

As if reading her thoughts, her phone rings and she leans over in her bed to see Smalls' name on the screen. She picks up the phone with a forced effort.

"Were your ears burning? I was just reaching for my phone to call you." Megan skips the usual pleasantries of answering a phone call and gets right to the point.

"Great minds, I guess." Jonathan chuckles uncomfortably. When Megan doesn't respond, he continues. "Look, Megs, I'm sorry about last night. I never should have…"

Megan cuts him off. "No, I know. Me too. I'm sorry. We both said stuff we shouldn't have. Stuff we didn't mean."

"Yeah. I was just trying to get mom to lay off. But I took it too far. I shouldn't have outed you before you were ready to tell mom."

"It's all good. I was just in a tough place already. This whole thing just…" Megan trails off, leaving her thought unfinished. She's always been good at brushing off how she really feels and when it boils over into an overreaction, she sweeps that aside too, as if it was nothing to be bothered with.

"This whole thing just what?"

Megan hears her brother's refrigerator close on the other end of the phone, followed shortly after by the beeping of a microwave.

Are you eating while we have a heartfelt conversation? Typical. Smalls apparently can't wait until they are done talking. Or wait for anything ever when it comes to food. When he's hungry, he eats. Megan rolls her eyes affectionately, recognizing his quirk.

Megan sighs a heavy breath, "I don't know. It's hard to explain. This whole thing just has me off kilter, I guess. It's like… growing up, I was so sure he loved us and he just didn't know how to be a proper dad. Then when we got older, I thought I was wrong. He never cared. He was just pretending, trying to convince himself. You know? I mean, he never tried to fix things with you." Megan hears Jonathan snort, as if mocking the very idea that Mark would even try.

"And then when I stopped trying, so did he. Now he's gone and… I don't know. I just have this feeling something is off and I don't know what it is. And no one believes me, so I'm just…" Megan's voice hitches. "It's just lonely being the only one in this, knowing everyone thinks I'm crazy."

"Josh and Katie are with you, though, right? In this investigation, or whatever?" Jonathan sputters the words out, as if thrown by Megan's uncharacteristic show of vulnerability.

"Yeah." Megan considers the truth of it. "Yeah, I mean they're helping me but, honestly, I can't always tell if they believe me or if they're just humoring me."

"Either way, they're being good friends. I'm glad you have them."

"Thanks, Smalls." They sit in silence for just a beat too long. The connection Megan feels to her brother is lost. "Anyway, I'll let you go now. I know this doesn't matter to you. And I get it. I really do." Megan lets Smalls off the hook, unsure why she unloaded on him to begin with when she hadn't confessed to anyone else yet.

"Ok, but… we're good?"

"We're good. Always." Megan replies. She means it. No matter how disconnected she and Jonathan were to their parents, each in their own way, Megan would never turn her back on her brother. One too many people who should have been there for him without question had turned their back to him already. She won't be one of them. "Call you later?"

"Sounds good. Later, Megs."

Megan hangs up the phone and drops it in her lap. She takes the backs of her fingers and nuzzles them into her eyes. Her circulation has always been less than stellar, her hands and feet always seem to run cold. The cool skin from her hands soothing the puffiness she can feel building under her eyes from the tears she held back during her phone call.

She goes to her bathroom to splash cold water on her face so she can get back to work.

Megan spends the better part of the morning reading. After four straight hours staring at boxy black lettering on a white background, which would normally sound like a dream, she needs a break. This doesn't feel like the leisurely reading she always looks forward to. This feels like work. Work of the most important variety. The pressure to get it right builds like a balloon inside her chest, threatening to pop any minute.

She gets up, grabbing her cell phone, and heads to the kitchen to refill her coffee. She doctors her coffee just the way she likes, with a packet of Truvia sweetener and an oatmilk creamer and then takes a deep drink.

She swaps her mug for her phone and taps to find Josh's name. She sends him a quick text message to ask if he's found any more details about where the mysterious sticky note came from, or who found it, or most importantly, why it existed at all.

She sits down on the couch, her thoughts flitting back and forth between what she knows so far and what she still needs to understand. After what feels like an eternity, her phone dings. She looks down to see Josh has replied, and only two minutes have passed.

He hasn't had a chance to look into it further because work has been crazy, but he'll try to prioritize it today.

Megan thanks him, telling him not to rush, hoping the three dots at the end of her message convey what she is thinking. *I'm telling you not to rush because I don't want to be impolite when you're doing me a solid. But please do rush. Just as soon as you can. If you're able to. No pressure. But thanks in advance for doing it today. As soon as you put your phone down. Again... no rush.*

She grabs her book and sits outside on her patio, leaving her phone on the kitchen counter to avoid any temptation of harassing Josh while he is working. Perhaps the sunlight will give her the boost she needs.

After another hour with nothing, she is about to throw in the towel when she sees it. There, on page 193. The words she's been searching for stare back at her.

Her dad has dog-eared the bottom of the page just a freckle, telling Megan this space is theirs. No one else would notice it, but both of them would know how to find it whenever they wanted to remember.

Her eyes linger there in this secret space, seeing both the words on the page and her dad's text message to her at once.

Remember, Aine, I have always loved you. Whatever happens, I trust you completely. This isn't goodbye, it's see you later.

Megan jumps out of her chair and runs inside, the book closed on her thumb to hold her place. She can't believe it. She throws her fists in the air, victorious. Her body has a sudden compulsion to dance around, her excitement manifesting itself in a burst of energy she doesn't know what to do with.

She was certain there was something here, but part of her never thought she'd really find the validation she so desperately needs. She collapses onto her couch. Her apartment is sweltering.

I found you, Dad. You were right here, in our Heaven. I just had to know where to look.

She sits up, the adrenaline drained from her body, mixed into the beads of sweat forming on her upper lip. The thrill of success propels her forward. She must keep going.

She tucks herself under a throw blanket, an odd chill taking over her, and picks up the book to read the words again, plunging them deeper into her heart, afraid they'll disappear when she looks away.

Shoving the thought from her mind, she soaks in the sweet words and prepares herself for more. She glides her fingers softly down the page, feeling the words, when her index finger catches on something. She rips her hand back to examine the tiny cut on her fingertip. Megan shoves the paper cut into her mouth to staunch the bleeding as she looks to see what nicked her finger.

It takes her a moment to see it. The familiar words were enough to affix her eyes to the page, but it isn't what makes her stay.

There, just where the quote begins, is a thin line, so thin, in fact, Megan might not have noticed it at all had it not sliced her finger. It is ever so slightly lighter than the rest of the page, a near perfect match in color. The line runs all the way from the spine of the book to the outside edge of the page.

As her eyes continue slowly down the page, she sees another line a few lines below the first. She squints to be sure of what she is seeing.

It looks as if someone replaced a block of text on the page, a near-perfect replica save for the almost imperceptible color distinction.

She traces her fingers horizontally over the lines, carefully this time, taking in the smooth texture of the old pages. But when she drags her fingers vertically down the page, she feels a minute bump where the lines appear.

It feels like a sticker, perhaps the thinnest she's ever felt. The text on the book continues flawlessly where the lines insert themselves, so Megan can't exactly decipher what this is.

She migrates to her junk drawer in the kitchen, where she riffles through and pulls out a pocketknife. When she sits down, she flips open the smallest blade available. She runs the tip gently along the edge of one line. She presses a little harder when nothing shakes loose, afraid she'll puncture the page.

On her second pass, a portion of the sticker gives way in one spot and her blade slides underneath, lifting it away from the original book page. Her eyes widen as she pulls the blade out, not wanting to damage whatever this is.

She checks she hasn't pierced the page and then pokes the blade back in softly and twists it ninety degrees to separate the two papers enough that she can look inside the gap it creates. She sees now this isn't a sticker at all, but a slip of paper, duplicated from the book and superimposed on top of its matching text.

It was so expertly adhered to the original that an untrained eye reading the book for pleasure might have assumed it to be water damage or, more likely, glossed over it entirely. Because Megan was focused on this page in particular, her eyes affixed themselves long enough to spy the inconsistency. Whatever adhesive was used managed not to create any glue-like bubbles or tugging of the paper as it dried. She pauses for a moment to admire her dad's ingenuity and skill. *This is very impressive, Dad. Well done.*

It occurs to her if his intent was to hide something, he may have been better off replicating the entire page rather than a snippet. She promptly scolds herself at the thought. Now isn't the time to be critical.

She goes back to gently lifting the rest of the duplicate paper. Once it's freed, she examines it. When she flips it over, she sees a note written on the backside. Even after all this time, she recognizes her dad's handwriting instantly.

432 Cosgrove Way Las Vegas 02/27 $25,000 11pm

A tiny gasp escapes her lips. *What the hell is this?*

While she has no idea what this cryptic message means, a darkness washes over her, sending a chill down her spine.

Her dad had a secret. Something possibly worth a lot of money. This is proof of as much, but what does it mean? A million thoughts cloud her mind, competing for her attention.

She looks back at the page where she found the bone to what feels like an enormous skeleton in Mark's closet. Page 193… those numbers. She's seen them somewhere else.

Megan is suddenly afraid to continue. She has opened a box and the lid can't be put back on now. She doesn't know where this trail will lead, but she knows she isn't prepared to continue down it alone.

She snatches her phone and sends a text to Josh and Katie.

I found something. I think it's bad. Can you guys come over tonight?

CHAPTER 17

Megan is pacing the living room, breathless from anxiousness or pure physical exertion, she can't be certain. Her head hangs, and she's chewing her nails again. She nearly jumps out of her skin when she hears the booming knock at the door.

Josh stumbles backward a step when Megan throws the door open. She steps towards him, rambling about her dad's books until Josh rubs her back, quieting her. "Let's go inside, Megs."

Josh guides her to the couch with a light touch between her shoulder blades and they sit with no extra space between them. Josh drapes his arm around her shoulders. "What's going on, Megs? You're worrying me a little."

"I'm sorry," Megan sighs. "I'm fine. But I didn't want to be alone. I think I found something, and I need help to make sense of it."

"Ok, we can work that out together." Josh's eyes are his best feature. Megan knows a lot of women feel that way about him. It's never bothered her before. They aren't wrong, but they also don't understand why they're so special. Most women agree the shocking blue-green color is rare and contributes to his overall attractiveness. But the truth is, his eyes reveal volumes of unspoken thoughts and feelings if you care to learn how to read them. Megan always knows what's brewing behind those eyes. She's been learning their language her whole life.

"Let's wait for Katie. She should be here soon." Megan says, checking the time before dropping her head to rest in the crook of his shoulder. "Thanks for coming, Josh."

"Of course, Megs. Always."

Katie arrives fifteen minutes later and Megan pulls her inside, pushing her over to the couch. Once Katie is seated, Megan picks up the copy of *Mania* she's been carrying around the apartment all day, afraid it might turn up missing if it isn't on her person.

Her recount of the day and her findings tumble out all at once. Megan is racing through the connection between *Mania*, Heaven and her dad's text message, when Josh interrupts, forcing her to hit the brakes.

"Megs, slow down. I'm not following. One thing at a time. You read the first book." In true police officer protocol, he tries to break her incoherent ramblings into short, succinct facts he can digest.

"Yes. And I found the quote my dad sent me in his last text. Look." Megan pulls out her phone and sets it down on the coffee table, Mark's message glowing brightly on the screen. She opens the book, jabbing a finger at the page showing the identical phrase. "I wasn't imagining it when I thought I'd heard those words before. Or read them, I guess." Megan shakes her head, annoyed with herself for feeling the need to clarify such an insignificant detail.

"Ok, so part of his text is here. And you got a paper cut from it?" Katie asks.

"Yes, exactly. I cut my finger, right here." Megan insists, pointing at the book, as if they might have forgotten where to look.

"And then you found something attached?" Josh drags the book closer to his face, squinting his eyes as if to get a better look. "Yeah, the page looks a little beat up," he says without looking up.

"And what did you find?" Katie sounds interested, but Megan can hear notes of skepticism slipping through. Katie waits while Megan picks up where Josh cut her off.

Megan walks over to the dinette and picks up the paper from the tiny tabletop where she'd left it, next to her notepad. She brings the paper to them. "This." She holds it out for them to see. "This was attached. One side matches the original page of the book, the other side has a note my dad wrote."

Josh and Katie lean closer together, inspecting the note simultaneously. Katie breaks the silence first. "So... what do you think it means?"

"I'm not sure yet. That's what I've been trying to figure out. Is it a place he gambled? It mentions Las Vegas. A drug pickup? Collection? A friend who owed him money? That doesn't feel like something worth hiding... But look at the page number." Megan walks back over to her dining table, this time grabbing her notepad. She sets it down in front of Josh and Katie and sits down on the floor across from them.

She flips the pad around so they can see the list of dates while she points to the date inside the cover of the first book.

01-01-93

"193". Megan waits for their shock, which never comes. "193!" She tries more forcefully, as if yelling the number might connect the dots for them.

She sees Josh purse his lips together. Katie's eyes never leave the list, a bit too intentionally.

Josh clears his throat. "Ok, I'm with you, Megs. I see the 193. But that only accounts for some numbers here. What about the rest? This is a date," he touches the pad with his left index finger, "and this is a page number in a book." He touches the book with his right index finger.

"Oh, right. I'm operating on the assumption there is a code here somewhere, but the dates are all mixed up. It looks random, but it's not at all. Like maybe my dad created a sort of filing system for these little notes. But I need help now. Because I'm not sure where to go next." Megan looks at Josh, hoping his police work might translate into code breaking somehow.

Josh runs his hand across the bottom half of his face and Megan notices a five o'clock shadow forming on his jawline. "Alright, Megs. Let's get to work. What have you tried?"

Megan smirks with satisfaction. "I'm presuming the last three digits are the page number since these line up." She gestures to the two different sets of matching numbers. "Then I thought maybe the first two digits of the date related to the book number in the series. He simply formatted them like a date so no one would think anything of it. So, month represents the number in which the book comes in the *Mania* series, while the last four digits for the day and year, when combined, represent the page number on which you can find a note like this one."

Megan holds up the scrap of paper. "I went to check the next number on the list, but it didn't work, see?" Megan points to the second date, 01-05-04. "If my theory is correct, this would correspond to page 504 in *Mania*. But *Mania* doesn't have 504 pages. So, I checked a couple more, and those didn't work either. Either the page number didn't exist in the corresponding volume, or the page had nothing attached to it. Then I wondered why, what could I have missed?"

Josh and Katie are staring at her. She can't be bothered to figure out what their expressions mean. Her wheels are turning too fast. Josh turns back around and, after a moment, suggests, "Maybe they're just out of order. Let's remove the dashes and put them in numerical order and then assume the pages numbers belong to the next book in the sequence."

Josh sets about shuffling the list around and when they are in numerical order, he points to the second number on the list, 010504. "That leaves us with the same number to work with, but let's check the page number in the second book of the series, which is…" He looks to Megan for the answer.

"*Mania's Child*," she says, grabbing the book then flipping to the back of it. "Which has a page 504!" She runs her finger and her eyes down the page but finds nothing odd about it. Her excitement wilts.

Josh goes back to the list in front of him. "Whoa. Let's press pause for a minute. Look at the fourth number on the list, 051005."

Megan checks the number. "What about it?"

"Do *any* of the books have over 1,000 pages? If not, then it seems like we're on the wrong track."

Megan eyes the box, plucking out the largest volume based on sheer size, and opens it up. Her shoulders sag. "Nope. This one has 687 pages, but that's a far cry from 1,000. Shit. What else could it be, then?"

Josh shrugs. "I'm not sure yet."

"Maybe the extra numbers are just there to throw us, and they mean nothing at all." Megan tosses the idea out half-heartedly.

Josh's face looks disappointed at the suggestion. "Then how would we even determine which book has the right page? I suppose we could go through and check every feasible option."

"Let's try a few and see if anything shakes loose," suggests Megan. She reaches for another book and prepares to check all possible pages from the list, when Katie speaks up.

"Hey, Megs. Remember how your dad had that one boss? He was German with a thick accent. We used to laugh at the way we could hear him smack his palm on the desk to make a point, even while your dad was on a conference call. So intense."

Both Megan and Josh whip their heads around at the same time. Megan had nearly forgotten Katie was here. She'd been so quiet and offered no help thus far. Megan tries to hide her annoyance at the nonsensical interruption. "Um yeah, I remember. What about him?" She returns to the book in her lap.

"He was super strict and so harsh. Hans… something. Remember, he used to demand your dad write dates in European format? He said Americans never understood it, but he insisted European dates were universally accepted." Katie pauses and Megan isn't sure what she is implying. When Megan doesn't respond, Katie continues. "Maybe you guys are overthinking this. Maybe they're dates like you thought, but he just put them in European format." Katie slurps the soda in her hand and sinks further back into the couch, checking for chips in her nail polish. "It would be kind of ingenious to bury such a simple solution in a system that looks so complicated."

Josh looks proud of Katie. "Dude, nice work!" Josh reaches over to high five Katie.

"I hate it when you call me dude," Katie says, reluctantly slapping her palm against his.

Josh rolls his eyes, sounding not the least bit contrite. "Think of it as a term of endearment."

Megan ignores the tiny voice whispering to her, *Josh never uses any terms of endearment with me*, and her mouth falls open as she stares at Katie. "Katie, you are brilliant! I can't believe I'd forgotten about that. Hans! Yes. For the longest time after my dad quit working for him, he kept writing dates in European format. It drove Annie nuts because it caused more than one date night mix-up and nevermind any kind of appointment." Megan turns her attention to Josh. "Let's reverse the month and day digits to convert them from European format." She can feel the anticipation building in her body as she watches him build the new list. Her heart thumps at double time in her chest and her pulse bangs against her throat and wrists.

Josh hands the paper to Megan and she looks at one number, 03-02-94. She grabs the third book, *Mania's Vengeance*, and flips to page 294. Gliding her finger down, she flinches ever so slightly when her finger passes over the bump. She looks up, beaming at Katie.

Josh bobs his head in appreciation. "Let's check the other books." He walks around the coffee table, pulling two of the books out of the box.

He flips open to the first page, checking the series list in front to determine which volumes he has in his hands. Megan checks another one herself, sneaking glances at Josh while he works.

He connects with her gaze and nods, pointing with his finger to show he's found what he was looking for.

Megan pauses and picks up the paper her dad used as a bookmark. "I still don't know what this means." Megan fingers the scrap spurred her further into this puzzle. *"There's not much time left.* How much time do we have? How will I know when time is up? What happens then?"

Megan looks down at the paper, the question she wants most to ask dangling from her lips. She doesn't look up, afraid of the pity she's sure she'll find in their faces. The question comes out in a whisper. "Do you guys think I'm crazy?"

Josh walks over at the same time Katie moves to grab Megan by the shoulders, forcing her to look into her eyes. "Megan, no. We don't think you're crazy. Look at what you've done here. Look at the lengths you'll go to find out the truth. This is next level loyalty and determination. So long as you're making sure you're allowing yourself space to process all of this too and not running from it all…" Katie doesn't finish the sentence and Megan wonders if it's because Katie can also hear herself echoing Megan's fight with Jonathan.

Megan hugs her to let her know she's alright. "I know, Katie. I'm fine. And I'm doing the therapy thing, so maybe my sessions will help somehow."

Josh smiles at Megan, the outer corners of his eyes crinkling as he nods once in agreement with Katie. "Look, I don't know what happens when time runs out. I'm not even sure what that means. But let's give it our best shot. What else can we do?" He tips his head toward the books. "Shall we?"

Megan nods and Josh carries the box over to the table, laying the books out in order. She grabs her notepad, and without speaking, they form an assembly line. Megan tells Katie which book and page to check. Katie flips through and looks for the seam of the superimposed section and passes the book to Josh. Josh takes the pocketknife and carefully removes the section with painstaking precision.

After they have linked all ten dates to a piece of paper, they turn them over to examine the notes on the back.

Each has its own address, date, time, and dollar amount. A very large dollar amount.

Immediately noticeable is how the addresses are spread over a large territory. A few are local, many are in Las Vegas, and one outlier is in Ahwatukee, Arizona.

They sit there quietly, each considering the magnitude of this discovery and what it might mean.

Josh blows out a long, full breath. "Well, Megs. I'll admit I may have had a few doubts this hunt would amount to anything, but this is impossible to ignore. If anyone thought you were crazy before, they won't anymore." Josh tries to lighten the mood, his words coming out like a half-hearted joke.

Megan returns his attempt with her own one-sided smile.

"Now, to figure out what this means. Josh?"

"I'm on it. Copy the addresses for me and I'll run them through the police database and see what I can find. This one here looks familiar. I can't put my finger on it," Josh says, ironically putting his finger on one address.

Megan starts a new piece of paper where she copies the addresses in a list format for Josh to take with him.

Josh reaches his hand out, reading it over. "Listen, Megs. Don't do anything until I get back to you on this, ok?" His eyes pierce into hers, blazing with seriousness.

"Like what?" Megan looks to Katie for a translation, and Katie shoots her a half smirk. When Josh whips around to confirm his suspected collusion, Katie quickly wipes her face clean and shrugs, as if to declare her innocence in this pretend debate.

"Oh, I don't know. Something like driving out to visit one of these local addresses to see what it's about before I've vetted the place." Josh shakes his head slightly.

"I wouldn't do that…" Megan avoids his eye. She's always been a horrible liar. The thought had absolutely crossed her mind already.

"Mm hmm…" Josh rolls his eyes. "I mean it, Megs. You too, Katie." He adds, looking directly at where she's sitting. "We don't know what this is yet. But no matter what is going on here, with money like this involved, this could be very dangerous. I don't have any family." Josh looks down briefly. "You two are all I've got." He stands up straighter, as if regrouping from his uncharacteristic display of emotion before continuing. "Promise me you will both stay put."

Katie speaks first and Megan can't help feeling like Katie is owning the lie, so Megan won't have to. "We will, Officer Pierce. Don't get so worked up."

Josh levels his brow at Katie's use of his professional title. "I'm mean it, *dude*. You could get hurt. Or worse." Josh hammers the point home.

"Alright, alright. Geez." Katie puts her hands up in mock surrender.

Josh releases his glare before changing the subject. "By the way, I was going to tell you when I got here. I talked to the coroner on the phone."

Megan perks up. She's been waiting for an update on this. "And?"

"I think I need to pay him a visit. Call it a hunch, but he's hiding something. He sounded shifty when I pressed him about the photocopied report in our file and he didn't have a suitable answer for where the original was or what might have happened to it. Then he said he spilled his coffee on it, so he rewrote it and filed the clean copy, not realizing it was the photocopy. I don't know what to make of it, but his story has changed and something is telling me to lean on him a little harder."

"I'm coming with you to talk to him." Megan leaves little to no room for argument, but Josh tries.

"That's a terrible idea. A man with a secret is always a threat. I'm more than capable of handling this. I know what we're after here."

"I know you're capable. And I trust you, Josh. But if he knows anything at all about what happened, I want to hear from him firsthand."

Josh adjusts his posture, providing an extra air of authority. "You can't, Megs. It's against protocol. I'm already sticking my neck on the chopping block for Chief by getting involved in the first place."

"If you're going to get in trouble regardless, then what difference will it make if I'm with you? Let me come. I can help."

Megan shoots him a pleading but decided look, letting Josh know she is both asking for his support and she is absolutely going with him.

Josh sighs, sounding exhausted. "Fine. I was planning on heading over there on Wednesday. My next day off."

"Perfect." Megan grabs her phone to block off the time on her completely open schedule and turns to give him a hug. "Thanks, Josh." She says, speaking the words to his chest rather than his face, since that's where her face lands on him.

"Alright, you crazy kids," Katie announces, louder than she needs to, as though reminding them she is still in the room. "If you don't need anything else, Megs, I'm going to head home and hit the hay. It's been a week, huh?"

"It really has." Megan turns, linking her arm through Katie's, walking to the door together. "We're good here. Thank you. For your help. For being here when I need you." Megan reaches for the doorknob before she can plead with Katie to stay longer.

Josh follows Katie out the door and turns to Megan one last time. "I'll get back to you as soon as I can. In fact, I'm kind of keyed up now. I may pop into the station on the way home to check out the addresses. I'll call you."

"Fifty bucks says I'm still awake when you do."

"Try to sleep. I promise I'll let you know if I find anything. Goodnight, ladies." Josh addresses them together, waving an arm over his head while he walks away.

"Night!" Katie and Megs respond in unison. Typical.

Megan locks the door behind her and gets ready for bed. She knows she won't be able to sleep, and she feels a headache coming on. She pops two aspirin in her mouth, turns the light down low, and opens her book to where she left off.

She glances at the clock on her nightstand. She likes to use a real clock instead of her phone. Her phone is too distracting. Every time she uses it to check the time, a million notifications beg her to be checked. So, she lays it face down on the nightstand.

She's been reading for close to two hours. Just when her eyes feel too heavy for her to hold open anymore, her phone dings.

Incoming text message from Josh Pierce (12:09 am):
I got something. Can you meet me for coffee in the morning before my shift?

CHAPTER 18

SUNDAY, SEPTEMBER 13TH

Megan strolls to her favorite table at Bean, Katie by her side. When they squeeze past the line spilling out the door, they spot Josh, a manilla file folder on the table right next to two grande coffee cups and two blueberry muffins.

"Chestnut praline lattes. Tis the season." Josh extends a cup to each of them, beaming, supremely proud at always knowing their coffee order.

"You're a saint," Katie says, taking a deep drink of the sweet, hot elixir.

They sit down, and Megan takes a tentative sip, checking the temperature. She can never drink it scalding hot the way Katie likes. When she finds the temperature just right, she looks at Josh to thank him.

"Katie's is extra hot. Yours is regular. I figured if I got here early, it may be cooled enough when you arrived." Josh looks smug and Megan can't even razz him for it because he nailed it.

Katie pretends to gag. "Wow, Josh. Think maybe you should try a little harder?"

Josh shoots her a look intended to shut her up. "Thanks for the advice, dude. I'll consider it." Katie rolls her eyes at him before looking away.

Megan turns her attention to the folder sitting on the table, pretending like her friends aren't behaving like toddlers right now. "Ok, now that caffeine is in route to my bloodstream, tell me about the addresses."

Josh opens the folder and pulls out his report. Handing each of them a copy so they won't have to share. Suddenly, he isn't Josh anymore. He's Officer Pierce. "The first section, highlighted in yellow, is all residences. The corresponding appendix has a list of the last known resident's name, age, and occupation."

Megan looks at Katie, pressing her lips together to suppress a snicker. Katie takes a drink, looking away from Megan so she won't burst into laughter.

Josh clocks the exchange immediately, almost as if he expected it, and sighs. "What's so funny?"

Megan rearranges her face in a serious expression. "Nothing. Honest. This is good stuff. You're just so formal right now. Is this what it's like to be on the job with you?" Megan turns to Katie. "I think we need to sign up for a ride-along. ASAP."

Josh remains stoic. "Yuck it up, ladies." He folds his arms across his chest and waits. "If you're finished now, I'd like to continue," Josh scolds.

Katie sits up straighter, clearing her throat. "Of course. Please proceed." Katie swipes her hand through the air as if presenting him with the floor.

"As I was saying, the yellow block is residences. The blue block underneath, is businesses. In the attached appendix," Josh pauses, checking that they are taking this seriously before continuing, "are the names of the businesses, the owners, and the business hours."

Josh brings their attention to the lone address at the bottom. "This is the one I thought looked familiar when I saw it last night. And I was right. I've seen this address before. This place is a known illegal gambling ring we've busted several times. The guys who ran it would vary their operation, shuffling rooms, business hours, and sometimes the floor they'd meet on. We were always on our toes. To our knowledge, they abandoned the location altogether last year after an FBI raid took down the head of the organization."

Megan takes in all the new information, considering her next move.

"Why do you think my dad had this register of both businesses and houses? If you had to speculate given your experience in law enforcement."

Josh considers her question, furrowing his brow as if choosing his words carefully. "If I had to guess, given what we know so far, he was either operating a small illegal gambling business and placing bets on behalf of his clients, or he was doing collections for someone else."

Megan evaluates the possibilities of this, bobbing her head. "You don't think it's drug related?"

"It's not outside the realm of possibility, but given the sheer size of the dollar amounts we're talking about, gambling is far more likely. I don't know of any drug kingpins who deal in those sums, let alone allow their clientele to rack up that much debt before collecting. Unless he was mixed up with a cartel somehow."

Josh lets his opinion linger between them and waits. Katie and Megan both glance at the lists, occasionally allowing their eyes to connect while silently communicating with each other.

"You're probably right, Josh. My dad was definitely dabbling in drugs and drinking far too much, on and off over the years, but I can't believe he'd have gotten in so deep or have had the presence of mind to work with a cartel. Not after seeing the video of him with his grandkids."

Josh nods in agreement and checks his watch. "I've got to head to the station."

Megan and Katie stand up to say their goodbyes. "I'll let you know what we find," Megan says as Katie releases Josh from a side hug.

"You'll do what now?" Josh turns to Megan, head cocked, one eye squinting in interrogation.

Megan looks around, pretending to collect her things, hoping her next words come out casually enough not to set off any alarm bells in Josh's head. She's never been able to lie to him. "We're going to go check out the local addresses and talk to the people there to see if they can tell us anything about what he may have been up to." Megan looks to Katie for support, and Katie nods her head vigorously in agreement.

"Like hell you are. Absolutely not. Two women rolling up to these places alone is probably your worst idea ever. I'll do it. I'll swing by in uniform." Josh's face looks as if it's made of stone, unflinching and immovable.

"How very piggish of you, Joshua." Katie chastises, adding a huff and an exaggerated eye roll for good measure.

"Damn it, Katie, this is serious!" Josh takes a breath and calms himself before continuing. "Call it what you want. You don't know what these kinds of people are like. They don't care that you're women, or innocent bystanders, or that you're just asking questions about your dad." He looks at Megan, his face unapologetic. "If you go snooping around where they don't want you, they will handle it any way they feel is necessary. This is not a negotiation."

Megan takes a step back, creating a bit more distance between her and Josh before she chimes in, squashing the conversation. "You're right, Josh. It's not a negotiation. If these people are really dealing in shady stuff, they'll never talk to a police officer. Katie and I are going together. And we'll be fine. We have our phones and the pepper spray you make us carry."

Josh is shaking his head disapprovingly at Megan. "That's not nearly good enough."

"And we will skip the gambling business you told us about. We'll only check out the two residences." Megan adds, breaking her own demand not to negotiate on the topic.

Josh's face drops, and he raises his hand to rub across his mouth, which is his nervous tick. Megan recognizes it immediately. "You're going to do this whether I like it or not. I can't talk you out of this, can I?"

Megan shakes her head, gently. "I have to know, Josh. I'm not asking for your approval." She knows it's killing him he can't protect them right now.

"Did you pick today on purpose? Knowing I have a shift and wouldn't be able to come?" Josh asks quietly, looking down at his shoes.

Megan doesn't answer. Her shoulders lift while she watches his jaw clench.

Josh relents. "Wow. Ok," he says as he pulls Megan into his arms. "Stay alert. Be careful." Megan can't tell if she heard the warning from his lips or his eyes as he stares at her with an intensity she doesn't recognize. He dips his mouth closer to her ear, and she hears him whisper, "I mean it, Megs. I can't let anything happen to you."

He backs away and looks at them both. "Text me immediately when you arrive and again when you leave each place."

Megan and Katie exchange a look of victory. It doesn't escape Josh's notice. "I mean it! If I don't hear from you within a reasonable time frame, I'm dispatching every unit I have. Don't make me use the resources if I don't need to."

"We got it, Josh. We promise." Megan says.

The trio parts ways and heads to their cars. Josh to the right, Megan and Katie to the left. It's a warm day, but Megan suddenly wishes she'd brought a jacket. With each step, she grows increasingly colder.

CHAPTER 19

Megan and Katie arrive at the first address forty minutes later. The neighborhood looks like it was once lovely and warm, but the upkeep has been abandoned long ago. The houses are modest, still made of wood panel siding instead of a more modern stucco, and the paint is severely chipped. Some yards have tired wooden fences, others have replaced them with chain link, some yards have abandoned fencing all together.

Megan double checks the address on her paper and sends the obligatory text message to Josh before glancing up at the house they're parked in front of. There is a small wooden porch, two steps off the ground, leading to the front door with a security screen attached. On the porch, to the right of the front door, there's an old, beat-up brown sofa sitting underneath a picture window with no screens on it. The curtains hanging inside are a crimson color, but there are some holes in the fabric. It occurs to Megan that while she can't see anything inside with the lights off, whoever lives inside could be watching them now. She thinks about how many times she's done exactly that when someone has come to her front door. How many times she's peeked just enough to watch what they do and then wait for them to leave. The feeling rattles her.

She looks at Katie, and the pair lock their tiny purses in the glove box after pocketing their pepper spray canisters. Megan steels herself before getting out of the car.

About halfway to the porch, Katie reaches for Megan's arm, stopping her in her tracks. "Wait, maybe this isn't a good idea. I've got a bad feeling about this."

"I know what you mean. I've been feeling uneasy since yesterday."

"Then maybe we shouldn't do this. We can wait for Josh to come check the place out. We should do that. Let's wait."

"Come on, Katie. It's going to be fine. This is just a weird situation. The guy probably won't even answer the door." When Katie says nothing, Megan tries again. "I need you. You're my ride or die."

Katie exhales, her eyes flicker around her, flinching at every tiny sound. Her words are just as frantic. "I know. You know I am, Megs. I'm down for the ride, but I don't want to do the dying part. This guy could be a total drugged out psycho." Katie's arm gestures wildly at their surroundings. "Look at this place. We have no idea what kind of person lives here! This is stupid."

Megan can see this goes beyond nervousness. Katie looks terrified. "Katie, it's ok. Why don't you go wait in the car? Keep your hand on your phone. I'll be quick."

"Ok… ok." Katie's breathing slows, and she backs away before pausing. "No. No, I can't leave you up there alone with who knows what on the other side of the door. Safety in numbers and all of that, right?"

"Are you sure?"

"Yes. Let's just get this over with."

They stagger toward the front door, and their arms link without either of them noticing.

Megan stretches out a tentative hand to ring the doorbell. When she doesn't hear any noise, she knocks on the door before she loses her nerve and takes a large step back.

A voice rings out from behind the door, sounding frenetic and too high pitched. "Who is it? What do you want?"

Megan exchanges an anxious look with Katie before replying loudly to be heard through the closed door, "Mr. Archers? My name is Megan Palmer." Megan and Katie both notice the curtains in the window are semi-sheer and they are now swaying back and forth. Being this close, they can only see the outline of the man behind them.

"I wanted to ask you about Mark Palmer," Megan explains, pulling a photo of her dad out of her back pocket. It's an old photo, but he looks the same, albeit younger and healthier. Besides, it's the only one Megan could find at her apartment.

She holds the photo up in the direction of the window, hoping he can see it. "Do you know him?"

"Waddya want? How you know him? We're square. I don't want nothing to do with him ever again. You git outta here right now." His words come out clipped and in triple time. Megan isn't sure if it's from fear, or drugs, or some combination of the two.

Katie's hand flies up to Megan's arm. "Come on, Megs. You heard him. Let's go." Katie's eyes plead with her.

Megan swallows down a lump in her throat and turns back to the door. She tries again, feeling like she's gliding over thin ice and it might give way any minute. "Please, Mr. Archers. I'm not here to cause trouble. Mark was my father, and he passed away." She listens, hearing nothing, she continues. "I found your address on a piece of paper in his things. Can you tell me why he had it?"

Megan waits for a response which never comes.

"Mr. Archers?"

"You get off my property right now! Now, I said! I ain't gonna tell you again. Tell Mark to go to Hell!" Somewhere behind the window, the sound of a shotgun being cocked rings out, loud and threatening. Megan is nowhere near ready to call the man's bluff.

Megan and Katie turn and run in one fluid motion, as quickly as they can, back to the car. Adrenaline surges through Megan's veins and her hand is shaking so badly she has trouble getting the car started. When the engine finally roars to life, she hits the gas and doesn't waste any time making a U-turn on the narrow street to go back the way they came. She goes deeper into the neighborhood, searching for another way out.

Once they find the main road, Megan pulls into a McDonald's parking lot and turns the car off.

The silence is thick. The sound of their hearts pounding against their ribs is the only noise, and it fills the car.

Megan wipes the sweat from her upper lip with the back of her thumb. When she finally turns to look at Katie, she sees her friend's face has become a bright and vibrant shade of red. "Katie, I'm so…"

"I told you I didn't want to go. I told you we should wait for Josh!" Katie cuts her off, her eyes piercing Megan, as her voice rings out.

"I know, I'm sorry. I didn't…"

"You didn't know. You didn't think… save it, Megan!"

Megan flinches at Katie's use of her full name.

"We could have died today. Do you even realize that? We don't know what your dad was mixed up in and that guy back there was off his rocker. If he's crazy enough to threaten us with a shotgun, you better believe he's crazy enough to use it, too."

Megan sits there, stunned, letting Katie scream at her. She deserves it after ignoring Katie's pleas to leave. She has never seen Katie like this. Megan doesn't know this rage filled version, and it frightens her.

But Katie is right. Megan knew Katie wouldn't let her go alone, and she took advantage. Unsure of what to say, she chews her bottom lip anxiously, using her teeth to pull the dry, cracked pieces of skin away as the taste of iron spreads across on her tongue.

"You're right. I shouldn't have asked you to come with me."

"You shouldn't have been there either! It was dangerous. Josh warned us. We should have listened." Katie turns her head to stare out the window, hard and unflinching. "Just take me home."

"Ok. I'll take you home. I'll let you know if I find out anything useful at the other address?" Megan's tone makes the tiniest inflection. Her words are asking, hopeful Katie is still interested in her pursuit. If she isn't, then Megan has done far more damage than she thought by dragging Katie into her search.

Katie whips her head around, her eyes so narrow they're nearly closed. "You can't be serious. You're still going to the next house? Megan, I know you're hurting, but do you have an actual death wish?"

"No, I don't, but I've come too far. I know something isn't right. I have to know. For myself." Megan hangs her head, staring down at her lap. She can feel Katie's judgment burning her skin and she retreats into herself for refuge from the pain.

"You don't have to do it like this. You can let Josh help. Or use the phone. Find another way."

"I'm the only one who cares, Katie. My dad trusted me with this. After all this time, he tasked this to me. He's still my dad. I owe him this much. I owe it to myself." Megan's voice cracks. Her eyes fall to her lap. The rest of her words come out in nearly a whisper. "Look, if I don't do this, no one else will. He'll be forgotten and all I'll be left with is wondering which pieces of him were real."

Megan's voice chokes out the words threatening to sink her heart with their weight. Vulnerability isn't something Megan is used to feeling. She can count the number of people she trusts on one hand. She's lived in fear those people will leave once they uncover the uglier parts of her life. The pieces she keeps buried. She can't show them everything, terrified they'll leave.

Now, because she's pushed her best friend too far, she is afraid she has lost one of the most important people she has left.

"You don't owe your dad anything. He messed up. A lot. The truth is he had no business putting this on you." Katie shakes her head, looking defeated. "If you get yourself hurt doing this, I'll never forgive you. I can't handle you becoming so reckless." Katie turns and rests her head on the window. "Take me home."

Megan is waiting to pull out of the parking lot when a police car flies past them on the road, sirens blaring, red and blue lights glowing hot on the roof. She remembers that Josh is waiting to hear from her, but she can't bring herself to reach for her phone and pretend everything is alright.

Megan drives the entire way in silence. Afraid if she says another word, she'll start crying and she won't be able to stop. She hasn't mourned the death of her father yet, but she can already feel the grief of losing Katie like a physical knife to her heart.

They arrive at Katie's apartment a half hour later. Katie reaches for the car door handle and stops. "Promise me you'll take care of yourself, Megs," she says without looking at Megan. It feels painfully like Katie is saying "goodbye".

When Katie closes the door to her apartment, Megan's wall crumbles. Megan sobs and she keeps sobbing until the reservoir dries up. She sits there, hoping Katie doesn't see her. Hoping she does. Katie doesn't come back out.

CHAPTER 20

The sound of her phone buzzing breaks her trance. Megan pulls her phone out of the glove box where she left it and finds seven text messages and five missed calls from Josh.

She scrambles to reply to his text message before he sends out the calvary.

Outgoing text message from Megan Palmer (11:04am):
Hey! Sorry, I left the phone in the glove box. All good here. Getting ready to head to the second address.

Josh doesn't text her back, he calls her. She hesitates to answer but can't find a good excuse not to.

"Hey Jo—"

"Seriously? That's all you have to say? I asked for one simple thing. Now I have to call off Sergeant Tompkins and explain to Chief why I demanded he be dispatched to Archers' house in the first place. Forget making detective. Chief is going to ship my ass off to archives. Why didn't Katie answer my calls, either?"

"Oh, her phone died. I've got it on the charger. It won't happen again. I'm really am sorry, Josh. ETA at the next location in fifteen minutes."

Josh's silence screams at her on the other end of the phone until he finally puts her out of her misery. "I'm standing by my phone."

The line goes dead before she can say goodbye.

Megan hates lying to Josh. His trust, like hers, is precious and earned. It's a risk that Katie might tell Josh about their fight, and he'll know Megan lied to him but, she pushes the thought to the side. She needs to see if the next address proves helpful.

She pulls away from Katie's curb, saying a silent prayer it isn't for the last time.

She arrives at the second house right on time and promptly texts Josh. He responds with a thumbs up and Megan can't decide if it's because he's working or because he's talked to Katie and now he's even angrier.

Megan looks around. This neighborhood is entirely opposite the first one. The homes are modern, cookie cutter stucco with only five different styles rotating down the block in varying shades of brown. The yards are small and well maintained. There are kids playing in the street.

Megan is both at ease and extremely confused about what her dad has been doing with people in these two locations.

She takes a deep breath and marches toward the front door, pepper spray in one pocket and her dad's photo in the other.

She raises her hand to the doorbell and forces herself to press it. She backs away from the door, apprehensive about what may come from the other side.

The door swings open and a young man who looks to be about the same age as Smalls appears and props himself against the doorframe in one fluid motion. "Can I help you?"

"Hi. Um... is your dad home?" She tries, hoping the man she's expecting is somewhere inside the house.

"I don't have a dad," the man replies plainly.

Megan feels quite certain now the person connected to her dad is no longer at this address. This boy isn't Richard Dennis, age 48, estate attorney. "Oh. Alright well... my name is Megan Palmer. My dad was Mark Palmer. I was wondering if you might have known him?" She reaches for her dad's picture, but before she can pull it out, he speaks again.

"Nope. Can't say I do." And he swings the door closed, leaving her alone on the porch.

Asshole...

Before she can turn to leave, Megan hears voices bickering on the other side of the door. One of them sounds like it belongs to a woman. She waits for a moment, against her better judgement, and suddenly, the door swings open once more. This time, an older woman stands in front of her with a frilly half apron tied around her waist, a rolling pin gripped in her hand. She looks the picture of a southern belle, an old-fashioned A-line dress jutting out at the bottom forms an upside-down cone shape. Her platinum blonde bouffant is perfectly coiffed, with a volume Dolly Parton would envy. Every strand has been tamed.

"Honestly, I don't know why he bothers coming over here at all if he's going to be such a beast." Megan isn't sure if the woman is talking to her or to herself. "I apologize for my son. Sawyer can be a real pain in the you-know-what sometimes." The woman rests the hand holding the rolling pin on her hip and swats at the air with the other, as if shooing her son away like a bug. "Is there something I can help you with, dear?" The woman's voice is soft, with a sweet southern twang.

Megan tries again. "Maybe. Hi, my name is Megan... Palmer. I was wondering if you might know my dad, Mark Palmer." Megan holds the picture up for the woman to see.

The woman leans in to get a good look and steps back, her face darkening. "Did he send you here?" She looks around frantically, as if expecting Mark to appear.

Megan stands still, trying to convey she isn't here to stir up trouble. "He died. I found your address on a piece of paper mixed in with his things, and I was wondering if you could tell me how you knew him."

"We have no business with him. And what business we had with him once is no business for a young lady such as yourself. You go on home now." The woman moves to step back and close the door.

Megan thrusts her arm forward to catch the door. "Wait! Please, ma'am." Megan appeals to the woman's obvious propriety. "I just want to understand what he was doing in his last days. I thought I knew who he was and... well, I'm learning how wrong I was." Megan pleads and crosses her fingers this woman's nurturing side will be touched enough to talk. "I don't have anyone else to ask."

The woman purses her lips, as if weighing her options. Then, her face slumps with a look of sympathy and she sighs. "Sit down, sweetheart." She gestures to the wooden porch swing to Megan's right.

Megan walks over with her and sits down. The woman sets her rolling pin down on the side table and smooths the back of her dress before sitting. She turns slightly to look at Megan, clasping her hands in her lap.

"You can call me Sarah Beth. How old are you, darling?"

"I just turned twenty-seven."

"So young." Sarah Beth's eyes soften as she looks at Megan. "And how is it you came to find us? You said your daddy had our address on a piece of paper. Did the paper say anything else?"

Megan sees an opportunity in front of her. Sarah Beth is asking Megan to confirm some suspicion, it seems. Perhaps if Megan is truthful now, Sarah Beth will return the gesture.

"Yes. The paper had your address next to a date, a time, and a large amount of money... $30,000, to be exact." Megan swallows, her throat suddenly drier than it has ever felt before.

"And what was that date and time?" Sarah Beth looks down at her lap and wipes her palms on her apron.

"January 16, 2009. 10:00 pm."

"I see." Sarah Beth nods her head, thinking. Then she seems to come to a decision, and it's as if a light turns on in her mind. If she'd been rattled before, she isn't anymore. "You're old enough to buy a drink. I reckon you're old enough to hear the truth."

Megan nods.

"My husband was a liar. And a cheat. To tell the truth, he was much worse. But I've never in my life used the kinds of words that would fairly describe him, and I won't give him the honor of being my first now. You understand what I'm telling you?"

Megan nods again, trying to picture this demure woman spouting off the filthiest of swear words. She suppresses a smirk. It would be a hilarious sight, unfitting of the grace seated beside her.

Sarah Beth continues. "Our entire married lives, Richard controlled everything. He managed everything from the dinner menu, which, naturally, I prepared, to our family's finances. I knew it wasn't right, his possessiveness, but he was kind to us. He never hurt us, ever. He was a very successful attorney, so I always thought he must have some quality that craved control and order. But one day, I learned the truth of why he kept such a watchful eye on our money." She closes her eyes and shakes her head sadly. "It was not because he cared about our family's financial standing."

When Sarah Beth stops, Megan just waits, afraid if she interrupts, Sarah Beth will change her mind.

"Your daddy came to our house last year, more than once, looking for my husband. It was Mr. Palmer and another man. Conveniently, Richard was never home, but Mr. Palmer and his partner kept trying, for a while, never telling me the purpose of their visit. They always said they were old friends. Mr. Palmer was always respectful to me. His partner was too, but something about them was awfully frightening. Then one evening, the very same night written on the note you found, I got a call from the local hospital informing me Richard was in critical condition and I should come straight away. When I finally got to see Richard, I wasn't sure he was breathing. Your father and his friend beat my husband to within an inch of his life and then dropped him off on the sidewalk outside the emergency room. I learned that once Richard came to, of course. Along with the true reason for their visits."

Sarah Beth pauses, looking down, and Megan is worried she's becoming overwhelmed. But when Sarah Beth looks up, her eyes are ice cold.

"Richard had apparently been gambling with our nest egg for years. He'd racked up $30,000 in debt and he hadn't been able to pay. On the day he was supposed to be released from the hospital, I went to go pick up his sorry behind, only to discover he'd left the hospital earlier that day. I never found out where he scampered off to."

Megan sits there, stunned. A million questions fly through her head as she tries to sort them in order of importance in case Sarah Beth's patience with her runs its course.

"What happened after that? I mean, did you see them again? Did they forgive the debt?"

Sarah Beth chuffs at the thought. "No, dear. Men like your daddy don't forgive a coward's debt." She sits up a little taller. "No, I handled it. When Mr. Palmer returned, I worked out a payment schedule with him, and I fulfilled the obligation. It's always a woman cleaning up a man's mess, isn't it?" Sarah Beth observes. "Anyhow, Mark warned me he was still looking for my husband. I assume to ensure he remains quiet. I told him Richard wasn't my concern anymore. Not that it ever stopped Richard from checking in."

"Your husband still came around after that?" Megan wonders if she could somehow get in touch with him. It would be a lot to ask of Sarah Beth, though. Too much.

"Yes, he comes around pretty regularly. Maybe once every other week or so. At first, he'd just linger until I threatened to call the cops, and then he'd slither off to whatever hole he was hiding in. But each time, he got more and more aggressive. He'd scream horrible names at me through the door as he tried to break it down. He smashed all the windows in my car and slashed the tires. Once, something woke me up in the middle of the night and I found him staring into the bedroom window."

Sarah Beth hangs her head. "My son has already had to cope with losing one parent. I shudder to think what it would do to him to lose two." She lets the thought float through the air, just for a moment, before she continues. "For a while, police sent patrol cars by for random checks as often as possible, but eventually, that stopped. Last I saw Richard was…" Sarah Beth gazes off into the distance, seemingly considering when she last chased him away. "Well, I guess it was just a little over two weeks ago, come to think of it." She shakes her head as if to erase the memory.

Megan moves on, unsure how much more time Sarah Beth will give her. "You mentioned my dad's *partner*. Several times. I'm curious. You knew my dad's name, but not his partner's?" Perhaps just an oversight.

"I never knew the other man's name. Your father introduced himself. Cocky considering his profession. But his partner never did, and I never asked." Sarah Beth sighs. "Now, I'm sorry about your father. This must be incredibly hard for you. But I really must get back to my day."

"Of course." Megan stands to leave before whipping back around. "Wait! One more question, please. Can you tell me what the other man looked like?"

Sarah Beth stands up and walks to the door as she answers. "He was quite tall, broad shouldered. He had dark, wavy hair. And when he smiled, he had a single gold tooth that stuck out like a sore thumb."

A gold tooth. Megan jots a mental note to tell Josh about it. Maybe it will help him as he looks into the people closest to Mark.

"Thank you, Sarah Beth. For you time and for your transparency. I'm sorry for what happened to your family." Megan looks down at the porch, shuffling her shoes.

"Well, that's not your fault, sweetheart. But I appreciate it just the same. We don't get to choose our parents, do we? You take care of yourself now." Sarah Beth gives her a tight-lipped smile before going back inside and closing the door.

Megan had wondered if her dad had been capable of extreme violence. Now she has her answer.

She pulls out her phone to text Josh, surprised when she doesn't find any missed messages from him. She tells him she is finished and asks him to meet her at her apartment when he is done with his shift.

CHAPTER 21

"You lied to me." Josh skips his normal greeting as he stands outside the door to Megan's apartment.

Megan opens the door wider for him, but Josh stays put. Megan knows she owes him an explanation. And an apology. But she isn't sure where to start. "Come inside, Josh." Megan jerks her head towards the living room.

Josh crosses his arms over his chest and adjusts his feet, planting them more firmly.

Megan sighs. "I'm sorry, Josh. I know I screwed up. But I needed to get some answers." Megan waits for him to move. Nothing. She starts to get frantic. "Come on, Josh. Please. I already lost Katie today. I can't lose you too."

Josh's face softens as his arms fall to his sides. He steps inside and wraps Megan in a tight hug. "You're going to have to try a lot harder if you want to get rid of me. But I'm still mad at you."

"I know." Megan whispers into his shoulder.

"And you didn't lose Katie. She'll come around." Josh strides over and plops down on the couch in his usual seat, which now has a Josh shaped indent molded into it.

Megan shakes her head. "You didn't see her, Josh. I've never seen her so angry, and it's all my fault. She could have gotten killed because I was selfish. I should have listened to her when she told me what she needed." Megan's head slumps down and she stares at the floor where she's drawing arbitrary shapes in the speckled brown carpet with her big toe.

"You could start by telling her that. Katie has her own baggage to deal with, but you two are like sisters." Josh shrugs like Megan's fight with Katie wasn't anything to be so worked up over. "Sisters fight, Megs. And then sisters get over it."

That eats Megan up the most.

Megan knows how traumatized Katie had been when Katie's father walked away from her and her mother. Katie was a little girl. Katie's dad wasn't a great dad. In fact, he wasn't much of anything at all. He offered nothing emotionally. He wasn't the breadwinner in the home. He didn't play with Katie or encourage putting Katie in group activities. Despite everything, he was Katie's dad. All Katie ever wanted was for him to love her enough to stay. Enough to try. She and Megan have that in common. When he left, Katie was never enough for anyone, ever again. Not even herself.

Megan knew better than to threaten to abandon Katie. Even unintentionally. It must have crushed Katie to think Megan didn't care if this whole thing got her killed.

Megan isn't sure what it will take for Katie to forgive her. Or if anything can. But she is sure an apology won't ever be enough.

Megan tells Josh everything that happened at the two homes she visited earlier. Her voice is quiet, as if the louder she speaks the words, the truer they'll become.

"Shit. Megs, I'm sorry. I know we were suspecting something like this, but I didn't want it to be true."

"Me either." Megan's shirt is damp as she repeatedly pulls the collar of her t-shirt up to soak up the tears before they fall. Each time she wipes them away, she hopes it's the last. But the well seems to be endless. "Ugh, sorry. I feel like I've been walking a tightrope this past week. It just feels like too much. I keep thinking I don't know who this man is and I should just let this go. This isn't worth it. Why should I even care? My dad obviously didn't. But I can't let it go… I feel so stupid. I'm sorry." She takes one more pass at drying her eyes.

"Don't apologize. Not for this. You're allowed to cry, Megs. Honestly, I can't believe you've held it together this long." Josh walks to the kitchen to grab a few paper napkins, which he hands to Megan.

"Thanks," she says as she blows her nose into one, then uses another to dab the corners of her eyes. "Anyway." Megan waves her hand in the air, shooing her silly emotions away. She slides her dad's wedding photo across the coffee table, closer to Josh. "This guy." Dan stands immediately to the right of Mark, but Megan taps her finger on the man on Dan's right. "Sarah Beth told me she never knew the name of the guy who would show up with my dad. We can't see his teeth since his mouth is closed, but this guy fits the other basic description she gave. Did you find out anything about these other people?"

Josh nods. "Yeah, I did actually." He sucks in a breath before he begins. "Dan's record is spotless. I couldn't find a thing on him. Not even an old parking ticket. He is a model citizen as far as his record is concerned. Annie is pretty clean, too. She has a couple of juvenile offenses for truancy and assault. She got into a pretty vicious fight with another girl at school in the seventh grade. They both did community service. Otherwise, she's been a witness for a couple of cases brought against the doctor she works for. They settled both cases in court. Beyond that, she's clean."

"Maybe they're both just fantastic at flying under the radar?"

"But for what? There's nothing to even hint at any duplicity." Josh asks, appearing confused and when he clocks Megan's look of outrage, he adds quickly, holding his hands up, displaying his innocence, "Just playing devil's advocate here. Trying to work through the information to form a theory."

Megan concedes she may have reacted too hastily. "I'm not sure exactly, but maybe they're involved in this gambling operation my dad seems to be mixed up in." Megan catches her mistake. "Or *was* involved in, I guess."

"Could be. But we don't know the extent of what your dad was doing. It's possible they were in the dark too, like Sarah Beth."

"Maybe so. But if it was *this* guy working with him," Megan points to the tall dark-haired man again, "what are the odds he's the only other one of the group involved?"

"Pretty small odds. I'll admit. Let's keep going. Before we get too sidetracked." Josh guides their attention back to the photo. "The women." Josh works his way through the women quickly, starting with the one closest to Annie and working his way out to the one furthest from her. "This is Sherri Armstead. She's an elementary school teacher and has worked at the same school for sixteen years. Her colleagues had nothing but good things to say about her. She never married or had kids of her own. Her students adore her."

Josh drags his index finger to the next women in line. "Next, we have Michelle Langford. She's a character, to put it kindly. She's been picked up several times over the years working various corners of Oak Park. Michelle changes her look constantly, probably hoping the cops won't recognize her next time. Her mugshots look like they could be a portfolio of movie roles. She's currently working as a masseuse at a shady massage parlor called

Happy Endings. God, you'd think people would at least try to hide that they offer a… full service menu…" Josh clears his throat.

A laugh escapes Megan's lips. As she whips her hand up to stifle it before it gets out of control, she notices Josh glance at her out of the corner of his eyes with a smirk.

"This last lady is another stand up citizen." Heavy sarcasm flows through Josh's voice, thick like molasses. "This is Donna Jenkins, aka Samantha Tomlin, aka Yvette Black, aka a bunch of other names. Ms. Whoever has a long rap sheet filled with fraud charges ranging from forged signatures to stolen identities. She never completed any formal education, despite having nearly perfect grades, until she dropped out in her sophomore year of high school. She's currently employed as a waitress at truck stop dinner down Highway 99, no doubt living a life free of crime." Josh rolls his eyes.

Megan sits back on the couch and pulls her knees up to her chest. "Wow. Quite the cast of women Annie keeps company with." Megan taps her finger to her lips a few times, piecing together her thoughts. "Ok, so let's see… if I had to venture some guesses, I'd say Sherri wouldn't dare be involved, Michelle wouldn't have the drive or the street smarts to get mixed in something so crazy, and Donna would be bored by it. She also lives a little too far away, which could either suggest she wouldn't be involved or that she stays away intentionally as a cover. Let's focus on the men, since we know my dad was working directly with at least one other male. How did I do, officer?" Megan shoots Josh a sly grin.

Josh nods in appreciation and gives a small slow clap. "Agreed. Plus, instinct tells me these women, however colorful they may be, aren't involved. I couldn't find another other connection to the group outside of the wedding photo. They don't seem to be in contact anymore for whatever reason."

"Ok then. Tell me about the other two men." Megan keeps the conversation moving while walking to the kitchen to grab two glasses of water for them.

"We know Dan. Next to him is a guy named Jeffrey Payne. He's an ex-marine Sergeant who was dishonorably discharged ten years ago when he was convicted of sexual assault against a female Private First Class. Payne maintained he was in a consensual relationship with Private Masula and the Corporal who reported them has caused disruptions among their platoon numerous times. But the Marines have codes and, consensual or not, relationships within a single chain of command are not allowed. Masula is suspected to have made a deal that she would be transferred to another platoon in exchange for her testimony that Payne's advances were unwanted. Payne has bounced from one construction job to another ever since, often working under the table."

"Sounds like a guy who could fit the bill. What do you think?" Megan asks.

"It's definitely possible. Men with stories like his rarely become productive members of society. If the sexual assault charges are true, and I believe they are, he's a dangerous man who operates outside the law. And if they aren't true, then he likely carries a chip on his shoulder and an angry ex-marine is never a good thing. Either way, if he's the man working with your dad, he's a lethal individual."

Megan chews on this.

"That leaves us with the last guy," Josh points to the last man standing on the end. His hands clasped behind his back, his chest puffed out in pride. His grin stretches ear to ear, exposing every tooth he owned. "This is Langford Downs. Langford Downs filed for bankruptcy eight years ago after his wife left him citing drug and alcohol abuse and impotence on the divorce papers. Brutal. He's been in and out of jail since then on various drunk and disorderly charges. He was last reported to be in a Utah drunk tank after he was found laying in the street wearing nothing but a t-shirt as a skirt. His head was wet on one side from laying a puddle of alcohol that spilled out of a bottle of whiskey he was still somehow holding, wrapped in a brown paper bag. I think we can safely cross him off our list of players. What do you think?"

Megan nods sadly. "I'd say we could." She can't believe how badly a person's life could spiral out of control. Where is rock bottom? How has Langford Downs not found it yet? Megan shakes the questions out of her head and refocuses.

These men are dangerous. She doesn't know how to figure out who is responsible for her dad's death without someone getting hurt. How much is she willing to risk to know the truth?

She is about to ask Josh what he thinks they should do next when her phone rings. Her heart swells, hoping it's Katie, and then quickly deflates when she reads Annie's name on the screen.

"What do you think she wants?" Josh asks, leaning over to see who was calling. From anyone else, save for Katie, such an invasion of personal space and privacy would have sent Megan reeling. From Josh, Megan never gives it a second thought.

"I called her on the way here to tell her I changed my mind and wanted my dad's photo albums. I was hoping I could go back and slip into the outdoor closet and grab the photo albums she's hiding. Maybe I can leverage them to get the truth out of her." Megan explains while her finger hovers over the green answer button.

"Hi Annie." Megan talks to Annie while she looks directly at Josh, borrowing his composure to anchor herself to the room. She doesn't break eye contact with him as she watches him listen to one side of the conversation happening in front of him.

"Yeah, I just wanted to see if I could swing by today and grab those photo albums from dad's room. I changed my mind... No, don't worry about it. I can let myself in since your headed out the door... Oh they're in the outside closet? I can come find them if you just leave the side gate unlocked... It's no trouble. Don't worry about it, you're headed out. I don't mind sorting through the boxes... Oh ok. Perfect. I'll be by in about thirty minutes... Ok, thanks."

Megan hangs up the phone.

"Well?" Josh sounds impatient.

"She said they were in the outside closet and she'd try to find them before she left. I insisted I could get them out of the closet and she got all dodgy and skittish. She told me she had time, so she'd leave them in the bedroom, and I could go inside and get them." Megan wonders if Annie knows she had been in the closet the last time she was there or if Annie doesn't know and is scared of the mere idea Megan might find what she's hiding.

"Do you want me to come with you?"

"You don't have to…" Megan pushes back, but she trails off when Josh doesn't argue. He sits there staring at her, his silence telling her he'll wait for her honest answer. "Ok, yes, please. If it's not any trouble." Megan adds an eye roll to put on record that she thinks he's being silly.

"I'll drive." Josh grabs his keys from the coffee table and holds the front door open for Megan.

They take longer than thirty minutes due to an accident on the road. As they turn onto Annie's street an hour later, Megan is fiddling with the radio stations when Josh slams on the brakes without warning, sending both of them flying forward until their seatbelts lock. Heart racing, Megan looks up. "What the hell, Josh."

But she sees what the hell right in front of them. She tries to say something, but her throat hitches. She finally tears her eyes away from the scene just long enough to check if Josh is seeing it, too. His face is all the confirmation she needs. This is actually happening.

CHAPTER 22

Emergency workers block the short street off from through traffic. Thick black columns of smoke roar up to the sky, while menacing orange and yellow flames consume Annie's duplex. Fire licks the trees and spits at the road. Firetrucks surround the area while the firefighters work to stop the spread and extinguish the blaze.

Onlookers and neighbors line the far side of the street, staying clear of the emergency workers but unwilling to walk away from the spectacle. Josh parks at the end of the road and they get out, weaving through the crowd to get a better look.

As they approach the scene, Megan watches flames pour out from the top of the outdoor closet, unable to look away. Her emotions swing like a pendulum from rage to devastation, wholly disappointed at the opportunity devoured by the flames in front of her.

Megan looks around her, taking in the damage. As she scans the onlookers, the vehicles, and the duplex on the far side of the firefighters, she notices an old woman sitting alone in the crook of a walker, wringing her hands together, and mumbling to herself. A flash of recognition, a memory from when she was young, pierces her mind. Megan knows her.

It's the neighbor who lives in the other half of Annie's duplex.

Megan motions for Josh to follow her as they skirt around the crowd and meander over to the woman.

They approach her slowly so as not to startle her and Megan reaches out to place a hand on her arm. "Mrs. Corsek?"

The woman turns her head slowly. Her eyes are cloudy. She looks not at Megan, but through her. "Hello dear. Where have you been hiding? You were supposed to come by for dinner last night."

"I've been around." Megan speaks gently. Even when Megan was growing up, the older lady was forgetful and fanciful. Often seeming to be in some other world. On her good days, she was lucid and lovely. On her hard days, she was lost. She's lived alone for as long as Megan has known her. Her daughter would come by often to sit with her, but they couldn't afford the live-in help Mrs. Corsek desperately needed.

"Mrs. Corsek, do you know what happened?" It's a long shot, but maybe today was a good day for the woman.

The old lady's eyes are suddenly shining with clarity. "Oh yes, dear. I've been trying to tell these gentlemen, but no one can be bothered to listen to the rantings of an old woman." Her eyes are clear, but her words are quick. Too quick.

"What happened, Mrs. Corsek? What were you trying to tell them?" Megan pushes gently, guiding the woman back on track.

"She warned me this was happening. In any other case, I would never have gotten out in time."

Megan and Josh exchange glances.

"Who warned you, Mrs. Corsek?"

"Annie, dear." Mrs. Corsek's words have slowed. They are careful, unambiguous.

"Annie warned you to get out? Are you sure? Annie isn't here. I'm not sure she even knows what's happened."

"I'm sure. I was sitting at the table having tea when I heard someone banging on my door. It was awfully loud. It gave me quite a fright. I got to the door as quickly as I could, which is not very quick, dear." Mrs. Corsek gives a wry chuckle. "I hollered I'd be just a minute while I fiddled with the darn lock. When I finally got the door open, I saw her at the end of the driveway. She got into her car and sped off, fast as lightning. I smelled smoke. Oh, so much smoke. Then I went outside to see if perhaps a neighbor was barbecuing. That's when I saw the horrible flames on her side of the building. I was too afraid to go back into the house," Mrs. Corsek points a gnarled finger to the duplex next to hers, "so I scooted over to my neighbor to call 911. Oh dear, I hope she's ok."

She returns to her mutterings, which Megan now hears are a sort of prayer. Megan rests a hand on the woman's back and waits.

"We can't leave her here alone." Megan looks over Mrs. Corsek's head to Josh standing on her other side.

"Of course not." Josh looks somewhere over Megan's shoulder. "Hey, I see Nelson over there. I'm going to go see if he can tell me what happened." Josh leaves to chat with the firemen.

When Josh returns, he tells them it looks like they nearly have the fire contained and then someone will go in and hopefully determine the cause.

Nearly an hour later, the fire is out and Annie's car rumbles down the street. When she gets out, she looks frantic, grabbing one firefighter to ask what happened.

"My god, what happened? This is my house. I live here!" Annie is hysterical.

Megan spots her and excuses herself to Mrs. Corsek. She strides over to Annie. Annie grabs her and pulls her into her arms, making Megan supremely uncomfortable. "Megan! Thank God, I'm so glad you're alright." Josh approaches right behind Megan, much to Annie's apparent surprise. "Josh. My goodness, I haven't seen you in…"

"It's been a long time, Ms. Stevens." Josh interrupts, in the politest manner.

"Please, you know you can call me Annie. We're family, Josh."

Josh cringes visibly and coughs into his shoulder to cover up the fact. Just as Annie opens her mouth to speak again, Nelson approaches the three of them.

"Ms. Stevens?" He inquires.

"Yes, I'm Ms. Stevens. Can you tell me how this happened?" Annie spits the words out between broken sobs.

"It looks like a fuse blew in the storage closet outside. The short must have sparked, lighting the surrounding boxes on fire. It spread up the back wall, connected to the second bedroom. Then back to where some flammable items in the hallway closet caught, accelerating the fire." Megan's mind flashes to the closet filled with medical supplies and medications.

"I'm sorry, Ms. Stevens. It looks as though the entire left side of the house has been destroyed. Do you have someone you can stay with?"

"Yes," Annie whispers.

Nelson nods, tipping his hat in her direction before returning to clean up.

Annie bursts out in frenzied angst. Megan looks at Josh as if to ask what to do. When Megan turns back to Annie, Annie grabs her again and pulls her back into her arms, her mouth close to Megan's ear. "Oh, Megs. I'm so sorry. I know how much you wanted those photo albums of your dad's."

"Don't worry about that right now." Megan looks over at Josh to see if he picked up on the apology. The frown on his face said he had. "Do you really have someone you can stay with?"

"I can stay with Dan. I'll call him just as soon as I call the insurance company. Thank God for homeowner's insurance, huh?" Annie sniffles. Her eyes are bloodshot.

"Right. Thank God." Megan steals a glance at Josh. "Annie, can you give me Mrs. Corsek's daughter's phone number? I want to be sure she can come take care of her."

"Of course, sweetheart. Give me just a minute." Annie turns to go and sputters to a stop. She whips back around, her face wiped clean of any emotion. "I'm just glad you weren't hurt. Thank God you weren't in the house when the fire took off."

The hairs on the back of Megan's neck stand straight up. Josh must have sensed it too, because he steps towards her protectively, putting his arm around her shoulder. Annie turns around and walks away, presumably to get her phone.

"Well, that was officially insane."

Josh nods, his eyes wide with disbelief. "No kidding. Annie was weird, right? She seemed both upset and yet… not exactly shocked?" Josh sounds like he was struggling to pluck out the right words.

"Yeah, that was definitely strange." Megan caught it, too. Something isn't quite right. For all the emotional show Annie had just put on, it hadn't escaped Megan's notice that not a single actual tear fell from Annie's very red eyes.

CHAPTER 23

TUESDAY, SEPTEMBER 15TH

By Tuesday morning, the adrenaline coursing through Megan's veins had finally subsided and the events of the weekend feel like a distant dream, the edges fraying, colors dulling.

Katie has returned none of Megan's calls or text messages, though she has apparently spoken to Josh. When he and Megan talked yesterday, he betrayed no details about how Katie was doing or what she's thinking. Megan tries not to be mad at him for telling her this was between her and Katie. She tells herself the fact that Josh isn't meddling and itching to repair them is a good sign. It tells Megan he's confident she'll figure out how to fix this on her own. She'd worry when Josh feels the need to mediate.

If Katie ever lets her back in, Megan will have more than earned it.

Megan has an early morning appointment with Dr. Glover today. She nearly cancels, her finger on the call button, ready to bow out, when Katie flashes into her mind again. She made a promise to Katie. If she breaks it when Katie isn't speaking to her, she isn't sure how Katie will let her come back at all.

When she arrives, Hannah looks especially professional in sleek new maroon glasses frames, her hair pulled up into a severe bun. Hannah's pencil skirt won't allow for her to cross her legs at the knee, so she sits with her knees together, leaning to one side with her legs crossed at the ankles instead.

"It's been five days since our last visit. How have you been handling things since we last met?" Hannah wastes no time in getting to the crux of their visits.

"I'm not sure. How do I know if I'm handling things well or not?" Megan returns her question with a question, punting her response down the road.

"That's a matter of relativity, isn't it? Are you feeling more at peace since we last talked? Or further from it?" Hannah watches Megan with her pen propped up in her hand, ready to write, the tip of the pen resting gently on the notepad in her lap. An image of a thoroughbred being held back by the starting gate flashes in Megan's mind.

"Further, I suppose is the honest answer."

"The honest answer is always the best response. We can only work with truth, regardless of what the truth is."

Megan is a bit thrown off because Hannah seems unusually chatty this morning, though Megan realizes that's a relative observation as well. Hannah is chatty compared to Megan's prior two experiences with her. Perhaps because it is her first appointment of the day and she's freshly caffeinated.

Hannah continues, "What do you think is causing you to move backwards instead of forward?"

Megan weighs the factors, contributing to her confusion, attempting to sort them out. She decides there are too many to list. It would take up the bulk of their hour together. So, she offers a summary statement to see how it lands.

"I think it's because in the last five days, I've learned several things about my father I hadn't previously known and it's causing me to question my relationship with him more than ever."

Hannah doesn't offer any further prompting, and after what feels like an eternity, Megan feels an overwhelming urge to fill the silence. Perhaps that was Hannah's goal all along, to coerce Megan into talking more. *Damn, Hannah is good.*

Megan's leg bounces nervously. She isn't willing to confide in Hannah about her findings, though she understands what she says in this room is privileged information. She doesn't trust Hannah with it. Not yet.

"The new information is almost certainly true, and it's at odds with the father I thought I knew. When I was a little girl, I thought my dad was the best dad a girl could ask for. I thought he loved me. When I got older, I thought he wasn't such a good person and he didn't care about me at all. Now I think he might be an altogether different person, capable of horrible things I never thought possible. So how do I sort through all of this? How do I make sense of it?"

"How do you think you accomplish that?"

Megan rolls her eyes, and upon realizing she'd rolled her eyes, she stares out the picture window, embarrassed to make eye contact with Hannah.

Megan huffs. "I'm not sure. Maybe it doesn't matter which is true. Maybe it only matters which one I decided is true."

"An awfully philosophical view for such a pragmatic woman."

"People don't like pragmatism. They prefer more idealistic views. Simplicity is the very definition of pragmatism and yet, it seems like people think it's too complicated to deal with being practical."

Hannah seems to evaluate Megan for a moment. "Would you like to talk about what you learned this weekend?" Hannah inquires.

Megan assumes Hannah means to get to the root cause of this discussion. Megan takes a drink of water, wetting her dry mouth. "Not particularly." She purses her lips together.

"You mentioned you learned your father was capable of terrible things. Do you believe now he was an inherently bad person?" Hannah tries a different route, but Megan knows it's to the same end.

"No. I don't think anyone is inherently bad. I think people learn to make horrible decisions, and sometimes even good people just get it wrong. It doesn't make it right, but it makes sense."

"What do you think taught your dad to do these horrible things?"

Megan relents. "That's what I'm not sure of. My grandpa committed suicide when my dad was just sixteen. But that alone doesn't seem like enough. Plenty of people experience that loss, but don't become vicious. And anyhow, I think it would support the idea that my dad committed suicide rather than…" Megan drifts off, catching her near slip.

"Rather than what?" Hannah clocks it.

"Nothing, I was just thinking. Anyway, I know he wasn't all bad." Megan thoughtfully pieces together what she will offer next. If she does it well enough, maybe Hannah will lose the scent of what Megan had meant to keep hidden. "For a long time, he was like a best friend. Not so much a dad, in hindsight. I knew I could count on him for help when I was in a jam and he never made me feel like he was judging me the way my mom did."

"It's interesting you use the term vicious to describe your father now. What had he done that you perceive as vicious?"

Megan thinks about the direction she'd like to take this. She could offer some examples, but that path would inevitably end with her confessing everything she'd learned this weekend, and she's already decided not to divulge that. She decides a different route, gazing up at her favorite sunrise ocean photo on Hannah's wall. "I may have been overly dramatic. Careless might be a better word. He was careless, with his kids, my mom, his jobs. He never gave much thought to what he should do or to what his daughter should be doing. It took years for me to see I couldn't count on him at all. He just did what he wanted to do. Selfish really…"

Megan drifts off. Hannah seems to notice her mind is elsewhere suddenly. "Is there a moment in particular you're thinking of right now?"

Megan doesn't answer her question. She just looks at Hannah and tips her head. Hannah gestures to the couch, an invitation to lie down and relax.

Megan obeys, hoping Hannah has been successfully redirected.

When I was fourteen, Brad, a boy I had a crush on, invited me to his house. We were on a summer break from school. He told me his older brother was having a party while his parents were out of town and he could invite some friends too if he wanted. His brother had just turned nineteen and had a fake ID. It felt important to go. Like I was finally being seen as one of the cool kids and not the poor, broken girl at school.

I told my dad about it, and of course, he said I could go. He didn't even need to think about it. He didn't ask where it was or who I would be with. He was the cool dad.

It wasn't the party I thought it would be. In fact, there were only four people there. Brad, me, Brad's older brother, Ryan, and Ryan's girlfriend, Felicity.

It wasn't long before alcohol appeared, and I took my first proper drink. I downed the first shot, as instructed. Bacardi O hit the back of my mouth with a slow burn, warming me from the inside out. It tasted sweet. I remember I liked it. Brad told me he asked his brother to get some when Felicity said girls usually liked sweet drinks.

Ryan suggested we play beer pong except he would put hard cider in my cups because I didn't like the taste of the beer I'd tried. I said yes. No one likes a goodie goodie.

Between rounds, Brad kept the Bacardi flowing.

It didn't take long before I was so dizzy I couldn't stand up on my own. I told them I needed to lie down.

Brad took me up to his room and told me I could use his bed. I laid down, and the bed spun in circles like a merry-go-round. I couldn't get off.

It was hard to keep my eyes open, but I felt hands on me. I tried so hard to understand what I was feeling as I rolled onto my side and opened my eyes. Brad had climbed onto the bed next to me and was grabbing at my shirt, pulling it up to touch my bra.

"What are you doing?" The question slurred out of my mouth like syrup.

"I know you like me. Just relax. You'll like this." He whispered in my ear. He clamped his lips down on mine and his hand moved down to my waistband as he tried to unbutton my jeans.

"Stop. I don't want to do this." I scrambled to get the words out before he could go any farther.

"Sure, you do. I know you've done this with a bunch of the guys at school already. But don't worry, I won't tell anyone." I had done nothing like this with anyone, but I knew girls talked about me because I got along better with some boys in our grade than I did with them. But Brad was telling me some boys said they had gotten some kind of sex from me. That's when I learned gossip and judgement wasn't exclusive to girls.

"No, I haven't. Stop it!" I pushed him, but the room was still moving, and it was hard to get my bearings.

He slid his hand down the front of my pants, under my panties faster than I could even process, as he pushed his mouth harder against mine. "STOP!" I hit him as hard as I could. He rolled backwards, yelling horrible names at me as I climbed out of his bed and raced to the bathroom and vomited. I threw up until the world stopped spinning, willing all the poison to leave my system.

I didn't understand yet what had really happened in his bedroom. Rape wasn't a thought in my mind. Rape was way more serious than I allowed myself to believe my experience had been. He never did more than touch me a little. This was nothing.

I don't know how long I was in the bathroom, but I knew I didn't want to come out. A knock at the door made me jump. Afraid it was Brad coming back for more, I sat in silence watching the footsteps under the door, willing them to go away so I could sneak out.

It was Felicity. "Is everything ok? You've been in there a while."

"I want to go home. Will you bring my purse?"

Felicity went downstairs and grabbed my bag for me. I opened the door just enough for her to slip my bag inside, and I locked the door behind me. I grabbed my cell phone and called my dad, knowing that would be my best option because I knew he would come for me if I was in trouble and the chances of being punished would be small.

My dad told me he had to finish up what he was doing and then he'd be on his way. I begged him to hurry and asked him to call me when he arrived so I could come out. I checked the time on my phone. It was nearly midnight. I didn't have a clue what he was doing, but we lived only twenty minutes away. Twenty minutes longer than I could bear being in this house.

I stayed in the bathroom alone until he called nearly an hour and a half later. I climbed down the stairs quietly, hoping I could creep out the door without drawing any attention to myself.

Felicity caught me and asked if everything was alright. I paused just for a moment, but I couldn't bring myself to look at her, afraid she'd know what happened. Hot shame filled me to the brim. I wondered if Ryan was the same way with her as Brad had just been with me.

I didn't bother to answer her. I grabbed the door handle and threw it open before the boys saw me and I ran to my dad's car and climbed into the back seat.

He asked if I was ok. "I'm fine. Can we just go, please?"

As he pulled away, I rested my head against the cool window, trying to shrink myself and disappear, tears of shame rolling silently down my cheeks, burning on the way down. I was stupid for thinking I could handle myself with boys like these. Ashamed so many boys believed I was one of the easy girls while I just thought we were friends.

My dad never asked me questions, and he never brought up that night ever again.

"I want to take a moment to remind you this is a safe space, and you have nothing to be ashamed of. You aren't responsible for the actions of others, and I am sorry that happened to you." Hannah says when Megan opens her eyes and turns her attention to the photo hanging above her. She rarely gets to look at this photo because it's displayed on the wall behind her when she sits on the couch. Only when she's reclined and sharing these delicate memories does she get to observe it. She's always appreciated the symbolism of the sunrise photos chosen for this room. It occurs to her only now that this photo is actually of a sunset. It's prettier than she remembers and in this moment, its dark hues draw her in.

Megan nods, and so Hannah continues. "It's interesting you climbed into the back seat. Why do you think that was?" Hannah asks. Only it wasn't interesting to Megan, because the answer was simple. She had climbed into the back seat because someone else was sitting in the front passenger seat.

"Do you know who was sitting next to your dad?"

Megan describes the man who was very tall. Though his head didn't quite reach the roof, his dark waves did. His shoulders reached all the way across the seat back.

"Did you know this man? Was this a friend of your dad's?"

Megan doesn't understand how this is relevant to her therapy and when Hannah asks a second time, a wave of nausea rolls through Megan and her stomach clenches. She makes a split-second decision. She lies. "No, I didn't." Hannah is quiet again, but Megan doesn't offer more. Not this time.

Hannah checks her watch. "Well, that's our time for today. I'll see you on Thursday." She folds her hands in her lap, waiting. A few moments pass and she stands as Megan gets up.

Megan exits the room, still seeing the back of the man's head in her mind's eye as she walks to her car. The circumstances of that night had long been forgotten, shoved away in an unlit corner of her mind. As the memory bubbled up to the surface, so had the details begun to focus. The man had never spoken to her, but he had glanced over his right shoulder to acknowledge her. As he did, a streetlight caught his smile through the window, sending a single beam reflecting off one of his teeth right into Megan's eye.

CHAPTER 24

Megan feels the throbbing of her pulse stretching the skin on her wrist. She waits in her car, thinking about the memory that arose in Hannah's office and the strange questions Hannah followed up with. Megan has her own questions about that night, which meant nothing at the time. They might mean everything now.

Why had it taken her dad so long to pick her up? Where was he when she called him? Had he been making one of his house calls and she had interrupted? Who is the other man with him? She's certain it was the same man Sarah Beth had told her about, but Megan had only gotten a quick glance at his face that night and it remains blurry in her head. Whether that's because of the alcohol in her system then or the time passed, she can't be sure. She relives the scene repeatedly, willing her mind to sharpen his features somehow.

She adds a task to her mental to-do list: Check the list of dates against the approximate time of this fresh memory.

She puts her key back in the ignition and then calls Grandma Barb. When she doesn't answer, Megan figures she's outside working and leaves her a message asking if she is free for dinner tomorrow night. Maybe Josh will join her. Grandma Barb would love that.

She sends a quick text to Katie asking her to please call. She just wants to talk. Megan decides she will keep bugging her. It's been three days, the longest they'd ever gone without speaking, which terrifies Megan more than she expected. But Katie has to crack eventually, even if only to tell Megan to leave her alone. And when she does, Megan will be ready to beg for her forgiveness.

After texting Josh that she is bringing him lunch and to ask what he wants, Megan starts her car and drives towards her apartment. Basic necessities are calling her, demanding her attention after being brushed aside for too long. Things like grocery shopping, laundry, another cup of coffee.

A few hours later, Megan arrives at the police station, two Styrofoam food containers containing jalapeno ranch burgers and garlic fries in her arms. For extra brownie points, she also brought in a couple dozen donuts for the rest of the station.

Josh finally comes out from the back of the station where Megan is chatting up some of his fellow officers over donuts. She turns just in time to catch him beaming in her direction. Perhaps at having such a thoughtful friend who gets along with his fellow officers. He smiles at her, each of his pearly white teeth on display. She drinks it in.

"Hey, Megs! Thanks for all this." Josh grabs the takeout boxes from the counter as she says her goodbyes to the team, and he leads her down the hall to one of the empty interrogation rooms, where they can talk in peace.

Megan jumps right in, opening her container and picking up the burger, appreciating the mess it makes in her hands. If a burger isn't messy, it isn't any good. Megan anxiously awaits the day when a team of scientists present her with a load of grant money to study this theory and prove it's actually a scientific fact. "Hey before I forget, I asked Grandma Barb if I could come have dinner with her tomorrow. Want to join?" Megan pops the tip of her finger in her mouth to clean the sauce from it. Her compulsion to estimate her calorie consumption is always forgotten when she's with Josh. "I want to check on her and see how she's doing, and I figured since we'll be together at the medical examiner's…" Megan lets the invite dangle there, not needing to be finished.

"Sure! Sounds great. I'd love to see her. I haven't been to a regular dinner with her since before your dad's wake. Or celebration of life, I guess."

Megan takes a large bite out of her burger and sighs. She closes her eyes and chews slowly, taking in the spiciness of the jalapeños, the tangy ranch dressing, and the warmth of the garlic. She wants to savor the delicious complexity of the flavors for as long as possible. When she's finished, she looks up, self-conscious when she remembers she isn't alone, and finds Josh staring at her with a silly half grin plastered on his face.

"What? Stop judging me. It's a good burger." Megan defends herself against the invisible attack his gaze launched at her.

Josh breaks eye contact and looks down, fiddling with his fries, like a kid caught swiping a cookie from his mom's baking sheet. "No, it's very adorable the way you eat a burger." He shoves three fries into his mouth at once.

Megan blushes, suddenly feeling like his commentary on her eating style was more than just a friendly compliment. She scrambles to reset the vibe in the room. "I mean it. A burger this good should be a crime." Megan slaps her palm down on the table with a loud smack. "Lock up the person who created it! See what I did there…?"

"Do I see you just made the world's lamest joke because we are sitting in a police station? Yes. I caught that." Josh rolls his eyes and suppresses a grin.

A laugh bubbles up from Megan's chest and she locks her lips just in time to keep the half-masticated fries in her mouth from spraying out and hitting Josh in the face, which, funnily enough, only causes her to laugh harder. "Damn it, Josh! I could have choked to death." Megan pretends to be appalled.

"It's not my fault you have no idea how to eat a french fry. Besides, I would have saved you." Josh throws the words out casually, but his eyes narrow, and Megan can see his jaw clenching.

Megan takes another bite, feeling lightheaded.

They finish lunch, while Josh tells her all about the different cases he's working on and the different calls he's gone out to over the last few days. Megan watches his face glow while he talks, taking in the way his cheeks lift, creating tiny crinkles at the corners of his eyes.

She wonders what it's like to love a job that much. It looks so good on Josh. Megan has graduated from college, gotten a steady job as a receptionist at a dental office and worked her way up to office manager. After years of searching, she still does not know what kind of career might make her feel the way Josh feels about police work.

When he finishes, Megan leans back in her seat as far as she can, stretching her whole body out. She rights herself quickly when she notices the bottom of her t-shirt sliding up just enough to expose a thin sliver of her stomach. She can feel Josh's eyes on her.

"I should let you get back to work. Big day tomorrow, though, right?" Megan puts their trash inside one of the takeout boxes and pours a little water from her water bottle onto a clean napkin to wipe down the table.

"Yup! I'll pick you up at your place around 9:00am and we'll head over. See if we can catch this guy off guard." Josh winks at her and coughs a bit to clear his throat. Josh is a serial winker. It's part of his charm. But this time it throws Megan off-balance, and she bangs her hip on the back of the chair when she moves away from the table too quickly, sending the chair crashing to the ground.

Megan springs upright, brushing off her thighs like nothing happened. "Ouch! Shit... sorry."

Josh is eyeing her like she's acting weird and she knows it's because she's acting weird. "Are you ok?"

"Totally fine. Hey, are you sure surprising him is the best idea?"

"Catching a person when they aren't expecting you doesn't give them the time or the space to fabricate a lie and then destroy any evidence that could expose them. Spilling coffee on original documents wouldn't render them illegible. They may be harder to read because they turned a particular shade of brown, but he should have produced them instead of creating a new report and then giving us a photocopy. Nothing about it makes any sense. He's hiding something. I can feel it."

Megan's hands begin to tremble and she busies them by picking up the empty takeout boxes. Maybe the crazy guy who pointed a gun at her affected her more than she's admitted to herself.

When Josh sees the boxes rattling in her hands, he takes them from her and sets them on the table. Clutching her hands in his, he steadies them and sits back, leaning his weight on the table to meet her eye line. "You don't have to come."

Megan nods and blows out a long breath she didn't realize she'd been holding. "I do actually. I need to hear it from the source."

"Ok. Remember, I'll be there, right next to you. And this guy isn't some drug runner or mob boss. He's a medical examiner. It's going to be alright. But whatever he's hiding could be big." He explains her nerves away so casually, putting Megan at ease.

Josh escorts her back up to the front and she can't help but smile as the other officers say their goodbyes, thanking her again for making their day.

She looks back one more time. Josh is watching her, never looking away, giving her one of her favorite smiles for the road. "See you tomorrow, Megs!" Josh says loudly so she can hear over the other officers' chatter. It catches a few of his buddies' attention who start whistling and teasing him.

"Oh, yeah… see you tomorrow, Megs!" they chirp.

Megan laughs, rolling her eyes. *Men are ridiculous.* She turns to leave, waving one arm high in the air without turning back around. "Bye, boys!" She rolls her eyes, smiling to herself, and walks out the door.

CHAPTER 25

WEDNESDAY, SEPTEMBER 16TH

Megan watches the clock vigilantly, waiting for Josh to pick her up for their visit to the medical examiner's office. She's operating with more energy than she knows what to do with after triply caffeinating herself when she couldn't sleep any longer. She woke up hours earlier than she'd meant to and began deep cleaning her apartment while listening to her favorite pick-me-up playlist to burn off as much of the excess jitters as she could.

When Josh arrives, she dances into the passenger seat of his car.

Josh leans away slowly, as if he's afraid to make a sudden movement around Megan. "Um, is everything ok?"

"Absolutely," Megan sings. "All good! Aren't I allowed to be in a good mood? Also, I couldn't sleep so I might have overdone it on the coffee this morning—even for me—but I just feel like this is going to be a good day.

This visit is going to shed a ton of light on our investigation. I just know it." Megan has apparently decided slowing down to breathe is overrated. "Oh, can we make a couple of quick pit stops on the way?"

Josh stares at her, his face blank, before turning to restart his car. His eyes are blinking rapidly as if he was clearing away the chaos Megan just brought into his car. "Sure, no problem. Where to first?"

"Coffee!" Megan blurts with a huge grin on her face.

"You can't be serious. In what world do you need more caffeine right now?"

Megan rolls her eyes. "It's not for me, silly. It's for Katie. We're going to go drop it off at her office."

"Megs, I don't know if this is your greatest idea ever. Are you sure you want to do this?" Josh's words sound timid. Cautious not to turn Megan's excitement into disappointment.

"Yes! Don't you see? It's brilliant. Since she won't talk to me, she's left me with no other choice. She works at the front desk; she can't leave it unmanned. So, when I come in with coffee, she'll have to look me in the eye. Maybe then she'll want to talk." The hope in Megan's voice feels fabricated, like Megan is convincing herself as much as Josh.

Josh flips on his turn signal as he pulls up to the stoplight in front of them. "Yeah, I think it's best to just give her space. She misses you, Megs. But pushing yourself on her before she's ready could send her running the other way, you know?"

Megan turns her head to stare out the window. Her heart tightening as she second guesses her master plan.

Josh moves the car forward again, glancing at Megan, who's slumped in her seat. "But hey, it also may be just the thing she needs. An in-person reminder you're here and the ball is in her court." Josh turns to give her a quick smile of encouragement.

Megan turns, nodding at Josh and her mood picks back up.

"Just promise me one thing," Josh adds casually. Megan waits to hear what it is before agreeing, realizing he's trying to manage her expectations.

"Don't force her to talk now. Just drop off the olive branch, tell her you're thinking about her, and leave."

Megan thinks about it for a moment and nods. "I can do that." Megan fiddles with the radio until she finds the right station, settling on a pop station playing "Bye Bye Bye" by N'SYNC. Megan bobs her head and picks up the song right where it is and her right arm juts out in front of her making a bird beak with her hand as she snaps it shut three times belting out *bye bye bye* which sends Josh into a fit of deep full belly laughs.

"Knock it off. I can't focus on the road with you practicing your American Idol audition over there." Josh chokes the words out between laughs and their eyes connect, breaking apart only so Josh can look at the road in front of him. Megan feels a rush of heat surge to her face as she turns away.

It occurs to Megan she would happily stay in this moment if she could. This tiny blip right here, huddled in Josh's car, surrounded with warm familiarity. Here, she and Josh are perfectly happy, together.

Megan plops down into her seat, puffing an exasperated breath out after dropping off Katie's coffee.

"Didn't go like you envisioned?" Josh ventures.

"Katie took one look at me and ran to the back. One of her coworkers accepted it on her behalf. I left a note." Megan straightens up and runs her hands down her face, resetting herself. "Oh well! I did my best. She still knows I was thinking about her."

"She does. Off we go?"

Megan gives a decisive nod and buckles her seatbelt. It was a short way to the medical examiner's office. Soon, she'll have some much-needed answers.

They drive in silence for a bit before Josh, apparently, feels the need to fill it with something. Instead of music, he opts for conversation.

"So, how's therapy going? I know you weren't thrilled when Katie suggested it."

Megan knows Josh's interest is sincere, but she doesn't want to bring him into the ugly parts of her past he isn't already privy to. "It's fine. Most of the time, she's just asking me to remember things from when I was younger. Like all the secrets to moving forward are locked up in the past somehow."

Josh nods, not forcing Megan to expand.

After considering it, she offers just a little more, holding back the pieces she is sure will hurt him. "What was interesting yesterday, or disappointing I guess, was in the memory brought up, I remembered getting picked up by my dad once super late at night, like past midnight and he had this guy with him. A guy with a gold tooth, just like Sarah Beth said. I can see the streetlight reflecting off of it so clearly in my memory. His face is hazy, though."

"Holy shit! Kind of insane you remember that. I'd say therapy is helping, at least in relation to your investigation. So your dad has been working with this guy for a long time, then?"

"It would seem so. I would have been about fourteen. So thirteen years ago, give or take."

"I guess that corroborates Sarah Beth's story." Josh's brow furrows, thinking hard about something. Megan watches his jaw grind back and forth as if literally chewing on an idea. A couple of minutes pass before he asks what's on his mind.

"Where was your dad picking you up from so late at night? Where was I? Or Katie? Were you alone?"

Megan doesn't answer right away. She can't. This was a moment in her life Josh wasn't there for and she just knows how disappointed he'll be in her if he knew what happened that night. "It doesn't matter. The important part is my dad took forever to come get me and we didn't live far away at all. Like twenty minutes. So what was he doing?"

They pull up into the parking lot of the medical examiner's office and Josh cuts the ignition. When Megan reaches for her door handle, he stops her. "Wait, just a minute. If it's not important, why are you hiding it from me? What aren't you telling me?"

Josh's eyes are like glass, a tiny flame housed inside, burning with determination. Megan wonders if she unknowingly triggered the officer in him. She suspects he will not let her off the hook. She closes her eyes and drops her head to avoid looking at him.

"Please don't be mad at me." She relives the entire memory with him. He doesn't interrupt her. Not even when she has to collect herself. When she finishes, her eyes open, and she sees two water drops on her jeans. She hadn't noticed when the tears slipped out, but she is sure they are filled with her shame. When she finally works up the nerve to look at Josh, he isn't looking back at her. His eyes blaze straight ahead. One hand grips the steering wheel so tightly she thinks it will leave an imprint. She watches as his other hand clenches into a fist.

"You must be so disappointed in me." Her words are barely audible.

"Who was he?" Josh's voice hardens, his teeth grit together.

"I'm sorry, Josh. You must think so little..." Megan's words get stuck in her throat.

Suddenly, it seems to register in Josh's brain what Megan is saying, because he finally turns to her, softening, and he pulls her across the center console into his right arm. "Megs, no. This wasn't your fault. How could it be?"

"I should have just gone home. I shouldn't have stayed. I... I..." Megan stammers the words into his shoulder. She isn't sure what she could have done, but she's certain the mistake had been hers.

"Who was he? Megs... please." Josh begs for a name.

"Brad." Megan whispers.

"Brad. Brad Donnelly?" Josh's face turns scarlet. "That guy's a total prick! He's always been a piece of shit. You have no clue what he was like in the locker room. He's still in town. I'll kill him."

"You can't, Josh. It was a long time ago. Just let it go." Megan pleads.

Josh turns to stone. His jaw sets, and in one swift motion, his fist comes up and slams into his steering wheel. "Fuck!"

Megan reaches out and folds his fist between her hands while he lays his forehead on top of his other hand, still gripping the top of the steering wheel. Megan knows Josh would never hurt her. But she also knows what his home was like growing up and he is no stranger to violence. It's rare, but his temper gets the best of him occasionally and it rattles her.

"Sorry," he mutters when the adrenaline subsides. "I just…" He doesn't have to finish the thought. Megan understands.

Josh's should sag and he moves to open his car door and get out. "Let's go."

Megan and Josh step into the medical examiner's building and find the front desk vacant. There is a small hallway to the left of the desktop that has swinging double doors with small windows in the middle and rubber door sweeps at the bottom. The room is spotless. Too bright and too clean to be the other half of a building that houses dead bodies. That she may be standing just a few feet away from any number of corpses sends Megan's stomach rolling.

Josh walks over and rings a small silver bell which sits on the front desk. A man comes out wearing a white lab coat and latex gloves. He pushes the doors open with his back and as he spins around to face them; he freezes in place. His eyes lock onto the gun at Josh's waist. Megan hadn't noticed he'd been wearing it and wonders if he always carries on his days off.

The man looks as if he's having to force himself to come closer, removing his gloves and tossing them in the trashcan under the desk. He smells of disinfectant and formaldehyde. Megan notices his hand shaking ever so slightly. "Can I help you with something?" His eyes dart back and forth between Megan and Josh, apparently unsure of where to settle.

"Dr. Oswald? I'm officer Joshua Pierce and this is my colleague, Megan Palmer." Josh presents his badge. The man flinches at the sound of her last name.

"Ok. What can I do for you? Would you like some water?" Dr. Oswald fidgets with his fingers for a bit before shoving them down into his pockets, hiding them away.

"We'd like to talk to you about a report you filed recently with the Sacramento Police Department. Is there somewhere we can go talk privately?" Josh oozes a calm authority, but Megan notices his hands are still clenched. Josh hasn't relaxed at all since he found out about Brad. Megan can see how tense he still feels. She can almost feel how much self-control he is exerting right now. He looks like a ticking time bomb, just waiting for the opportunity to explode.

They follow Dr. Oswald through the double doors and into the first room on the right, which is an excessively minimalist office. Inside is nothing but a desk with a few drawers in it, and two large filing cabinets on which a few medical reference books sit.

"Please, sit down." Oswald waves his hand at the chairs by the far wall without looking at them before struggling to seat himself. He's quite jittery.

"Doctor, you recently examined Mark Palmer. You provided our department with a photocopy of your report, which, as you must know, is highly abnormal. I'm going to need to see the original report. Coffee stains are of no consequence."

Oswald's eyes flit around the room as if assessing his options. "Of course. Of course. I've got it right here." He leans over to shuffle through the files in his desk drawer, but he is having a lot of trouble thanks to the shaky fingers that have now evolved into a full-blown tremor. Megan presumes he has Josh's forceful presence to thank for that as she watches the man fumble through his folders.

"It must be here somewhere…" Oswald mumbles. Megan isn't sure if he's speaking to them or to himself. Megan is, however, sure the man is stalling. She can tell Josh knows it too, and he's growing impatient.

"Dr. Oswald, the report." Josh pushes.

"Yes, yes, I'm just having some trouble locating…"

Josh cracks his knuckles before whipping around in his seat to talk to Megan, looking eerily calm. "I left my phone in the car. Could you please run and grab it for me?"

"Seriously? Can't it wait?" Megan's heart beats faster, not being privy to whatever Josh is communicating to her.

"It's important. I'd appreciate it, Megan."

Megan glances at Josh, then at Dr. Oswald. "Alright… sure."

Josh spins back to face the doctor as Megan stands to leave.

Megan returns a minute later empty-handed. Dr. Oswald is lowering himself back into his seat. The lapels of his lab coat are rumpled and the collared shirt beneath it is twisted and wrinkled as if he'd grabbed on to it too tightly. When she looks at Josh, she can't read the expression on his face.

"Sorry about that, Megs." Josh pulls his phone out of his pocket. "Looks like I had it all along. But good news. Dr. Oswald decided he's ready to tell us what happened to the original report." Josh's eyes pierce into Oswald's and Megan watches as the man dabs his brow with a handkerchief.

Oswald gulps before speaking. "I—I—I don't have the original report. A man was here before. He burned it. I swear."

Megan sits up a little straighter. Josh was right. Dr. Oswald was hiding something and now they are getting somewhere.

"Who burned the original report?" Josh's voice sends a chill down Megan's back, the tiny hairs on her arms all stand at attention.

"I don't know. It's the truth. I didn't get his name. He just barged in, and held me at gunpoint," Oswald's eyes flit to where Josh's gun may be on the other side of his desk, "demanding to see the original report. When I gave it to him, he burned it and ordered me to write a new one."

"What did he look like?"

"It's hard to say. He was quite tall. And wearing a black sweatsuit. His hood was pulled up over his head, and… and… he was wearing dark sunglasses." Oswald hasn't moved a muscle the entire time and sweat now pours freely down the sides of his face.

"Any distinguishing features?"

"Not that I could see. I think I saw a few strands of dark curly hair sticking out from under his hood. But I can't be sure. I was frightened."

Josh pauses for a moment to look at Megan. Then he continues. "What was in the original report?"

"He made me write a new cause of death and to alter my findings." If Dr. Oswald thinks this is enough explanation, he is sorely mistaken.

"Keep going. Leave nothing out." Josh's tone is a warning. He won't ask twice.

"To begin with, the body was in poor shape, beyond what would be expected in a simple suicide. The damage was concentrated in areas with a distinguishing feature. Several tattoos were badly bruised. A scar that ran the length of the forearm was bruised over. And a large pear-shaped birthmark on the back of the shoulder was nearly missed due to the amount of discoloration that lay over the top of it."

Megan perks up. "My dad didn't have a scar on his arm. Or a birthmark on the back of his shoulder."

Dr. Oswald wipes his brow again. "The scar was only a few years old, judging by its texture and color. Is it possible you simply weren't aware of it?"

Megan considers this, knowing full well it's possible. "Could be. Keep going, please."

Oswald's Adam's apple bobs up and down as he swallows. "The fracture patterns on the back of the skull were quite fragmented, but the first thing I noticed was the exit wound."

"What about it?" Josh prompts him.

"It did not have the correct trajectory to match the entry wound. They were just slightly off." Oswald looks up to meet Josh's eyes. "Upon closer examination of the exit wound, I noticed a tiny piece of the skull had groove patterns that support a bullet going *in*, rather than a bullet coming out."

Josh frowns. "You're saying he shot himself in the back of the head?"

Oswald sits up a little straighter and finally puts his hands down to rest on the arms of his chair. "Or someone else did."

Megan feels her heart pick up speed and Josh stands to pace beside her. "What else?"

"There was also a discrepancy in bullet size," Oswald says. "His scalp showed abraded and blackened skin, suggesting he was shot at close range. The largest section I had been able to measure, had it been a clean entry, would suggest a smaller bullet like a .22 caliber. And the shot was angled downward." Oswald's first two fingers form a gun shape which he points towards the desktop. "Such that the bullet would have exited through the mouth cavity, which could be how the assailant collected the extra casing."

Josh pauses mid-pace. "So what's to say that the bullet didn't start at the mouth and exit through the back of the head?"

"Because the section I was able to measure inside of the skill suggests a bullet larger than a .22 caliber." Dr. Oswald is stabilizing, appearing comfortable in his element, discussing his forensic findings. Megan watches Josh absorb the information, trying her best to keep up. She turns back to Dr. Oswald, who hasn't broken stride yet. In fact, he seems to be gaining momentum. "Upon closer examination, I believe the discrepancy between the two sections I measured is due to the fact that I was looking at two different bullet holes."

"What are you saying?" Megan interjects, struggling to put the pieces together.

"Mark was shot twice?" Josh asks.

Oswald clears his throat. "I'm suggesting, when all of my findings are taken together, it's possible that a shot to the back of the head came first. The killer then came around to the front," Doctor Oswald touches his pointer fingers to the desk and drags one around the other to demonstrate visually, "and shot the victim through the mouth, approximating the path that would allow the second bullet to pass through the entry wound on the back of the skull. An arduous task indeed."

Dr. Oswald's hand flies up to his collar and he stretches it open, as if he needs a little more air. He releases the top button before continuing. "He would have needed a much larger bullet to ensure the original wound was sufficiently altered."

"Something like the Western .38 special that was found on the scene," Josh says, his eyes locked on Oswald's desk as if lost in thought.

Oswald nods. "The casing he used wasn't one I'd personally seen before. It was slightly heavier than the typical Western .38 special, and it had a deep groove around its middle. However, the weight could explain the damage to the smaller entry wound on the backside of the skull."

Josh frowns. "He? You said he. How do you know the killer is a man?" Josh cuts in.

"Ah yes, indeed there is no forensic evidence to support this, but given the nature of this particular homicide, it is a reasonable assumption. Statistically speaking, an execution style killing suggests premeditation at a minimum. And the calculated composure exhibited during an execution is most often characteristic of a male killer. In cases of a female suspect, it's highly more likely to be messy. A crime of passion, if you will."

"Agreed," Josh adds. "If your theory is the killer shot Mark first in the back of the head and then a second time in the front, how did you explain the lack of blood and spatter from the first bullet?"

Megan whips her head around, staring at Josh in awe, as if realizing for the very first time just how very good he is at what he does.

"There were no samples taken from the scene, so I can't be certain. But as I swabbed the victim's…"

"His name was Mark." Megan interrupts, suddenly overcome with the need to remind Dr. Oswald that he's talking about a human being, one who meant something to her, and he had a name.

"Yes, of course, my apologies. Mark." Dr. Oswald swallows before proceeding. "As I swabbed Mark's face for gunshot residue, the standard chemistry test ran showed traces of a few different chemicals, all of which can be found in common household cleaning products. Glass cleaners, hand soaps, laundry detergent. Things of that nature. It wouldn't be unreasonable to think the killer may have placed something around Mark's head to catch most of the initial spatter and blood until the killer could come around to the front. He might have used a pillow, a thick towel or bed sheet. He could have wiped down the face afterwards before shooting again from the front and then disposed of the supplies, or burned them, perhaps. It's difficult to say with any degree of certainty. Because police did not classify this as a murder investigation, I had no reason to request any additional tests and analysis. I'm sorry."

The doctor hangs his head in his hands and his chest heaves up and down, but no sound comes out. When he rights himself once more, his cheeks are soaked, and his eyes are bloodshot.

Josh sits back in his chair, his arms draped casually across the armrests. "Is there anything else?"

"I didn't want to falsify the report. I didn't. He threatened my life. My wife and kids. He told me if I ever spoke of this to anyone, he would kill my family first, then he would come for me. He threw $1,000 on the desk before he left and told me it was for my silence. I'm sorry. I'm so sorry." Dr. Oswald lays his head on his desk between his folded arms and weeps.

Josh stands, and Megan follows. "Well, doctor, now you're going to stay quiet again. And keep yourself available in case we need to speak to you again."

Megan follows Josh out the door and breaks into a jog. The walls of death close in around her and she is surrounded by the smell of decay. She can hear Josh's voice behind her, but she can't understand the words. She doesn't stop until she reaches his car, and she feels the world tip over and fade to black.

CHAPTER 26

Megan's eyes flutter open to find Josh staring down at her, his face twisted with concern. "Hey, welcome back." He sounds like a dream, soft and whispery.

"What happened?" Megan is groggy, her head still spinning slightly.

"You passed out. You're lucky I caught you, you could have gotten a nasty bump." Josh pushes her hair back away from her face and drapes it behind her ear, exactly the way she does a hundred times a day.

"Sorry. I guess it's been a while since I've eaten. I've only had coffee today," Megan admits.

"Way too much coffee. Drink this," he says, passing her a bottle of water. "Let's go get some food."

Megan watches Josh at the counter, ordering their food. The girl on the other side bats her eyelashes. She looks to be about Megan's age, but the way she's acting makes her seem much younger. Josh chats with the girl in the friendly way he does. Megan watches the girl toss her head back, giggling. Giggling too much. Josh isn't that funny. The girl touches a light hand to Josh's arm and Josh stands up, relaxed, removing his arm without drawing attention to it.

When Josh sits down, Megan catches him before he gets comfortable. "So how come you aren't seeing anyone?" Megan lobs the question out into right field.

How come you're not seeing anyone? Am I sure I didn't hit my head…?

Josh sets the tray down on the table. "Um, what?" He shakes his head. "Where did that come from?"

Megan nods in the cashier girl's direction. "In case you're blind, she's interested. She didn't even try to be cool about it. I mean, you're a catch and I just realized I never hear about you dating anyone." Megan had never thought about how it would feel if Josh were dating someone, but she suddenly feels like she may not be entirely fine with it. Megan takes a huge bite of her burger and looks up to find Josh staring at her with a dopey grin. Her mouth is full, but she mumbles a noise that sort of sounds like "what?".

"You think I'm a catch?" Josh flashes his teeth at her, only to be met with a roll of her eyes, as if Megan is now dealing with a pesky child.

"I regret asking now. Forget it."

"Ok, seriously. I don't know. I just haven't met anyone I'm interested in. Besides, I'm focused on my career right now. My line of work isn't exactly made for the casual dater." Josh turns back to his food.

Megan pretends not to notice the pang of disappointment she feels when Josh says hasn't met anyone. She tells herself it's because she wants him to be happy and he deserves an exceptional partner. It has nothing to do with the fact that she is included in the group of women he's not interested in.

The pair eat in comfortable silence for a few minutes. The burger in Megan's belly is exactly what she needed. She can feel her energy returning and the fog lifting from her head. "Oh, my god this burger. Why have I never eaten here before?" Megan asks with her mouth full.

Josh chuckles. "Well, if I'm understanding you correctly, probably because you don't live nearby and it's a hole in the wall."

"How do you know about it?"

"I know a lot of places you don't. I cover a lot of ground when I'm on duty."

Megan smacks her palms on the table. "That settles it then. You are officially taking me on a burger tour when this is over."

Josh smiles. "A burger tour. I like it. It's a date. I just made a mental list of four places already."

A date?

"You're quiet. What's going on in that head of yours?" Josh is staring and Megan realizes she's been zoned out.

She pops a french fry in her mouth, buying herself another moment before she answers. "I'm just still trying to come to terms with all of this. As a kid, there's so much that you see but don't understand. When you grow up, in hindsight, it's clearer. But until then, it just is what it is, and doesn't mean anything."

Megan takes a drink of her soda, which she doesn't drink often but thought the sugar might give her a quick spike in energy. "When I was sitting with Sarah Beth, thinking *how could my dad possibly be capable of this*, I remembered the time Annie told me my dad had taken their dog as a hostage. She said he took the dog away and said he'd bring the dog home when Annie gave him her wedding ring. He pawned it to pay one of his drug dealers. Or so said Annie. That's a sick individual. Desperate, right?" Megan's mind wonders off again, weaving through her thoughts, lost.

"I guess what I mean is, I can see all these moments when I just thought he was being a terrible dad. I had no idea he was just being a terrible person."

Josh finishes the bite he'd been chewing, then he sets his burger down and wipes his hands on a napkin. He lays his palms face down on the table with gentle purpose and looks up at Megan. "You know it's ok, right? That you love your dad. It's ok to miss him. To be sad about what should have been. And it's definitely ok to be pissed at him. I know you feel like you can't have all those feelings at the same time, but you can. He was your dad. He was there for you for a long time until he wasn't. And even then, he should've been."

Megan musters a weak smile. As much as she wants to thank Josh for giving her the permission she so desperately sought, the words are too hard to find. She nods, hoping he'll feel the sentiment all the same.

Her mind skips ahead. "You know what else is bothering me? The birthmark. I don't remember him having a birthmark on his shoulder. I keep trying to picture it, trying to remember if I could see it in the home video Annie was watching, but I can't. The scar I can buy off on since I wasn't around for thirteen years. But I'd remember a birthmark. Wouldn't I?"

Josh thinks about it. "I don't remember it either, but I'm not sure why I would. You could ask Grandma Barb."

"Good idea. Maybe I'll do that."

Josh grabs a fry and dips it into the tiny cup of ranch sitting between them. "Should I change the subject now?"

Megan perks up. "Oh, my god yes, please."

Josh reaches into his back pocket and pulls out a folded pamphlet. He slides it across the table for Megan to look at.

The brochure is a colorful display showing the Las Vegas strip with a large, brightly lit casino in the center. Inside shows photos of patrons gambling at tropical themed tables and slot machines, a stunning glass bar area with bronze trimmings and a vast selection of top shelf liquors, and promises of unbelievable daily payouts.

The Grand Oasis Casino in Las Vegas. Leave your baggage at the door. Your dreams await you.

"What is this? Are you trying to tell me something? Are you living a secret double life, too?" Megan tosses the joke out to mask her confusion.

"Ha ha. Hilarious." Josh rolls his eyes for dramatic effect. "This is a casino established in 1982 by Nathanial Walker. The place became famous for its *No Shoe Policy*. People could yell 'daddy needs a new pair of shoes' before placing a bet and then take their shoes off. If they lost on that next bet, they surrendered their shoes and left barefoot if they couldn't afford to buy new shoes from the in-house luxury shoe store. But if that person won, the house would provide them with a brand-new pair of shoes for free."

Josh takes a sip of water. Megan looks at him, still confused, and ventures a new guess. "Ok, so you need new shoes?"

Josh's laugh rings out across the courtyard. "Yup. Why buy them myself when I could gamble the pair on my feet? No... about ten years ago, Nathanial passed away, and his nephew inherited the place. Daniel Walker."

Megan nearly chokes on her soda. "Dan? Dan is running this place? How did we not know this sooner?"

"He's running it under a pseudonym. In the casino, he goes by Damien Wallace. Once I figured out his alias, I dug a little more, and it looks like he keeps his identity muddled because he also deals in a lot of underground, illegal sports betting. He's been at it for a very long time. Apparently, the D.A. in Nevada has been building a case with Homeland Security for years, but they can't get anything concrete to stick. He keeps his hands pretty clean somehow..."

"Using people like my dad to handle the dirty work?" Megan finishes the thought as Josh nods at her.

"Most likely, yes." Josh holds Megan's gaze, his eyes sad at the acknowledgement, until she breaks away.

Megan hunches over the table, staring at the pamphlet as if there are answers tucked away between its folds. "So, what do we do now?" This feels like too big a decision to make on her own. She needs Josh to tell her what to do.

"For now, let me keep digging. I'll ask around. See if anyone has some confidential informants out there who they can get in touch with. I'll let you know as soon as I feel like I've got something we can use."

"Josh?" Megan doesn't want to ask the question creeping around in her brain like a cockroach, looking for a dark corner to hide in. "What would happen if someone who worked for an operation like this decided he wanted out?"

"Let's not think about that until we have to. Let's be sure of the connection first. Maybe someone out there can tell me if they know Mark."

Megan swallows the question back down, despite her intuition telling her it will scream to be answered again soon.

"What time are we going to Mrs. B's for dinner?" Josh's question snaps Megan back to present and reminds her their day isn't over.

CHAPTER 27

Megan and Josh pull into the driveway of her grandma's little ranch promptly at 6:00pm. The crunch of the gravel shifting under the tires rattles the whole car. Megan can feel her body relax as the house comes into view. The house is modest and comfortable but sits on ten acres of property with a large barn at the end of a trail winding downhill behind the house. The barn is home to two horses, a dairy cow, three goats and four pigs.

Megan hates that her grandma lives out here alone and insists on working the ranch without help. If anything happened to Grandma Barb, if she fell and hurt herself, her nearest neighbor is a mile up the road and isn't prone to spontaneous visits. Megan reminds her grandma on every occasion that the very least she can do is take her cell phone with her when she goes out to the barn. And on every occasion, Grandma Barb insists having it in her pocket is uncomfortable and gets in the way. She's stubborn, but she'd be wrong to think Megan won't remind her again tonight.

"Whose car is that?" Josh asks as they get out and walk to the front door.

"It's Jonathan's." Megan's tone betrays her surprise.

"You didn't know he was coming?" Josh notices the inflection and turns to find Megan's head shaking.

Grandma opens the door and when they cross the threshold, they're transported back in time to when Elvis reigned supreme. Grandma Barb only keeps two types of décor in her home. The first is family mementos including photos, trinkets, drawings given to her by her grandchildren when they were little, and heirlooms passed down through the generations. The second is Elvis memorabilia. Collector's plates, figurines, and records adorning the walls. Megan smiles, thinking about how the drawers of the entertainment center hold nothing but Elvis CDs and DVD copies of his many movies.

Megan can smell the warm tomatoes baked between layers of cheese and wide, flat noodles. Notes of garlic float through the air as greetings are exchanged, and Grandma ushers Megan and Josh down the entryway and into the living room. When Megan turns the corner, her brother peeks over the back of the La-Z-Boy he's sitting in.

Jonathan stands up to hug Megan. "Hey, sis." He turns to shake Josh's hand, but Josh pulls him into a brotherly hug and they pat each other firmly on the back. "Hey man, how have you been?"

"It's good to see you, Smalls. It's been too long." Josh is beaming, his face soft.

Megan glances at the television and chuckles, looking pointedly at her grandma. "Braveheart? Since when are you a Mel Gibson fan?"

"Since Jonathan turned this movie on an hour ago. Who knew Mel was such a dish? Consider me a new Mel-lady." She winks at Josh. "That's what they call his lady fans." Grandma Barb's face is painted in coyness.

"Wow. I don't even have a response to that." Megan's eyes glitter with affection.

Josh laughs. "More power to you, Mrs. B. But I don't think Mel can handle you. You might be too much for him." Josh rarely skips a chance to tease Grandma Barb and simultaneously pay her a compliment.

Grandma Barb pinches his cheek, making a mock exasperated face at Josh. "Now just what am I going to do with you?" Then she flutters off to the kitchen, beckoning them to take their seat at the table. "Jonathan, come help me bring out the food."

Megan's brother shuffles off to do as he's told.

"Mrs. B, this looks amazing. If this tastes half as good as it smells, I can die right now, a happy man." Megan swears she hears the saliva filling Josh's mouth as he speaks. She's about to second his compliment when his head whips up towards Grandma, and he winces. "Shit... sorry. I mean shoot!"

Her eyes are kind, knowing he meant no harm in his choice of words. "Nothing to be sorry for. I accept your kind words and I'll let you off with a warning for cursing at the dinner table since it's been a while since you've been over. Next time, it's a dollar to the swear jar." She winks at Josh, putting an end to the matter.

Megan proceeds with cation. "So, how are you doing, Grandma?" Megan stares at her plate and pokes a piece of lasagna onto her fork, not drawing too much attention to her grandma's response.

"I'm just fine, dear. Don't I look fine?"

The women in Megan's family have a long history of keeping their mouths closed. Best to be seen, not heard. They are always fine. Megan looks to Jonathan for help, as if he can talk some sense into their grandma and keep her from skirting around her feelings. Jonathan just shrugs at her, bowing out.

"Grandma..."

Before Megan can argue, Grandma Barb cuts her off. "I'm just sorry Katie couldn't make it tonight."

Megan drops her hand to the table a little too hard and her fork bangs on her plate. She clears her throat. "You talked to Katie?" Megan looks back and forth from her grandma to Josh, trying to decide if the pair are in cahoots. Josh is busy putting on a show of being consumed by his favorite dish in front of him.

"Well now, I couldn't have dinner with three of my favorite young people without also inviting the fourth, now could I? It's a shame she had to work late tonight…" Grandma lets the words hang there like a carrot dangling in front of a horse.

Megan plays her game, albeit poorly. Too poorly having been unprepared. "Oh right, of course. She's been working a lot lately."

Grandma Barb calls her bluff immediately. "Didn't you know? You and Katie are practically glued at the hip. Are you two having a fight?" Grandma's voice is sickeningly sweet, dripping with innocence.

Meddlesome woman…

Megan looks to Josh, then to Smalls for anyone to intervene, only to find them both avoiding her gaze. No one is willing to try to slip one past Grandma Barb and risk having her turn her focus to them when it isn't their battle. Megan doesn't bother to mask her annoyance and gives a half confession. "We aren't in a fight. We just haven't connected in a few days. That's all."

"Now that just won't do. Two girls as close as the two of you can surely work this out, whatever it is. It's not over a boy, is it?"

Megan's grandma glances at Josh as she asks, but the moment is gone as quickly as it came. "No, it's not over a boy." Megan looks at the boys sitting at the table, trying to decide which she'll divert attention to first. Josh is inhaling his food, so she settles for her brother. "So, Smalls, how are things at work?"

Grandma perks up politely.

"Oh, things are good. My boss seems to have calmed down. And this customer brought in an old '57 Thunderbird he wants restored. He doesn't have the time to work on it himself. Sam put me on the project in my downtime, so that's been cool."

Megan loves the way talking about cars draws her brother out. She's worried about him her whole life, not having a father figure of any kind around. Smalls kept to himself growing up, painfully shy, and it always took him a long time to trust other people. Cruel kids pick on the loners because they're easy targets. Smalls was no exception to the social order. He's endured a lot.

Megan has always felt fiercely protective of her brother. Hannah says this is Megan's subconscious effort to heal her own child self, whose basic needs went repeatedly unmet. But truthfully, Megan regrets she wasn't there for Smalls as much as she could have been. She got to keep their dad for far longer than her brother did. Naturally, it divided her focus, and they didn't grow up to be as close as they could have been.

Seeing Smalls lately feels like meeting someone new. She sees him blossoming, settling into himself, and letting other people see him too.

Megan's heart swells as she watches Grandma and Josh share in Smalls' joy, asking questions, showing interest. Sometimes, the sharp reminders of how unfair his upbringing was dig into Megan's side. Knowing how Grandma Barb pulled Smalls closer when Mark pushed him further away provides a bit of solace. At least Smalls knows their grandma never forgot about him.

Megan knows she isn't Smalls' only protector.

The evening draws to a close and Grandma Barb directs Jonathan to clear the table, and he brings the dishes to the kitchen where Megan stands at the sink washing, and Josh loads the dishwasher and hand dries the larger items.

Megan can feel the eyes on her before she sees them. She turns around, not the least bit surprised to find her grandma behind her, casting sly looks in her and Josh's direction. Megan turns back around, shaking her head at her grandma's nosiness as she approaches and stands between them. She drapes an arm across each of their shoulders and pulls them into an uncomfortable side hug, their heads mashed against hers. "Aren't you two just sweet as punch? Thank you both for coming to have dinner with an old woman."

"You know we love it, Mrs. B. We won't wait so long next time, will we, Megs?" Josh pecks Grandma on the cheek before resuming his task. Megan catches the way Josh refers to them as a pair and her cheeks start to burn.

"No, we won't," she agrees. "But I won't come back unless you promise to take your phone with you when you go out to work in the barn…" Megan's voice gets increasingly louder to ensure her grandma hears her as she scoots away.

"What's that, dear? I couldn't hear you. Let me just see Jonathan out."

"That woman is exasperating." Megan tells Josh. Josh just chuckles at the beginning of an exchange they've had too many times to count.

Grandma Barb returns just as Megan and Josh are finishing up. They dry their hands and take turns hugging Grandma goodbye as they meander slowly towards the front door.

"Shall we plan for a couple of weeks from now?" Grandma asks Megan.

Megan's mind is elsewhere, and it takes her a moment to register her grandma talking to her. "What? Oh. Right. Sounds great. I'll call you this weekend and we can pick a day. Would that work?"

Grandma Barb tilts her head. "Are you ok, sweetheart? Something on your mind?"

"Actually, there's something that's been nagging at me. I've wanted to ask you all night, but I didn't want to talk about it in front of Smalls because it's awkward for him." Megan catches Josh looking curiously at her over her grandma's shoulder. "Do you have any idea why dad left a note telling police to call you instead of Annie? It's feels like such an odd thing to think about before…" Megan can't bring herself to finish the sentence in front of her grandma.

Grandma Barb shakes her head slowly and closes her eyes. When she opens them, they glisten with a thin layer of new moisture. "No, I can't say I do. Maybe he just wanted his mama." Grandma pulls Megan into one more hug. Her voice is low and soft next to Megan's ear. "You know, it doesn't matter how old your children get. Your babies are always your babies. Nothing can change that."

Megan can't tell if Grandma Barb is referring to her bond with her own son. Or to her son's bond with Megan and Smalls. Perhaps it was a bit of both.

Megan turns to leave when she's reminded of the other thing poking at the back of her mind. "Oh, one more thing. Did dad have a birthmark?"

A dark look crosses her grandma's face. Megan can't quite decipher it. "Oh yes. He had a pear-shaped one on the back of his left shoulder. About the size of a silver dollar. Why do you ask, sweetie?"

"No special reason. I just realized I wasn't sure. It was bothering me that I couldn't remember." Grandma Barb gives her a sad look and Megan feels like she's somehow disappointed Grandma Barb. "Good night, Grandma."

CHAPTER 28

THURSDAY, SEPTEMBER 17TH

Megan throws on a pair of black leggings, an oversized sweatshirt, and a ball cap to cover up her unwashed hair before leaving her apartment. She walks into Bean to find it unusually crowded for so late in the morning. She hoped she would hit a sweet spot, just after the morning rush, but early enough that she could make it to her appointment with Hannah. As she looks at the crowd, she mutters curses at herself for underestimating Bean's popularity. She could have made coffee at home, but she was coming to love the routine of Bean's lattes before her therapy sessions. For that reason alone, she risked the time it would take.

She grabs her coffee, pleasantly surprised at how quickly the line moved, and strolls toward the door when her phone chimes. She pulls it out to see who is texting her and turns around to push the door open with her back, since her hands are full. Luckily, someone pulls the door open for her.

She looks up from under the bill of hat to thank the person, only to find herself face to face with Katie.

"Katie!"

"Megan!"

They speak simultaneously with equal measures of shock and unease.

"I wasn't expecting to see you here so late in the morning," Megan says, wondering if Katie came at this time specifically to avoid her. Not wanting to be proven right, she quickly goes on, "It's great to see you."

"Yeah, it's good to see you, Megs."

Megan feels a gush of fondness at hearing her nickname in Katie's voice again. Megan moves outside when a pair of customers excuses themselves to squeeze past her in the doorway.

"Do you have a minute?" Megan asks. Katie checks the time, as if calculating whether she did. Or if she could find an excuse not to. "I promise I won't keep you. I have therapy this morning." Megan prays silently her admission will soften Katie's resolve.

"I have to get to work... but I guess I have a couple of minutes. Let me get my coffee first."

Megan watches Katie move to the front of the line as she thinks about what she is going to say. She isn't sure how much time Katie will afford her, so it needs to count.

Megan stands on the sidewalk just outside the door, watching people walk by while she waits for Katie. A part of her thinks maybe Katie will slip by her and bolt, or have a fresh excuse why she can't stay by the time she returns. When she sees Katie come through the door, she releases a breath she didn't know she was holding.

"Katie, I'm sorry. I am *so* sorry. When you told me you wanted to go back, I should have listened to you. I should have turned around with you. I should have taken the risk more seriously. This isn't your fight. It's mine. I put you in danger."

Katie looks anxious, like each passerby reminds her they are in a public place. She murmurs, as if not wanting anyone to overhear their private moment.

"That's not it. Megs, I appreciate the apology. I do. But it's more than that. I want to be here for you through this process. I want you to heal and move past all the stuff with your dad. But when you took off without me, I realized how deep you are in this whole thing. It's like you're obsessed, and it just felt like..." Katie chokes up and swallows. "It felt too reckless, like you didn't care if you die in the process. Like you hadn't thought about what it would be like for your grandma, or your brother, or Josh..." Katie gulps, "or even me, if we lost you to all of this. And *that* really hurt, Megs."

Megan hears the pain rippling through Katie's words. Katie's right. Megan hadn't thought about anything beyond getting the answers she was looking for. Defensiveness roars up in her chest like a reflex. She wants to unleash everything building inside of her. To scream that Katie doesn't understand what Megan is going through. That Katie doesn't understand her. But that isn't true. Katie understands Megan better than anyone and if there are pieces of Megan she's unaware of, it's because Megan has kept them from her.

Instead, Megan takes Katie's hand in hers, and looks her in the eyes. "You're right. I was selfish. And I'm not the only one whose feelings matter. I should have realized before, but I didn't. I see it now."

A single tear falls out from underneath Katie's sunglasses. "You know how hard it's been for me since my dad left. I don't have many people I can count on. If I can't count on you, then..."

Megan forgets people are watching them. The background fades away and Katie comes into sharp focus. Megan pulls Katie into her arms. "I know. I know, I'm sorry."

The pair breaks apart, remembering they both have people expecting them and their time has run out, for today. Megan doesn't want to leave Katie this way. "Unfortunately for you, I'm not going anywhere, so you're going to have to put up with me for at least…" Megan checks the time on her phone, "sixty more years."

Katie gives a tiny chuckle. "Make it one hundred."

"Ok, deal." Megan holds her hand out to shake on it. "Ok, so you'll go to work. I'll go to therapy. And you'll stop pretending like you don't know me?" Megan cocks her head, trying again to lighten the mood before they go their separate ways.

"Sounds like a plan." Katie nods with her full smile on her face.

Megan gives Katie's hand a light squeeze and they turn to walk in opposite directions. Megan gets a few steps in before turning around to yell, "by the way, Grandma Barb missed you at dinner last night!"

Katie turns around, walking backward, "I missed her too! Next time!" She winks at Megan and turns back around

Megan sits in her usual seat on the couch, staring out the window. A voice disrupts her thoughts, though she can't make out its words.

She tears herself away from the gorgeous morning view of the cityscape to find Hannah looking at her curiously.

Megan realizes Hannah must have said something to her while her mind was wandering. "I'm sorry. What?"

"I said you seem cheerful today. Is there something specific to thank for that?"

"Oh! Yes, I do feel good this morning. My best friend and I had a bit of a disagreement, but I ran into her this morning, and we talked through it." Megan sips a cup of water casually, careful not to pique Hannah's interest. Especially since it has been at least semi-resolved at this point.

"Well, that certainly is something to feel good about. Is there anything in particular you'd like to talk about in our session today?"

Megan isn't sure where the line is drawn in terms of patient and therapist confidentiality, but she's already decided she will not risk telling

Hannah about her dad's involvement in an illegal operation. Especially when she doesn't even understand all the details just yet. "I don't think so."

"Does your newfound mood translate to how you are feeling about your father? In our last session, we discussed how you felt conflicted in your understanding of who your father was. Do you feel you are gaining more clarity?"

Megan's eyes flicker up to the photo of the ocean on the wall directly across from her, feeling the similarity between the movement of ocean waves and her own relationship with her father. The similar way they roll up to the shore, stretching as far as they can, reaching out to latch onto something new, only to watch it slip away as they retreat, sliding backward into the painful sea they already know.

"Sometimes I feel like I'm so close to understanding everything. Other times, I feel like I might never know what happened or how to feel about him."

"Is it fair to say you feel stuck? Unable to move forward."

Megan nods. She hasn't made any progress processing her dad's death.

Hannah seems to consider Megan. After a moment, she shifts in her chair slightly before tipping her head to the side. "Have you grieved your loss yet?"

"What does that have to do with understanding who my dad was or how I should feel about him?"

"There is no one correct way to feel about another person. We're not here to discover how you *should* feel. Try to keep that in mind." Hannah sits up straighter. "Grief is illogical and malleable. It changes shape, springing up when you least expect it, latching onto you long after you've had enough, leaving a hole that can never be filled even after it lets you go. It's often missing when you search for it. Megan, those who deny themselves permission to grieve when grief presents itself, also deny themselves permission to feel a much wider range of emotions. Without the ability to identify what you feel, you also reject the ability to process those feelings."

Megan considers this. Logically, it makes sense. And with that, she concedes Hannah may have a point.

"You're saying I won't be able to move forward without allowing myself to grieve. But how do I give myself permission to grieve a monster?"

"Is that who your father is to you?"

"Sometimes."

"And the other times?"

Megan chooses not to answer this, assuming Hannah means for the question to be rhetorical.

Hannah continues, making an uncharacteristic recommendation. "Can you agree to give yourself permission to mourn the parts of your father that made him human? Leave the monstrous pieces for another time."

Megan nods, promising to try, praying she can deliver.

When Megan offers no more, Hannah changes the direction of the conversation. "Let's shift to another dynamic. You seem to be stuck on expectations. What you expect yourself to feel, what you expect to learn about your father, even what you believe I expect you to say during our sessions. I'd like for us to explore what kinds of expectations you feel your parents placed on you, starting with your father. Are you open to that?"

The question surprises Megan. She wasn't sure where Hannah would go next, but this wasn't what she would have guessed. She has to search for her answer.

"I guess… he expected a lot. Or at least I felt like he did."

"How so?"

"Well, I always tried to bring home good grades. I tried to get chores done quickly and then ask what else I could help with. Things like that."

"Did your father ask you to do those things?"

It occurs to Megan the answer is *no*. "He never actually said he expected those things. But then, he never treated me like a child. He always treated me like an adult. I guess I thought those are things adults would do."

"How do you feel about that today?"

"Resentful. I never got to just be a kid. I always had to be better."

"Why do you think that was?"

"I'm not sure." Megan waits, and so does Hannah. Megan can feel this is a moment where Hannah will outlast her, forcing Megan to proffer a response. "Maybe because my brother was just a kid, and my dad abandoned him. Maybe he wouldn't abandon me if I could act more like an adult. Be less of a hassle."

"Can you recall one such instance where too much was expected of you?"

Megan nods, because truthfully, one particular memory springs up immediately.

I grew up fast, learning at an early age that my parents were too young when they had me. I see now they didn't know how to handle a child's development and help them navigate childhood.

By the time I was twelve, I was regularly caring for myself and hanging out with my dad and Annie's friends. They told me I was an old spirit, and I'd lived many lives before, which I learned later is just hippie lingo for "mature for my age." It's true I was more mature than most kids my age. It wasn't by choice as much as spurned from necessity.

I was close to turning thirteen years old when I went to a restaurant to celebrate my stepmother's birthday.

I was the only kid there, which was typical. I'd never invite any of my friends from school. Just the idea of it was humiliating. My dad and stepmother's friends didn't have kids my age. It seemed like my dad wished that were true for him as well. But since it wasn't possible, and it was his weekend to have me, he toted me along. His social life wouldn't stop because his child should be in bed.

I was even around for their grown-up Halloween parties if it coincided with a weekend on which he had custody.

The night of Annie's birthday, we didn't sit in the restaurant area, where all the cozy booths were lined up, filled with families enjoying a meal together. We sat in the bar area, with the people who were more thirsty than they were hungry. One by one, her friends stopped by to toast to her. I knew by then what kinds of things they were drinking. I was regularly offered small tastes of their drinks and then ordered a virgin version of whatever fruity concoction was being served. The coconut drinks were my favorite.

I couldn't tell how long we stayed because I was watching the clock. I could tell because I was counting the number of times "one more round" was shouted and the waitress moseyed over to replace the empty glasses.

The night went on and after some hours had passed, my stepmom was very drunk. She excused herself to go to the bathroom, except she didn't come back for what seemed like a very long time.

My dad eventually noticed. This wasn't the first time I'd seen adults drunk. However, it was the first time he asked me to check on her instead of doing it himself. He told me she might be coming down with the flu and asked me to go check on her and be sure she hadn't fallen asleep on the floor.

After years of this kind of stuff, he still somehow thought I didn't understand what was going on. All adults were once children. How is it they forget how much they absorbed at a young age? Why do adults think their kids can't possibly figure these things out? I'm not sure I'll ever know. Maybe they feel better if they pretend.

I walked into the bathroom & the smell hit me first. It was like ten children had gotten ill and vomited collectively.

I checked the stalls, and my stepmother was huddled in a kneeling fetal position over the porcelain toilet. Her hair was long then. It draped down to her waist. I remember sitting with her in the mornings, transfixed, as she expertly French braided her thick chestnut locks in less than five minutes. She always offered to do my hair too.

Now her long hair was cascading around a toilet, grazing the floor. It appeared all the sick had made it into the toilet. At least there was that.

"Annie?" I called gently. She didn't respond.

I took a couple of steps closer & touched her back. "Annie?" I gave her a little shake. Still nothing.

I shook her shoulders a little harder, and she finally stirred. I pulled her hair back & tied it in a loose scrunchie. "Can you stand up?"

"No. Go get your dad." She sounded so small. So weak. I never knew her to be either of those things. I wasn't sure yet how I felt about seeing her this way.

"Sure."

I left to look for my dad. I looked through the cracks between the groups of grown-ups and finally spied him in a corner off to the side of the bar.

He was alone with Dan, the two of them separated from the rest of the group. It looked like they were arguing. My dad's back was to me, so I couldn't see his face, but I could see Dan's. My dad's arms kept shooting out to the sides as if the topic exasperated him, while Dan's face looked wild and red. I almost didn't recognize him. They kept their voices low, but I watched Dan's finger slam into my dad's chest over and over. So hard I wondered if my dad might have tiny fingertip shaped bruises in the morning.

I walked over slowly so I wouldn't sneak up and surprise them. Dan's face changed the instant he laid eyes on me. It was as if lightning struck and the power surged, flipping a circuit breaker. It was that quick.

His eyes softened and the smile I knew and loved stretched across his face as he lowered his hand, stretching it towards me for a low-five. "How ya doing, kiddo?"

"Fine", I told him as my dad turned to look at me. "I checked on Annie". I told him she wasn't looking good, and she needed his help. We went back to the bathroom. I stood outside the bathroom door, arms folding across my chest, trying to make myself invisible, praying I didn't run into anyone from school who might be here with their family. I waited by the door to stop anyone from going in while he was in there helping my stepmother.

Once they emerged, my dad helped her out to the car. It was his old 1995 Ford Mustang convertible. It had a bright sky-blue body with a white fabric top. I loved that car. When we sped down the highway with the top down, I could close my eyes and pretend I was flying high above the rest of the world to places I only ever dreamed of seeing. I remember feeling heartbroken when he sold it. I never knew for sure why he let it go.

I crawled into the backseat and my dad lowered my stepmom into the front passenger seat and reclined the seatback so Annie could lie down. He explained again that she wasn't feeling well. Though he seemed ok, I wondered if my dad was feeling well enough to drive.

I didn't have much of a choice. It was late, and I was so tired. I buckled my seatbelt and slipped out of the chest strap so I could lie down across the backseat.

My dad put on the Eric Clapton song, "Change the World". It was one of his favorites to serenade my stepmom with. Usually when he sang a song, he changed a few of the lyrics to something silly. But not this song. He would look at her tenderly and sing, slightly off key. Such a sweet gesture. It never sounded bad to me.

The song broke my heart every single time. It was a reminder of the happy life I should have had. The one where my dad loved my mom, and my mom loved my dad, and they both loved me and my brother. That life was over if it had ever really existed to begin with.

I listened to him sing her to sleep like a lullaby. I willed myself to go to sleep too, but each time I closed my eyes, a few more tears leaked out silently, sliding sideways down my face.

I never told my dad how much I hated that song.

Hannah guides Megan gently back to the present with her soft tone and classic question. "How do you feel, having remembered such an intense moment?"

"Angry. No. I'm not just angry. I'm fucking pissed." Megan opens the door to her thoughts without meaning to, and now they are spilling out in no particular order. "I'm pissed because he left me with more questions than answers. Pissed because he chose another family over me and my brother. I'm pissed because he chose not to be there to walk me down the aisle or play with his actual grandkids one day. I'm pissed because he told me how much he loved me and that I was his world and now he's gone, and it was all a big fucking lie. And I'm really pissed that everything I've been doing is probably for nothing." Megan crashes to a halt, thankful at having caught herself before she told Hannah everything she's been up to. She pulls a huge breath into her lungs, realizing how badly she'd needed it. "Mostly, I'm just pissed that I still care so much about him when he didn't care about me or Smalls at all."

Megan screws her jaw in tight, so it doesn't come loose again without her permission.

Hannah waits a few minutes and Megan resolves not to be the first to break the silence this time. It's Hannah's turn to give her something.

Hannah leans forward slightly in her chair. "Your feelings are valid. Your anger is normal, and it is ok."

"Yeah, the seven stages of grief and all that," Megan replies, flapping a hand in the air.

"It's five stages, but yes. Anger is one of them."

Of course she needs to correct me. Know it all.

Hannah continues. "It's the second stage, after denial. You've been denying since we started our sessions together. Ready or not, you are finally moving forward."

Megan's body slouches down, drained from the emotional toll her outburst had taken on her. She looks back at the ocean photo, daydreaming about running off to the beach, far away and basking in the sun, forgetting the mess she'd left behind. "Is there any way we can just skip ahead to the acceptance part and be done with it? I'm so tired."

"I'm afraid not. The five stages aren't a race. There are no shortcuts, Megan. They are a natural human progression through grief. With your permission, I'd like to offer a suggestion."

Megan furrows her brow and pinches her lips together as she looks at Hannah.

"I'd like for you to take a day trip. Many people find as they dig deeper into their therapy, a change of scenery can be beneficial. Both in relaxing their physical tension and clearing their minds, creating the space needed to process everything they've been uncovering. It can be a small trip to a nearby park or something further if you wish."

Megan scrunches up her nose.

"Consider it a homework assignment for next time." Hannah scribbles something in her notepad before looking back up at Megan.

Megan drops her head onto the back of the couch and closes her eyes. Just as her head hits the backrest, it ricochets back up, her eyes wide and glowing. Her mouth stretches into a tight smile. "Actually, that's a great idea."

Hannah looks surprised at the rather quick attitude change. But as always, her face betrays very little. "Wonderful. Do you have a place in mind already?"

"I do. Las Vegas." Not wanting to reveal her actual motive for going to her therapist, Megan adds, "I can let the city that apparently meant a lot to my father speak to me too. Maybe it will tell me something I don't already know."

Hannah frowns and then quickly rearranges it back to its neutral position, but not before Megan catches a glimpse. "Megan... that's not what I intended with this homework assignment. The idea is to put yourself in a cheerful space. Not directly in the middle of the experience which brought you to me in the first place. The idea is not to intensify the trauma you are working through."

"No, I've never been to Las Vegas. The lights, the shows, the food. People seem to love it and it's not too far. I think this is really going to help." Megan stands to her feet, grabbing her purse and starts inching towards the door before Hannah can argue. "Thanks again! Great idea. See you next time."

Megan takes a couple of strides backwards, waving goodbye, then turns to let herself out, closing the door on Hannah as she is speaking.

"Megan, you shouldn't..."

CHAPTER 29

When Megan arrives back at her apartment, she writes a list of things to do before she leaves tomorrow.

Pack a bag.
Book a motel room.
Let Josh and Katie know where I am going.
Bow out of family dinner tomorrow night.
See if any decent shows are playing in Las Vegas (since I'm already there…)

She's done the math and even if she leaves first thing tomorrow morning, she won't arrive in Vegas until early evening. If she were to turn around and drive home immediately, she wouldn't get home until four in the morning the next day. Unrealistic considering she needs to visit a few places while she's there, so she'll need a place to stay the night.

Megan pours herself a cup of coffee and sits down at her laptop, searching for an affordable place to stay for one night since her bereavement leave only pays her for five days off. Her boss encouraged her to take at least two weeks, but anything beyond that will use her vacation stockpile if she wants to be compensated. She checks a couple handfuls of options based on location, rating and price, before settling on The Pink Flamingo Motel, rated highly for its cleanliness, staff responsiveness and well-lit property.

She enters her credit card information and completes her reservation before doing a quick search to see what concerts or shows have tickets available.

Chumbawamba? Who even knew they still existed?

Megan isn't interested in seeing them get knocked down or get back up again, so she heads to her room to make some phone calls while she packs.

She dials Katie first, knowing the chances of her picking up right now are slim since she is at work. Katie never listens to voicemails, opting instead to just return the call and force the person to relay their message twice, so Megan sends a quick text letting her know it's nothing urgent and can she call when she's off work.

Next, she tries Josh, but again, no answer. So, she moves down her list to her mom. No answer.

Well, thank God this isn't an emergency…

Megan tries her brother, who finally picks up. "Smalls! Finally. I was beginning to wonder what a girl's got to do to get someone to answer her call."

"Well, it is Thursday afternoon, sis. A lot of people are working."

Megan hears the clinking sounds of metal on metal through the phone. "Oh right, of course. You must be at work, too. Why are you answering the phone?"

"I'm in the back working on the T-bird I was telling you about. Anyway, I thought it might be an emergency. It's not, is it?" Jonathan's voice is muffled off and on, like he's using his shoulder to hold the phone up to his cheek.

"No. Not an emergency. I was just trying to get a hold of mom to let her know I can't come to family dinner tomorrow, so I'll have to catch her next time. If she doesn't call me back, can you apologize to her for me? Maybe make up some excuse?"

"Yeah, I can. But why aren't you coming tomorrow?"

Megan sits down on the edge of her bed and props her elbows on her knees. She doesn't want to tell Smalls the truth. She doesn't want to lie to him either. "I got a homework assignment from my therapist to take a quick trip somewhere to clear my head."

"Oh, actually, that sounds kind of cool. I mean, if you have to do homework. So, where are you headed?"

Megan closes her eyes and sucks in a breath. "Las Vegas."

"Las Vegas? What are you doing, Megs?" Smalls' voice is getting pitchy, his words quickening.

"I'm just going to check out a few things. See if being there will give me some closure."

"Check what things out?"

Megan can't decide how much of the truth to share. "There are some people Dad was working with, and they might be able to tell me about him. I feel like I need to check on Dan. Something isn't right with him."

She hears her brother sigh on the other end of the line. "This is so incredibly stupid." Megan can tell he's talking through gritted teeth. "Megs, don't do this. Don't go out there alone. Have you told Josh about this?"

Megan is pacing around her apartment now, as she does when she's getting worked up. It gives her something else to focus on. "Josh is not my keeper! And who are you to tell me if this is a good idea or not?"

"Are you listening to yourself? You want to go hunt down men that our upstanding father was mixed up with? Alone. Ten hours away. Am I hearing you correctly?" Jonathan doesn't even try to hide the sarcasm and arrogance in his words. "This is insane. This sounds dangerous, and I'll bet Josh would agree with me."

When Megan didn't respond, he continues. "Megs, I'm worried about you. You are falling so far down into this hole you created for yourself. What is it going to take for you to see that?"

Megan falls onto the couch. The adrenaline has faded, and her body feels too heavy. "Smalls, I need to do this. I feel like it's my last shot at the truth. I'm going and I just wanted to let you know I won't make it to dinner tomorrow night."

"Shit… fine. Will you at least check in, so I'm not worried you've gone missing? Please." He adds one final dig before letting her go. "This is a horrible idea."

"I leave tomorrow morning and I will check in with you. I'll only be gone for one night. Don't worry. But have mom call me if you can and tell her next week for sure, in case I don't get to talk to her."

"I will. Be safe, Megs."

"I promise."

Megan hangs up the phone and tosses it to the far end of the couch, suddenly needing a nap. She also needs to put on some SWAT gear for when Josh barges into her apartment after she tells him what she's doing.

She settles on a compromise, finishing her cup of coffee and then closing her eyes for a twenty-minute *caff-nap* while the caffeine kicks in. She read somewhere that corporate employees working long hours do this to increase productivity.

When her alarm goes off, she grabs her phone and dials Josh's number again before she can talk herself out of it, while her brother's words are still ringing in her ear.

This is a horrible idea. Please. Don't do this.

CHAPTER 30

FRIDAY, SEPTEMBER 18TH

Megan buckles her seatbelt and double checks she has both a giant tumbler of coffee and her bag. She feels every minute of the sleep she didn't get after having the same argument three times last night with Smalls, Katie and finally Josh. Josh had tried to come over, but Megan stopped him by explaining that if he came over, she would inevitably be too tired from arguing with him to drive safely this morning.

Katie's had been the conversation Megan was most afraid of. She was terrified Katie would think she was going rogue again. On the phone, however, Megan noticed Katie sounded equally nervous, maybe worried Megan would find her unsupportive. It breaks Megan's heart that their bond is so fragile right now, but with Katie speaking to her now, she knows time will solidify them again.

They all agreed Megan will keep them in the loop at every opportunity. Josh threatened to send police units to pull her out again. This is only the second time he's used that threat, and Megan has already grown tired of it. But she knows it's the best he's got, and a piece of her feels safer at the promise of his protection.

Megan informs everyone of her departure before opening her copy of the police report. She soaks in the photos of the parking garage, memorizing again each detail. She sets the folder down on the passenger seat and plugs in the location of her first destination.

The parking garage for the Viva Las Vegas Wedding Chapel.

It's just after 5:00pm when Megan pulls into the parking garage. Four levels of concrete building sit directly ahead of her, but she's frozen at the entrance, intensely aware that despite her destination sitting in front of her, she still has a little further to go.

A driver honks their horn behind her, impatient to enter the garage. She jolts forward, though she isn't quite ready. But then again, she realizes, she'll never feel completely ready.

She pulls into the garage and begins the ascent to the top level. There are a few cars on each floor, but as she climbs to the top, it's as if she's transported somewhere else entirely.

The top level is deserted, and unease settles into her chest. She parks by the entrance to the floor, near the car ramp, and turns off the ignition. Her awareness of her surroundings heightens as she assesses the area before leaving the relative safety of her car.

The parking garage is small. It's made of nothing but concrete, and the pale grey color reminds her of death. There are four rows in which cars can park and spaces for perhaps fifteen cars in each row. The top floor is open, enclosed on the sides by a short concrete retaining wall. Across the way, she sees an entrance to an elevator. A small section of wall juts out next to it with a sign indicating the stairs are located behind it. A weak overhead light flickers on and off.

She pulls out her phone, unwilling to break her promise to the three people waiting to hear from her, and sends a text to each confirming her safe arrival. Immediately after she taps the send button, a phone dings. It's the same sound hers makes when she receives a text message. She checks her phone. Nothing. She'd left her window cracked and decides it must have been someone's phone on the level below her and perhaps the sound carried up the garage.

Megan looks around to confirm once more that she is alone and then refers back to the police photos, locating the spot where her dad had last stood alive.

When she gets out of her car, the air is sucked from her lungs like a punch to the gut. While the lot felt small before from inside her car, the openness of the top floor is suddenly vast and endless, leaving her completely exposed. And utterly alone.

A feeling of hopelessness swirls around her and she wonders if the city itself creates it, stealing the life from its visitors. Or do the visitors bring it with them, binding their sorrow to the city forever when they leave Las Vegas behind? The air feels murky, and she wades through as it veils her in despair.

One foot in front of the other.

It occurs to her that the sound of a gunshot would be lost up here, floating up into the sky, drowned out by the noise of the city below.

She wonders how many souls met their end here, like her dad, and now haunt the space they last inhabited.

Maybe others can feel it too. Maybe it's why this floor is desolate.

She's close now. Just a few more steps.

Though she isn't aware of crossing the last few feet, Megan finds herself standing just across the aisle from the space where it happened. The exact spot where Mark died, leaving a permanent blemish on Megan's world.

She sits down on the parking curb of the space she stands in, staring at the parking spot directly across from her. The ground where it happened has a dark stain on it. She tells herself it's dirt. Wear and tear from car tires pulling in and out of that parking space. Someone spilled a sticky drink. A soda maybe. It could be true, and it feels a hell of a lot easier than wondering if it was stained by blood just weeks ago.

She knows from the police photos her dad's car was parked two spaces to the right of where his body was found. He was near the wall, facing it like he was looking at the cityscape. His body had crumpled in a way that suggested he dropped to his knees before pulling the trigger.

Megan stares, her eyes glassy. She wraps her arms around her knees and waits. For what, she isn't certain. It's as though she expects the city itself to speak to her. To whisper the truth of what happened that night. Now that she's here, she isn't sure she really wants to know.

The air shifts and a chill races down the length of Megan's spine. Tingles on her forearms make the tiny hairs stand at attention. Megan springs to her feet at the sudden feeling she's being watched.

She looks around, assessing her surroundings, cursing herself for trusting the solitude and leaving her purse containing her pepper spray in the car.

There's nowhere for a person to hide on this floor. It's completely open, with no extra structures to hide behind. Unless someone slipped in by her parked car when she wasn't looking.

She stays where she is, a good distance away from where she parked and steps to the left and then the right, checking for a person crouched by her car. When no one appears, she drops to the ground to check underneath the car for a pair of feet. Nothing.

She staggers slowly to her car, doing exactly what Josh taught her to do. Though she's confident no one could have gotten into her car without her notice, she approaches the side of the vehicle and looks down into the window, looking for anyone who may be laying down on the seats or the floor.

The car is empty, but her heart is still banging against the back of her ribs.

She gets in the car and locks the doors while she reaches for her purse. She puts the police report in the glove box and locks it, as she thinks about how she wants to proceed.

Her next stop is The Grand Oasis Casino to do some reconnaissance on Dan, as if she knows how to do reconnaissance. Maybe she'll work up the courage to talk to him.

The casino is only one block away. It seems ridiculous to drive over there, but her pulse hasn't steadied and she's on edge. She imagines the path her dad might have walked from the casino to this garage at some point and decides she will walk, but she will be smart about it.

She will not go into the elevator alone, and she will not walk all the way across the lot to take the stairs alone. She can hear the conversations of people on the floor below her, so she will walk down the ramp to the third level and then mingle in with the others leaving the garage.

She loops her purse over her shoulder and palms the canister of mace, spinning the trigger so it's ready to be fired. She steps out of the car and closes the door behind her.

As she turns to leave, there's a flash of movement by the stairwell. Someone turning to go down the stairs. She only sees a portion of the figure from behind, but they were tall, the top of their head hunched over like they were ducking down. It's hard to tell, but she thinks they were wearing a hood or had dark-colored hair, and a long sleeve in a dark color. Like a faded shade of black. Then again, it isn't well lit over there.

Her flight response kicks in, and she turns to run down the ramp and into the safety of a crowd. When she gets down to the next level, she looks across the way, hoping to spot the person who had been lurking on the top floor. Megan imagines a handful of innocent reasons a person might have popped up to the top floor. A drunk person looking for their car in the wrong place. A couple sneaking up for the thrill of a technically public display of affection. Or someone like her dad.

As she stalks across to the elevator with a group of people, she can't find a single person who fits the description in her mind. Neither can she shake the feeling of being followed.

CHAPTER 31

As Megan leaves the garage, she squints against the combination of the strip lights glowing and the setting sun pointed directly at her. In the time she was sitting in the garage, the sky has grown darker, and Las Vegas' nightly transformation is underway.

People surround her as she wanders down the block, glancing over her shoulder every few steps.

The entrance to The Grand Oasis finally appears in front of her. The building towers over its neighbors, gold embellishments adorn the entrance. Rows of huge, live palm trees line the walkway to the automatic double doors at the entrance. She walks through to find a second set of automatic doors that open into the casino floor, but not before passing a man dressed like a Tommy Bahama model holding a sign which beckons her to "Take off your shoes. Stay a while." *Clever sign. Ridiculous job.*

She steps through the doors and gets pummeled by flashing lights. Her ears are hit by a wall of noise. The chimes of machines declaring their winners, dealers calling for patrons to place their bets, the cheers of crowds gathered around the felt tables, and the collective groan of the losers.

Megan presses forward, taking in all the colors and décor while keeping her eyes open for Dan.

To her right is a row of cashiers standing in tiny cages, taking people's money and exchanging it for chips. She wanders deeper into the casino. Along the back wall is a row of shops, and as she passes the windows, she notes the brand names and exorbitant price tags. She passes the shoe store Josh told her about and wonders how many people here could afford to be gambling and purchasing such high-end items. She supposes that must be exactly the temptation that causes you to gamble your own shoes.

She meanders through the middle of the large floor, passing by the tables, looking at the different games being played.

She passes by the famous glass and gold bar. It is a stunning sight. It somehow fits the tropical décor perfectly, but also stands out. She wonders what it cost to build such an extravagance.

As she approaches the far side of the casino, she stops abruptly, spotting a man standing across the way in front of a set of solid black double doors with no windows in them.

Dan.

He's whispering in the ear of one of two men who look every bit the security detail they must be. They stand perfectly still and attentive, one in front of each door. Their presence is large and looming. Dan looks out over the floor, surveying the scene. His hands are clasped together in front of him, his arms framing a round belly that pokes out just enough to create a tiny dome under his shirt. When he disappears back through the doors, the two men move closer together, standing guard outside.

Suddenly, Megan is struck from behind as a man drunkenly stumbles into her, sending her crashing to the floor. He slurs something that sounds possibly like an apology as a different arm reaches out, helping her to her feet.

A gruff voice is attached to the hand that pulls her upright. "That's enough for you tonight, Paulie. Go home. You can settle up tomorrow." The voice is calm, but firm, appearing to let Paulie know he won't tolerate any argument on the matter. Paulie wobbles towards the door and down the street.

Megan steadies herself and turns to thank the man who helped her, but her voice catches. The man still holding her arm looms over her, well over six feet tall, with shoulders twice as wide as Megan from end to end. He's wearing a long sleeve slate button down, tucked neatly into pleated black slacks, both of which look to be tailored to his frame. On top of his head is a layer of soft dark curls with product raked through them, helping them to lie down neatly. She knows his face. She's been memorizing it for weeks.

"Hello, Megan." He smiles kindly at her. His teeth are off white and lined up neatly until their order is interrupted by a single gold tooth.

Megan wants to run, but her feet feel like they're stuck in a vat of quicksand. She opens her mouth, but no words come out.

"Follow me." It's an order, not an invitation. Megan is afraid to go with him, but she's more afraid not to.

They plod over toward the same doors that swallowed up Dan, and the bouncers part at their approach. No questions asked. Once inside, a long brick hallway lies in front of them, with several doors along either side. The doors are all solid, painted black, with no markers of any kind showing a room number or what might be behind them. The only distinguishing features on the doors are three separate locks and a peephole in each one.

The hallway ends at a set of decorative mahogany double doors with ornate designs carved into the wood. Megan looks up. A tiny camera is mounted in each corner above the doors. She turns around and notices cameras above every other door in the hallway. No one could sneak through these rooms unnoticed.

A voice calls out from inside. "Come in."

The man with the gold tooth holds the doors open for Megan and she steps inside as he herds her deeper into the room.

Dan sits in an oversized tufted brown leather chair, behind a large wooden desk, light bouncing off the glossy finish. He extends a hand, offering Megan a seat opposite him. "I won't bite. Please, sit."

She looks back at the man hovering over her and then takes a seat in the chair furthest from him. The entire room smells of freshly cut wood, with a waft of smokiness floating through it. Megan turns to see a small fireplace on the far side of the room.

"How are you doing, kiddo?" Dan's eyes sparkle, the way they always do, but Megan bristles at the familiar greeting. It no longer feels endearing.

Her eyes narrow, challenging Dan. "How do you think I'm doing?"

He leans back in his chair, ignoring her cockiness. As he raises his arms to cradle his head in them, she hears the crinkle of the leather as it strains under his new position. "I see you've met my associate, Jeffrey Payne. We've been expecting you."

Megan looks at Jeffrey, sizing him up. "I know who you are."

He tips his head towards her courteously. "You can call me JP. All my friends do."

Megan notes his friendly tone, wary of it. "It would be a mistake to think I'm stupid. We aren't friends." JP's mouth ticks downward, like he's suppressing a smile. Megan looks to her right where rows and rows of TVs are lined up, showing every angle of the casino outside the solid black doors.

"How did you know I was coming?" Megan asks turning back to look at Dan.

"Hannah called me when you left her office yesterday." Dan watches her as confusion settles over Megan's face. He explains further, as if she were a small child. "Annie told you a friend gave her the referral."

"You were that friend."

"Hannah and I go way back. We just wanted to be sure you're ok. She's very good at her job." Dan answers, as if it were perfectly reasonable.

"You mean you wanted to keep tabs on me." Her instincts had been right from the start. Dan and Annie had been trying to hide all this from her, making sure she didn't learn too much. "I hope she's ready to retire because when I get back, I'm going to make damn sure she never practices again, having violated my patient therapist privilege. What we discuss is confidential."

"She's obligated to report when she suspects you to be a danger to yourself or others."

"Not to you."

A dark look flashes across Dan's face. "Oh, I assure you, she is very much obligated to me."

Forgetting herself, she jumps up and starts yelling. "How dare you! You had your big stupid goon following me around since I got here? Trying to scare me into going away and forgetting you killed my dad! It was you!"

Dan's eyes blaze, and his voice freezes over like a thick sheet of ice. "Lower your voice, Megan. Sit down." His words sear through her.

Megan realizes her mistake instantly as Josh's warning screams inside of her head. She's known Dan for most of her life. But suddenly, she's a girl nosing around, trying to expose the people who murdered her father. She cannot underestimate their ruthlessness. If they had anything to do with Mark's death, they probably won't have any issue making sure she stays quiet as well.

She sinks back down into her chair and crosses her arms over her chest like a petulant child. It's all the protection she has right now.

"I didn't kill Mark. I would never do that, Megs."

Megan watches as Dan's eyes dart from her to JP, as if exchanging some secret knowledge with him. Dan reaches into a cigar box sitting on the side of his desk and pulls out a cigar. She watches as he lights it, puffing out the old smoke until he's ready to take in a mouthful.

She can't take it anymore. Megan keeps her voice low as she reprimands them, daring them to show her what they are capable of. She throws what she knows at them like daggers, trying to draw them out. "Then you had someone else do it. Same difference. I know you did. I just don't know why. He was your friend. He dirtied his hands so you could keep yours clean. You were both in his wedding, for God's sake." Megan looks back and forth between them. "How could you?"

Megan closes her eyes, fighting so hard not to cry. But the tears leak out against her will, betraying her. She furiously pushes them aside with the backs of her hands, sets her lips in a tight, thin line and forces herself to look at Dan, goading him to deny it.

He leans forward, resting his forearms on his desk, one hand neatly stacked on top of the another still holding his cigar. Megan can see the wheels turning behind his eyes, calculating. Fabricating a lie to placate her, or determining how much of the truth to give her? She isn't sure. She braces herself, the way Hannah would, and resolves to let Dan break the silence first.

"Ok, Megs. The truth. Yes, your dad worked for me. It was a good setup, mutually beneficial. He came to me years ago needing money for child support. So, I gave him a job to do. A trial run. He handled his business so well." Dan looks off somewhere else, his face shimmering with admiration. "Above and beyond, really. He asked for more work, and I was happy to give it to him."

JP brings over a crystal tumbler with brown liquor in it. Dan sets his cigar down in a crystal ashtray and takes a drink before continuing. Megan looks over his shoulder at the picture frames on the wall. Each frame displays a photo of the casino at various stages of building over the years or a framed article of praise for The Grand Oasis. All but one. One photo is smaller than the rest. Inside the gold frame is a copy of Mark and Annie's wedding photo. She scans the faces, knowing each of them by name now. They all look so happy. Especially her dad. You'd never know from this picture how much cruelty lurked behind the faces.

"A couple of years after Mark married Annie, he wanted out. He told me he didn't like who he was turning into. You need to understand something, Megan. Your dad was excellent at his job, but he was never made for it. His heart wasn't in it. I brought him in and sat him down. Right where you're sitting." Dan nods to Megan's chair and Megan shifts uncomfortably. "I explained to him I wanted to let him go, but it was impossible. You don't just walk away from this business. There's too much trust on the line. But unstable people are challenging to manage. People who want out are a liability, Megs. But I loved your dad. He was one of my best friends. I'd never kill him."

Dan reaches into his pocket. Megan sits up nervously. He holds up the other hand, declaring peace, while his wallet appears in the other. He opens it up and pulls out a black poker chip and pushes it across the desk towards Megan.

Megan reaches for the chip, seeing what it is before she picks it up. Stamped on one side, in gold lettering, are Mark and Annie's names and their wedding year. Written around the edges is the name of the chapel, the Viva Las Vegas Wedding Chapel. She turns the chip over and traces her finger over the initials.

DW. Dan Walker.

"I'd never kill your dad, Megs." His eyes are sincere, but Megan can't let herself trust him. "I reassigned him. Partnered him with Payne," he says gesturing to JP with a nod of his head, "and they worked in tandem. In fact, I have you to thank for that, don't I?" Dan's smile twists.

"What are you talking about?" Megan's face feels hot and sweat begins to bead on her upper lip.

"You sent him crawling back to me. That last night. You two had a horrible fight. You said some very mean things." He wags a finger at her. "Didn't you, Megan?" Dan's words slither out of his mouth, like a snake coiling around Megan's neck. Her mind jumps back to that night involuntarily. She sees herself standing in the driveway. Her words infused with as much venom as she could muster.

"Smalls had it right, didn't he, Dad? He was only five, and he knew to leave you even then. That you'd never be good enough. He was smarter than all of us."

Megan watched her father's face change from hurt to anger to resolve. She stood her ground as he returned fire.

"Go home, Megan." She didn't move. "Go! Get the hell out of here!" He took a step forward and Megan stepped back, afraid of what might come next. She turned on her heels and ran to her car, her dad's voice booming behind her. "I don't want to see you here ever again! Do you hear me? Don't ever come back here!"

She slammed her car door and sped off. That was the last time she listened to her father.

Megan's eyes glisten with pain. The weight of her guilt crushes her until she nearly disappears inside herself. She drags herself back up to the surface when she hears Dan still talking.

"When Mark told me what happened, I knew I could still use him. Mark kept working and Payne stepped in when Mark couldn't. I kept a pair of eyes on him, but that was the end of it." Dan relaxes back into his chair, taking a puff of his cigar.

Megan wants to believe it was that simple. That her dad endured years of emotional torment and violence until one day, he couldn't bear it anymore. But Josh had warned her about men like this. Even the closest of friends wound up dead when they betrayed the organization. She doesn't trust Dan as far as she can throw him.

"I don't believe you."

Dan smiles at Megan's defiance and lets out a tut as he shakes his head. "You know, Mark thought he was protecting you when he pushed you away. But look at you, Megs, here in the thick of it anyway. Like father, like daughter. Throwing your life away like it's nothing."

Mark's words bounce around in Megan's brain alongside images of his coded dates.

There's not much time left.

"Like father, like daughter." Megan agrees. "Fortunately for me, you're absolutely right." Megan pushes a lock of ash blonde hair behind her ear and looks up. "I'm willing to wager you aren't aware of the meticulous records my dad kept regarding his various… *jobs*. You wouldn't be, since they were coded so well. But one of us figured it out and I'll give you a hint; it isn't you." Megan snarls at Dan, egging him on as they stare each other down. "I know exactly who you are, and I have the records to prove it. So, why don't you grow up and take some responsibility for what we both know really happened so we can stop dancing around it? Or are you afraid, like you were too afraid to kill my dad yourself."

Dan's eyes narrow until they are barely slits and he nods once at JP, apparently indicating he desires some privacy. "Go make the rounds."

JP turns on his heel with no argument and Megan watches him leave. When the door closes, the temperature drops. Megan is frighteningly aware that she's alone with Dan, and the nearest person to her is the bouncer outside the door to the casino who would never be able to hear her scream. Hell, he'd probably look the other way anyhow.

She turns back to find Dan already looking at her. "You're a smart girl, Megs. You always have been. But before you go and do something rash, you need to think about who else is at stake here."

"What do you mean?"

"Save it! I know you've been poking around my business with Josh. It stops right now." Dan jams a finger into the top of his desk.

Megan feels the seriousness of the implicit threat. Dan may have left it unspoken, but it feels anything but hollow. "I just want to know the truth about my dad…"

Dan cuts her off. "Cut the shit, Megs. Josh has been tracking me for years now. Making friends on the force while he was still in the academy, snooping around my case files. I like the boy, I always have. But this chip he's been carrying is going to get him killed if he doesn't stop. *You* are going to get him killed."

His words catch Megan off guard, hitting her in the chest. "What are you talking about? I only just asked him to look into you last week."

Dan throws his head back and laughs, his voice squealing in sick delight. "He didn't tell you. Oh god, you really didn't know?" His voice is breathy as he pushes the words out between chuckles.

He swivels his chair to the side and unlocks one of the desk drawers. Rifling through some folders, he carefully pulls out a plain manilla file and tosses it to Megan's side of the desk. "Megs, be careful around that boy." He narrows his eyes at her, shaking his head. "Looks like you and I aren't the only ones who've been keeping secrets." His twisted smile is still glued in place.

He pokes at her like a predator toying with its prey. His finger jabs her wounds to see how much more she'll bleed.

Pulse racing, bile rising in the back of her throat, Megan slowly opens the file. She flips through the documents, finding time-stamped photos of Josh at the casino last year, transcriptions of phone calls in which Officer Josh Pierce requested information about Dan and a copy of what looks to be a police report filed against Payne.

Megan's face sinks and despite of being surrounded by lights, the room grows darker around her.

"You're lying. Josh would have told me if he already knew everything about you."

Megan wants to run, but she finds herself stuck in the chair.

"Open your eyes, kiddo. The proof is there in front of you. You need to be careful with that one. Josh has been carrying a grudge against Mark since he was a teenager. And a man with a grudge is a dangerous man indeed."

Megan shakes her head, vehemently rejecting the words she can't unhear. She can feel the tide of the conversation shifting. "No. I don't believe you. What would he be holding a grudge for?"

Megan's mind ricochets back and forth in her memories, flashing pictures behind her eyes of the times Mark and Josh would argue only to quiet when she appeared. Of each moment that led to Josh coming over less frequently.

"I think you know the answer already." When Megan doesn't respond, he leans back in his chair again and cradles his head in his hands once more, like he couldn't possibly be more relaxed. "That boy has been carrying a torch for you his entire life. But your dad made one thing clear to him several times. He wasn't good enough for you. Mark saw the road Josh was traveling down and he'd be damned if he was going to let Josh take you with him."

Dan sits forward, resting his forearms on the desk, clasping his hands together as he leans closer to Megan. "Josh was creeping around, and he followed Mark out to a job one night. Josh wanted in, thinking if he proved himself to Mark, then Mark would sign off on Josh dating you. He tried so hard until Mark told him to stay the hell away from him, and from you. Josh finally screwed his head on straight after that and stayed out of Mark's crosshairs. But he's nothing if not persistent." Dan leans a little closer to Megan, dropping his voice down low. "Did he stay away from you after that?"

Dan already knows the answer, but Megan whispers involuntarily anyway. "No."

Dan shakes his head, smiling. "Ah, young love. The heart wants what it wants." He sneers with satisfaction.

Megan stands up, shoving the chair backwards until it nearly tips over. Dan won't get any more from her tonight. "Josh isn't a murderer. My dad tried to help him, he took him in. He wouldn't do that to my dad. He wouldn't do that to me." Megan won't admit Dan's suggestion is under her skin now, making it crawl, but she says the words like they are fact. She almost convinces herself.

"I wouldn't count him out. Officer Pierce would do anything for you. Probably anything to be with you. People have killed for a lot less, Megs. Believe me."

If Megan wasn't sure what the face of evil looked like before, she is now. Her heart is thumping wildly, she can hear her pulse behind her ears. Dan planted a new and devastating seed in her brain. She knows Dan can't be trusted. But Megan also can't discount the notion that maybe some fragments of truth are hidden in his words, and he'd twisted them into something more sinister.

Dan presses the intercom on the phone sitting on his desk. Jeffrey Payne reappears in the doorway. "Payne, see to it Megan returns safely to her car." Dan stands and turns to Megan. "Take care of yourself, kiddo. And be careful who you trust." Megan cranes her head around to watch him, and he winks at her just before the doors latch shut behind her.

Megan walks for a while in silence. They are nearly at the parking garage when Payne speaks, catching Megan by surprise.

"There's something you should know about Dan."

Megan's ears perk up and she drags her eyes away from the ground to steal a glance at Payne, who isn't looking at her.

"Look straight ahead," he instructs. "Dan is a very dangerous man. It's true he and Mark were close. But when Mark told him he wanted out, it changed everything."

"How?" Megan can feel how important this conversation is. Payne's size is terrifying, and she hasn't forgotten some of the vicious things he's done. But Megan suspects he's the only person who might tell her the truth.

Payne's posture is rigid and unyielding. He keeps walking with the same air of authority he's had since he picked her up in the casino, but his words are softer now. "Dan didn't just have a chat with Mark and then everything was fine. These things are never that simple. Dan was never going to let Mark go. Men like him have ways of... forcing your hand." He glances around, scanning their surroundings continuously, though a passerby would likely assume he's taking in the sights.

Megan's hands start shaking. It's a warm night, but she folds her shaking hands across her chest and rubs them up and down the goosebumps on her arms, chilled to the bone.

"Dan devised a plan. He got Annie to agree to it. Together, they made it look like Mark was physically abusing Annie. Dan beat the hell out of Annie one night and they took pictures of it. Dan brought the photos to Mark and told him they would destroy him if he ever talked about getting out ever again. They held those pictures over his head for years."

"But why would Annie ever agree to that?"

"Annie and Dan have been masterminding, coming up with different schemes since they were kids. She helped recruit your dad. She has her own side prescription business too. Dan blamed her for bringing in someone weak, so she paid for it. But her compliance in these photos made it up to him. Proved her loyalty. Dan took it too far that night, if you ask me. I didn't want any part of it. But Annie probably had some great meds to help her through it."

Megan feels drunk though she is stone cold sober. Her brain bobs around in her skull like she's swimming underwater and her body feels like jelly.

"Why are you telling me all of this?"

Payne stops and looks around before finally looking down at her. They've made it to the top of the stairs in the parking garage. "Because I worked with your dad for years. I trusted him with my life and I knew who he was. And I know what it feels like to be set up. To sit back while people lie about you. Knowing there's no way out."

Megan remembers what Josh told her about Jeffrey Payne and the way the military buried the truth about his rape charges. How it destroyed him.

Megan considers everything he's just told her. "Why do you stay? Why are you still helping them?"

His brows pinches together, and the corners of his eyes crinkle. "There's nothing else for me to do. It's too late now. Mark got soft, letting customers slide here and there. Look what happened to him. He wanted to get out." Payne pauses and his eyes flick down. "And in the end, I guess he did."

Payne's eyes close for a second as if blinking away some regret. "We've all done things we didn't want to. God knows I have." Megan isn't sure which things he's referring to, but it sounds like a confession.

Payne turns and looks Megan right in the eye. "But you should know your dad loved you. He kept a picture of you and your bother in his pocket. I'm sorry, kid. I'm sorry it ended up this way."

Megan nods, acknowledging the kindness he's just given her, but she's unable to thank him. She turns to walk across the parking lot to her car and glances over his shoulder to see Payne walking towards the stairwell. She opens the door to her car and slides into the front seat. Payne is gone.

She waits for a moment, trying to steady herself. She remembers to send a quick text to the people waiting to hear from her and gives the parking garage one last look before she leaves.

She stares out through her windshield at the space in front of her and whispers, "Goodbye Dad".

The sad, small area of pavement ahead of her was the last thing in the world to feel her father alive. To hear the sound of his breath, to see the curves and angles of his face. She isn't sure which is more heartbreaking. That, or the man he turned out to be.

Just as she is about to turn the key in the ignition and pull away, something catches her eye. Tucked away behind the wheel stop of the space where her father died is a small piece of what looks to be black plastic. It would have been hidden from view from where she sat earlier. She can't see what it is, and her curiosity gets the best of her. She looks around to ensure she's still alone before getting out of her car.

She walks over to retrieve it. The eerie silence wraps itself around her, squeezing until it's hard for her to breathe. She feels a pair of eyes on

244 | MARISSA VANSKIKE

her that she can't see. As she approaches the wheel stop, her eyes connect with the trinket. A gasp escapes her mouth, and her hand flies up to stuff it back inside.

She picks it up delicately, as if it may crumble in her hands. Her eyes drink in the details.

A small, black custom poker chip. "Mark and Annie '96" is stamped in shiny gold lettering right in the center of the chip. The edges display the Viva Las Vegas Wedding Chapel name.

How is this here? Is it possible the police missed this? Did they think it was an ordinary chip and ignored it?

Her hand tremors so violently she nearly drops it. The chip feels like it weighs one hundred pounds. She knows she has to turn the chip over to see the initials printed on the backside and she is terrified.

She closes her eyes and flips the chip over in her palm. She counts to three in her head before opening her eyes to look down.

A scream catches in her throat, and she's grateful it hasn't escaped. She whips her head around, checking that the stairwell is still empty and then sprints to her car as fast as her legs will carry her. She throws herself into the seat and slams the lock on the door. Her tires screech as she spins the car around to leave, narrowly missing a traffic cone outside the garage that wasn't there when she arrived.

Once she is outside the city limits, she pulls over to catch her breath. It's late, but she knows she won't be able to fall asleep if she goes back to her motel room. She decides instead to load up on energy drinks and snacks from the gas station and drive all night. She just wants to go home.

She sends another message to Josh, Katie and Smalls and waits for the inevitable return messages demanding she think twice before driving all night.

Outgoing text message from Megan Palmer (8:17pm):
I can't be here tonight. I'll explain later, but I swear to you I will pull over if I get tired. I'll let you know when I'm home.

She copies the message and pastes it in each of the text windows. Her mind races After finding directions to the nearest gas station, Megan pulls the chip out of her pocket and into her hand, checking it again to see if her eyes had deceived her.

The chip hasn't changed. The initials burn into her eyes.

J.P.

CHAPTER 32

Megan pulls her shades closed and pours herself into her bed, fully clothed, just after 7:00am the next morning once she's made the mandatory check-ins. It occurs to her it's somewhat miraculous she made it home in one piece. Not just because she's been awake for twenty-four hours, but because of how difficult it was to focus on the road for over ten hours with her head spinning in endless circles trying to process everything that just happened.

In all the time she spent sifting through the new information, the lies, the threats, the stories, she still hasn't figured out where to begin untangling the web she walked into.

And she hasn't yet decided what to do with the poker chip.

Is it proof enough to confirm her suspicion? If she told Josh about Payne and his confession, it could send Josh spiraling, chasing after some very dangerous men.

And then, of course, there's Josh. If any part of what Dan said is true, then Josh has been lying to Megan since they were sixteen. And if Josh can keep his feelings and what he's been looking into hidden from her all this time, what else might he be capable of?

Megan eventually drifts off to sleep. She wakes to her stomach rumbling painfully, making her aware of how long it has been since she ate anything other than Quick-e-Mart snacks. The clock on her nightstand tells her it's dinnertime.

She rolls out of bed, stumbling to the bathroom. When she comes back, her phone is buzzing wildly on her side table.

She sees Josh on the screen and accepts the call.

"Hey, Josh. What's up?" Megan feels like her voice sounds odd, but she can't remember what she normally sounds like.

"What's up? Megan, you've been MIA all day after you said you made it home! It's been thirteen hours since any of us heard from you. We are worried sick." Josh sounds more concerned than angry.

"Sorry. I didn't mean to sleep for so long. I'm just... drained. And starving."

"I'm coming over. I'll bring pizza." Before Megan can get a word in, he stops her. "Don't argue with me."

She smiles weakly. "See you soon."

She hangs up the phone, hopeful that seeing Josh in person will prove he is the man she knows. That he's not the man Dan spat at her.

Megan types out some texts to Katie and Smalls, letting them know she is alive, and that Josh is bringing her food. She'll call them later. Then she heads to her master bathroom to take a long shower and wash off the layer of filth Las Vegas left her coated in. She hears a knock at her door just as she's slipping into some heather grey jogger sweatpants and a fitted white tank top. She can't help her smile when she slips her hands into her pockets. *Rich man sweatpants.*

Seeing Josh standing there is like breathing in fresh air. She hugs him and he sits there, one arm wrapped around her back letting her pull away first. He walks in, closes the door behind him, and sets the pizza down on the coffee table. He hands her one of the paper plates from the bag and lifts the lid for her.

Hawaiian with pepperoni and black olive.

She smiles. "Thank you."

He beams back at her and slides two pieces onto his plate.

They sit there in silence as they eat their first slices. Once the pangs in Megan's stomach subside, she turns her body to face Josh and pulls her legs up onto the couch, sitting cross-legged. She can't ignore the fact that she feels safe here, sitting with Josh. She always feels safe with him. She wonders if her intuition is failing her.

"I don't know where to start."

"How about at the beginning?" Josh suggests.

Megan spills nearly everything, carefully omitting the pieces about Josh and the poker chip she found on the ground. Something is holding her back from divulging those parts to him just yet.

"Megs, this is insane. I don't know what to say." Josh admits.

"You? Speechless? *That's* insane." Megan swats Josh playfully on the shoulder. "Josh?" Megan glances up. He's focused wholly on her, making her a little nervous.

Megan looks down at her hands, picking at a jagged fingernail, and swallows. "Why did you stop coming over when we were teenagers? What was that last fight about?"

Josh flinches, so subtly, but Megan catches it. "It was so long ago, Megs. It wasn't anything specific. Your dad and I were butting heads a lot, and I was a stupid teenage boy…"

Josh is lying. He gave her an answer, but not the one she asked him for.

Megan nods, as if she accepts his response.

"What brought that up, Megs?"

Megan considers telling him it's nothing. Just something she's been curious about. But if she wants the truth from him, she decides she has to offer it in return.

"Dan told me you and my dad had a falling out. A bad one. That you'd known what my dad was doing and tried to become a partner in it. When my dad rejected you, you got it in your head that you would bring them all down." Megan looks up at Josh.

Josh's knee begins to bounce gently, a nervous habit he'd broken long ago. He puts a hand on his knee to steady it.

"Is it true?" Megan pulls her own knees up to her chest like a shield.

Josh looks down, not making eye contact. "Come on, Megs. You know me better than that." He sounds offended, even saddened by the question.

Shaking her head at his avoidance, she asks again, her voice firm, demanding an answer. "Is it true?"

"No! Of course it's not true!"

Lie.

His explosive response rattles her a bit. Megan treads lightly, carefully trying to extract the truth from the man sitting next to her. "Did you know about Dan's casino and illegal gambling ring this whole time? Have you been looking into him for years?"

"No." Josh's eyes meet hers just for a moment before he rips them away, as if he can't hold on any longer.

Lie.

Megan nods her head slowly, and Josh interrupts her thought. "Why do I feel like you don't believe me? What's happening, Megs?"

Megan wasn't prepared for Josh to be dishonest with her. He's never hidden anything from her before. At least, not that she'd known about. She's even less prepared for the sudden urge to be very careful around a man she's known her whole life.

"Just one more question." Megan is rarely so forward, and she isn't confident she'll know if he is lying. Everyone has tried to push Megan and

Josh together, but Megan kept him at arm's length, unwilling to accept that maybe their chemistry isn't only the type that makes up close friendships. Maybe in part, but it isn't all of it. Josh just confirmed, through omission, that some things Dan told her are true. What if all of it is?

Since Dan breathed life into the idea of Josh's feelings for her, she hasn't been able to ignore her own feelings for Josh any longer. Amidst everything else, Megan replayed their entire history together in her mind while she was driving home. Dan forced her to when he told her what he knew about Josh. Her eyes are clear. She can see now how others might conclude there is more between them.

She picks her chin up from off her arms and locks eyes with Josh, swallowing her fear. "Do you love me, Josh?"

His eyes are a vibrant shade of emerald. He scratches the back of his neck, his brow furrowing, jaw etched with tension. "You know I do, Megs."

Megan pushes her lips together and then tries again, drawing out the true meaning in her question. "No, Josh. Do you love me?"

His mouth falls open, but no words come out. Megan instantly feels foolish and turns away, ready to explain how Dan planted the idea when she hears his answer.

"Yes." It comes out just barely louder than a whisper.

She looks back at him, his eyes glistening. He turned his entire body to face her.

Truth.

Heat radiates through her body, a flush creeping into her face.

She shifts her weight forward, rolling onto her knees. Her body falls into Josh and he catches the side of her face in one palm, her hip in the other. Their mouths are so close together Megan can feel the warmth of his breath rolling in and out between his lips.

He grazes her cheek with his thumb, then runs his fingers back through her hair, as if savoring the feel of her. His eyes never leave hers and she inches forward. Her skin is prickling, her lips are warm. He meets her halfway and when his mouth touches hers, there's a spark.

Megan melts into him, drowning in the feel of his lips on hers. His tongue is soft and slow, like he's relishing the taste of her. They fit together like they were made to, their kisses growing hungrier from years of holding back.

Josh breaks away to leave a trail of eager kisses down her cheek and neck while Megan runs her hands up the length of his arms and down his chest, memorizing every curve and every edge of the body he's diligently carved out. Her bee-stung lips continue to swell.

The touch of his hands makes her forget everything. She wants to forget everything.

Josh slowly wanders back up, pausing for moment. Resting his forehead against Megan's collarbone, he whispers, "Everything I ever thought was about me, was always about you, Megs. Every fight with your dad. Every time I asked your grandma for a ride home from school. Every time I ask for black olives on our pizza. I don't even like olives, Megs."

She pushes herself away with great difficulty and stands up. Holding her hand out to him, she invites him to follow her. "Come on," she says. He slips his hand into hers and Megan leads him to the bedroom.

I'll be careful around him. Tomorrow.

CHAPTER 33

SUNDAY, SEPTEMBER 20TH

Megan listens to Josh snoring lightly. Though she'd fallen asleep curled into the nook of his shoulder, her head on his chest, they'd separated at some point and now she sees how he really sleeps. On his stomach, one arm under his pillow, the other wrapped over the top. One of his legs juts straight out, and the other knee is pulled up towards his chest at a ninety-degree angle.

She watches him for a moment, her fingers grazing her lips, still tender, before slipping silently out of bed and tiptoeing to the bathroom to freshen up, not nearly ready for the intimacy of smeared mascara and morning breath.

As she climbs back into bed, Josh stirs, groaning as he stretches. When he rolls over to look at Megan, his smile reaches all the way up to his eyes. He hooks and arm around her waist and pulls her into his arms.

"Good morning," he breathes into her hair as he nuzzles her with his nose.

"Good morning back." Megan smiles back, soaking in how natural it feels to wake up this way.

"Last night was…" Josh starts.

"Perfect," Megan finishes.

Josh is quiet, his eyes running over Megan's face, like he's seeing her for the first time. He leans over, kissing her firmly, yet gently, on the lips. When he pulls away, his eyes shine as he confesses softly, "I love you, Megs."

"I love you too." She replies, feeling the truth of it in her bones. She kisses him one more time and lays on his chest, afraid to let go of this moment. Knowing she'll only ever have it once.

Eventually, Megan sits up. "Katie will be here soon. She said she wants to hang out today, but I think she just wants to be sure I don't run off again." Megan chuckles, but as soon as the words have left her mouth, reality floods her mind, reminding her she has some decisions to make with the information at her disposal. She isn't sure who to involve or who to trust. She isn't sure what to do with the knowledge she can now, literally, hold in her hand, printed on a tiny black poker chip.

Josh sits up, and starts to get dressed. He collects his things and walks over to kiss Megan on the cheek. "I don't want you running off, either."

A shiver zips up Megan's spine. "Josh? Can we keep this between us for now? I want to talk to Katie first and…"

Josh cuts her off. "Of course. I get it." He takes both her hands in his and steps towards her so there's hardly any space between them. He looks down at her. "I'll do anything for you, Megs."

She can feel the truth of his words and goosebumps pop up on her arms. Josh notices and begins rubbing her arms to lay them back down.

Megan walks him to the door. He gazes at her, a dopey close-lipped smile on his face. "See you later."

254 | MARISSA VANSKIKE

"Goodbye." Megan says to his back. He hesitates for a moment and cocks his head. But he doesn't turn around. Instead, he ducks his head and trots off to his car.

Megan locks the door behind him and walks over to her purse, pulling out the poker chip, running her fingers over the initials.

She knows what made Josh do a double take because she felt it, too. She had meant to say "see you later". When "goodbye" slipped out instead, it sounded like forever.

Megan rolls the poker chip between her fingers, reading the initials, tracing them with her fingertip as if it will either confirm or contradict her knowledge of its owner. A knock at the door gives Megan a start, though she's expecting Katie. The air in her apartment is charged with secrets. Megan tosses the chip onto her nightstand and arranges her face in a way she hopes won't give her away. Katie is one of very few people she's never been good at keeping secrets from.

When Megan opens the door, Katie sweeps into the room and wraps Megan in her arms. "Oh my god, Megs…" For a minute, Megan just stands there, letting Katie hold her, returning the hug. "I will not pretend like it wasn't completely idiotic for you to run off to Vegas *alone*, but I'm so happy you're alright."

"Come in, sit." Megan instructs Katie. Megan pulls a cream-colored stoneware mug out of her cabinet for Katie, and a vibrant turquoise mug for herself before pouring them each a cup of coffee. She sets the cups down on the coffee table and plops down on the sofa next to Katie, letting out her breath like a whoosh.

"I'm not sure where to start." Megan admits, overwhelmed by the amount of information she's holding onto.

"First things first, did you get what you needed by going there?" Katie asks.

What Megan gained in the last forty-eight hours is far more than she ever went searching for, but Katie doesn't know that. Megan thinks about her answer and instead says, "Yeah, I think I did." Megan can feel the meaning in Katie's stare, asking her for more. "Katie, if I'm being honest, I'm not sure how much I can give you right now."

Katie frowns, knitting her brows together. "What do you mean?"

Megan considers her response, thoughtfully piecing the right words together in a way Katie might accept. "When you went with me to Archers' house, I didn't think about how you felt, or the danger I put you in. I should have. And I don't want to make the same mistake again."

"Alright… but it's fine to get Josh mixed up in this?" Katie retorts.

"Josh is a police officer. He has resources I don't have access to…"

Katie interrupts, "Exactly. You're fine jeopardizing him. Putting his career at risk to help you. That's ok, but Katie can't help so let's leave her out of it…"

Now, it's Megan's turn, before this turns ugly. "Hold on Katie, let me finish." Megan pauses to regroup. "The nature of Josh's job is dangerous. He knows how to protect himself and has resources we don't in order to do just that. His helping me has nothing to do with my protecting you. I put you at risk before and I almost it almost broke us. I won't do it again."

"How are you putting me at risk by just keeping me in the loop?"

Megan understands. The three of them have always been a trio. It breaks her heart to put Katie on the outside. Megan is too familiar with the feeling. "The men in Las Vegas are dangerous. You do not know what they are capable of. *I* didn't know. But now that I do, I won't put you in the crosshairs by involving you anymore than I already have, knowing it isn't safe."

Katie doesn't look convinced, so Megan leans forward and grabs her hand.

"Katie, I promise. As soon as I figure out what to do with all of this, I will tell you everything. Can you be ok with that?"

Megan searches Katie's face for any sign of which way she'll swing. Katie's face is hard with determination and for a moment, Megan is certain Katie is prepared to fight. Then suddenly, Katie's shoulder slump and her face hangs soft, the corners of her eyes turning down. Katie has been by Megan's side long enough to know if she continues to push, Megan will clam up. But if she rides it out, Megan will tell her when she's ready.

"I can." Katie squeezes the hand Megan is still holding and Megan relaxes into the back of the couch.

"Does this mean you were right? About what happened to your dad?" Katie asks.

Megan just nods, looking at her.

"And you think you know who was behind it?"

Megan feels a surge of respect for Katie, for the way she will let Megan keep her answers close to her chest, but she isn't willing to sit here with no information at all.

"Yes, I do. I'm certain, I just— "

Megan is cut off by her cell phone ringing on the couch between them. They look down at the same time and see Josh's face appear on the caller ID. Katie looks at Megan, brow knit together. Megan shrugs.

She answers the call, putting it on speakerphone so she won't have to relay the conversation to Katie afterwards. "Hey. What's up?"

"Megs! I just got called in to work. Dr. Oswald was found dead in his office. He was shot."

Megan covers her mouth with her hand, stifling a gasp. "Shit. Suicide?" As horrible as it sounds, Megan prays Dr. Oswald just couldn't live with what he'd done. The alternative is too devastating to consider.

"He was murdered. An investigation is underway, but forensics could tell immediately."

"Oh my god, Josh." Megan locks eyes with Katie.

"That's not everything, Megs. There was a note. It was… stapled to his chest. ***The investigation ends now.***"

Megan is speechless. She pulls the question she's afraid to ask from out of the depths of her gut somehow. "Did we do this, Josh?" Megan looks down, unable to look at Katie as she asks. She can't handle the look of horror Katie must surely be wearing.

"I don't know. But I have to go in, they called me out specifically. I'm coming to your place, first. I think I might have dropped my wallet on the floor by the bed and it has my badge in it. Be there soon."

Josh hangs up without saying "goodbye". When Megan sets the phone down, she takes her time raising her head to see which part needs explaining first. Katie is sitting there, arms folded across her chest, her expression a mess of tangled bits and pieces.

"Well?"

Not wanting to divulge anything unnecessary, Megan infuses as much innocence into her voice as she can. "Well what?"

"I know you want to keep me out of the investigation stuff, so I'll give you that. For now." Katie holds a finger up to Megan. "But would you like to tell me why Josh's wallet is on your bedroom floor?" Katie manages to look both stunned and smug somehow.

"Yeah, I was going to tell you, I swear." Megan spills everything, leaving out the sordid details, but including the nuts and bolts. "Are you angry? It won't go any further. It was just an emotional moment, and I will never jeopardize our friendship. Do you hate me?"

"Megan! I've been waiting for you both to stop pretending you aren't into each other for years! I'm mad you didn't lead with this information when I got here, but oh my god I'm so happy for you guys! Was it magical?"

Megan blushes, feeling heat rush into her cheeks at the memory of Josh's hands on her body. "It really was."

"Wait. You said it won't go any further. Why not? Did something happen?"

Megan suddenly feels on the verge of tears, but she blinks them back. "It just won't work. It can't…" Before Megan can finish, Josh is at the door. She opens it and steps back to let him in. He's staring at her like he hasn't seen her in forever and he can't believe she's standing there. Megan pulls her eyes away, aiming them at the floor.

If Josh is bothered, he doesn't show it. Katie jumps up and is across the room, hugging him before he knows what's happening. "Josh, Megan told me about you guys, and I just want you to know I think it's great and I fully support this. I don't know what happened, but I'm sure you guys can figure it out."

Josh looks at Megan. His forehead creased, one eyebrow raised. Megan knows he is asking what Katie is talking about. Dragging his attention back to Katie, he replies, "Thanks, Katie. I appreciate it." He sidesteps around Katie and she moves with him. "Look, I can't talk right now, but maybe when I'm done working? I need to grab my wallet and get to the crime scene."

Josh backs away and spins around, heading down the exceptionally short hallway to Megan's bedroom. Megan doesn't follow him, staying close to the front door, and to Katie.

When Josh doesn't come back right away, Katie jerks her head awkwardly towards the bedroom, motioning for Megan to go check on him. Megan gives a reluctant eye roll before trudging down the hall.

Megan enters the room, and Josh is just turning around to face her. He freezes in place, standing in front of her nightstand. He locks onto her gaze, just long enough to cause the tiny hairs on the back of Megan's neck to stand at attention.

Megan swallows nervously. "Did you find it?"

Josh holds the wallet up in the air, displaying it to Megan. "Yup. I did."

He walks towards her slowly and stops directly in front of her. Megan's fight-or-flight response is urging her to run, but her feet remain rooted in place. Josh leans down slowly, too slowly, and drops a light kiss onto her cheek and whispers, "I'll see you later, Megs". He steps to the side and leaves her standing alone in the room.

Megan hears him say goodbye to Katie and the front door closes. She releases a breath and moves towards her nightstand that Josh had just been standing in front of. She stares down at the poker chip sitting on top. She reaches down and slips the chip into her pocket, suddenly certain she shouldn't leave it laying around unattended.

CHAPTER 34

MONDAY, SEPTEMBER 21ST

There hasn't been a word from Josh since he left her apartment yesterday. Neither has there been a lull in her unease since then. Right now, she can't afford to think about it. Megan is getting ready for dinner with Smalls and their mom to catch up after the missed Friday dinner. She will need all her focus to be on staying sane and civil tonight. She slides the poker chip in her pocket before heading out the door. It suddenly feels like the key to everything and she can't shake the feeling that if she leaves it behind, it will disappear.

She arrives at their mom's house at 5:00pm sharp and she double checks the time they'd decided on after noticing Smalls' car isn't there. He must be running late, she decides, though he's always early to dinner.

It might be good for her to have some time alone with her mom before he arrives and consumes every spare ounce of her attention.

Megan steps up to the door and knocks. She hears her mom calling from inside the house. She steps through the doorway. "Hey mom, where are you?"

"We're in the kitchen, dear."

We're?

Megan walks into the dining room attached to the kitchen to find her brother helping her mom put some finishing touches on the dishes she's working on. The smell of spiced beef, tamed with the sweet smell of cream cheese drifts over, finding Megan's nose.

"Beef stroganoff?" Megan asks, hopefully.

Megan's mom winks at her. "I know it's your favorite. I thought it sounded delicious tonight."

Jonathan peaks over his shoulder, taking care to stop chopping the bell pepper in front of him first. "Hey, sis."

"Hey, Smalls. I didn't see your car outside." Megan walks over, giving him a side hug with one arm.

"Mom picked me up this afternoon. I've been helping her with a few things around the house. Can you give me a ride home after dinner?" He resumes chopping when Kathy shoots him a reminder with her eyes.

Megan swipes a stick of red bell pepper and pops the end into her mouth, savoring the sweet crunch. "Sure. No problem."

Her mother looks at her, her face disapproving of Megan speaking with food in her mouth. Megan holds up her hands apologetically. "Sorry. Anything I can help with?"

"No, dear, we're just about finished. Why don't you go sit down?" Kathy instructs.

Megan sits down just as Kathy and Jonathan bring food out. They take turns passing the dishes around, making sure everyone gets a bit of everything. As usual, Kathy dishes Jonathan's portions for him.

Megan pokes a bite of stroganoff onto her fork. Normally she'd start with her salad, filling up on greens before carbs since they contain far fewer calories, but she can't resist starting with her favorite dish of her mom's, eating it with a clean palate. "Everything looks great tonight, mom."

"Thank you, dear." Kathy says, pausing mid-bite to look at Megan. "I'm just so glad we could get together tonight. I know you couldn't help a last-minute work seminar popping up, but when Jonathan told me he had to go into work also, I can't pretend like I wasn't disappointed."

Megan looks up at Jonathan. Jonathan never bails on their mother, that she knows of. "You got called into work? On a Friday night?"

"Yeah. The guy with the T-bird is putting pressure on us all the sudden to get it finished. They needed some extra hours." Jonathan explains, without looking up from his plate. "How was your trip?"

Megan's insides clutch at the mention of her trip. Not wanting to get into any more arguments about it, she brushes the question under the rug. "It was fine. Pretty uneventful, actually. I probably shouldn't have gone."

Kathy sits up and takes a sip of water. "Of course you should have. When your boss pays to send you to office management training seminar, you go. You are obviously being groomed for another step up."

Megan shoots her brother a grateful smirk. She hadn't known what excuse he'd given their mom for Megan's absence, but he'd clearly kept his word by not divulging the truth. "I'm already an office manager, mom. It's no big deal. Besides, I'm not going to be there forever."

"And what is your plan? You graduated with a degree in psychology, but you haven't done a thing with it."

"I'm not sure yet, mom. Geez, I'm twenty-seven. Don't you think I have time to figure it out? You became a vet tech at forty-three years old."

"And I hope you won't take nearly as long as I did." Kathy lets out a little humph before returning to her plate.

Jonathan breaks the silence. "And how is your hunt for a killer going, big sis?" He shoots her a wide smile, displaying his fictitious innocence in asking.

Megan fights her natural inclination to argue with him, knowing it will go nowhere good, and that she can't tell them anything even if she wanted to. For their own protection.

Megan sets her fork down. "It's not. You were right. It was stupid of me to think it was anything more. And even if it was, who am I to figure it out, you know? I was just grasping at straws."

"So, I guess you can cross detective off of your list of possible career paths then, huh?"

"Ha ha, very funny." Megan throws a piece of bread at her brother, causing him to jerk backward, his fork slipping. A piece of pasta falls onto his hoodie.

"Shit," he says, grabbing his napkin to wipe off the mess.

Kathy interjects, scolding them both. "Remind me again, how old are my children? Megan, we do not through food across the dinner table. Jonathan, there's no need to antagonize at family dinner. Honestly, you two…"

Megan and Jonathan's eyes connect, and they stifle a shared chortle.

"You need a new sweatshirt anyway, Smalls. I don't think I've seen you in anything but that old black hoodie for the last month. I'll buy you a new one myself. Just promise to wear it around me so I can pretend like you own more than one article of clothing."

Jonathan gasps dramatically, feigning offense. "How dare you. This is my favorite sweatshirt. Besides, black is a neutral color. It goes with everything."

"That doesn't mean it should be the only color you wear."

Kathy rolls her eyes. "Ok, enough picking at each other for one evening."

They somehow get through the rest of the meal without deviating from friendly conversation. As the evening comes to a close, Megan and Jonathan stand up to clear the table. As her brother gets up, his keys hit the floor with a loud jingle. He crouches down to pick them up and stuffs them back in his pocket. They amble over to the sink and Megan loads the dishwasher while her brother puts the leftovers into Tupperware containers to take home.

Megan and Jonathan say goodbye to their mom and Megan says a silent prayer of gratitude that they made it through the evening without argument. In fact, it was a pleasant evening.

"See you next week, mom." Megan calls over her shoulder, smiling at her mom who is watching them leave from the doorway.

CHAPTER 35

The drive home is relaxed. Megan and her brother say little for a while and somehow Megan feels at ease. Without the added formality of family dinner and their mother's hovering, Megan sees an opportunity to learn about who her brother is when she and Kathy aren't around.

"So, Smalls, are you seeing anyone right now?" Megan dives in, ready for him to blow her off. She knows he isn't dating anyone. Their mom wouldn't be able to shut up about it if he were.

"Actually, yes." Jonathan leans forward and scans the radio stations.

"What? You are?" Megan sputters. "Wait, have you been hiding this from mom?"

Jonathan chuckles. *He's enjoying this.*

He settles on a station playing classic rock. "Mom knows."

Of course she does. Megan was left out. Again. How had she missed that her brother was dating? "Well, go on then. Spill it. Who is she?" She flips on her left turn signal as she approaches the red light in front of them.

Jonathan doesn't hesitate. "Her name is Christine. She's a total bombshell, a redhead. She always wears caramel brown leather, and all she wants to do is go out cruising every night…" He gives Megan a side eye and the pieces click into place.

"You're talking about the Thunderbird you've been working on." Megan rolls her eyes. "Ok, you got me, Smalls."

Jonathan laughs as he turns to look out the window. "You're too easy, sis." A classic muscle car pulls up next to them at the stoplight. Megan can't even fathom a guess as to what kind of car it is, but it is pretty. The exterior is a pearly shade of aquamarine, the engine grumbles loudly as it idles. She watches the way her brother looks it over, reading it like a book. Megan sees how his eyes flit back and forth from the front to back before he gives a polite nod of appreciation to the driver.

Megan's phone dings with an incoming text message. She glances down to see it's from Josh.

Incoming text message from Josh Pierce (8:03pm):
Megs, where are you right now? Are you ok?

She looks up to be sure the light is still red before replying.

Outgoing text from Megan Palmer (8:04pm):
I'm fine. Giving Smalls a ride home. What's going on?

Incoming text message from Josh Pierce (8:04pm):
Wait for me when you get home. You're not safe.

Outgoing text message from Megan Palmer (8:04pm):
What are you talking about? You're scaring me…

Incoming text message from Josh Pierce (8:05pm):
Please Megs! It's Dan. Don't go inside without me.

A car honks behind them, snapping her attention back to the road. Jonathan is looking at her phone. "Megs, the light's green. Who was that?"

Megan presses the accelerator a little too quickly and the car jerks forward, bumping their heads against the headrests. "Sorry. Just Josh. It's nothing. He's working a case right now, and he was just giving me an update."

Jonathan looks satisfied and turns back to the window, watching the city glide by. "Gotcha. What case is he working? Anything interesting?"

"The city medical examiner was murdered." Megan leaves the explanation short, still feeling that more information would only put the people she loves at greater risk. Megan reaches to move her cell phone from her lap, where she dropped it, to the cubby in her dashboard where she keeps it. She can feel her hand shaking and she looks at Jonathan in her peripheral to see if he's noticed.

Jonathan nods his head, betraying nothing in his face. "Shit. That sucks. Any idea who might have done it?"

Megan presses on the gas a little harder to beat the yellow light ahead rather than slow down and wait at another red light. "Not yet."

Megan turns onto Jonathan's street and then into the apartment complex. She navigates the miniature roads between the apartment buildings, but her mind is somewhere else. She must have looked it because her brother reaches a hand across and rests it lightly on her shoulder.

"You ok, sis?"

She looks at him to find his eyes searching hers, his forehead crinkled and eyes squinting. "Oh, yeah. Just spaced out, I guess. Why?"

He turns back, facing forward. "I was asking you about your trip, but you didn't seem to hear me."

"Sorry, try again. I'm listening." Megan sees his building ahead and slows down, rolling gently over a speed bump.

"I asked if it helped. Seeing the parking garage. Did you get the closure you were looking for?"

Megan pulls into a parking space in front of the staircase which leads up to her brother's apartment and cuts the ignition. Something about his question is poking the back of her brain. She hears him shifting in his seat, and her eyes snap open, as if she just remembered something important.

"Yeah, actually I did." She nods at her brother, managing what she hopes is a smile.

He gives her a tiny nod and his own half grin in return. "Good. I'm glad, sis." He reaches for the door handle and Megan does the same so she can get out and hug her brother. As she gets out, she hears his keys hit the pavement with a loud clink.

"Geez, Smalls. I've never known you to be so clumsy. That's the second time you've dropped your keys tonight." Megan points out.

"Yeah, I found a hole in my sweatshirt pocket. I keep forgetting about it when I toss my keys in it." Smalls closes the door and bends down to retrieve his keys.

As Megan stands up, a tiny gulp catches in her throat and a shiver rolls down the full length of her back. Her brother walks around the car to give Megan a hug.

"Thanks for the ride. Get home safe."

"Of course. Any time." Megan hugs him, gripping him a little tighter than normal. "I love you. You know that, right?"

He lets her go and takes a step back. "Love you too, sis." He shoots her a confused smile and turns to hike up the staircase.

Megan lets him take a few strides before calling out to him. "Smalls! You forgot something." He turns around, and she tosses the poker chip she'd been carrying into the air. He catches it and turns it over in his palm. "It must have fallen out of your pocket last weekend."

Jonathan looks up and takes a step forward. Megan reflexively takes a step backward. He looks hurt at the sight of Megan afraid of him and he raises his hands in the air. "I'm not going to hurt you, Megs. I'd never do that."

"How can I trust you?" Megan keeps her distance, needing his entire body in full view, just like Josh taught her to do when she feels threatened. "It was you this whole time, wasn't it? You let me go on and on about everything when you *knew*. You knew! How could you do this to me? To him?"

"I'm not a monster. I can explain! It…" Tears fill his eyes, spilling over the edge. "I'm so sorry, sis. I never meant to hurt you. I swear——"

"Then why did you kill him?" Megan cuts him off, afraid of letting her guard down at his uncharacteristic display of emotion. "What about Dr. Oswald? You killed him just because he talked to us. He told us about your visit." Megan's whole body is shaking, frightened of what Jonathan is capable of. Equally frightened of the voice inside of her telling her Jonathan isn't going to hurt her.

Jonathan looks at her, confusion gleaming in his eyes. "What visit? I didn't kill Dr. Oswald." Jonathan sniffles, finally lowering his hands and hooks his thumbs into his pockets, leaving the rest of his hands visible.

Megan shakes her head, taking in her brother's tall stature, curly hair, and black hoodie. "Dr. Oswald described you perfectly. So tell me why, Smalls? Why'd you do it?" Her eyes plead with him, begging for the truth.

Jonathan looks around, scanning for anyone who may overhear. When he finally speaks, his voice is low and controlled. "Ok, yes, I visited Dr. Oswald. But I didn't kill him. I just made him change his report, that's all! I'm telling you the truth."

Megan hasn't missed the fact that Jonathan addressed her accusation about Oswald, but not the one about their dad. "But you killed our father, didn't you?"

Jonathan's face hardens. "Megs, our dad was a monster. Look at the damage he's done. Forget for a minute about the fact he abandoned his son at five years old, or how he's abandoned you, over and over. He hurt everyone he touched. It's a miracle Josh swung in the other direction and became a cop." His voice is growing loud and wild with rage. "He hurt people for a living, Megan. Jesus. The money he gave our mom every month was blood money." His arms fly out to the side as if this is the most obvious thing in the world. "He couldn't just get a job like a man is supposed to. I stood by for years, watching him hurt you, and when I found out how he was making his money, I couldn't take it anymore."

Megan listens carefully, making sure she hears him correctly. "How did you find out what Dad was doing?"

"Dan told me. He caught me following Mark one night and I asked him to tell me the truth about Mark." Jonathan looks down at his feet, shuffling them back and forth on the sidewalk, as if he's ashamed of the admission.

Megan scowls at him. "Why? I thought you didn't care about Dad."

Jonathan sneers like he's disgusted by the idea that he would ever care about Mark. And then his face changes, drooping down, and it appears his features themselves are tired from holding up his wall of callousness any longer. He sniffles again and wipes his nose with the back of his hand. "I wanted to know what was so much more important than me." Jonathan gathers himself before continuing. "Dan remembered who I was. He knew my history with Mark. He told me what Mark had been up to and how sloppy he was getting. Dan said he was a liability." Jonathan averts his eyes, avoiding Megan's gaze. "He said he wanted my help in taking care of Mark."

Jonathan pauses, taking a deep breath. "Dan said I was the perfect man for the job because Mark would never see me coming. So I kept following Mark around, studying his movements. He never even noticed." Jonathan snorts and looks back at Megan, his eyes drooping, shoulders sagging. "When Dan told me about how Mark destroyed my friend's family, I said I'd do it."

"Your friend's family?"

"Yeah, Sawyer Dennis. His dad got mixed up with Mark and gambled away all of their family's money. When he couldn't pay up, he bailed and left Sawyer and his mom to clean up his mess."

Megan tries not to dwell on the question of whether her father knew he was destroying a family connected to his own son. "What happened when you told Dan you'd help him?"

"Dan said he would make it worth my while to do the job." Jonathan shrugs as though none of this matters much. "We met a few days later to work out the details. Then I called Mark and told him to meet me on the top floor of the Viva Las Vegas parking garage that night."

Megan presses the heel of her hand to her forehead, between her eyes, desperate to relieve the dull throbbing. She doesn't want to hear this. She doesn't want to know, beyond a shadow of a doubt, that her brother is a murderer. But Jonathan is still talking.

"I followed him up to the parking garage. I knew it would be safer if he didn't see me, but before I knew it, I was marching towards him screaming at him that I knew who he was. I knew what he did." Jonathan hangs his head and two tears hit the pavement leaving twin spatter marks. "He couldn't even be bothered to turn around. He was messing with something in his car, just standing by the open door."

Jonathan stares off somewhere on the sidewalk and Megan wonders if he's seeing it all again. "Dan gave me a gun to use. But when I went to pull it out, Payne got out of the passenger side and stepped between us. He dragged me back a few steps, and he told me he knew what I was there for."

Megan stares at him, struggling to concentrate, struggling to breathe. "You knew who Payne was? How?"

"He was with Mark the night Dan caught me. Dan told me who he was."

Megan doesn't want to hear the rest of the story, but it's too late for that. "What happened then?"

Jonathan shakes his head, not meeting Megan's eyes. "He asked me if I had the gun Dan gave me. I nodded and Payne stuck his hand out and told me to give it to him. He said I didn't want this kind of blood on my hands and told me to go. He would take care of it, and I'd done my job by getting Mark out into the open."

"And then?" Megan is suddenly desperate to know the ending. The truth dangles in front of her, so close she can reach a hand out and grab it if she's quick.

"And then nothing. I glanced over Payne's shoulder to see if Mark had heard us talking. Didn't seem like it, but when he stepped back, I saw Mark loading bullets into a gun in his hand."

Jonathan shakes his head. "I don't know why but I yelled at him. I asked if he was going to kill me to shut me up. I called him a fucking coward and told him he'd be better off using that thing on himself!"

He drops his eyes, defeated. "When he finally swung around to face me, I got scared and I ran back to my car and got in. I tore out of there and didn't even look back." Jonathan collapses to his knees with his face in his hands and sobs.

Megan stands there, processing her brother's confession. She isn't sure how long she's been silent.

"I heard the gunshot as I drove down the ramp." Jonathan chokes out. "I swear, Megs. I didn't do it. I couldn't. Even if Payne hadn't—." His voice hitches and he lifts his face from his hands. "What happens now, sis? Are you going to call Josh? Turn me in?" Jonathan watches her intently.

"Turn you in?" Megan can't even begin to comprehend what her brother means.

He nods. "Mark is dead because of me. He was dead the second I made that phone call and I knew it." Jonathan's voice drops to barely a whisper. "And…I wanted it to happen. I wanted Mark to die."

"Stop calling him Mark!" Megan screams, feeling the pain and fear and grief come roaring to a head inside her chest. "He was our dad! Before everything else he became, he was our father first."

Jonathan winces and his shoulders cave in. He shakes his head. "Maybe he was yours. But he was never mine."

As she listens to him, Megan hears the angry words of a hurt little boy all over again. Except this time, someone ended up dead. Was her father's death ultimately caused by his own inability to be a father to his son? Can she forgive that Smalls felt he was acting on a misplaced sense of heroism confronting their dad?

Megan's mind races through her options, trying to untangle her personal feelings from her moral sense of right and wrong. From justice to some horrible kind of understanding. How will Jonathan live with this guilt? He did not murder their dad, but he is complicit.

Megan has heard Josh discuss his job enough to know that her brother could be charged with accessory to murder if it's proven that he withheld information about a murder. Or worse, that he planned to murder Mark himself. God knows if there is any video evidence linking Smalls to Dan and Payne. Jonathan is only twenty-five years old. If he is convicted, his life will be over.

But maybe it's all mute. Dr. Oswald's original report is gone. As far as anyone knows, Mark's death was a suicide.

Megan drowns in her thoughts as she stands in front of her brother, holding his fate in her hands. The course of his life is hers to determine and the weight of it is unbearable.

No matter which path is taken, she can't see how Jonathan will come back from this. How will she come back from this?

Jonathan looks up at her, his face swollen and red. "What happens now?"

Megan bites her tongue so hard she tastes blood in her mouth. "Now...nothing. You weren't the one who pulled the trigger, even if—." Megan pinches the bridge of her nose and takes a deep breath. She doesn't finish the sentence.

"I'm sorry, Megs."

Something in Megan snaps. "You're sorry? Well, shit, Smalls! That just fixes everthing!" Megan balls her hands into fists. She shakes her head, suddenly exhausted, and she takes a step backwards. "I have nothing to say to you. Just go, Smalls. I have to get out of here. Josh is waiting for me."

Jonathan nods, seemingly resigning himself to Megan's judgments. He climbs back to his feet and turns to go when he stops, looking sideways over his shoulder at Megan. "How did you know? That the chip was mine."

Megan looks at him with a halfhearted shrug. A single tear rolls silently down her cheek. "You slipped. I never told you I went to the parking garage in Vegas."

Megan climbs into the front seat and watches her brother walk up the stairs to his apartment before she drives away.

"Bye, Smalls."

As Megan pulls away from her brother's apartment building, she thinks about how much of a person's life is determined by choice rather than chance. The unexpected happens. It requires a choice to be made. That choice leads to the next chance event. And so it goes on, each choice a fragile link to the next. Any other response could have altered the course of a life.

Now Megan sees what's at stake when a father doesn't choose his own family. The ripples that roll through those nearby can be devastating. Sometimes the consequences are forever.

If only her father had chosen differently. If only Smalls had chosen differently. Her heart cracks at the realization that she is pushing her brother further away. It feels too much like abandoning him.

But, it didn't have to be this way.

CHAPTER 36

Josh is waiting in his police cruiser when Megan arrives at her apartment. He gets out of the car and jogs over to her. He pulls her close. His urgency is making her nervous. He steps back, keeping his hands on her shoulders while he looks her over. "Are you ok? You're not hurt?"

"I'm fine, Josh. Really. I was just with Smalls. What's going on?"

Josh reaches out a hand. "Give me your keys. I'm going to make sure your apartment is empty."

Megan does what he asks, dropping her keys into his palm. His insistence tells her not to argue. Not right now.

"Go wait in my car," he orders. He watches her get in and waits for the car door to latch closed before heading to her door, his gun aimed down at the ground, ready to deploy. She looks around, newly aware of how poorly lit her building is. It's dark now and there are very few places around her she can see clearly.

She watches him enter her apartment. She follows the tiny beam of his pocket flashlight bouncing around behind the curtains in the windows and sliding glass door.

A few minutes pass before Josh reappears. His gun is holstered, and his flashlight is put away. He waves for Megan to get out of the cruiser. "All clear."

"Are you going to tell me what's going on now?"

They walk to her apartment together before he answers.

"We found out who murdered Dr. Oswald. I thought he might come for you next." Josh squeezes her hand. "I was so scared I wouldn't get here in time."

Megan pulls her hand away, remembering the secrets between them. "I don't think we need to worry about that anymore." Megan brushes past him to set her purse down on the table in the dinette area.

"What are you talking about, Megs?" Josh asks, hovering her over protectively, never more than six feet away. If he'd been bothered by her retreat, he doesn't show it.

Megan walks over to the refrigerator and grabs a bottle of water before slumping down onto her couch. "I know who killed my dad, and it's all over now."

"Wait, how do you—", Josh is interrupted by communication over his walkie.

"10-26. Repeat, suspect apprehended, 10-26."

Josh turns to Megan raking his hand down the side of his face and then back behind his neck. "We caught him, Megs. You're safe now."

Megan barely registers that Josh is talking, replaying the day over and over in her mind, trying to change the outcome.

Her angst must be apparent on her face, because Josh tries again. "Did you hear me? You don't have to worry about Dan or Payne anymore. We got him. We got Dan, and the team is in pursuit of Payne as we speak. He's not in custody yet, but we'll catch him too."

Megan tilts her head and squeezes her brows together, perplexed. She plucks out the only words that she heard. "Dan? And Payne?"

"Yes, Dan murdered Oswald. He did a pretty good job covering his tracks. He scrubbed the camera footage from the time we visited on." Josh steps forward and reaches for Megan's hands. "But, Megs, listen to this. The bullet recovered from the scene at Oswald's office is the same bullet Oswald described in his autopsy report for Mark. A Western .38 special with a deep groove around the middle. Ballistics is confirming the weight of the casing, but I'm certain it's the same type of bullet that was used on Mark. And I'm going to make damn sure your dad's case is reopened and we nail Dan for his murder, too."

In any other moment, Josh's promise would have meant everything. But Megan isn't sure it matters anymore.

Josh hesitates before continuing. "Look, there's something I need to tell you, in case it comes out. When we visited Dr. Oswald, and you left to get my phone. I roughed him up a bit."

Megan takes a step backwards and Josh scrambles to explain. "I didn't hurt him, Megs. I would never do that. But I scared him a little bit when I grabbed his collar and got in his face. That's all on camera and I'm in deep shit with Chief over it. I know I've been a little MIA, but it didn't look good for me when Oswald turned up dead. But for now, the focus is on Dan. He didn't know Oswald had a hidden camera tucked away in the book spines on his shelf. The footage shows the whole thing." Josh takes a step closer to where Megan is standing, closing the gap between them. "I'm so sorry, I wanted to tell you, but it was imperative we didn't blow the investigation and Chief already knew I was reopening things I shouldn't have been. I was on thin ice. I think my personal connection to Dan was the only thing that saved my ass, to be honest." Josh chuffs at the irony as he traces the outline of her hand with the tip of his index finger.

Megan grapples to understand everything he's telling her. She has a million questions, but a minute passes and all she can manage is, "The investigation? Our investigation?"

Josh sits on the couch and motions for Megan to join him. She hesitates before lowering herself to the cushions, keeping some distance between them. "We have been helping Homeland Security for years to build their case against Dan. When I came onto the force, my relationship with Dan made me a valuable resource. I've been helping them because Dan seems to have never considered me a threat. I could filter in and out of his casino without him giving it a second thought. He just assumed I had a personal grudge. But I had to tread carefully not to compromise the work we were doing with Homeland Security."

Josh shifts in his seat, twisting to drape one arm across the back of the couch behind Megan, resting the opposite palm on her knee. "Then we got the call that Oswald was murdered and I came over here and saw the poker chip, Megan..." Josh's voice hitches. "I was just so scared you'd be next. That Dan and Payne would find out you knew they killed your dad and would come for you. It killed me that I couldn't tell you, so I bolted to make sure we caught them first."

Josh's walkie rings out once more, announcing that Payne had escaped. "Repeat. Suspect evaded. Police in pursuit. Suspect is considered armed and dangerous. Looks like this guy had help." Megan's stomach turns in a knot, but her thoughts feel like a tiny metal ball launched deep into a pinball machine. They bounce around from wall to wall until they land on something simple, saving complicated things for later.

"Why did Oswald have a hidden camera to begin with? He's a medical examiner."

"It looked to be installed fairly recently, possibly after he had been threatened, just in case something happened, if I had to guess." Josh explains.

Megan pinches her mouth shut, afraid to reveal how much she knows about the intruder who forced Dr. Oswald to alter his report.

"What about Annie?"

Josh pinches his lips together as one side of his mouth ticks upward. "We have nothing on Annie, but I'll keep an eye on her. I don't think she's a threat, but I won't let anyone hurt you." He reaches for Megan before stopping midway to her. "Wait. Payne is still out there. But before… you said you knew who murdered Mark. And it's over now. How do you—"

Megan closes her eyes. Payne could have killed her already if he wanted to. He may have pulled the trigger, but in the end, he isn't the one responsible for her father's murder. Dan is. Dan and… She swallows, unsure of how to hide the truth from Josh.

She's not ready.

She looks at him, drawing her shoulders upward. Josh pulls her close and kisses her on the head, resting his cheek in her hair.

CHAPTER 37

SATURDAY, SEPTEMBER 26TH

It's been nearly a week since Megan's search came to a head. It's been quiet. Not a word about Jeffrey Payne. He seems to have vanished into thin air. He's out there somewhere, but somehow Megan isn't afraid. Everyone has started to relax, the chaos of the last month settling into a new, easy cadence. The details becoming fuzzier.

Megan walks to Bean to meet Katie. This time, she's not alone. She strolls down the sidewalk, her hand swinging more heavily now with the weight of Josh's fingers weaved through her own.

It's sunnier than usual and impossibly warm, considering the weatherman boasts a high of sixty-eight degrees.

Bean comes into view, and across the way, they spy Katie, holding their table. Katie waves enthusiastically and Josh waves back. He brings

Megan's hand to his lips and drops a quick kiss before releasing it and disappearing into the coffee shop.

Megan slides into the chair next to Katie. "Oh, I love your nails! Blood red. A bold choice."

"I thought they looked fun. Though I prefer to think of them as candy apple red."

When Josh sits down and passes Megan her latte and a muffin, Katie looks at him. "So Josh, how's life as a desk jockey? Any interesting cases you've gotten to read about this week?"

Josh pulls his lips into a tight line. "You know, *dude*, snide really doesn't suit you. Not a good look. Though it certainly goes with your nails." Katie rolls her eyes. "And I'm not a desk jockey. It's more like probation with an emphasis on clerical work. But since you asked, guess who filed a missing person's report?" Megan shakes her head, unable to even offer a guess. "Sarah Beth Dennis. Dick Dennis apparently hasn't shown his face in a while."

Megan looks stunned. "But Sarah Beth hates her husband. She told my dad not to worry about telling her if he found Richard. Why would she bother filing a report?"

"According to her statement, he came around regularly, almost never longer than two weeks between visits. He'd harass and torment them. She started to worry when she hadn't seen him in over two weeks. She was nervous about where he'd pop up and what he might do to her or their son. He sounds like a pretty bad guy according to her description."

Megan looks at Katie, speechless. Katie drums her fresh manicure on the iron tabletop. "So what's this guy even look like? Where was he last seen? Any leads?" Ever since their decoding of the *Mania* books, Katie had officially caught the detective bug. Megan doesn't mind. She knows talking about his cases takes Josh's mind off of his probation.

Josh shakes his head. "Not much yet. We tracked his credit card to a gas station just outside of Reno the evening of August 28th. He was last seen wearing khaki pants with a white ribbed tank top tucked in. He bought a bag of peanuts and a KitKat bar, got some cash back and he left." Josh shrugs and takes a sip of his coffee. "His normally sandy brown hair was dyed black and tucked under a baseball cap but the clerk said he remembered the tattoos and the huge tear drop mole on his shoulder when he walked away. Camera footage confirms the attendant's account and shows Dennis getting into the backseat of a black SUV with no plates and driving off." Josh tears off a piece of Megan's muffin and pops it into his mouth.

Megan casts a disbelieving look before letting out a *hm* to acknowledge Josh's information without committing to any particular feeling about it.

Katie snaps her fingers. "Just like that? He's gone?"

Josh shrugs. "For now. I'm sure he'll turn up eventually. Guys like him don't stay hidden for long."

An image is buzzing around Megan's head like a fly. As Megan tries to catch hold of it, Katie changes the topic. "How's your mom doing, Megs?"

"She's a mess, honestly. She's trying to keep it together, I can tell, but she ends up sobbing every time I talk to her."

When Jonathan didn't answer their mother's calls or return any of her text messages for the past week, Kathy became increasingly worried. When Megan said she hadn't heard from him, Kathy called the auto shop and Sam informed her Jonathan hadn't shown up for his shifts and wasn't answering their calls. When Kathy called Jonathan again and found his cell phone disconnected, she and Megan drove to Jonathan's apartment together to find out what was going on.

Jonathan didn't answer his door and Kathy barged into the apartment manager's office, screaming that something was wrong, demanding the superintendent let her into her son's apartment. The superintendent came out and calmly tried to explain there was no issue. The resident, Mr. Palmer, moved out earlier in the week. He turned in his keys and dropped off the fee for terminating his lease early before he left. After much arguing, he conceded to open the apartment for Kathy.

The apartment was bare, as if Jonathan had never been there. It had taken nearly twenty minutes for Megan to get Kathy off the floor and out of the apartment while the superintendent explained how most everything had been left behind and was moved temporarily to a storage unit.

Megan thanked the super as Kathy wailed. "What is going on? I don't understand! How could he vanish without telling anyone?"

Megan and Kathy went to the police station to file a missing person's report, but nothing had turned up yet. Megan was thankful for that. She'd gotten Josh into enough trouble. Josh was assigned desk duty until Dr. Oswald's murder case was officially closed, and then he was on probation until further notice. Megan wouldn't ask him to dispose of the report. Besides, her mom was calling the station multiple times a day, requesting an update. A vanished report with a connection to Josh would probably ruin him.

"That's awful. I can't believe he just disappeared. It's just so shocking. I guess you never really know a person…" Katie trails off, lowering her eyes to the table before taking a sip of coffee.

Neither Katie nor Josh have come out and asked Megan if Jonathan had anything to do with their father's death. Megan knows they suspect it to be true. The timing of his disappearance is too glaring to ignore. But they never ask. And Megan never tells them.

She never will.

Megan's phone dings with an incoming text message. She picks up her phone and smiles. "It's Grandma Barb. I asked her to call me. I wanted to see how she's doing." Megan taps out a quick reply and sets her phone down. "I'm going to head out to the ranch for a late lunch after I help my mom go through some of Smalls' things."

Josh and Katie smile at her. "Tell her we say hi and we owe her a dinner." Josh says. Katie nods in agreement.

When they finish coffee, they get up to leave. After exchanging goodbyes, Katie walks in one direction, while Megan and Josh walk in the other. The trio's new dynamic will take some getting used to. But as they go, Megan's world is vibrant and alive. Everything is different. And somehow, it feels as though nothing has changed.

CHAPTER 38

M egan pulls onto her grandma's gravel driveway a few hours late, after getting trapped underneath her mom's emotional baggage while sorting through Jonathan's things. She knows her grandma won't hold a grudge, but even so, Megan hates being late.

She walks up to the door, noticing the way the sunlight softens everything around her as it begins to set. She smiles at the sound of Elvis singing from somewhere inside. Megan lets herself in, calling out loudly to announce her arrival, careful not to startle Grandma Barb.

Megan hears nothing in response, and she creeps uneasily deeper into the home, calling for her grandma.

When she enters the kitchen, she finally finds her. Grandma Barb is out on the back porch throwing a log into the fire pit and poking it while the flames inside roar higher. Megan breathes a sigh of relief and opens the sliding glass door.

286 | MARISSA VANSKIKE

"Oh Megan! There you are, sweetheart." Grandma Barb sings out, walking over to pull Megan into a hug. "So good to see you."

"Geez, grandma. Do you think your music is loud enough?" Megan teases.

"Well, I couldn't hear it out here on the porch. I just put a casserole in the oven, so we have about an hour until it's ready. Sit sit, make yourself comfortable." Grandma Barb gestures to the chairs seated around the fire pit and disappears into the kitchen.

Megan sits down and a minute later, the music quiets and her grandma appears holding two glasses of iced sweet tea. She passes one to Megan and takes a seat next to her. They clink their glasses together. "To moving forward," her grandma says.

"I'll drink to that." They sip their tea and recline back in their chairs.

"So how are you, grandma?" Megan turns to look at her grandma, one hand positioned as a makeshift visor to shield her eyes from the sun.

"I'm fine dear. Worried about you, though. Given everything that's happened, what with Mark's friend getting arrested and then Jonathan running off, of course."

"He wasn't dad's friend, Grandma. And honestly, I don't know how to feel about Smalls. Or what to think." Megan lays back with her eyes closed for just a moment. Her phone dings.

Incoming text message from Josh Pierce (6:26pm):
Sorry, Megs. I'm stuck at work while longer. Not sure I'll make it. But good news. We got Annie! I'm meeting Dillard down at the precinct now to book her. Chief's even talking about ending my probation! Call you when I'm done. Love you.

Megan's heart fills up at this win for Josh, and she can feel her grandma's eyes on her as she taps out a response. "That must be Josh." Her grandma's eyes twinkle.

Megan purses her lips together before admitting her grandma is right. "He can't make it tonight. They found something on Annie, and they picked her up not long ago."

"Ah. I see." Grandma Barb sits there with a knowing look on her face as she sweetly sips her tea.

"Alright, out with it. What aren't you telling me?"

"Nothing dear. I just heard through the gossip chain that the police got an anonymous tip about some side business she'd been running not entirely… above board. Something about insurance fraud, medical malpractice, and falsifying medical records." Grandma Barb's nonchalance is about as suspicious as it gets. "The whistleblower apparently revealed the location of some evidence hidden away in her house. Anyhow, I don't know all the details…" She shoos away the matter as Megan just shakes her head, at a loss for words.

Grandma Barb sits quietly for a moment before getting up out of her seat. "I'll be right back." She goes into the house, and Megan turns her gaze back to the land in front of her, staring out over her grandma's property. Her friends always seem to desire the city, drawn to the hustle and endless list of things to do. But here, Megan sees the appeal of a simpler life. The peaceful beauty in a patch of earth left wild and undisturbed.

Grandma Barb returns carrying a small stack of papers. She walks over and sits down again. "These are for you." Megan takes the stack warily from her hand.

"What's this?"

"I know you're disappointed by not having many photos of your dad, so I had copies made of some I had in an album. You're welcome to more if you want them."

Megan thumbs through the photos. A candid shot of a young Mark cooking in the kitchen. A picture of Mark reclined on the couch, Megan tucked into the crook of one arm, Jonathan in the other, both of them asleep.

Megan pauses longer when she flips to a photo of Mark holding her as a little girl. They are standing in front of Grandma Barb's barn. Mark's back is to the camera and Megan is peeking over his shoulder at the lens. Mark is wearing a white muscle tank and he's looking sideways at Megan. Behind them, next to the barn is the old oak tree she'd climb as a little girl, its branches perfectly positioned to help a child on the journey upward, lifting them higher until they reach the top so they can marvel at just how big the world is. She and her dad used to pretend this was their own little piece of heaven. The tree had so many branches jutting out in every direction that when the sun went down just far enough, the lines and angles of the tree sliced the sunlight into a thousand tiny rays. Megan used to pretend that every ray of light touching the earth was an angel coming down from heaven to play. She would race across the path to scramble up the tree, hoping the angels would let her join their games.

A thought pokes around in Megan's head but she can't quite latch on to it. She sets the picture on the top of the stack and holds up an envelope situated behind the photos.

Megan turns the letter over, examining her dad's handwriting and her grandma's address. Her eyes float up to the postdate. "Grandma, what? The date…"

"The day your daddy died. I'll give you a minute, sweetheart." Her grandma squeezes her hand before going back inside.

Megan doesn't open the letter right away. Its contents rattle her, even though she doesn't know what lays inside. She taps the envelop to her palm a few times, noticing the way the address blocks are a little smudged, like the author was rushed. Finally, she breaks the seal and opens the flap. She slides the paper out of the envelope and slowly unfolds it.

Megan, my Megan,

If you are reading this, then you know two things are true. First, the man you once knew so well is gone. Second, your search has come to an end. I knew you'd make it this far. You were always one of the most capable people I've ever had the pleasure to know.

I'll never be able to fix the mistakes I made with you or your brother, but I can tell you, for once, how deeply I regret my failure as a father to you both. Telling you I'm sorry will never be enough. I do not write this now, dreaming of forgiveness. I'm far too pragmatic for that. I do, however, hope you both will eventually come to understand everything I've ever done was for you. I had to protect you both, from what I found myself involved in, from the people I worked with, and from me. No matter the cost. I can't bring myself to regret my choice, even though it cost me everything.

You came this far in search of answers. I won't keep them from you now.

I tried, Megan. I tried to get out. To make amends for the damage I'd done. But I couldn't. Not without putting you and your brother in danger.

Jonathan knows who I am, or rather, what I am. He's been appearing for a little while now. I pretended not to notice. I didn't want him to be connected in any way. But Dan got to him, and there's only one way forward from here. I wish there wasn't. Dan will kill your brother if he thinks he's strayed. I won't let that happen. Everything is in motion and it's no one's fault but my own. It cannot be stopped now. I want you to know that it's not your fault. Or Jonathan's.

I'm choosing to tell you this now, because I'm afraid of what will happen to him. I'm afraid of what will happen to you, if you find out any other way. I hope you respect my wish to protect your brother.

Forgive him. He did nothing wrong. He will need you now more than ever.

I understand his anger. His hatred for me. That isn't his fault, it's mine. And I bore that cross every day. But you have always been better than me. You are the strong one, Megan. You can see what you'd be throwing away over a choice that was never yours to make. The choice to go was mine. I am at peace with it, though it pains me to know all the ways you and Jonathan will struggle with it.

I wasn't good to you, and I was even worse to Jonathan. But I love you, Megan. I love your brother. I always have.

The days to come will be a time of love and a time of grief. Keep your brother safe. Keep yourself safe. This isn't goodbye, it's see you later.

I'm sorry, Megan. I'm sorry this is how it had to be.

All my love,

Dad

Megan watches the way the ink bleeds across the page beneath her tears. She wipes her cheeks just as her grandma comes back out and sits down once more in the chair next to her.

"Do you know where Smalls ran off to?" Megan looks at her grandma, noticing how the setting sun behind her creates a halo of soft, angelic light around her head.

Her grandma doesn't reply. "Of course you do."

Grandma Barb leans over and takes the letter from Megan's hand. She stands up, tossing it into the fire. "Jonathan called me a few days ago. Asked to be left alone. But he wanted someone to know."

Smalls is safe.

Megan watches the paper burn, the white of the page turning black, little by little, until its pieces crumble, and disappear into the ash beneath the log.

"How do we come back from this? How will it be ok ever again?" A tear rolls down Megan's cheek. She looks at her grandma, her eyes like steel, and she's grateful when Grandma Barb doesn't answer the rhetorical question. Megan always admired her grandma's resilience.

Megan slides the photo of her and Mark back out. Her eyes run over the colors, taking in the memory printed on the tiny paper when Grandma Barb speaks again. "That is one of my most favorite pictures in the world. I remember the moment so vividly. Every little detail captured perfectly."

The thought bubbling up in Megan's brain resurfaces and she squints at the photo. "Grandma… you said Dad had a birthmark on his shoulder. But there's…there's nothing here."

Her grandma's knowing silence is all the response she needs.

Your search has come to an end.

Megan's mind is racing and she nods her head. "I think I'll go for a walk, if that's ok with you."

"Of course, baby girl. You go."

Megan walks slowly down the dirt pathway to the barn. The same ring of sunlight shines behind the building, cutting through the oak tree standing beside it. What she's thinking is impossible, but she's never felt more sure.

I'll see you again one day, in Heaven. Their own little piece of Heaven.

Megan smiles to herself, thinking how much it feels like an angel leading her to sanctuary.

I'll never be too far away again.

As she approaches the barn, Megan sees the huge barn doors on both sides are open and the sunlight pours through the breezeway. The only thing obstructing its path is the outline of a man holding a pitchfork, tossing hay from a wheelbarrow into one of the horse stalls.

You just have to know where to look.

She opens her mouth to speak, but her voice catches in her throat as the man rights himself and turns towards her. The sunlight coming in from behind him obscures his features, making them hard to distinguish, but Megan knows exactly who he is. He's somehow taller than she remembers. His hair has grown out, and he looks older. His forearms peek out from under his rolled-up sleeves, tanned from the sunlight.

A soft smile spreads across Megan's face as the man rests his hands on the end of the pitchfork. Their matching brown eyes connect and she hears his voice, so sweetly familiar.

"Hey, Megs."

ACKNOWLEDGEMENTS

Apparently, you're allowed to say "based on a true story" whenever you want. Even if it isn't true at all.

Well, this is based on a true story, and I've been writing it since I was a little girl.

But this is no memoir. And those who know any part of my story might be tempted to try to dissect the truth from the fiction. Separating the two would be like plucking the thorns from a cactus with nothing but a pair of tweezers. Tedious work, though not impossible. But to strip a cactus of the sharp edges that make up its essence feels like a crime. I suggest you try not to strip these pages of the edges that make up their essence, either.

Acknowledgements is the section where an author thanks all the people and groups that helped push their story out into the world. And I intend to do just that.

But I also intend to acknowledge the truth within this novel. Because without it, this story wouldn't exist.

That said... while writing often feels like a solitary endeavor, books are never made by a single person. My name may be listed as the author, but there are many people to thank as I went on this journey.

First, to my husband, who, when I randomly turned to him one night over a year ago and said, "I want to write a book", just looked at me and said "Great, do it. What's it about?" Everything became real that night, and everything felt possible. Thank you.

To my writing partners, Jessica Jones and Greta Ford, who read countless versions of this story and never failed to tell me what it lacked or where it shined. Your critiques were invaluable. This story and my writing are stronger because of you. Thank you.

To my editor, Jamie Warren, who read through revision after revision with a fine-tooth comb, providing me with your writing expertise. Though the limit does not exist for how many typos, grammar mistakes, or plot inconsistencies I could throw at you, you caught them every time. I shudder to think how this story would read without your keen eye. Thank you.

To my many beta readers and testers. Without your honest feedback on early versions of this story, I wouldn't have been able to finish it the right way. I hope this final version tops the one you read. Thank you.

To all my friends who let me pick your brain in your areas of expertise as I traveled the road into authorship, giving me tips on writing, publishing, graphic design, marketing, and more. Thank you.

To the influencers, bookstagrammers, librarians and bookish friends who took the time to read and review this book. Your opinion means far more than you might realize. Your support can change an author's life. Thank you.

And last, but far from least, to my family, friends, and community, who must surely have been shocked when I announced that I'd written a novel. You met me with nothing but excitement, love, and unflagging support. "Thank you" isn't enough. But thank you all the same.

To anyone I've forgotten, please forgive me. Everything they said was true. This section is infinitely harder than the 38 chapters that precede it.

For bonus content or to connect with the author, visit:

www.marissavanskike.com

www.instagram.com/marissavanskike